A LIFE SINGULAR

PART TWO; VOLUME ONE

BY

LORRAINE PESTELL

Cover designed by Shawline Publishing Group

Lorraine Pestell
Visit my website at https://www.lorrainepestell.com

Printed in Australia

Shawline Publishing Group Pty Ltd
www.shawlinepublishing.com.au

First Printing: November 2020

Paperback ISBN- 9781922444110

Ebook ISBN - 9781922444127

For Jed,
my ever-loving and much-loved companion.

*Huge thanks to Bradley Shaw and Steph Huddleston from
Shawline Publishing for showing faith in my writing and for their
valuable advice and assistance.*

*I'm also grateful for the loyal band of readers who have encouraged me
to continue with my life's work.*

*Sale proceeds of this book series will be donated to EdConnect Australia
and The Smith Family for the ongoing support they deserve.*

REVIEWS FOR A LIFE SINGULAR

There is so much happening in what is a beautiful story about life and love. Even more appealing than your typical love story is how the author has embedded into the storyline some of the more difficult social questions that we often avoid addressing, making it more intellectual than your typical love story. I can't wait to read the next book in the series! **Jenny, 5 STAR review**

Contemporary Fiction with Love & Loss - A Life Singular Part One is the first book in the Life Singular Drama. This is a love story that deals with social issues of today including mental illness and loss of a spouse. It is captivating, yet emotional. Sad yet lovely. A truly real story that could be taken straight out of today's newspaper headlines. Highly recommended extraordinary read!! **5 STARS, Anonymous Goodreads review**

I'm always looking for quality series as I like being able to continue on with the story. In this book, the first book of the series, the author sets the stage for what is to come. I've also read the 2nd book but there will be no spoilers given. The only thing I'll say is the author does a good job of letting you think one thing and then doing a really nice twist when you definitely don't expect it. It kept me on my toes throughout the story. If you're like me and like solidly written stories with plenty of details and no lags, I think you'll become a fan of the author and move straight into each book that follows the one you are reading. I've just finished the second book and found the quality of writing to be as good as this one. If you are looking for a good series – put this author on your list... **Diana L 5 STAR review**

A great read by a great author! The description for this book hooked me instantly and I began reading the second I downloaded this book. This was a great read with zero lags. A good portion of this book centred around finding the person responsible for a high-profile murder and then the subsequent court trial. It was hard for me to put this book down at night as I wanted to know what would happen next. I definitely recommend this author as rarely does a book keep me as interested as this one did... **Beverly Clark, 5 STAR review**

A Wonderful Series Begins Here! There's a strong romantic element at the beginning of this story that really sets the stage nicely for the reader to understand the two characters (Jeff and his wife Lynn). When there is a tragic turn to their 20-year anniversary, the author smoothly takes us into the mystery of what happened and also the matter of how one person moves on after a tragic loss. The characters are well created and there is plenty of details to give this story the layers needed to keep one reading. The author has the ability to move the reader through the emotions being experienced – from love to anguish to feelings raked raw – the reader has his finger on the pulse of what is going on (said and unsaid) with each character. This book definitely hooked me on wanting to know what would happen next and I'll say now – I liked the second and third book too... **Wilson R 5 STAR Review**

PICKING UP THE PIECES

Matthew and Rhiannon ran to open the front door for two of their favourite visitors. The Diamonds had fallen into line with Michelle's insistence that they come to the Hadleys' for dinner instead of *vice versa*. It not only saved the family from finding a babysitter but also encouraged the matching pair out of their penthouse prison. Jeff accepted on his daughter's behalf, knowing she would have felt obliged to prepare something special for dinner, as her mother would have done.

'Hey, kids!' Jeff shouted, grabbing hold of both youngsters and tickling them until they crumpled to the floor. 'What's up?'

The ten- and seven-year-olds escaped the tall man's powerful grip, and Matthew laid straight into him with a barrage of punches, leaving Kierney to deliver their wine and beer to the kitchen where Michelle and Alan were waiting.

'How is he?' her mum's best friend mouthed, cocking her head towards the peals of childish laughter.

'This was a great idea,' the eighteen-year-old sage replied. 'Thanks for making the counter-offer. It's really good for *papá* to be somewhere other than the apartment in the evening. How are you all?'

'Oh, we're just fine, thanks, Kierney,' Alan answered, kissing her on the cheek. 'Tell us how *you* are?'

'Getting there, thanks. Good days and bad days.'

The empathetic doctor nodded. 'To be expected. And your dad?'

'Mostly bad days.'

Michelle smiled at the pretty teenager, hearing her parents' dry humour emanating from her youthful mouth. She was relieved to find Kierney looking bright-eyed and relaxed, remembering the stories Lynn would tell about Jeff's depression and how difficult it was sometimes to cope with his anger and mood swings. It appeared the young lady was surviving fairly well in spite of the tragedy that had befallen them in February.

'So you're not going to Sydney after all?' Alan asked.

'No, not yet. I've signed up for a research programme at Melbourne Uni' instead. It's only for this year, and then I'll take up my place at Sydney Uni'. They've agreed to keep me on their list. That's the plan at the moment anyway...'

'Alan!' Jeff shouted, extending his hand to Michelle's husband and winking at his daughter. 'Sorry, Kizzo. Didn't mean to interrupt.'

Kierney smiled. 'You didn't. I was finished.'

'Thanks for having us over,' the songwriter continued. 'It's actually refreshing to be out of that bloody apartment.'

'That's what Kizzy said,' Michelle chuckled, walking over to kiss their handsome visitor. 'How are you?'

'Bruised,' Jeff answered, rubbing his stomach and thighs where the couple's children had beaten him to a pulp. 'How're you guys going?'

'Stop avoiding the question,' their host scolded her best friend's husband.

'He's an expert at doing that,' Kierney laughed, poking her father in the ribs. 'Too thin, look! You need to make sure he clears his plate, like the kids, Michelle.'

The rock star pretended to wring his daughter's neck with long fingers. 'Ah, yeah... Don't mother me, *gorgeousita*,' he threatened, kissing the top of her head before hugging her close.

Alan placed a glass of red wine in each guest's hand and ushered them through to the lounge room, where the Matthew and Rhiannon had put on a video. He asked for the television to be switched off, beckoning for the new arrivals to sit down. Immediately, the kids leapt on the friendly billionaire again, almost spilling his wine.

'Hey, watch it, guys,' Jeff warned, passing his glass into his daughter's safekeeping. 'Let's all sit quietly now. I don't need any more battle scars tonight.'

'So Michelle tells me you're looking for a house to rent,' Alan opened.

'Yep. That's right. Somewhere close to the city, but closer to sea level.'

The surgeon laughed. 'Penthouse not good enough for you these days?'

Their good friend shrugged. 'Something like that. So how's work, mate? Any major repairs lately?'

'Yes. Pretty good, thanks. Busy. One of my colleagues was offered his dream job in Boston, so we're a man down. I had a bloke in yesterday with a severed hand. Six hours he was on the table!'

'Wow! Did you stitch it back on? How did he lose it?' Kierney asked, screwing up her face at the grotesque image.

'Accident at work. Not sure of the details, but the hand was badly damaged. He probably won't get all motor function back, but we're hopeful. Very abusive actually, the git! Sometimes you wonder why you bother...'

Jeff smiled, miming a quick slice with a scalpel. 'Whoops! Sorry, mate,' he joked, turning wild eyes towards young Matthew. 'Didn't see your ear there. You didn't need it, did you? You've got two. You'll be fine.'

The boy gasped, instinctively grabbing both sides of his head. It made the others laugh, which embarrassed the youngster, much to his little sister's delight. Kierney stood up to see if Michelle wanted any help in the kitchen, and the children followed her like puppies.

'She's doing well,' Alan observed, once the teenager was out of earshot. 'Or is it an act?'

'Sometimes,' the father confessed. 'But overall, she's pretty good. She watches me like a hawk, as you saw. I love it... crave it, in fact... but she shouldn't be focussing her attention on me like this. I kick her out regularly, insisting she spends time with her mates, but then she tells me as soon as she gets out, she can't wait to be home. *Vat* can you do?'

His host shook his head, chuckling at the famous man's hark back to his Yiddish boyhood to mimic his paternal grandparents' accent. 'She obviously wants to be there with you, so I shouldn't worry. You're onto her motives. As long as you both know the situation, I'm sure it'll balance itself out.'

'Cheers, mate,' Jeff nodded, raising an empty wine goblet. 'I agree. This bereavement lark's a bloody long, painful process, that's all. Two steps forwards, one step back. Or *vice versa* when it comes to me.'

Dinner was served with far too much ceremony for a mid-week *soirée*. Alan refilled their glasses while Michelle and Kierney distributed plates piled high. The conversation stayed light and fluffy in front of the children, but nevertheless the widower could feel all adult eyes boring into him, as if they were monitoring his every move.

Don't be ungrateful, he chastised himself. The Hadleys cared about Lynn's bereft family, and this latest diversion had originally been his idea.

After the main course, Michelle excused herself to put the children to bed while the men started on a third bottle of red. The parents held firm as all manner of youthful objections were voiced, even after the thoughtful teenager's offer of assistance.

After half an hour's intellectual discourse while the women were away, the men tackled such wide-ranging topics as Melbourne's social issues, its ageing hospital system and the new football season which was about to start. Alan was more than ready for dessert by the time it was served.

'So, Jeff... Are you going to answer my question from earlier?' Michelle asked, giving the musician's daughter a sideways glance.

'Which question was that, Mish? The one about wanting more wine? Yes, please. That'd be great.'

'*Papá*, you've been warned,' Kierney scolded, wagging her finger. 'Last night you said you needed to talk, so talk, damn you!'

Their hosts laughed at the matching pair of Diamonds sitting at their table, so alike in every way. They had watched on with great interest as Jet and Kierney grew up in the blinding spotlight of celebrity, and the cluster of inherited family traits never ceased to amaze them, whether gained through nature or nurture.

'Yes, ma'am,' Jeff saluted. 'Anything you say, *pequeñita*. You're right, as ever. What would you like to know, Your Honour?'

'Everything,' the redhead shrugged. 'How you are. How we can help you recover from this huge loss. Is there anything you need?'

'Thanks, guys. It's great that you're so worried about us, but there's nothing I need from you. Plenty I need, however,' her famous friend issued a half-hearted smile. 'Y'know, what I really need is to stop being a millstone around my friends' and family's necks and for people to stop fussing around me like I'm incapable of taking care of myself.'

Michelle brushed tears from both sides of her face. 'But we care so much, Jeff,' she insisted. 'Lynn was my best friend for more than thirty years, and God knows I loved her heaps and heaps. I can only guess how much worse you feel, and how much you three must be missing her. We really want to help.'

'Jeez! I'm grateful, Mish. Really I am, but what the hell could you guys do, apart from listening to me moaning and blubbing all day long? I'm in a very dark place and would rather not drag anyone else along with me. Let's talk about something else. Have you guys decided what you're doing about a school for Matt?'

'Not yet,' the lawyer shrugged in resignation. 'He's bright enough for MA, but I don't think it's the right school for him. Al wants to do all boys.'

'Why?' asked Kierney, relieved that her dad had managed to stem the tide of overwhelming pathos coming their way. 'What's wrong with girls?'

'Nothing but distraction,' Alan offered, lifting his hands in front of his face as if expecting a missile to be launched in his direction. 'He knows how to interact with girls through his sister. He needs focus and discipline, and to learn *self*-discipline.'

Jeff smiled at his daughter's mock rage. 'So why not MA?' he quizzed. 'It's all about focus and discipline. Why the hell do you think it's top of the Dyson league table? Didn't you enjoy your time there, Mish?'

Michelle shook her head. 'Too much pressure. I think Matthew'll buckle under the strain. And he's not sporty or musical either, so he wouldn't take advantage of all the extra-curricular stuff there.'

'Quite a few kids are like that though,' the recent graduate recounted. 'Isn't that the same at any school?'

The protective mother agreed with a sigh. 'Probably. Perhaps I'm biased 'cause I found it so hard.'

'Where did you go to school, Al?' Jeff probed, scratching his shirt where his dream girl was transmitting her amusement at the great egalitarian's sudden interest in Melbourne's elite school system.

'Scotch,' the doctor replied. 'And you're right, Kierney. They are the same, pretty much. Just slightly lower down the pecking order, but all the same benefits in terms of *cachet*. We need to decide soon. His name's down for both, so we'll end up paying double fees.'

Michelle rolled her eyes. 'Don't be such an idiot, Al. This is serious, and I'm glad Jeff's forcing the issue. We've been avoiding this for a while now. Can I ask you a question you mightn't want to answer, Jeff?'

The curious man frowned. 'I guess so.'

'Would you have sent your two to MA if Lynn hadn't been their mother?'

'Was I in Melbourne?' the mischief-maker countered.

'Yes,' their host groaned, having forgotten how exasperating it was to play hypotheticals with her old friend's intellectual powerhouse. 'Of course.'

'And why d'you suppose I'd have had kids if Lynn hadn't been around?'

It had taken no time at all for the game to be on! Kierney leant forwards with her elbows on the table, eager to see her father spar with the part-time solicitor, as he had so many times before. This was a very good sign.

'For God's sake, humour me! If it's not too much trouble, imagine you had a daughter and son by someone else,' the woman insisted. 'You're so bloody infuriating sometimes.'

The joker shook his head. 'I can't. It wouldn't have happened.'

'Oh, do play along, Jeff,' Alan chuckled. 'There's a good chap.'

The charismatic world-changer grinned, leaning back in his chair and crossing his legs, the fingers of his left hand drumming his thigh as his nicotine craving mounted. 'Very sorry, Mish. Are they smart, these kids of mine?'

'They're your kids,' Michelle retorted.

'Of course they're smart,' Kierney interjected. 'And you have enough money.'

'Thank you, Kierney,' the older woman smiled. 'Your dad hasn't lost the ability to be bloody infuriating, has he?'

'You stay out of this,' Jeff warned his daughter, blowing her a kiss. 'Glad to be of service. It'd depend on whether there was a good public school in the neighbourhood.'

'There is,' the redhead replied. 'Walking distance too.'

Removing the cigarette packet and his lighter from his pants pocket, the Sydneysider paused for a second or two, realising the passing years had altered his opinion of private schools. Melbourne Academy had played a significant role in rounding his children out, and he couldn't be certain they would have turned out the same if they had attended the local high school.

'And where are you planning for Rhiannon to go?' Jeff asked. 'Why wouldn't you send them to the same school?'

'Excuse me! I'm asking the questions, if you don't mind,' Michelle objected with a chuckle. 'Would you have sent both of your kids to the same school?'

'More than likely, yeah. It gives them more in common for when they go through tough times. They can relate to what each other's going through. Wouldn't you think, *pequeñita*?'

'Yes, I would,' she affirmed. 'Like when Jet remembered Mrs Stavrakakis the other day... It does make a difference when you know someone's sharing the experience with you, good or bad.'

'So, Scotch is out then,' Alan declared with an impish grin.

'Either that or you give your daughter a sex change,' their facetious visitor offered.

'Jeff!' Michelle cried out. 'Don't say that! He probably would.'

'Well, at least there's a fair chance of the surgery going well.'

Everyone laughed at the showman's quirky humour, especially his daughter. It was encouraging to see him taking part in this jocular discussion with such enthusiasm. She wondered whether her mother was here tonight, keeping tabs on them and lifting their spirits.

'So then you're looking at church-affiliated schools or independent,' Jeff continued, changing the subject for fear of offending his hosts. 'Firbank, the Catholic, Anglican or Jewish schools, or MA. Back to where we started!'

A whimpering sound caused all four heads to turn, their conversation cut short by the appearance of a seven-year-old at the dining room door.

'I can't sleep,' Rhiannon announced. 'I want Uncle Jeff to read me a story.'

'Oh, do you now?' Alan replied. 'Uncle Jeff's our guest. You should go back to sleep.'

The little girl began to cry, running over to her mother and burying her head in her lap. The visiting father felt jealous of the affection, thinking back to his raven-haired gipsy girl at the same age.

In a similar situation, she would have sidled up to him almost unnoticed and propped herself up on his knee, always outlasting his resistance to stroke her hair or adorn her temple with a kiss. Those had been sweet moments indeed, and judging by the sustained tingling in his chest, her mother thought so too.

'I'll read you a story,' Kierney offered, noticing a faraway look in her father's eyes. 'Is that OK, Rhiannon?'

The tears stopped as quickly as they had started, and a wide smile spread across the child's face. Jeff's hand grabbed his daughter's arm as she passed his chair, cottoning on to her motive. Still blessed with her *mamá's* enduring patience, she had been angling for a chance to make herself scarce in order that he might speak freely with Michelle and Alan. Flashing her eyes in shared recognition, Kierney exchanged a modern-day sweet moment with him, bringing tears to his eyes.

Michelle nodded, stroking her daughter's back. 'Thanks, Kizzy. You're sure you don't mind?'

Alan scowled, clearly thinking his wife too much of a soft touch. The teenager held her hand out to the little girl, and they both trotted back to her bedroom.

'Sorry, Jeff,' Alan apologised.

'It's fine. She did it on purpose.'

'Who? Rhiannon?' Michelle pounced. 'What do you mean?'

'No,' the widower smiled at the over-reaction. 'Kierney. She's astute enough to know we want to talk about Lynn, and she also knows I don't want her to have to hear it morning, noon and night. I bet she's been looking for an opportunity to desert us ever since we finished dinner.'

'Oh, OK,' the defensive mother responded. 'Well, she's right. I do need to know what's going on for you. Kizzy said you drove over to Escondido last night on your own. Was that a good idea?'

'Ah, yeah. It was a shit experience, but a good idea. I wanted to find out if the place still meant anything to me, before I board it up and find somewhere else to live.'

'Wow,' Alan murmured. 'It must've been hard to go back there. That house was built for your family, mate. You designed it, didn't you?'

'Yep. You're not wrong, mate. We did design it, from scratch. I was looking for a sign to feed my senses, which are starved to the point of atrophy at the moment.'

'What's atrophy?' Michelle interjected.

'Wasting away,' her husband answered. 'Undernourished. It's a great way to describe it.'

'Cheers, Al,' the widower sniffed. 'That's exactly right. It's like I can spend all day and all night looking at photos, or put Lynn's CDs and videos on any time I like, but they don't feed me. And in fact, it's the opposite. They leave me wanting. Even emptier.

'It's the spontaneous appeal to the senses that you miss most when someone's no longer around. Even Jetto. Y'know... His obnoxious retorts and sharp tongue. Like Lynn's frustrated laugh at my lame jokes, or a heart-stoking smile in response to random acts of love.'

A lone tear rolled down the superstar's cheek, smartly wiped away while watching his wife's friend do the same. 'Sorry, guys. Ignore me,' he said. 'There's nothing I can do about my emotional responses, so I just have to ask you to put up with it, please. I'm long past caring who sees me cry.'

'It's quite alright, Jeff. You're excused,' Michelle chuckled. 'If you'll also excuse me.'

'Sure. Thanks, Mish. Y'know, it's at these times that I think back and wish we'd made some salacious home movies,' the middle-aged rock star carried on, a wry smile on his face, 'just so I can hear the sound of Lynn sighing and moaning as she came to orgasm, and to see my hand on her breasts, and watch her close her eyes when my fingers brushed her skin...

'I apologise, guys, for the graphic commentary, but that's the way it is. Seeing her standing on stage and hearing her sing songs with full production quality is nowhere near enough. It's impersonal, and it just makes the yearning worse.'

'I'm so sorry. You're always so good at bringing scenes to life,' Michelle asked, noticing her husband's glazed eyes. 'Too good! So what does all that have to do with Escondido?'

Jeff sighed and shifted in his chair. 'I went there to make sure the inspiration I'm seeking isn't locked up in that house,' he explained, knowing by the expressions on their faces that the couple at whose table he sat were unable to relate. 'There was the odd thing that stimulated me visually to a mild extent, such as our bedroom and sitting on the balcony.

'But that's easy. It was no different to being in the apartment. I can feed my eyes when they're closed just as well like that. Same with sounds; piano there or piano on the sixteenth floor... What I miss is the touch of her skin and the taste of her kiss. I can't get that anymore at Escondido than I can in the city, and I won't get it less in a rented house because a big fat zero's where I'm at. There's nothing less than zero, is there?'

The others shook their heads. Tonight's dinner guest had painted an accurate picture of someone grieving for a lover, and there was no disputing the distraught man who got up from the table and made his way to the bathroom. The Hadleys stared at each other for a few minutes before clearing the table while they waited for him to return.

'We can't begin to know, can we?' Alan said to his wife. 'It makes me feel very grateful we're together.'

'Thanks,' Michelle nodded, accepting a kiss. 'And he's right... Apart from listening, there's nothing we can do. We can't bring Lynn back. There's no substituting for that sort of loss.'

Jeff came back to the dining room to find it empty. He slumped down onto his chair and closed his eyes, still struggling to contain his sorrow. He decided to suggest they go home as soon as Kierney returned from Rhiannon's bedroom, not wishing to abuse the Hadleys' friendship by overstaying their welcome.

Lynn's school-friend walked back into the room and placed a gentle hand on the musician's shoulder to avoid making him jump. 'Coffee?'

'Yeah. That'd be great. Cheers, Mish.'

'You know what?' Alan declared, clapping his hands. 'I actually know of a nice house in the Richmond area coming up for rent. You might be interested in taking a look.'

'Ah, yeah?' the billionaire perked up. 'Where?'

'On the corner of Rose and Mary Streets in Burnley, opposite a park,' the surgeon answered. 'Not too far from the river either. An Indian doctor at the Epworth owns it, and he's going back to India for a while because his mother's sick. Or his father? Can't remember which.'

'Sounds good. What's it like?'

The surgeon stood up as his wife entered the room carrying a trayful of coffee cups, clearing some space on the table. 'I haven't been all round it, but we went to a party there once,' he replied. 'Do you remember, honey? Pramod and Nisha's house?'

'Yes, I remember. Older style, mock-Tudor or whatever they call it. Depends what you're looking for, Jeff. It's a big house; must be at least four bedrooms and huge downstairs. Quite a lot of work to keep up.'

'The block has three street frontages, from what I remember, but there are high walls and hedges all the way round, so nice and private,' Alan explained. 'I'll make some enquiries tomorrow if you're interested.'

Jeff nodded, opening his arms for his daughter to walk into on her return from story-reading duties. 'I am interested. Cheers, Al. As long as they wouldn't mind me strengthening the security some more if it needed it. I'll take my flatmate over there in the morning to have a look at the outside. Can't visualise exactly where it is.'

Kierney accepted a cup of coffee from and took her seat again. 'Were you talking about a potential house?'

'Sí, pequeñita. These guys know of a house belonging to one of the doctors at Epworth. It sounds worth a look.'

'They're both doctors, aren't they?' Michelle corrected. 'Nisha's in paediatrics, I'm sure.'

'Even better,' the larrikin teased, seeing her husband's dismissive expression. 'Might be a material fact, mate. You never know.'

Jeff didn't feel like going to bed that night. Instead, he chose to stretch out on the couch in front of the television. His brain was full of questions that no-one could answer. It felt like the old days, before his beautiful best friend had woven her magic on his damaged inner child, with a multitude of anxieties and compulsions setting in again.

Would he spend the rest of this lonely life filling in time, waiting to die? Or could he somehow behave like the children and move on to other worthwhile pursuits which would bring some meaning to his continued existence? Why couldn't he be like the kids? And furthermore, why did Lynn not expect him to recover after all these years of healing? Although still buoyed by her fervent wish to be together again in the next life, it still amazed him that she had professed to be of the same mind.

If the intellectual were honest with himself, there was considerable doubt in his mind that his *regala* would have followed through with her apparent willingness to terminate her existence if their fates were to have been interchanged.

Would Australia's princess really have thrown in the towel if he had died first? With the overwhelming amount of support on offer from their friends, family and friends, the grieving husband was beginning to drown in guilt and shame for the irrepressible urge to go after her.

Had his dream girl only taken such a stance in her letters because she knew he would want her to? If not, he had better not wait too long, for if their souls were to find new bodies to occupy, the age difference ought to be minimal.

Imagine if he were to survive another twenty years and then trust his new incarnation to fall in love with a woman old enough to be his mother? Bizarre! Lighting another cigarette and closing his eyes, he wondered whether this was why one saw such strange pairings every so often. Not the rich, old codger with the gold-digging, Barbie doll girlfriend, but ordinary folk who were drawn to each other inexplicably and became extraordinary couples.

With no contribution from his lover's ghost coming to the fore, the widower grew drowsy. Perhaps in the meantime, to avoid the endless probing questions about his state of mind, he might be better off leaving Melbourne and all his significant others behind. He could start a fresh life in France, as he and Lynn had planned for their retirement. Would the better half of the Diamond pantomime horse's drifting soul still be able to locate him when so far away?

'Where are you now, angel?' Jeff cast into the air. 'Would it matter where I was? Could you still find me? How far can you travel? Jesus, Lynn, I wish I knew what was going on. Is this all in my head? Am I trying to make the impossible happen, or do we really have a future together?'

No hint of a response came his way, confusion giving way to despair. The songwriter stood up to close the lounge room door and switched on the television, searching for some mindless entertainment to which he could fall asleep. How many nights like this would he need to endure? Tomorrow must be different, surely? It was up to him and him alone to make the remainder of his life more bearable; no different to his teenaged years. If he had triumphed before, he needed to knuckle down and triumph again.

The dejected man's mind turned to the upcoming trial of Lynn's killer, Juan Antonio García. How was the short, beige, rat-like man passing the time these days in his six square-metre cell? Was he remorseful or angry? Regretful or satisfied? What sort of a man was he? Was he resigned to spending the rest of his useful life in prison, or did he expect to escape a sentence? The Spaniard had confessed to the shooting, yet after twenty years traipsing through the corridors of power, the seasoned world-changer knew enough about the justice system not to presume conviction to be a foregone conclusion.

Jeff did his best to rid his mind of the man responsible for extinguishing the life of the only woman he had ever loved by imagining how the Sydney courtroom would look. After a few minutes, he drifted off to sleep.

The widower woke at three minutes after midnight on the first of April, to the sound of his own voice shouting. He was directing people away from the crime scene for the umpteenth time, preparing to run after a man he could see leaving the hotel. His father was there, doubtless laughing at the futility of his cries, as were the Jaworski brothers. His nightmares these days, though less frequent, certainly boasted an all-star cast.

April Fool's Day, Jeff rued, returning to consciousness. *How apt.*

Sweat-drenched and wretched, he slid off the couch and made sure the lounge room door was closed. Slightly late admittedly, but he didn't want Kierney to come in and find him in this state, especially doing what he was about to do. He grabbed a notebook that sat on the coffee table's shelf, drew a timeline and mapped out the next few months' milestones.

It was now six weeks since Lynn's death. He took some solace that he was thinking with greater clarity recently. His hours of soul-searching had resulted in a few vital tasks he needed to accomplish on behalf of his absent wife, and some of his own records to set straight once and for all. These would all take time, hence the sudden, secretive pressure to work out how many days, weeks or months were at his disposal.

'Where are you, angel? I need to know how to find you. When, where, *et cetera*... I need to get serious about our plan.'

The bereaved man sat on the floorboards, resting the notebook on the coffee table and with his long legs stretched out underneath. An empty whisky glass sat in front of him, tempting him to have another, but he resisted. He wanted to create his schedule with a clear head, so he could put hand on heart and claim to have covered every eventuality.

Lynn's anniversary letters were etched onto his brain. He took her photograph from his wallet and placed it on the table in front of him. "Please, please find me," she had written in her very first letter, way back in 1981. Tears welled up in the forty-three-year-old's eyes when he envisioned the beauty languishing in the great beyond, eternally exasperated that her lover didn't know more.

'Christ, angel,' he cursed. 'You might've given me a bloody clue!'

The celebrity had spent the last few weeks immersed in bureaucracy, eager to be free of it and to dedicate time to a joint autobiography. There was a great deal to sort out, what with staying in touch with the trial preparations and making sure everything in Lynn's estate ended up where she had intended.

As part of this new master plan, he needed to instruct Gerry to help him redirect his own assets too. He had no desire to make any more money, but neither should his fortune sit idle. Paragon Holdings and the Diamond Celebration Foundation were two complex money-spinning beasts with metaphorical fingers in so many pies.

What was the best for Jet and Kierney? Their parents hadn't wanted them to inherit much directly, preferring them to be granted decision-making powers over the organisations they could bequeath. Albeit for differing reasons, he expected both kids to call the USA home in the fullness of time, which led him to ponder the best place to domicile this diverse set of legal entities. No doubt the indomitable Mr Blake would know someone who could advise him well on this front.

Kierney was desperate for a career at the United Nations in New York. She was identical to her teenaged father in this respect, except with infinitely more opportunities dangling just beyond her reach. For the last five years, changing the world for the better was all the dusky, serious-minded teenager had desired, and he had felt continually frustrated on her behalf during this prolonged period of enforced inertia.

In fact, as the industrious superstar sat facing backwards on his life, he realised an entire generation had passed, depositing his daughter at the same stage of rapid ripening whence he had found the girl of his dreams. How had his sixteen-year-old girlfriend described herself when the soul-mates first met? Plenty of opinions, but no power? Jeff smiled to himself. This was Kizzy to a tee; so fired up with ambition but way ahead of her time.

This trait ran in the family, along with independent driving! How ironic that Lynn had agreed to give their daughter the name "Freedom" but couldn't stick around long enough to see her use it...

And Jet? He wouldn't come into his own for another five years, the widower calculated. Their firstborn was destined to live out his Dyson dreams with his usual exuberance before the closet intellectual would bubble up to the surface. Life nowadays was all about cricket, swimming and sex, earning his degree and making West Coast rock music with his university buddies.

The proud father pictured an older version of the muscular, blond teenager living in the mountains of Colorado, dreaming up movies in the cool, clean, rarefied air. Subtly teaching the world how lessons from the past could fashion a better future.

Ryan Diamond's passion slept deep within him, a few more years of maturity necessary to recognise his vocation. The forever couple had made plans over the recent festive season for the father and son to spend a month in the English summer, riding motorcycles and tempting some of these more introverted ideas from the hidden recesses of the lad's brain.

Yes, Jeff nodded, marking a few more milestones on his timeline. His month in the UK must still go ahead. Both men stood to benefit from burning across the countryside on the days when there was no cricket, during his son's summer holidays from Cambridge. The leadership of Paragon Holdings belonged to Jet. He would, with

Gerry's tutelage, make the best custodian of his father's dream of delivering technology and information into the hands of the masses.

Jeff marked another date by which to establish a new Ethics Board to oversee the company's venture capital decisions, and he would make their children joint Chairs. Unable to pinpoint at this moment a worthy appointee for the third decision-maker, it was patently obvious that a casting vote was imperative for the occasions when his offspring didn't see eye-to-eye.

Not Gerry this time, the pioneer of progress chuckled to himself. The conservative buffoon lacked both his daughter's compassion and his son's vision, therefore only playing an arbitration role at best. Paragon Holdings' current Chairman needed to take care in appointing a successor for this important voting position before vacating its present informal equivalent.

The projects that the Massachusetts Institute of Technology was running on behalf of the Diamonds' communications endeavours often unearthed complex moral questions, such as scientists developing the capability to mess with the very fabric of the human brain and body and the possibility of collected behavioural information to be put to evil use as well as good.

"Social engineering", as the venture capitalist had labelled this path to innovation a few years earlier, had the potential for dangerous consequences in the absence of diligent overriding governance. It made no sense to retard scientific development, or even to control its advances, yet there was an inevitable opportunity cost to progress the impacts of which were as yet unknown.

"Property," Jeff marked on the timeline. He would keep the luxurious penthouse apartment and divide it back into its original two again. One for each child, he thought, long settled on this idea. The future of Escondido remained unresolved in his mind, so he underlined its name as a reminder and appended four large question marks.

The Diamond Celebration Foundation's many charitable trusts would prove more difficult to allocate. Africa concerned him, the original intent of the famine relief movement beginning to stray from its original quest of empowering people to bring themselves out of poverty. Such was public generosity all over the world, with citizens and governments alike endlessly pouring cash into the deserving continent, the wash of easy money was breeding a culture of dependence and even the expectation of a future based on handouts rather than hand-ups. This knotty conundrum was Kierney's job, along with fighting the inevitable corruption that arose from human greed. He felt convinced she could turn things around with the right partners in the right places.

Childlight Worldwide would go to Kiley Jones and Guy Kahn; the easiest choice of all. The jazz trumpeter, who had stolen the violinist's heart and with whom she now had three children, had always been the most in tune with him on this subject.

The Fellowship work would need a new patron too, someone with first-hand experience of mental illness and ideally of recovery through a respectful and loving support network. The appointment of his successor to this mammoth organisation was much trickier since it was a heavy responsibility to give to someone who might break under its weight.

Much more thought required, Jeff rued, adorning this item with another row of question marks. Chewing absentmindedly on the end of his pen, he sighed, hoping his beautiful best friend could hear these deliberations.

'Whoa, angel. Why the fuck are we doing this now?'

The couple hadn't planned on dividing their mighty empire until their seventies or eighties at least. They had spoken endlessly about phasing out of various aspects of their life singular over ten or so years. "Together, old and grey," they had laughed, imagining the replacement slogan for one of their most memorable fundraising campaigns. The leftover Diamond world-changer was now faced with setting himself a considerably shorter timeframe. The gestation period of a human being, in fact.

No sweat, Jeff smiled to himself, remembering the news Marianna had told him in confidence at Lynn's memorial service; that Anna and Brandon were expecting their first child in September. 'Look what we made in nine months, baby,' he prompted his wife's ghost. 'If we can make such perfect beings in nine months, I can sort out all our shit too.'

"Name" was scribbled onto the schedule as the song the superstar would release for the birth of the new Dyson baby. He had written it when Jet was on his way, nearly twenty years ago, but he had never released it. Though Lynn's sister and her husband worked hard at their research into killer diseases, making more than adequate salaries, they could count on this song to generate a tidy trust fund for their next generation.

Suddenly disoriented, the uncle-to-be lay down on the floor with the ceiling whirling overhead. He rubbed the tattoo on his chest, willing it to send him a restorative message.

'I'll pick the day we're going to be closest, angel. Trust me. I want to be with you so badly. *Je t'aime tanto-tanto, mon amie.*'

Jeff closed his notebook and tucked it between two glossy coffee-table books which hadn't moved for a good few months, hoping Kierney wouldn't be seized by an urge to purge tomorrow. He would find a better place for it in the morning. Stretching out on the couch, he wondered if he might escape the nightmares in the short interval between now and dawn.

He pictured Lynn lying next to him in bed, her body touching his at the shoulder, hip and foot. The image was so powerful that he could almost sense the contact. He fantasised her hand reaching for his and forced imaginary bedclothes to shift as he took hold and slipped her fingers across his chest towards the cherished "JL" symbol.

'*Gracias, Regala*,' he whispered. 'I need you. I love you so much. Will you meet me in June for my hundred-and-forty-fourth birthday, gorgeous?'

The widower wept anew. His dream girl had always spun time backwards so cleverly while they had been together. Each year of their marriage had made him feel more youthful and relaxed, healthier and so much happier. The odometer in his diseased mind had wound back to its actual age during the time the pair had been granted in each other's earthly company. Since she had been taken from them, his desperation was magnified by all those discarded extra years rushing back to reunite with the tortured boy they had not forgotten.

THE QUEEN VERSUS GARCÍA

An expressionless and taciturn Juan Antonio García stood in the dock in the Supreme Court on one side of Queens Square in Sydney's CBD. The bailiff read out the same three charges on which he had been arraigned at the committal hearing, stating allegations that he had intentionally murdered Victoria Lynn Shannon Dyson Diamond on the 16th of February, 1996, using an unlicensed firearm, after having intended to murder Jeffrey Moreno Diamond.

The jury and a packed public gallery were told that García entered The Pensione Hotel at approximately nine o'clock that morning, armed with a handgun and silencer, and had waited for Mr and Ms Diamond to arrive. When the opportunity arose, he had fired four rounds at his chosen subject. The hushed and spellbound courtroom heard the Accused had intended the bullets for Mr Diamond, but that he had turned the gun on the celebrity's wife instead once he realised his original target was not present in the hotel lobby.

One bullet had entered the victim's skull through her forehead, killing her instantaneously. Two other bullets may not have proved fatal but had inflicted serious injuries, one resulting in significant blood loss and potential organ failure. A fourth bullet was later found embedded in the leather sofa to the left of where Ms Diamond had been seated.

Surrounded by eager onlookers, the aforementioned Mr Diamond was in court to hear these words, along with the couple's eighteen-year-old daughter. They sat in the front row of the public area, flanked by two uniformed security staff. Jeff had been in two minds whether to allow Kierney to attend, coming down on the side of total transparency. She knew all the facts, and hearing them relayed in a clinical, dispassionate manner might even help to bring closure to the nasty mess which had culminated in the loss of her mother.

Rosemary Milne, Queen's Counsel, explained to an agitated courtroom that the onus was on the Prosecution to prove beyond reasonable doubt that the man in the dock committed the crimes with which he was charged, and that he did so in full knowledge of his actions and their potential consequences. From their elevated position in the public gallery, the widower sighed at the untold number of complications in this opening sentence alone. Kierney looked into her dad's eyes and pecked his tense cheek for good luck.

Judge Milne asked the Defence bench if it was satisfied that the Accused properly understood the Prosecution Counsel's charges, the evidence its legal team would present to the court and the plea it was entering on his behalf on each count. Stephen Greenshaw, head barrister defending, stood up and addressed the bar, confirming García was in a fit state to be tried, but with the *caveat* that he was under considerable mental strain as a result of the surfeit of publicity surrounding this case.

Graham Winton, the Crown's chief prosecuting solicitor, had told the victim's husband a few days earlier that the Crown's own psychiatric report did not substantiate the Accused's mental incapacity. The judge had advised Defence Counsel not to put too much emphasis on the fact this was a high-profile case. She had apparently indicated, since this case was high profile for both sides, that their respective legal teams were therefore on a level playing field.

Despite the complexity of the charges the Prosecution was required to prove, watching the first few minutes of Judge Milne presiding over "Lynn's case" furnished Jeff with optimism that his beautiful best friend was in excellent hands.

Winton had also let slip that the court officials considered the Defendant to have had a surfeit of similar opportunities to stalk and kill his famous prey throughout his apparent obsession. The fact that he chose this particular day made it difficult to believe he had acted without forethought.

García's Defence lawyers again laboured the point of his diminished mental state. In fact, they went as far as reporting he had regularly contemplated this crime, as substantiated in the media by his former spouse. The dark-haired Diamonds turned and gaped at each other in the peanut gallery upon hearing this statement.

'What a stupid thing to say,' Kierney whispered.

'Yep,' her father replied with a half-smile, putting his finger to his mouth to request her silence.

The young woman crossed fingers of both hands on her lap and fixed her eyes back on the judge, now looking leftwards at a woman who immediately rose to her feet. For the benefit of the jurors and the packed rows of seating upstairs, the court officer read out the legal definitions of murder and manslaughter, urging all present to take time to recognise the difference.

Her Honour next turned to the members of the jury, arranged in three banks of four over to the right-hand side of the courtroom from where the Diamonds were sitting. To Jeff's relief, they were quite a diverse bunch; a little nervous, but eager to understand the case. He really hoped his dream girl was floating around nearby, so she could also achieve some ghostly form of closure over the coming days.

'How do you plead?' asked the judge, requesting the Defendant's response.

'Not guilty,' García answered in a strong Spanish accent, looking anxiously across to the Defence team's bench and offering nothing further.

'To all charges, Mr García?'

'Yes.'

The court officer coughed. 'Will you please address the judge as "Your Honour", Mr García. Do you plead "not guilty" to all three charges?'

'Yes, Your Honour.'

Kierney gasped, even though the Diamonds had been warned by the prosecuting barrister that the Defence had changed its plea. Her father had been waiting to hear these words too, putting a reassuring arm around his daughter. The man had a right to defend himself, regardless of how they felt about him.

The judge gave the Defence team a perfunctory nod. 'Is your client aware that changing his plea during trial proceedings may result in a longer sentence if he is found to be guilty by this court?'

'Yes. He is, Your Honour,' Stephen Greenshaw replied.

'They're going to argue there was no premeditation to kill *mamá*,' Jeff explained. 'Just me. And they're bound to throw in "diminished mental capacity" because he was consumed by jealousy.'

Kierney longed to learn everything she could about the judicial process, so the patient man to her left described the various players and their function in the trial. The court reporter typed furiously while the prosecuting barrister gathered up several folders of paperwork.

The trial now officially open, Graham Winton did his best to iron out any ambiguity in outlining the facts on behalf of the Queen. Jeff shuddered as he remembered the parts of the story he had witnessed. He could still picture the bullet hole in his wife's forehead and smell the blood congealing on her clothes.

Tears pricked behind his eyes, but he couldn't cry. He was racked with anger and rendered confused at reacquainting himself with the man who stole his lover's life on that sunny Friday morning; a man who might well have absconded, had his original target not intercepted him on his way out of the hotel building.

The press and public had already crucified García a hundred times over, to the point where even the victim's husband and his spokespeople had considered it prudent to issue their own statement regarding the Accused's right to a fair trial. The closer the nominated date had approached however, the more anxious the rock star became that the scales of justice might tip the other way. His conscience troubled him greatly, fuelled by his own father's situation and also because he knew how close to the edge a desperate person could skate.

The Australian people were collectively baying for blood to avenge their favourite lady's death. The front page of most newspapers this morning carried the same close-up picture of Jeff and the children taken at Lynn's memorial service, showing their grief at the loss of the famous wife and mother. The story was inset with pictures of Bart and Marianna Dyson and the Accused's own wife, who had publicly filed for divorce shortly before the murder trial commenced.

García stared at the floor while the Prosecution's chief lawyer delivered his opening address.

'This is a *prima facie* case,' Winton told the jury, with expansive hand gestures and exquisitely rounded vowels, 'which means the Crown believes it has sufficient reliable evidence to convict the Defendant of the charges you have just heard.'

Jeff studied the man in the dock for any sign of remorse. At one point, the barrister pointed into the public gallery to where he and Kierney were sitting, referring to the victim's family. A ripple of whispers went around the courtroom as all eyes lifted. García's eyes too flashed upwards for a moment, and the widower's grabbed them for as long as they could. Although the Accused's expression didn't change, his body language became defensive, shuffling in his chair and releasing eye contact almost immediately.

'Ladies and gentlemen of the jury,' Graham Winton announced to the twelve people on the judge's left, proceeding to outline his responsibilities during the trial.

The jury members nodded their understanding of the Prosecution's responsibilities.

'If that's clear,' he continued, 'the Crown intends to prove beyond reasonable doubt that the Accused, Juan Antonio García, is guilty of all three charges brought before the court.'

'You OK?' Jeff asked the teenager, once the prosecutor had sat down.

She nodded and gripped her father's hand. 'Are you?'

He smiled. 'Yes, thanks, gorgeous. Just relax. It's early days.'

The barrister representing García took the stand and presented the opening address for the Defence. An equally impressive orator, Greenshaw's assertions caused some restlessness in the gallery by describing the Spaniard as a hard-working family man who had been poorly served by society since arriving in Australia over thirty years ago.

'There are heaps of people in that category,' Kierney whispered. 'Does that mean it's OK to shoot someone?'

Judge Milne cautioned members of the public to remain silent during the Defence's opening statement, drawing their attention to the security staff stationed at the back.

'Lock 'im up for good!' came a shout from somewhere over the Diamonds' left shoulders.

Kierney tensed up and giggled. Jeff had noticed she was dressed in Lynn's clothes from head to toe. He still had difficulty coping with this recent practice of hers, but it made the youngster feel closer to her mother, which was enough reason for him not to mention his discomfort.

'They're fighting a losing battle,' the empathetic man's voice remained calm as he referred to the court officials. 'If she thinks people are going to be quiet, she's a little naïve. We're probably adding to her problems by sitting here, but what the hell. And hey, Kizzo... If anytime you want to go, we can go.'

The judge repeated her request for silence, threatening any future outbursts with removal from the gallery. Kierney shook her head vigorously.

'No. I have to be here.'

Her dad smiled. '*Bueno*. Me too. I'm going to get slaughtered by the papers for bringing you, but I don't give a shit.'

The barrister for the Defence resumed his opening remarks, urging the jurors to ignore any comments they might overhear from the public area. He stated his team's intention to call witnesses and exhibit evidence in dispute of the charges and the exact circumstances which drew the Accused to commit his actions.

Greenshaw explained that the Defendant had come to Australia as a boy from an agricultural region in southern Spain, with his father and two younger brothers. Their mother was not mentioned, the Diamonds both noted. He told how García's father had struggled to make a living in Sydney, unable to speak much English, unskilled and uneducated. A saintly picture was painted of the young Juan Antonio, who played the guitar and had been a regular churchgoer all his life.

Jeff and Kierney avoided each other's gaze during the rest of the statement, not wishing to draw attention to themselves and risk causing another bout of unrest. Except for a barely audible whistle at the fact that the immigrant married at eighteen years old and had fathered five children, neither passed any comment on the Defence's story.

So what had driven García to commit these alleged crimes? This was the question the victim's husband was desperate to have answered. How long had he been waiting to do this? Was he part of a bigger operation, or had he worked alone? Was it a snap decision to kill him that day, or had the insignificant-looking bloke planned it over months or even years? *Be patient*, the famous man requested of himself. It was weird in the extreme to be attending his wife's murder trial, learning the truth of his own bungled assassination attempt.

From his vantage point high above the wooden box enclosing the Accused, Jeff felt closer to Lynn, gradually sensing her sharing the experience. Instinctively, he rubbed his chest, causing Kierney to glance across and issue a questioning smile. He acknowledged her with a flick of his eyebrows, in response to which his daughter rested her head against his upper arm.

After the Defence's barrister had finished, the judge called a thirty-minute recess and everyone stood while she and her entourage left the court. The security guard at Jeff's side also jumped up and pointed into the aisle, signalling for both Diamonds to follow him.

'Where are we going?' the young woman asked. 'A break already?'

'There's a room reserved for you to wait in during breaks, Miss,' replied the second bodyguard on the other side of her, 'for morning tea, lunch. You know...'

The teenager nodded, invited ahead of her father to follow the uniformed man. They were shown into a wood-panelled office serviced with pots of coffee and tea and some pastries. Jeff dropped his tall frame down onto a chair and let out a deep sigh.

'Jesus, Kizzo. Recess already. We've hardly started, and I'm bloody exhausted. Maybe it'll be too much to attend every day.'

'How long do you think it'll go for?' Kierney asked, pouring cups of coffee and stirring two heaped spoonful's of sugar into her father's cup.

'Who knows? But I suspect we're going to get pretty familiar with this room.'

His daughter chuckled. 'I'll bring a book tomorrow in that case.'

There was a knock on the door, and in walked Graham Winton, the chief prosecution attorney, minus his flowing gown and dusty-looking wig. He strode straight up to the celebrity and extended his hand.

'Jeff, good morning,' he said with well-practised sincerity, his eyes travelling upwards as the great man's head rose to well above his own. 'How are you?'

'Fine, thanks, Graham,' he replied. 'This is our daughter, Kierney. This is Graham Winton. He's the head honcho for the Prosecution.'

The senior counsel held out a gracious hand to the young woman. 'It's a pleasure, Miss Diamond. My daughters love your music.'

'Thank you very much, Mr Winton, and thanks for representing us too.'

The three sat down to coffee and cakes as if they were attending a regular business meeting. Jeff playfully kicked his gipsy girl's foot under the table, and she returned a coy grin, happy to be included in the grown-up world at last.

Graham continued. 'We're not actually representing you, Miss Diamond. We're representing the Commonwealth of Australia, but we *are* here to make sure justice is served for the loss of your dear mother.'

Kierney nodded her gratitude. This imposing man reminded her a little of her grandfather.

'This morning, we went through the jury selection process,' the barrister explained. 'The Defendant can request three jury members be changed out and three new ones to be called. Today only one person was challenged. A woman of roughly your age, Jeff, who they thought would be unfairly biased towards the Prosecution. We didn't seek any changes. It tends to make the Defence nervous if we tell them we're happy with the jury as it is.'

The seasoned negotiator laughed when he heard this. He doubted whether the esteemed Senior Counsel for the Defence, Mr Greenshaw, would ever be nervous.

'How bloody awful would it be to get picked for jury service this week?' the superstar smiled. 'Of all the weeks. Double-edged sword, I guess. What a responsibility they must feel.'

The youngster frowned. 'Yeah. Especially with the two of us watching them.'

'Indeed,' Graham affirmed. 'That's why the judge will take extra time with them, to make sure they're not bamboozled by any technical jargon. Greenshaw and I were given strict instructions on Friday in our pre-trial conference to be very explicit.'

'Great,' the celebrity sighed. 'I like that. How long d'you expect the trial to last?'

'Oh, not more than ten days,' Senior Counsel answered matter-of-factly. 'That's what they normally schedule for a murder case. Juries are allocated on the basis of no more than two weeks out of their workplaces, so the judge will do her best to have it wrapped up well within that timeframe.'

Jeff sniggered. 'Very business-like,' he stated, doing well to mask his frustration.

Kierney felt angry too, picking up on her dad's sarcasm. The barristers had already discussed how many witnesses were to be called for each side and the testimonies likely to be presented. It all seemed a bit of a show, with much of the important detail worked out in advance behind the scenes between the rival lawyers.

'So what I don't understand, Mr Winton, is why Mr García's allowed to change his plea,' she asked. 'If he confessed to the murder, why can't the case go forward on that basis?'

Jeff smiled without looking in her direction, not wishing to put the clever teenager off her stride.

'The Defendant gave his confession before the lawyers representing him now were engaged, Miss Diamond,' Graham responded.

'Please call me Kierney,' the polite young woman interjected, having heard her parents do the same so many times.

'Of course, Kierney. The police assigned him a brief who supposedly did not give him thorough advice, according to Defence Counsel. Now I don't know if that's true, but he is entitled to take further advice and change his plea. It makes little difference in this case because he didn't plead guilty to any of the charges, that is to murder or manslaughter.'

'If he'd offered a guilty plea to manslaughter, and we try him on the basis of manslaughter, then he should get a more lenient sentence if convicted. But the Defence has not requested the charges be downgraded, and we shan't offer either.'

'I see,' the serious student responded. 'Thank you. That makes perfect sense, but aren't you taking a risk that he may be acquitted of murder but would have been convicted of manslaughter?'

'Yes, we are, angel,' her dad replied. 'They are, I mean. But public opinion's on our side. The fact he fired the gun four times suggests it was no accident.'

The barrister nodded, looked at his watch and gulped down the rest of his coffee. 'Absolutely correct, sir. Sorry, good people, but I must be off. We're due to resume in five.'

Kierney nodded. 'Thank you, Mr Winton. It wouldn't have taken so long on the original plea though, would it?'

'Nope,' the widower sniffed, picking up on the subtext of his daughter's line of questioning. 'I wonder which paper's underwriting their bill.'

Winton raised his hands as if to say, "No comment," and the others laughed. A bailiff knocked at the door and entered. The judge was ready to continue. Graham jumped to his feet and clattered his cup back onto its saucer.

'I'll call by over lunch,' he promised, almost running out of the door.

'Right,' the superstar replied to the back of the man's head, before turning to his daughter. 'What did *mamá* used to say?'

'Argh!' they groaned in unison.

Kierney hugged her father tightly as they absorbed this painful reminder of their missing loved one and her endearing way of dealing with bothersome people. Both wiped away tears and filed back out with the security men, ready to take their places in the public gallery for the second session.

As if sitting in the dress circle in a theatre, the Diamonds prepared to watch the next few scenes of Lynn's tragic play unfold beneath. Several fans behind attempted to pass on good wishes, but the vigilant bodyguards prevented anyone from making contact. The crowd had called out a few encouraging comments as they walked down the steps, which Jeff had acknowledged with a smile and a quick wave.

'Y'know...' he muttered, as they waited for the officials to return, 'this trial could go wrong in so many more bureaucratic ways than you'd think.'

His eager pupil grimaced. 'Really? Instead of the jury's decision going against us, you mean?'

'Yeah, exactly. I was talking to Gerry's mate, Bryce, yesterday. You remember him? With the two boys at MA.'

'Yes, I know. Connor and Aidan.'

The celebrity shrugged. 'I don't know their names. Anyway... All the Defence has to do is prove García didn't understand what he was being charged with, or if they pick up an inconsistency in someone's statement, or someone once said something that García considered overly threatening. The list goes on... It gave me a much better appreciation of why we have to pay solicitors such a huge pile of cash, because they need to be extra careful with every tiny detail.'

The crowd seemed to have increased in size during the break, with a line of latecomers now standing at the back. Jeff discovered via their security firm that a queue of people hoping to secure a seat in the gallery had snaked all the way around the building since before six o'clock that morning. With a fresh dose of caffeine inside them, the atmosphere felt more highly-charged than earlier too.

'We're in for a bumpy ride,' the forty-three-year-old warned, putting his arm around his gipsy girl and surveying the scene. 'Just remember... Don't focus too much on any one phrase or question. They're going to try to trip witnesses up and deliberately provoke them into saying something rash. It'll be fun to see the lawyers squirm if their witnesses let them down.'

García was already installed in the dock, with a uniformed custodian stationed by his side. He looked slight and inadequate, hunched over. The court stood to attention when the judge re-entered the room, followed by the associates and officer, all taking their seats together with a shuffling of feet and creaks of aged joinery.

Winton was ready and waiting when the judge moved to question the first witness. 'The Prosecution calls Detective Inspector Robert Fisher from the New South Wales Police.'

A gust from front to back signalled the audience's collective inward breath, and the familiar figure of Bob Fisher took the stand. He was in full dress uniform with a strip of multi-coloured ribbons above his left breast pocket, his peaked cap under his arm and shiny buttons on his *épaulettes*.

'He looks like he's about to burst into song,' Kierney giggled, 'like in a Gilbert and Sullivan operetta.'

Jeff nudged his daughter. 'Shhh! That's very good, but shut up.'

The tattoo behind the musician's own breast pocket flared suddenly. The handsome man lifted his eyes to the ceiling and wondered briefly where Lynn's ethereal seat might be. Heartened, he focussed back on Fisher and the sheets of notes spread out on the lectern in front of him. The experienced police officer gave an air of considerable ease with court processes, which also boosted the famous pair's confidence.

Winton directed the inspector to describe the sequence of events leading to the Accused's capture and subsequent arrest. Staring directly at García, the polished performer gave evidence.

'Thank you, Your Honour, and good morning. The Accused, Juan Antonio García, was detained at the scene at around nine-twenty on the morning of the sixteenth of February, nineteen-ninety-six, by hotel security staff with reasonable grounds for suspicion he was involved in the fatal shooting of Ms Lynn Diamond at The Pensione Hotel on George Street in Sydney's Central Business District. As the Prosecution has already stated, this constitutes a "Class One" offence.'

Fisher then shifted his stance to face the jury, who were listening with bated breath. 'The Accused had been apprehended upon attempting to leave the hotel by the Victim's husband, Mr Jeff Diamond, at the request of the hotel manager in the aftermath of the shooting.'

The proud teenager looked up at her father's handsome face while the crowd broke into spontaneous cheers and clapping upon hearing this fact, which had been widely publicised on television and in the newspapers.

'Good on ya, Jeff!' came a yell from behind them. 'We're all with you here.'

The superstar acknowledged the kind advocate before making another, more direct hand gesture to request quiet, and the judge's stern voice demanded there be no further utterances from the gallery. She reminded the jury again to disregard any comments made by people other than those representing the Crown or the Defendant.

Fisher coughed but continued unfazed. 'My colleague, Detective Sergeant Andrew Waters, detained him for questioning in relation to the murder of Ms Lynn Diamond based on information that her husband had supplied us, concerning a remark the Accused had made to him.'

'And what was that remark, Inspector Fisher?' Graham Winton prompted.

'The Accused spoke in Spanish, Your Honour, which is his native language. Mr Diamond is also fluent in Spanish. Forgive my pronunciation as I read it out for the court.'

DI Fisher picked up a piece of paper and put on his spectacles, preparing his rehearsed line. '*Quería matarlo Ustéd, pero es mejor así,*' he enunciated with care, daring to glance up at Jeff and Kierney in the gallery.

The uncharacteristically reserved star gave a slight nod in reply, causing subdued laughter to break out around the famous pair. Judge Milne called the court to order and requested an English version from the Prosecution's first witness.

'Your Honour, the Defendant's comment has been translated by an accredited translation service as, "I wanted to kill you, but it is better this way."'

A loud gasp went up in the public gallery, and the Diamonds remained motionless while the excitement died down. Members of the jury stared at one another in amazement, and the judge asked the witness to repeat the phrase once more in both languages.

After Fisher had done so, Graham Winton turned to the jury and raised his hands as if to say, "There you have it," before urging the Detective Inspector to continue with his summation of the events. The witness removed his glasses and rested them on top of his papers.

'The Accused accompanied DS Waters into an office, where he was given a verbal caution, and his rights were explained to him. Ascertaining that English was not his first language, the sergeant radioed back to Surry Hills Police Station to send an interpreter to the scene as soon as possible. The Accused became agitated when he was detained but did not resist. A search subsequently located the weapon used to shoot Ms Diamond, buried in a large plant pot in a corridor leading off the main foyer.'

The court officer circulated two photographs. One was of a semi-automatic firearm and silencer which were recovered soon after the police's arrival, covered with markings in white powder denoting fingerprints. The other was of an underarm holster, spread out on a flat surface, with the gun inserted, which García had been wearing under his blouson jacket. The victim's relatives watched each juror take a careful look at both pictures before passing them to the next person along.

'DS Waters indicated that the weapon smelled like it had been recently fired and was warm to the touch,' DI Fisher continued. 'And as you can see in the photograph, there were several fingerprints matching those of the Accused, and no prints belonging to any other individual. The Accused did not resist arrest and was taken to Surry Hills Police Station, where he later gave a full confession to my superior officer, Superintendent Frank Corelli.'

Winton interrupted the witness. 'Inspector, to which charge or charges did the Accused confess at this time?' he asked, gesturing towards the jury.

Fisher nodded, reminded of their questioning plan. 'At this point, the Accused was charged with one count of murder, that of the Victim, Ms Lynn Diamond, and with possession of a firearm without a permit. He had informed us that he had applied for a licence at the same time as he bought the firearm, in the Victorian country town of Mildura, but there's no record of a licence in any state in the name of Juan Antonio García.'

'So please inform the court at what stage the third charge was brought?' Winton asked.

'Shortly after three o'clock that afternoon, Your Honour, after I had returned from the press conference held to formally alert the media of Ms Diamond's passing.'

A hush descended over the public gallery, and a shiver ran down Jeff's spine. Imagining that if he were to look round, every single sad eye would be on him, he threaded an arm around Kierney's shoulder and squeezed her into his side. She was weeping into a tissue, and her body felt rigid against his. García slouched like an unfinished statue in the dock, eyes directed to the floor in front of his feet.

Fisher went on. 'I returned to the investigating team to review their case file. I remembered again the words the Accused had used, which suggested to us that García had intended to murder Mr Diamond himself, and had in fact turned the gun on his wife when the original target was not present in the hotel lobby.

'I conferred with my colleagues and my superiors, and we decided to add the third charge at this time, i.e. intent to murder Mr Jeffrey Moreno Diamond, as a result of the comment the Accused made when prevented from leaving the hotel.'

'Detective Inspector,' the barrister prompted again. 'Was it only those few words that gave you to believe Mr Diamond was the Accused's original target?'

Fisher shook his head. 'No, Your Honour. Hotel staff provided statements testifying that Ms Diamond took a telephone call on behalf of her husband, which was later on established to have come from a public phone in the foyer. The hotel reception staff reported taking a call from a man with a strong accent asking for Mr Diamond...'

Fisher picked up his notes and spectacles again, re-familiarising himself with the quotation he had extracted from the dazed hotel worker's statement. 'Yes, here,' he continued. 'Hannah Elizabeth Todd, receptionist at The Pensione Hotel. Witness statement taken at five minutes past eleven on Friday the sixteenth of February, nineteen-ninety-six.

'Miss Todd states, "Ms Diamond checked into the room which had been booked for her and her husband for that night. I handed her the room key and two envelopes that had been left for them, and then the phone rang on the desk. I answered it and couldn't understand the voice very well. It was foreign, a strong accent. I asked the caller to repeat what he said. He asked to speak to Jeff Diamond, so I told Ms Diamond the call was for her husband. She said she would take it, and my co-worker said she could take it at the courtesy phone on the other side of the lobby. The next time we looked at her, even though we didn't hear anything, she had been shot in her head and was completely still."'

Jeff let out a slow breath, tears overflowing from his eyes.

'It wasn't your fault,' Kierney whispered. 'You couldn't have known what was going to happen.'

The jury sat motionless and mute, as did the public gallery. The whole courtroom seemed to be set in stone, until someone's telephone rang a few rows behind the celebrity. Furious, the judge commanded a bailiff to eject the person responsible for such an impertinent interjection and reminded everyone to ensure no further calls would disrupt the trial.

'Shit!' Jeff whispered, grateful that the tension had been broken and reaching for his own handset. 'That could've been mine. Look! Gerry rang two minutes ago. Lucky I remembered to put it on silent during the recess. Is yours off?'

Kierney grinned in relief, seeing the name on the screen which looked so small in her father's hand. 'Are you alright?'

'No,' he nodded.

The teaser's tired, old trick made his daughter laugh, as it always did, and his chest twitched again. '*Mamá* liked that too,' he confessed, rubbing his tattoo and kissing the teenager's forehead.

Sitting back to pay full attention, the widower's heart leapt into his mouth when fingers with long nails pressed lightly on his right shoulder. He twisted round to see a woman's tear-streaked face smiling down upon him and his miniature. The security guard advised her to sit back, but the celebrity intervened.

'It's fine, mate,' he said, doing his best to hide his disappointment.

'I just wanted to say you two are so lovely together. I'm so sorry Lynn's no longer with you.'

Jeff gave the well-wisher a melancholy smile. 'Thanks heaps. It's tough, but we'll get there.'

The judge focussed once more on the jury before posing a question to DI Fisher. The Diamonds' sympathetic fan sat back, and their minder relaxed again. Jeff pitied everyone around him. Who would be the next in line to pose a potential threat? Why now did all these kind-hearted, ordinary citizens deserve to be treated like would-be assassins? And yet, who said lightning didn't strike twice?

'Detective Inspector...' Judge Milne addressed the witness. 'How did the Accused react to being charged with these three serious offences?'

'Your Honour,' Fisher replied. 'The Accused had adopted a belligerent attitude when brought into the interview room at first. However, he broke down in tears just before confessing to shooting the Victim. García spoke in rapid Spanish, which the interpreter had difficulty understanding due to his distressed state. The only charge he disputed was in regard to the firearms permit. At seventeen-fifteen hours the same afternoon, the Accused appeared before the magistrate and pleaded guilty to all three charges.'

After listening to a few sentences of the inspector's intricate explanation of the police process in relation to homicide investigations, Judge Milne interrupted and addressed the Defence's bench. 'Mr Greenshaw, please would you confirm to the court that your client does not wish to use the services of an interpreter during these proceedings?'

'That's correct, Your Honour,' Stephen Greenshaw responded, checking with the hunched man in the dock, who shook his head. 'The Defendant does not wish to use an interpreter.'

Jeff couldn't help but draw comparisons between García and his father, and also between García and himself. The similarities were as complicated as the differences: he and García were similar in age, but in not much else; his father and García were both born outside Australia and had arrived as children in a strange country.

Although, he mused, his father must already have understood and spoken English well by the time he arrived in Sydney, since he had spent a year in an elementary school in the New York borough of Queens. García and Jeff were both hard-working men, whereas to the songwriter's knowledge, his father had never held down a real job.

All three were family men. By all accounts, the Spaniard had been a good father; an accolade to which Jeff's father most definitely could not lay claim. It appeared García had been without a mother from an early age. His father had been blessed with one, but her influence had been negligible. The billionaire had always wondered why this was. The younger Diamond had grown up with a mother too, but she had neglected her accidental son from the outset.

As the big-hearted philanthropist toyed with these various ideas while Fisher droned on in monotonous detail, they only proved to him further how challenging it was for a society to create services to assist disadvantaged families. Each individual presented with a composite of unique differences.

Acknowledging this problem was unlikely to be solved during the inspector's testimony, the intellectual dragged his mind back from his parallel universe to where Fisher was now explaining that no recording was available of the telephone call made to the hotel seeking information as to the whereabouts of one Mr Diamond; the one his wife had taken on his behalf.

Jeff exhaled, the memory of his own part in this torrid scenario weighing heavily on his conscience. His tattoo itched again, and he took heart that Lynn didn't blame him.

'Poor bastard,' he murmured to Kierney, nodding at García. 'He has no idea what's going on.'

'Why do you care?' she replied. 'He shot *mamá*, didn't he? And he wanted to shoot you. Why are you so sympathetic towards him?'

Jeff's stomach flipped over, and his head filled again with thoughts of his own father. Disoriented, he battled to stay conscious while his persistent psyche alternated between his father and himself in the dock in García's place.

'I don't know, *pequeñita*,' he whispered, sweat forming on his brow. 'Probably because of Granddad, or even because I know how it is to feel overwhelmed with anger for a long time and to have bottled stuff up inside for so long. All it took was one bad decision for García, just the same as my dad, and bang! No more freedom. *Adiós a la esperanza.*'

The celebrity stood up, to the astonishment of those around him. Kierney rose halfway, expecting to follow him, but he eased her shoulder back down. The security guard at his side led him up the aisle, determined to prevent supportive hands from reaching out and touching the bereft superstar as he sprinted up the steps towards the exit.

The same kind lady from a few minutes ago leant forward to speak to the youngster who had been left behind. With swift reflexes, her bodyguard lunged over and motioned for the stranger to sit back, which she did. The teenager smiled through tearful eyes at the woman who only wanted to reassure her.

'I'm alright, thank you,' Kierney assured her. 'My dad'll be OK too. It's good for him to have a break. He won't be able to stay away for too long.'

The woman blew her a kiss, and the dark-haired student faced the front, gritting her teeth to stave off tears again.

Down below, Fisher continued to speak to the jury. 'The Accused asked if he could telephone his wife, but they did not have a conversation. The officer who accompanied him couldn't tell if he had failed to contact her or if she had refused the call. He was then given access to a Legal Aid lawyer who spoke fluent Spanish. The Accused did not request to contact any other family members. In fact, no other person, Your Honour.'

Graham Winton thanked the senior policeman and advised the court to be satisfied that nothing had been overlooked. A couple of jury members nodded their apparent understanding, but others merely stared towards the bench. Kierney wished she could be a fly on the wall to listen to the first conversation between these twelve strangers, her stomach hinting that the lunch break must be imminent.

In the restroom, Jeff bent over the basin, splashing water over his face. His insides still felt queasy, conscious of the awkward security guard loitering by the door.

'Sorry, mate,' the widower said, sucking in large breaths and blowing them out noisily. 'All good. I'm just going to check this message and make one phone call, if that's OK. Then we can go back in.'

The burly man said nothing while the well-respected celebrity listened to his voicemail. It revealed that his business manager was flying up to Sydney and would see his clients in the landmark building soon after lunch. He couldn't keep away, according to the message.

Jeff shook his head and smiled. 'Thou shalt not turn this into a circus,' he mocked, dialling his friend's number.

'Mate! How are you?' Gerry's voice sounded anxious. 'How's the trial going?'

'Hey, Gez. We've hardly got started really. Where are you?'

'In a car, about five "K" from the CBD. Have you broken for lunch? Is it OK if I sit with you?'

'Sure. Absolutely, mate. It's tough; slow going, y'know. DI Fisher's still setting the scene. They're taking a whole heap of extra precautions to prevent misunderstandings, which I guess is good. But it makes it so agonisingly tedious.'

'Fuck that,' the businessman replied, laughing. 'Maybe I should turn around and go back to the airport.'

Jeff laughed too. 'No, mate. Don't do that. I'm grateful for your support. I expect the umpires'll call lunch soon.'

The security guard waved to his charge, having received a message via his earpiece. 'Lunch recess has started, sir.'

'Cheers, mate. Thanks,' the great man acknowledged, lifting the telephone back to his mouth. 'Gez, I've just been told they've already called time for this morning. Let me know when you get here, and I'll send someone down to find you. We're on Level Three, I think.'

The security guard nodded.

'Yep. Three, mate. See you soon.'

Jeff ended the call, and the two men left the bathroom. only to be confronted by hordes of people streaming out of the public gallery and swarming towards them. Hysteria erupted around the Australian hero, with people scattering in every direction, some too scared to approach him and anxious to stay out of his way, and others who were determined to speak to him and even touch him.

The security man looked on dumbfounded while the authoritative songwriter kept walking at a steady pace through a crowd that parted at his will. Jeff Diamond had done this before, the young man realised. He provided a somewhat redundant rear-guard action and watched the handsome star let himself into their temporary home and disappear inside.

Safely behind the closed door, Jeff walked up to his daughter and gave her a big hug. 'Sorry to abandon you. I didn't realise we were so close to lunch.'

'I think the judge broke for lunch because you left,' Kierney replied. 'I saw her look up because everyone else did.'

Her father shook his head. He was turning the trial into a circus after all. Perhaps they oughtn't to attend. Maybe they should content themselves with an update at the end of each session. The last thing he wanted was to jeopardise the outcome simply by sitting in the dress circle.

The teenager began to unwrap the plates of sandwiches on the table, while her dad poured three glasses of orange juice.

'Three?' Kierney asked. 'Is Mr Winton coming to join us?'

'No, Gerry is. He rang to say he couldn't keep away. D'you mind?'

'No, of course I don't mind. Do you?'

'Definitely not. I'm bloody glad he's here.'

The pair sat eating their lunch, each deep in thought. It was a relaxed, comfortable silence.

'That woman was kind,' the young woman broke the spell, setting her plate down. 'The woman behind.'

'Yeah, she was,' the sad man agreed, opting not to let on about the trick his mind had played on him.

'After you left, she tried to console me, but the security guy wouldn't let her talk to me. I felt embarrassed for everyone. And then she blew me a kiss, which made me want to cry.'

Jeff sighed. 'Whoa, baby. I'm sorry. D'you think we should leave? I'm wondering if we're too disruptive.'

Kierney scrunched her pretty facial features. 'No, *papá* . I'd prefer to stay. What about sitting at the back?'

'No way! That'd be excruciating,' her father declined with a chuckle. 'We wouldn't be able to see properly. I'd rather not be there at all than not be able to see what was going on.'

'That's so selfish,' the precocious student chided. 'Halfway up then.'

Jeff laughed again, raising his hands. 'Alright, already. You're too good, Miss Peacekeeper. Good idea. It's a deal.'

'Is *mamá* here?' his daughter asked, her eyes diverting downwards to her father's chest.

'Sometimes. I hope she's causing an icy cold wind to blow down García's neck.'

'*Papá!*' Kierney yelped. 'One minute you're saying "poor bastard" and the next you're hoping he's freezing to death. Make up your mind!'

'I feel sorry for him,' the master clarified his position to the willing apprentice. 'I didn't say I wanted him to feel good. I'm quite happy to feel sorry for him suffering for as long as it takes.'

The youngster's face assumed a confused frown. 'That doesn't make sense. What's the point in feeling sorry for him if you don't want him to feel better?'

'Aha! That's the difference between empathy and sympathy, Kizzo,' her father explained. 'You can understand someone's plight without having to agree with them.'

The teenager beamed. 'Wow! I never thought about it that way. That's brilliant! I completely get that. *Gracias.*'

'*De nada, pequeñita,*' her dad responded, toasting her with his glass of orange juice. 'Glad to be of service.'

'See?' Kierney whined. 'I *do* still need you. You said you could retire, but I'm not ready.'

There was a knock at the door, and one of their security guards entered, shadowed by the family's smartly-dressed business manager. Jeff stood up and strode over to shake Gerry's hand, indicating that the dutiful sentry should allow him in. The door closed quickly behind them, shutting out the hubbub in the background again.

'G'day, mate,' the victim's husband welcomed his friend. 'Can't miss it, huh? It's a sell-out show. You'll have to sit on Kizzy's lap.'

'Hello, Kizmet,' the new arrival said, bending over to give his favourite girl a kiss on the cheek. 'I'm not sure that'd be too comfortable for you, but I'd certainly enjoy it.'

The youngster rolled her eyes. 'Hi, Gerry. Don't listen to him. He's in one of those weird moods.'

'Well, it's completely manic out there,' the accountant reported. 'The concierge, or whoever she was, who directed me here, said they had to turn away four hundred people this morning.'

'Four hundred?' Kierney gasped. 'How many do you think are in the public area, *papá*?'

'About the same,' Jeff guessed. 'Told you it was a sell-out. There've been some interesting moments already, with people shouting out.'

'Yeah,' his daughter joined in with a ready smile. 'Someone yelled, "Lock 'im up!" right at the very beginning. It was funny, but the judge is good at taking control.'

Gerry grinned. 'Good thing too. I didn't know whether you'd be enjoying it or not, but you seem OK.'

'Jesus, mate, it's not enjoyable,' the grieving man scoffed. 'It's terrible actually, but it's like a morbid fascination. You don't want to know, but you need to know. That's how I feel anyway. What about you, *pequeñita*?'

'Not as bad as you, but similar, yeah. The process they're going through is interesting. Only it'd be much better if they weren't talking about *mamá*.'

'Hey, mate,' Jeff interjected, momentarily distracted. 'You know what that reminds me of?'

Gerry shook his head.

'Remember when Big D was trying to ride me out of town, back in 'seventy-four, when Lynn came home from the US?'

'Oh, yeah,' his long-time manager nodded.

'I remember saying to you then what a fascinating exercise it was, but such a damned shame it was my life he was fucking with.'

Kierney's eyes widened. 'Grandpa? What was he trying to do?'

'You know all about that, baby,' Jeff said, overcome with emotion again. 'When he was hoping your *mamá* would've forgotten all about me, but she hadn't. And I had to prove myself worthy of her in his eyes.'

The former lost boy leant forward on the table and began to sob. 'And then I didn't protect her, and he was right all along.'

The young woman rushed to hug her father, confident that it was sympathy she was feeling this time. She didn't want him to beat himself up any more about how his wife had died.

'Grandpa doesn't think that way now.'

'Ah, I bet he does,' the man sniffed. 'I'd be very surprised if he hasn't had that very conversation with Grandma. A quiet "I told you so" moment. "My daughter should've married Prince Charles after all."'

'Bloody nonsense, mate,' Gerry scoffed. 'Dyson respects you enormously. You proved him wrong on all counts, so get those stupid ideas out of your head right now.'

'Argh!' Kierney groaned, desperate to pull her dad out of the doldrums. 'Prince Charles! I'm relieved he's not my father. Just the thought makes me shiver! *Cállate, papá. Mamá* would've gone crazy long ago if she had.'

Jeff smiled. 'Thanks, *pequeñita*. That was different; an arranged marriage that should never have happened. He never loved her. They're divorced.'

'Oh, for God's sake,' the teenager objected again. 'Stop it, please. No-one blames you for *mamá's* death. No-one except you, that is. That's why we're here, isn't it? To see García get put away? If you'd already been in that hotel lobby when he phoned, you'd be dead now and probably *mamá* too. Then Jet and I would be orphans, so I'm not blaming you for it turning out this way.'

'Hear, hear,' the new arrival agreed. 'Listen to mini-me, mate. She makes a lot more sense than you do.'

The widower sighed. 'Thanks, but it's not going to work, guys. I know what you're saying, Kiz, and I can't dispute any of it. But regardless, she's fuckin' dead, and I couldn't stop it happening. I failed to protect your *mamá* from that bloody weasel and his unlicensed gun.'

'Christ, mate,' Gerry raised his voice, grabbing his friend round the base of the neck with both hands and shaking him roughly. 'How many times do you think that bloody weasel, as you call him, stalked you before he got his opportunity? You protected Lynn all those times, and from all the other fuckers who wrote those crank letters over the years. You couldn't know if and when some crazed idiot would do something like this. Just try and tell me you could.'

Kierney was crying, more out of frustration than sadness. 'Thanks, Gerry,' she said. 'Very true. If Grandpa'd been right back then, someone related to your past could've got to *mamá*, or any of us, years ago. Please stop thinking this way. We have to listen to all the witnesses this afternoon and tomorrow. Who knows how many days it'll take? And you've got to be a witness yourself, so please try and shake this off.'

'Your dad'll be fine when he takes the stand, Kiz,' their manager consoled her. 'You know how good he is on his feet. That'll be no problem. Come on, mate. Eat another sandwich and have some of this revolting, lukewarm coffee.'

Jeff stood up and stretched his arms high into the air, in an attempt to release some tension from his shoulders. He paced up and down in the small room, accepting a cup of the unappetising beverage with little enthusiasm.

'Is it going well, so far?' Gerry changed the subject, addressing the younger Diamond.

'I think so,' she replied. 'Hard to say. Mr Winton's very impressive. Super-confident. But so's the other guy. What's his name?'

'Greenshaw. Stephen Greenshaw. Yeah, they're both at the top of their game, that's for sure. And I like the judge. She's already made up her mind. You can tell.'

The executive directed his old friend towards a chair. 'Sit down, mate. That's good then, isn't it? I know Steve Greenshaw. We went to school together, if he's who I think he is. I've met him a few times over the years, and his kid sister and I used to have a thing for a while. He's got an excellent reputation by all accounts.'

Blake & Partners' VIP client did as he was told, not surprised to hear about yet another of his old friend's silver-spoon female conquests. 'I'm sorry, guys. Thanks for putting up with my spoilt brat ways. It's been a long time since I've felt this desperate and out of control. Lynn was so expert at handling me. She never let me behave this way, so I apologise. I love you guys so much.'

Kierney leant over and kissed her father hard on his left temple. 'I love you too, and so does *mamá*.'

'Come here, you gorgeous thing,' Jeff grabbed his daughter and swung her round onto his lap, cuddling her in close. 'You say all the right things. You're very good to me, just like your *mamá*.'

'OK, OK,' the older man said, uncomfortable to be sharing this rather intimate moment between grieving family members. 'Isn't it show-time yet?'

The youngster checked her watch. 'One-thirty, they said. Ten minutes. I'm surprise we haven't had a visit from the Crown.'

'When are you up?' Gerry asked.

'Number Three,' the widower replied, suddenly listless and purged of energy. 'Tomorrow, I expect. Or the next day even, at this rate. The Defence has to cross-examine Bob Fisher next. Then it'll be the hotel doorman, Fruity, or whatever his name is.'

Kierney giggled. 'Fruity? Oh, Karl Fruchtmann! That's not fair! Now I'm not going to be able to take him seriously at all.'

'You should yell that out when it goes quiet in there,' the insolent man suggested, pleased to see his daughter happier again. 'Hey, Fruity! Will you go out with me?'

Kierney screwed up a paper napkin and threw it at her father. He caught it and tossed it back, hitting her squarely on the cheek.

'I'm sure the security guard next to me was chatting me up when you left just before lunch,' she told the two men. 'He got very friendly once you were out of sight.'

'Doubtless,' Jeff chuckled. 'The slime-bag. Can't blame a man for trying.'

It was all Kierney could do to keep a straight face when the aforementioned slime-bag knocked on the door at the very same moment and entered to tell them the court would resume in five minutes.

'Thanks, mate,' the celebrity said, reaching for his daughter's hand. 'We're all yours.'

The youngster shot him a perturbed glare and made a swift exit to the ladies.

'Who needs a brother when she's got a father like you?' Gerry teased his long-time friend.

'Shut up! She's fine with it. We're only mucking around. She's only just coming to terms with how attractive she is as a woman. I'm building her confidence, that's all. She knows exactly what's going on.'

Jeff flinched as a sharp sensation shot through his left pectoral muscle. A good sign, he thought, instantly more positive about the rest of the day's proceedings.

Thanks, angel, he mouthed, watching through the open door and seeing Kierney on her way across the hall.

'Shall we go?' the security guard asked.

37

POLICE REPORT

Jeff informed both bodyguards of their plan to seat themselves somewhere higher in the dress circle during the afternoon's performance. Kierney sat between her father and Gerry, craning her neck to see the participants as they filed back into the courtroom below. The officer requested everyone to rise, and the judge and her entourage took their seats.

A full five minutes went by while Rosemary Milne outlined each type of evidence to the jury, along with their relative importance. Kierney looked from Gerry to Jeff, and then down at the members of the jury. She was beginning to understand the burden of responsibility on these twelve ordinary citizens much better. There were so many nuances to consider, which made the truth difficult to work out.

And if the three types of evidence weren't complicated enough, there were also all the technicalities which her father had described earlier. Did the police follow proper procedure? Did anyone tamper with the evidence? Was the Accused given ample opportunity to exercise his rights? Was he informed of his rights properly and at the right time?

'I know what you mean now about García not knowing what's going on,' she whispered.

'Yeah?' Jeff answered. 'Cool.'

'It's so complicated,' the teenager mused. 'You need to be pretty smart to figure out if you're being treated fairly, don't you?'

'Yep. Ain't that the truth.'

'Is that why Granddad was convicted?' she asked in a hushed voice.

'Who knows?' the celebrity replied with a wry smile. 'I hope he was convicted because he was guilty, but we'll never know. Money talks, baby. If you can afford the smartest lawyer, you're more likely to get off. That's the way of the world. And another thing you should seek to change when you get to the UN.'

Kierney smiled. 'I know. That's what I've been thinking. They say the justice system is fair, but that's only on the surface, isn't it?'

'Absolutely, *pequeñita*,' the proud father agreed, nudging her so hard that she bumped against Gerry's arm on the other side.

'Oi! What's going on?' the accountant teased. 'Stop it, kiddies. Behave yourselves.'

'Remind me to talk to you tonight about the impact of prejudice too,' Jeff whispered. 'That's a whole other angle.'

The enthusiastic youngster nodded. '*¡Excelente!* I'd love that.'

The cross-examination of DI Fisher had begun. Stephen Greenshaw was a tall, willowy man, whose gown seemed to be equipped with invisible fans to give it a life of its own.

'Inspector, could you please tell the court how you determined the hotel receptionist could be sure the telephone call transferred to Ms Diamond was made by the Accused?'

'Yes, Your Honour. Miss Todd was asked to listen to the tape recording of the Accused reading his statement of confession. From this, she confirmed it was the same voice she had heard over the telephone,' Bob replied without hesitation.

Kierney saw some jury members nod to each other. Fisher went on to answer questions about the warrant obtained for entry into the Accused's home.

'An order was issued to search Mr García's place of residence, Your Honour. The Defence is in receipt of all related paperwork and has indicated its satisfaction. The Accused gave his consent for New South Wales Police to search the rented house in Parramatta, and a contingent of forensics specialists was dispatched there at sixteen-twenty on the afternoon of Ms Diamond's murder. The house was not occupied when the team reached it, and the officers were obliged to force the lock. They seized several letters and notes that were thought to be in the Accused's handwriting. They were compared at the scene to a handwriting sample he provided us with.'

Fisher paused and directed his gaze towards the jury to ensure they were clear about his testimony. Defence Counsel urged him to continue.

'These notes were written in English, describing feelings of inadequacy and jealousy towards the Diamond family. There was also a sentence in a note we found written to his wife. I quote, "I will get rid of Jeff Diamond because you are in love with him and he is nothing but an immigrant murderer's son."'

The public gallery gave a collective gasp. Jeff and Gerry frowned at each other over the teenager's head. She reached out her hand, and her dad took hold of it, resting it on his left thigh.

'Sounds like intent to me,' the business manager whispered to the others.

'Shhh,' his client requested, feeling sick as García's written proclamation rang around the courtroom. 'There are ears all around us, mate. Just keep it to yourself for the moment.'

The older man frowned. 'Sorry, mate.'

Greenshaw passed a dossier of documents in clear plastic protectors to the jury. One by one, each person leafed through what must have been the various pieces of paper retrieved from García's house. A fresh round of whispering had whipped up in the gallery around them, and Kierney turned to gauge her father's reaction. For his part, Jeff had long thought his past was by now common knowledge, yet it was obvious that some had been selective when deciding which reports they believed about public figures held in high esteem.

Greenshaw posed another question to the senior police officer. 'DI Fisher, can you be sure the Accused was not detained against his will prior to arrest?'

The witness' body language impressed Jeff as he straightened up and responded with authority. This was the grey area to which the senior officer had alluded in their meeting after the committal hearing.

'Yes, Your Honour. In response to a request by the hotel manager, who was the person in authority prior to police attendance, the Accused was prevented from leaving the scene of the crime by Mr Jeff Diamond. The Accused initially stood without restraint between Mr Diamond and a member of the hotel's staff. This sequence of events was corroborated by one of the hotel's doormen, who I believe is the Prosecution's next witness.'

The Defence barrister interrupted to ask a follow-up question. 'He was detained by civilians?'

'No, Your Honour,' Fisher replied with care. 'The Accused was not detained, as such. Hotel security staff were almost immediately on the scene, I'm told, and the Defendant did not attempt to leave the building again, although free to do so if he had so wished.'

Greenshaw interrupted. 'Detective Inspector, if I may... My client reported that Mr Diamond manhandled him. Ladies and gentlemen of the jury, manhandling, to me, suggests an element of force, does it not?'

Jeff tensed up and caught his old friend's eye. Neither spoke, and the celebrity felt his heart rate increase. Again, the detective kept his cool. He was as experienced at providing evidence in criminal cases as the barristers were at questioning witnesses. They were worthy adversaries, and it was clear they held a healthy respect for one another.

'Your Honour, I cannot comment as to whether the Accused used the word "manhandled", nor whether Mr Diamond used force when preventing the Accused from leaving the hotel. The first police car arrived at the scene some ten minutes after the scene in question took place. Therefore, neither myself nor any of my colleagues observed this.'

'Thank you, DI Fisher,' Greenshaw cut him off, annoyed not to have caught the officer out. 'Once the police had arrived on the scene, could you tell us how they identified the Accused?'

'The hotel manager, Mr Christopher Nichols, met us at the entrance of the hotel, Your Honour. After his brief description of what was alleged to have taken place, I directed two officers to the scene of the crime. Myself and one other officer approached the three men who were stood together, near the reception desk. One of these men was hotel security, one was Mr Jeff Diamond, and the third was the Accused, Juan Antonio García.'

'And what was the Accused's state of mind upon seeing the police approach him?' Defence Counsel asked. 'Did he attempt to flee?'

DI Fisher turned to the second page in his pile of papers and read from a statement from the arresting officer.

'Your Honour, the words I'm about to read come from Detective Sergeant Andrew Waters' testimony. He states, "A man of between forty-five and fifty-five years of age, approximately one-hundred-and-seventy to one-hundred-and-seventy-five centimetres tall, with dark, thinning and greying hair, a grey moustache and of medium build, was standing between Mr Jeff Diamond, who I recognised instantly, and a tall, heavy-built man in his twenties dressed in the uniform of a contract security firm. I was directed to this group of men by the manager, who told me the man in the centre had tried to leave the building immediately after the crime was reported."'

Fisher again paused, allowing the jury to process this information before reading further. 'DS Waters goes on to say, "The person of interest was wearing a beige jacket and beige pants, with a white shirt buttoned to the neck. He appeared nervous but was not restrained and did not attempt to leave when approached by police officers. His jacket's zip was not fastened and, having been informed by Dispatch that a fatal shooting had taken place in the hotel, I had reason to believe this man may be a suspect and that therefore he may be concealing a weapon.

'"I asked for his name, which he gave as Juan Antonio García. His left hand was in a position on his hip that led me to suspect he may be concealing a weapon in the belt of his pants. I asked him to raise both hands in the air. The side of his jacket fell open to reveal an empty leather underarm holster. At this point, I arrested him on suspicion of inflicting serious injury."'

The witness put his papers down onto the lectern in front of him and fixed Stephen Greenshaw with a stare.

'DI Fisher,' the lawyer rebutted in a forthright tone, 'why did Sergeant Waters not arrest the Accused on suspicion of murder at that time?'

Bob puffed out his chest, stealing a glance in the direction of the prosecution bench. 'DS Waters had not yet received confirmation that the Victim of the shooting was in fact deceased. He could not be sure whether a murder had been committed at that stage. It was not until a few minutes afterwards that the Victim's death was confirmed.'

The gallery fell quiet. Jeff relaxed a little, feeling Kierney exhale with the distress of having to hear the events surrounding her mother's violent end dissected with such cold precision.

'Thank you, DI Fisher,' Defence Counsel replied. 'Is it fair to say, sir, that Sergeant Waters could not at that stage determine whether the empty holster he found on the Accused's person had in fact held the firearm that was used to commit the fatal shooting?'

The inspector smiled and answered with a hint of sarcasm, his sentence building into a distinct *crescendo* as he made his point. 'Yes, Your Honour. I concur with Defence Counsel that my colleague could not be absolutely confident at that stage that the suspect had been carrying the weapon used to shoot Ms Diamond. But it's fair to say that identifying someone in the hotel lobby wearing a holster such a short time after a shooting had occurred constitutes significant probability that he was a person of interest for the investigation.'

Greenshaw gave an affected nod, as dramatic as ever. Jeff exchanged sideways glances with his daughter, reading from her expression that she was as conflicted as he was between her desire to understand the intricacies of the judicial process and the pain she felt about the clinical way these men were discussing their loved one's murder.

'But the Accused was of the opinion the firearm was legally licensed to him,' Defence Counsel continued. 'Therefore, he was within his rights to walk through a hotel lobby carrying his firearm, wasn't he?'

'Mr Greenshaw,' Judge Milne interjected. 'You are technically correct, of course, but the jury should disregard the Defence's last question to the Witness. The Accused was found to be wearing apparatus used to conceal a weapon at the scene of a fatal shooting. This represents ample reason to question his involvement with the crime and to arrest on suspicion, despite not yet having found the weapon at this point.'

'Thank you, Your Honour,' Graham Winton chimed in. 'You are quite correct.'

Jeff shook his head.

'What's the matter?' Kierney asked.

'They're playing around down there,' he murmured. 'I don't like it. They shouldn't make it so obvious they think the guy's guilty. They might alienate the jury.'

'Mmm,' Gerry agreed. 'I wondered that too. That's the trouble with these Supreme Court barristers. They know each other so well. They probably all drink together on Fridays after work. Their kids go to the same schools. They play golf together on cool summer evenings. It's all too incestuous for words.'

'Nepotistic,' the wordmonger corrected. 'I hope they're not incestuous too.'

His daughter giggled. 'Stop splitting hairs, you two. Is there even such a word as "nepotistic"?'

'Probably not,' her father smiled, 'but you knew what I meant.'

The court officer distributed another folder of documents to the jury. These were the signed statements of each person present at The Pensione Hotel that morning, along with transcripts of the formal interviews which had taken place at the police station over the ensuing days.

'DI Fisher,' the barrister for the Defence began again. 'Once the Accused was in custody, did the New South Wales Police consider any other suspects in this case?'

The noise level rose once again in the public gallery, but the experienced officer was expecting this question. 'Yes, Your Honour. We followed up all leads and also pursued additional lines of enquiry recommended by the Australian Federal Police, to whom we were asked to refer the case owing to the high profile of the Victim and her family. However, once we had a confession and all the evidence pointed convincingly to the Accused, there seemed little point in proceeding with other lines of enquiry.'

The jury members became a little confused, the star observed, and he anticipated Stephen Greenshaw would be keen to pounce on their uncertainty. And pounce he did.

'Your Honour,' Defence Counsel resumed in a loud voice. 'We are all aware of the phenomenon that murders are frequently committed by close family members or friends, are we not? I'm curious to know whether the New South Wales Police ever questioned the Victim's family in connection with Ms Diamond's murder.'

The packed public gallery jumped to its feet *en masse*, many joining the prosecution team in their objection to Greenshaw's suggestion. Jeers and shouts abounded at how ludicrous an idea they thought this was. The grieving lover closed his eyes and waited for the ruckus to die down, sensing the whole crowd willing him to stand and echo their opinion. He remained seated, gripping Kierney's hand.

Judge Milne was at pains to prevent the onlookers from stating their piece. Her eyes were searching for the Diamonds in the front row, where they had been spotted prior to the luncheon recess.

'She can't see us,' Kierney whispered. 'She'll think we've gone.'

'Doubt it,' her father replied, breathing deeply.

The pair couldn't tell if the judge had spotted their fine-tuned vantage point in the shoal of animated bodies, listening to her direction to the jury.

'Silence, please, ladies and gentlemen. As we can all hear, there are powerful feelings being expressed by people in the public gallery. I must ask you to keep these thoughts and emotions to yourselves. We have all known the Diamond family for a long time, and the Dysons too. They are people we respect for their many talents and the hard work they do. We see their faces on television and in the papers regularly, which means you may think you know them well.'

Gerry put his right arm on Jeff's left shoulder, across the young woman's back. The judge was about to support Greenshaw's position.

Rosemary Milne carried on. 'However, I must insist on silence in my courtroom, or I shall request that the bailiffs remove you. Ladies and gentlemen of the jury, let me remind you that any opinions expressed by the gallery are not relevant to this case and are therefore to be disregarded.

'Counsel for the Defence has rightly reminded us that many assaults and murders are perpetrated by a person whom the Victim knows and trusts. Mr Greenshaw is entitled to suggest the police include Ms Diamond's family as Persons of Interest in this case. However, Counsel for the Defence is not assuming any guilt on the part of Mr Diamond, nor any other friend or family member. Do you understand, ladies and gentlemen?'

The jurors nodded despite the continuing disquiet in the public space above. Stephen Greenshaw posed another question.

'Detective Inspector, I put to you again whether you have fully considered any suspects other than the Accused, particularly members of the Victim's family and their circle of friends?'

Fisher nodded. 'Yes, Your Honour. The New South Wales Police and the AFP are both satisfied that this murder was not committed by Mr Jeff Diamond, any other member of their family or anyone in their very wide circle of friends.'

Greenshaw persisted. 'Did it cross your mind, Detective Inspector, that Mr Diamond might have used a man such as the Accused to carry out such a crime on his behalf? It may explain why Mr Diamond knew to stop the Accused from leaving the hotel after the shooting.'

Jeff swore under his breath, feeling dirty as he heard his character being dragged through the mud. These were questions the Defence was duty-bound to ask, but the mere suggestion that he might hire a middle-aged amateur nobody to kill his beautiful best friend filled him with revulsion. He felt Kierney's head lean onto his shoulder and Gerry's hand pressing harder on his back, neither uttering a sound.

For the first time during his time on the stand, Bob Fisher showed a modicum of frustration. 'Yes, it did cross my mind, Your Honour. Our investigation followed this lead thoroughly and found no evidence to support that assumption. Mr Jeff Diamond will take the stand later on in this trial, and I'm sure Defence Counsel will put these questions to him at the appropriate time. The New South Wales Police is satisfied that Mr Diamond had no motive to murder his wife, either himself or through a third-party.

'We're also satisfied the Accused and Mr Diamond were not known to one another prior to the shooting on the sixteenth of February, nineteen-ninety-six. At the time of the murder, we have three separate witness statements telling us that Mr Diamond was parking a rented vehicle in a car park next-door to the hotel. According to both their statements, Mr Diamond and the Accused found themselves simultaneously in a set of revolving doors in the hotel's entrance, and the doorman's identification of both persons puts their chance encounter at just two or three minutes after the shooting.'

'Thank you, DI Fisher,' the barrister for the Defence said, sensing antagonism brewing in the public area above and keen to bring the policeman's testimony to a close.

'Get on with it!' came a shout from the back of the gallery. 'Everyone knows Jeff didn't kill Lynn. Move on, for God's sake!'

Gerry slapped his friend on the shoulder, and the widower shook his ponderous head. The teenager in between the two tall men was both smiling and crying, no doubt feeling the strain of a confusing day. Her father fixed his dark eyes with hers and cocked his head towards the exit at the back, anxious to find out if she wanted to leave.

'I'm good,' she answered. 'It's like a see-saw, isn't it? Like the worm they use for elections, tipping above and below the line all the time. I never realised it would be this stressful, did you?'

Jeff nodded. 'Hang on in there. Let it wash over you. You know what you believe. Listen carefully, but just keep believing in what you think is right.'

Judge Milne issued another stern warning to the gallery to remain quiet or risk being escorted out of the building. She told the jury to concentrate on the floor of the court rather than on outbursts from the public or press personnel, before turning back to Greenshaw for any further questions for the inspector.

The court learnt the Crown had served an indictment on the Accused, signed by the New South Wales Attorney General within two weeks of the committal charge, and that it had been filed in the court registry on Wednesday the 13th of March. They also discovered that García was unable to provide an alibi for his whereabouts on the morning of Lynn's death, that the Accused was not under the influence of alcohol or drugs when he committed the alleged offences, nor was he acting on anyone else's instruction, to the best of the witness' knowledge.

Having excused DI Fisher from the stand, the judge asked the Defence team whether it was satisfied with the disclosure of evidence from the New South Wales Police. It was, and the uniformed officer stepped down from the box. As the senior detective made his way back to his seat at the back of the courtroom, he too glanced upwards to where he thought the Diamonds were sitting. Jeff didn't attempt to make eye contact, and Fisher walked out of the courtroom with a relieved look on his face.

The judge then granted everyone a few moments to stretch and reflect upon the first witness' evidence before her associate called proceedings to order again. A third folder was opened and handed to the jury for their examination.

'Ladies and gentlemen,' the judge announced, 'the court officer is about to read out the Victim Impact Statement for this case. I instruct you that this is a factual document drawn up by Crown prosecutors to summarise the effects the crimes under trial have had on their victims. You may find the contents of this statement distressing, and I urge you to remain silent until the officer has finished reading, so we all have the chance to hear it clearly.'

'Do you want to go?' Gerry asked his pale clients. 'This is going to be nasty.'

'No, mate. I want to see the bastard's reaction. And it'll be good to hear Lynn's loss being acknowledged in public.'

'Kierney?' their manager asked, concerned for the youngster.

'I've read it already,' the teenager told him. 'I agree with *papá*. I want everyone to hear what she meant to us.'

A male court officer rose to his feet with several sheets of paper held up in trembling hands. He took a large gulp of water before coughing politely and taking a deep breath.

> 'Her Majesty, Queen Elizabeth the Second, leader of the Commonwealth, represented by this Court, is today trying a man for murdering and intending to murder two of Australia's most prominent and well-respected public figures, Lynn Dyson Diamond and Jeff Diamond, respectively. There are many victims of these crimes, as has been noted in hundreds of tributes and public outpourings of grief all over the world.'

The civil servant paused and took another long breath to steady his nerves. He who was most impacted among those remaining on Earth wondered how this poor bloke had ended up with such an awful task.

> 'The murder victim, Victoria Lynn Shannon Dyson Diamond, aged forty years, received three bullet wounds to her head and body, the first of which entered through her forehead and extinguished her life in a matter of seconds. A second bullet also inflicted life-threatening injuries on her vital organs, from which she may never have recovered. The third bullet entered her shoulder, causing some internal bleeding.'

The dark-haired Diamonds steeled themselves for what they knew was coming next, recognising the potential to cause a great deal more disruption in the courtroom.

> 'Lynn Diamond leaves behind a husband of twenty years' marriage and two teenaged children, all of whom are well known to the Australian people and internationally. Not only have the Diamond family members suffered the loss of a loved one, but they have also had to endure intense speculation about the Accused's original intention to murder Mr Diamond. The knowledge that his wife died instead of him is an additional heavy burden of guilt to bear on top of the grief of losing one's wife.
>
> 'Ryan and Kierney Diamond have lost their mother, Bart and Marianna Dyson and their children have lost a daughter and sister. Her many friends and associates in the music business and sports world,

not to mention the beneficiaries of the family's numerous charitable organisations will also suffer in losing the Victim's public patronage.

'In conclusion, the Crown wishes also to acknowledge the impact of Ms Diamond's loss on her large number of fans, especially those she mentored. She was a much-loved role model for young people beginning musical and sporting careers, and her loss is bound to damage their motivation to succeed.'

For the first time since the trial began, Juan Antonio García showed a flicker of emotion. His eyes reached up into the dress circle to where there remained a substantial amount of background noise and the occasional shout or cry. The bereaved man noticed him blink several times, as if trying to clear his eyes, before burying his head in his hands.

'Look,' he whispered to his daughter. 'He's breaking.'

The rest of Lynn's Victim Impact Statement was read out in the packed courtroom to stunned silence. It told of her career past and present, the grief of the extended family, of the sporting dynasty, of members of teams and musical groups in which she played a vital role. Lastly, there was the general public, having turned out in their thousands to mourn in Melbourne and at other venues reserved around the country and internationally, all listed as victims of this heinous crime.

Kierney watched her father fight back tears during the long, overly-dramatic statement. She was glad to hear the detail broadcast loud and clear, and she was glad that the journalists in the media gallery would have the opportunity to supply an accurate report for the next day's newspapers.

Jeff grabbed her hand and kissed her temple, making her dissolve into tears too. 'Good girl,' he whispered. 'I love you. *Mamá* still loves you. Listen to all those people who miss her. We're all with you and your brother.'

'Do you really think they'll ask you all those horrible questions about being a suspect after this?' the teenager asked. 'How could anyone ever think you'd want to kill mamá?'

'That's right,' Gerry agreed, also trying to reassure the young woman. 'People would have to have been living on another planet not to notice how much your parents loved each other. I'd be very surprised if they try hard.'

'Cheers, mate. I'm sure they'll have a go, if only to reinforce the point for the other side. Look at García. He's fucked and he knows it.'

'*Papá*, be quiet,' Kierney urged her father, whose knees shook from holding the tension at bay. 'How about a ciggie break?'

Jeff shook his head. 'No, not yet. I need to hear how Fruity goes. I can't risk my story contradicting his, or we'll confuse the jury.'

Gerry laughed. 'Steady, mate. Methinks a break would be a good thing. Come on, you know what he's going to say. You're vibrating so hard, I fear the balcony'll become structurally unsound if we don't get you out of here.'

The celebrity smiled, gripping his thigh muscles and massaging his knees to calm his nerves. 'No, I'm OK. I'm hanging on by the skin of my teeth. Sorry if it's freaking you out.'

Accepting the man's word, the businessman's hand reached deep into his left trouser pocket and pulled out a small packet wrapped in waxed paper.

'What's that?' Kierney asked with a look of dread on her face.

Her father's best friend showed her the label, trying not to laugh. It was nicotine chewing gum, used for giving up smoking, and the teenager breathed a sigh of relief.

'You two *are* stressing me out,' she sounded exasperated. 'Can I have one, please?'

All three took a piece of gum and unwrapped them together, much to the amusement of their neighbours. It was a valuable moment of respite not lost on anyone.

The court officer called Karl Fruchtmann to the stand as the next prosecution witness. Graham Winton stood up and stepped forward, ready to take the nervous doorman through his paces, asking him to recount the sequence of events before the police arrived.

Kierney listened intently to his description of what had taken place that awful morning, long before she reached The Pensione with Gerry and her grandfather. She scanned the jury's faces, trying to read their minds. How would she react to the responsibility of putting someone behind bars for the rest of his or her life?

Her thoughts turned to her paternal grandfather, whom she had met on only one occasion; one which she scarcely remembered. For someone who had spent most of his adult life in prison, he hadn't fared so badly. As far as she could glean from her parents, Paul Diamond had been treated well under the circumstances.

These jurors would shortly decide whether to deprive this man of his liberty and the right to make his own choices. Her deceased mother had been deprived of these rights too, and so in many ways had her father. The distinction was perfectly clear to her at this moment: García had made a choice, whereas this tragic situation had been foisted upon her parents.

The Prosecution seemed intent on rushing through its questions for Fruchtmann, eager to bring the Defence barrister once more to centre-stage. Winton's first question was predictable and drew a frustrated sigh from the public gallery.

'Mr Fruchtmann,' said the bold barrister, 'for how long did you detain the Accused before the police arrived and questioned him?'

The doorman was on-message, having rehearsed several times with members of the Crown's team. 'I did not detain the Accused, Your Honour,' the heavy-set man told the courtroom, revealing another foreign accent. 'I alerted hotel security, who sent two men to the foyer to assist with the commotion after the shooting. As soon as security arrived, I left the Accused and Mr Diamond together. I was called to help to screen off the scene of the crime.'

Winton continued. 'And can you please describe to this court how the Accused was prevented from leaving the hotel?'

'Yes, sir. I heard my manager tell people not to leave the building. I saw a man walking towards the main doors and started to run after him to ask him to stop, but at the same time I saw Jeff... I mean Mr Diamond, I'm sorry... pushing the revolving doors and talking to the man I was chasing.'

'Do you see the man you were chasing in this courtroom, Mr Fruchtmann?' the barrister interrupted, with a wide arm gesture around the large room.

'Yes, Your Honour,' the doorman replied with a decisive air, pointing to the hunched figure of García. 'It was this man. The Accused. Sorry, Your Honour. I'm very nervous.'

The public gallery gave another collective gasp while the jurors' eyes scanned from the dock to the witness. The Defence bench offered no objection, and the dozen turned back to the smug prosecution attorney.

Gerry put his right hand on Kierney's knee and shook it back and forth. 'That's what we wanted to hear,' he whispered.

The teenager wasn't so sure. She was already attempting to formulate the Defence's version of this interrogation, and by the concentration on her father's face, so was he.

'The Prosecution has no further questions for this witness,' Winton announced to the judge with a flourish.

Rosemary Milne acknowledged him and signalled to defending counsel to begin his cross-examination. Stephen Greenshaw's gown spirited him to his feet again.

'Mr Fruchtmann,' the barrister addressed him with a smile and a gentle opener. 'How long have you been working at The Pensione Hotel?'

'Just over six months, Your Honour.'

Greenshaw continued. 'And in that six months, what training have you received in dealing with criminal offences committed on hotel premises?'

'Nothing in particular, Your Honour,' the German answered, his eyes seeking urgent advice from the prosecution bench. 'Mostly emergency evacuation procedures; fire drills and that sort of thing. We are told to alert security if there is any sign of trouble, which is what I did on this day.'

'Thank you,' Defence Counsel said. 'Were you born in Australia, Mr Fruchtmann?'

Winton jumped to his feet. 'Objection! Irrelevant question, Your Honour.'

'Mr Greenshaw,' Judge Milne addressed her Defence team. 'Please explain the relevance of your question to the jury.'

'Certainly, Your Honour,' the barrister replied. 'I am seeking to establish the level of understanding the Witness had of his duties and the decision-making power The Pensione Hotel affords its floor staff. Oh, and whether these measures suffice to protect hotel guests adequately.'

The intellectual scoffed. 'Dumb move,' he whispered to his companions.

Sure enough, the judge pounced on the taller attorney with commanding force. 'I fail to see what relevance Mr Fruchtmann's place of birth has on his ability to make decisions that protect hotel guests, Counsel. The Prosecution's objection stands. The witness is not obliged to answer this question.'

Graham Winton appeared pleased with himself, but Greenshaw was unfazed. This was only a game to these two privileged gentlemen.

'Fair enough, Your Honour,' the bouncing man went on. 'Mr Fruchtmann, please could you tell the court whether you had any trouble understanding the training you were given, and whether you therefore feel well-equipped to make decisions about the safety and security of hotel guests?'

Even if Karl Fruchtmann hadn't been confused on the 16th of February, he definitely was now! 'Err... I called security when my manager wanted to stop people leaving the building. I felt well-equipped of making that decision, yes, Your Honour. Everything was happening so fast that I did not have the chance really to think about it.'

'And, in your opinion,' the Defence lawyer carried on, 'do you think your manager had the authority to prevent members of the public from leaving the hotel at this time?'

The doorman nodded. 'Yes, I think so. A crime had been committed. My manager needed to keep everyone in the hotel and preserve the crime scene, I think, before the police arrived.'

'You *think*?' Greenshaw laboured.

'Objection!' Counsel for the Prosecution piped up again. 'The Defence is badgering our witness, Your Honour. The onus is not on Mr Fruchtmann to know what his manager's responsibilities are in such an extreme event. As the hotel's doorman, he was simply following an instruction to prevent people from leaving the building.'

Again the judge upheld the Prosecution's objection, and again Greenshaw continued unabashed. 'Thank you, Your Honour,' the snide man said. 'Mr Fruchtmann, did you witness Mr Diamond preventing the Accused from leaving the hotel that morning?'

'Yes, Your Honour,' the Fruchtmann answered, 'but at the time, I did not know for sure it was Mr Diamond's intention.'

'Did you see Mr Diamond using any force to change the Accused's mind about leaving, Mr Fruchtmann?' Greenshaw pushed. 'For example, did you see any physical contact between the two men or did you hear raised voices?'

'No, Your Honour,' the doorman answered without hesitation, pleased to be brought back to a line of questioning he had rehearsed with Peter and Moira from the prosecution team. 'I saw Mr Diamond and the Accused talking on the other side of the revolving door. I could not hear what they were saying. Mr Diamond pointed back into the hotel, and the Accused went back through the revolving door in front of Mr Diamond.'

'You did not see Mr Diamond touch the Accused?' Greenshaw pressed.

'No, I did not. The partitions of the revolving door kept them apart.'

'And how about on the other side of the door?' the barrister persisted.

Jeff turned to Gerry, over Kierney's head. 'They're labouring this point so hard. It must be all they have.'

'That's good, isn't it?' the accountant shrugged.

His friend shrugged back. 'Yeah. Guess so.'

The German replied to the latest question. 'I could not see perfectly, Your Honour. Mr Diamond may have put his hand on the Accused's back or shoulder. I don't remember. There wasn't any force used, like pushing or something, I'm sure, and the Accused did not try to leave again, even when the police sirens started.'

'Thank you, Mr Fruchtmann,' Greenshaw muttered, before continuing in a louder voice. 'Did you think at that time that Mr García was the gunman who had perpetrated the crime?'

'No,' the doorman replied. 'It all happened so quickly, Your Honour. I did not know really what had passed. I was more interested in helping my boss organise the crowd and make less the noise in the lobby of the hotel, where Mrs Diamond was shot. After security arrived, I was not thinking about this man at all.'

Greenshaw switched tack, appearing to be inspired by a new idea. 'Mr Fruchtmann,' he began, almost excited, 'when you observed Mr Diamond and the Accused talking outside the lobby, did you get the impression that they were strangers or that they already knew each other?'

'Objection!' Winton leaped to his feet again. 'The witness has just answered that he was unable to see clearly or hear what the two men were saying. To answer the Defence's latest question would be pure conjecture.'

'Noted, Counsel,' Judge Milne almost smiled, 'but I'll allow it. Mr Fruchtmann, in your opinion, and from what you could observe of the Accused and Mr Diamond's behaviour at the time, was it your impression that these two men were speaking as acquaintances? In other words, people who already knew each other?'

'I'm sorry, Your Honour,' the hotel employee became frightened, beginning to babble. 'I cannot answer this question. It is my impression that most people already know Jeff Diamond. The Accused can know Mr Diamond for that reason, I think. And Mr Diamond is a most friendly man. When he visits our hotel, he speaks to all staff and guests like a friend. Perhaps Mr Diamond thought the Accused was a guest at the hotel and was taking care for him to know my manager's instruction. I don't know. I could not hear what he was saying. I'm sorry.'

The judge raised a hand to signal to the witness that she would not press him for any further information. If she and the lanky barrister had sought to tease out any conspiracy, Fruchtmann's evidence was inconclusive, and Jeff watched the pair exchange looks of frustration.

Defence Counsel had one more question for the flustered doorman. 'Please could you tell the court whether you heard the Accused speak at all before the police arrived, and what he said?'

The doorman paused for a moment, looking up at the high ceiling while he formulated his answer.

'Take your time, Mr Fruchtmann,' the judge instructed. 'It's important to remember things as accurately as you can.'

'No, Your Honour,' Karl replied. 'I don't remember the Accused speaking at all while I was near him. I'm pretty sure he didn't say anything.'

Stephen Greenshaw raised his hands towards the judge's bench. 'Thank you. I have no further questions for the Witness, Your Honour.'

The jury members shuffled in their seats, surprised that the questioning had come to such an abrupt halt. Kierney gazed into her father's eyes for answers.

'Maybe Fruity gave him the right answer he wasn't looking for,' Jeff offered. 'He didn't say anything, which is what I remember too. Maybe the Defence was trying to trip him up?'

'Oh, I see,' his daughter frowned.

The handsome man nudged the teenager's arm. 'Convoluted, isn't it?'

Nodding, she smiled and saw the songwriter check his watch. It was almost four o'clock, and her *papá* recalled from Winton's running sheet that he was the next witness to be called. There was bound to be another recess before the Prosecution continued.

'We're going to be postponed,' he announced to Gerry and Kierney. 'I doubt they'll want to start again this late.'

Jeff's assumption was valid. After a few minutes explaining the jury's obligation to keep all matters discussed in court confidential, especially from the many newspaper and television reporters hovering around the Supreme Court, a recess was called until nine o'clock the following morning. The court officer asked those present to rise, and the judge left the room without further ceremony.

Like a classroom of naughty schoolchildren abandoned by its teacher, the public gallery transformed into a raucous and restless rabble. A number of them chanted, "Guilty! Guilty! Guilty!" as an armed police officer led the Accused out of the dock. Other onlookers tried to quieten them down, but the pent-up emotions had become too hard to rein in.

The two bodyguards on either side of the Diamond party stood up and requested their three charges follow them towards the exit. Obediently, the well-known figures rose to their full height and faced their ardent followers.

'Jeff, we love you!' came a loud female voice from one of the top rows.

A tremendous cheer went up, followed by clapping and more shouting. The megastar raised his hands to thank them for their support, which only served to increase the volume. With Kierney sandwiched between the two men, in turn sandwiched between the two security guards, the Diamond cohort filed up the stairs and out into the court building's main thoroughfare, as if following each other in a bizarre conga.

Jeff felt his mobile vibrating in his pants pocket. Reaching in to retrieve it, he saw Graham Winton's name on the screen.

'Counsel for the Prosecution.'

The tired man heard the barrister chuckle on the other end of the line. 'Mr Diamond, are you still at court?' he asked with some urgency.

'Yep. We're close to the room where we've been hiding during recesses. Why?'

'Good, good. I thought you'd decided to leave earlier. We couldn't see you. Are you in a rush to get going?'

'No, I guess not,' Jeff replied, smiling at the latest game. 'D'you want to come to my office?'

Kierney and Gerry locked eyes with each other, wondering what had amused the dark humourist this time. Their companion motioned for them to head towards the same wood-panelled meeting room, and the group secreted themselves within.

'Sure, Graham,' he continued, hearing the lawyer say he would be there in a short while. 'Just come up whenever you're ready. I need a cigarette almost as much as I need my wife back, so give me ten minutes, please.'

With the call ended, Jeff stood facing his daughter and his old friend, all three stunned and exhausted. 'They want to talk to me before we go tonight,' he sighed. 'You guys can go on ahead, if you like. I'll meet you back at the hotel. I don't know how long this is going to take.'

'No, papá,' Kierney disputed. 'I don't want to leave you on your own. I'd rather stay, if that's OK.'

'Of course it's OK. I just thought you'd be tired and hanging to escape, that's all. It appears they have a proposition to put to me.'

'Then I should definitely stay too,' Gerry added. 'I am still your manager, am I not?'

Jeff shrugged, slumping down into a chair. 'Bloody well hope so, mate. You looking to resign?'

The accountant guffawed. 'What? Now life's so exciting? I should've called it quits years ago when things were boring and uneventful.'

'When was that, mate?' his client forced a wan smile, clutching his aching head.

'Exactly. Let's get that cigarette. You must be ready to climb the walls.'

'I thought you were about to say, "You must be ready to murder one,"' he intellectual scoffed.

'I nearly did,' Gerry admitted. 'My tactfulness filter worked, for once.'

Kierney gave an exasperated groan. 'Please stop messing around, will you? It's been a horrible day, and we shouldn't joke about things.'

'Right,' Jeff snapped out of the boisterous mood which was bordering on the hysterical at this late hour. '*Pissoir*, cigarette, fine wine, dinner. In that order. OK, Kizzo?'

His daughter nodded her gratitude, and the trio headed out of the room, tailed by their attentive minders. Once down on the ground floor, they were shown into a small arboretum reserved for Supreme Court smokers. Gerry passed round his packet of cigarettes, and all five accepted. Jeff watched with interest as the younger of the two security guards positioned himself next to the pretty teenager, knowing by her disinterested facial expression that the poor bloke was about to be disappointed.

'Did you or *mamá* ever get called for jury duty?' Kierney asked.

Jeff nodded. 'I've been called five times. Twice I couldn't go because I was overseas. And the other three, the Defence released me 'cause they thought I'd be too opinionated.'

The young woman grinned. 'Oh, really?' she quipped, hearing over-enthusiastic laughter from over her right shoulder. 'Wonder where they got that impression. How about *mamá*?'

'She was called three times, I think,' her dad answered. 'Similar thing. She was released twice without being assigned to a case, and the other time, she was out of the country too. So neither of us got to exercise our privilege to bang someone up.'

'*Papá*! You can't say that,' Kierney cried out. 'Objection!'

'Overruled!' Jeff snapped back, stubbing out his cigarette and passing round his packet. 'I'm the dad. I can do that.'

The gipsy girl pulled a face, deciding for now to be lenient with her highly enervated parent. The others passed on his offer, so the widower lit his second cigarette while they finished their first.

'I'm knackered,' Gerry announced. 'Hope tomorrow's easier going.'

The celebrity sniffed. 'For you, maybe. I have to face the inquisition at some point,' he said, standing to attention and turning to face an imaginary barrister. '"So, Mr Diamond, did you manhandle the Accused on his way back into the hotel?"'

The uniformed man sitting on Kierney's right shoulder chortled. 'Is your dad always this funny?'

His daughter's suitor had made his unsubtle move. Jeff caught her eye and winked, rendering her self-conscious. No matter how close a girl was to her father, there were some things she would rather he didn't observe.

'Did you think that was funny?' she enquired of the hapless twenty-something. 'I thought it was distasteful.'

The young man backed off as a chill wind blew in his direction. Trying not to smile, the widower longed for his tattoo to itch and let him know Lynn was watching her good teachings being put into action. To his disappointment, nothing happened. His wife must agree with his daughter, he concluded with a distinct sadness.

'Sorry, gorgeous,' he said, stubbing the rest of his cigarette out. 'We should be getting back upstairs. The Queen's expecting us.'

In the meeting room on Level Three, Graham Winton and Peter Yun were waiting patiently for their star witness to return. A decanted bottle of red wine took pride of place on the table, next to a tray of four glasses. Both men stood as they saw the others approaching.

'Sorry, gents,' Jeff said, reaching to shake Graham's hand and then Peter's. 'It's been a long day. We had to blow off some steam down there.'

The eighteen-year-old frowned a little, stepping forward to greet the Crown prosecutors.

'No, actually. Let me correct that,' the tired man changed his tune. '*I* had to blow off some steam. These guys indulged me, as usual. Kierney, this is Peter Yun, Graham's associate. Peter, this is our daughter, Kierney.'

He beckoned for the teenager to accept the young lawyer's outstretched hand, which she did. Sweet relief washed over him as the muscle under his precious tattoo twitched once, rewarding him for respect shown towards the gracious young lady. He turned away for a few seconds to recover his composure from the effects of this private delight. Throwing his suit jacket over the back of a vacant chair as a valiant decoy, he removed his tie and rolled the cuffs of his shirt sleeves over.

In the meantime, Gerry re-acquainted himself with both men, and everyone took their seats. Sneaking a quick look at the dark-haired teenager, the business manager sensed her fear that the immense presence which was Jeff Diamond was near the end of its tether, concluding that it would be in everyone's interest to speed things along as fast has he could.

'What's the occasion?' the suave accountant asked, pointing to the wine. 'Have we won already?'

'Round One perhaps,' Graham nodded, 'but it's much too early to say. I thought you might appreciate a loosener at close of business. Your client's penchant for fine reds is well understood.'

'Thanks. Much appreciated, sirs, but we're a glass short.'

'No, thanks,' Kierney jumped in, anxious not to cause anyone any embarrassment. 'I don't want any.'

Winton watched the celebrity smile at his daughter from under a furrowed brow, a prize for her politically motivated compliance. No doubt about it, these Melbourne household names were special people who communicated without words and who possessed the uncanny ability to influence a situation with a few well-chosen tugs at the heartstrings. There was a reason they had stayed at the top of their many professions for so many years, and now he was being treated to first-hand insight into the inner workings of the Dyson-Diamond family.

'Peter,' the barrister turned to his associate, 'would you mind sourcing a can of Coke or similar for Miss Diamond?'

'Thank you,' the teenager acknowledged. 'That'd be great.'

The young man obliged and returned in no time with a bright red can. He dutifully cracked it open and poured the liquid into a water glass. All five people lifted their drinks into the air but proposed no toast.

'So, what are these developments you wanted to run past me, Graham?' Jeff asked, his eyes checking with Gerry's that his trusted adviser was ready to jump in at any time.

'García's wife wants to testify against her husband, as an additional witness.'

'Really? Absolutely not!' the widower swallowed his mouthful of wine and crashed the glass back down onto the table. 'Is she serious? Are *you* serious?'

The barrister was clearly disconcerted. 'The Crown considers her a powerful witness. Second to yourself, of course.'

Jeff rested both hands on the varnished mahogany surface, twisting the base of his wineglass round and round with his fingers. 'It's your case, Graham, not mine,' he acquiesced a little. 'But I think it'd be a bad move.'

'Why, if I might ask?' Senior Counsel asked. 'She's unlikely to suddenly change her story. She's filed for divorce. She despises him for what he did.'

Gerry stayed silent. He agreed with Winton and couldn't think of anything to say which would back his client up.

'Mrs García might feel differently if she sees her husband looking so pathetic in the dock,' Kierney interjected. 'She might change her story, or the jury'll feel sorry for him because his wife turned against him in his hour of need.'

Jeff picked up his glass and raised it to the teenager, again proud of her maturity and confidence. With a single, simple sentence to demonstrate the difference between empathising and sympathising, he had turned his daughter into a negotiator.

'What she said,' he smiled, deferring to the pretty, young woman growing up before their eyes. 'Couldn't have said it better myself. Don't push the jury, guys. We need *them* to despise him. *You* need them to despise him, I mean. Me, I couldn't give a toss.'

'Cool it, mate,' Gerry warned, sensing another shift on the widower's emotional barometer. 'Let's sleep on it. It's been a taxing day. There may be some mileage to be gained when she talks about his obsession with you.'

'All right. So answer me this...' Jeff asked, forcing himself to calm down. 'When would you propose she take the stand?'

'Immediately after the Accused, tomorrow morning,' Winton responded. 'That way, his cross-exam' will have finished leaving certain conclusions in the jury's mind, and we could go straight from that to questioning her about his motive, either to reinforce or influence their thinking.'

The celebrity sighed. 'Wait a minute,' he said, with a playful smirk on his face. 'First, I thought I was next up tomorrow, so now you tell me that's changed. And second, we know his motive already. He confessed to it. Do we really need to hear her rubbing his nose in the dirt? Is that what you think'll win this case?'

'Sorry, Jeff, yes. We ran out of time to catch up with you during lunch today,' Graham accounted for his decision. 'We were talking to García's wife at the time. The Crown wasn't originally going to call anyone related to the Accused as a witness, but when she came forward to say she was prepared to testify against him, it made sense to change things around. We can always redirect if the Defence's cross-exam' doesn't go well for us.'

'You could,' Jeff nodded, suddenly drained. 'You're the experts.'

Winton was also tired, and he saw red. He didn't take kindly to being pulled up on a point of process, especially in front of a junior associate.

'This is the trial of your wife's killer, sir. Do you want us to put him away or not?'

Both Kierney and Gerry knew this was an unwise question to have asked the Bohemian figurehead and braced themselves for the full force of his reaction. After pausing for a couple of seconds, the handsome widower span his chair round to face the barrister, whose belly was doing its best to pop his shirt buttons.

He took a slow, inward breath. 'For this exquisite lady over there,' he affirmed, pointing to his daughter, 'and her brother, I want you to put him away.'

Jeff's hand diverted to his old friend, who was staring out of the window. 'And for him and his family, I do too. For the Queen, the Commonwealth and all of you, I do,' he continued with a heavy sigh. 'For me, I'm not so sure.'

'*Papá*,' Kierney whispered.

'To be honest, I couldn't give a flying fuck,' her father leant forward, raising his voice and focussing back on the prosecution team with bestial eyes. 'You got some way of bringing Lynn back, I'm listening.'

Silence echoed around the room as if an invisible energy source had extracted all the air. It left their eardrums pounding with jittery pressure, and the red-eyed eighteen-year-old shot an adoring glance at the inimitable figure of whom she was so in awe.

'Of course he does, Mr Winton,' Gerry took over. 'My client wants your client to win this case. Just take a few moments to hear him out, would you, please?'

Jeff stood up and began pacing up and down one side of the table, with a barely discernible nod to his long-time business partner. Kierney was reminded of the benevolent lion to which her mother had likened him in one of her letters. The image sat well with her too. This was a man who believed in fairness and justice for all, even if it meant the man who killed his best friend and forever lover got off lightly. She was full of admiration, fighting back tears as she watched him take another deep breath and launch his attack.

'This man...' the bereaved husband began. 'García, that poor bastard, is already breaking. I can see it from ten metres up in the air. He did it, ladies and gentlemen of the jury. He's already told us he did it. For Christ's sake, we found him within spitting distance of a warm, partially loaded gun.'

'Jeff, mate,' Gerry warned, standing up but receiving an immediate sign to sit back down again.

'The jury's nearly fifty percent female. They already hate him for taking Lynn out, 'cause they can see me and Kierney in the gallery. If you put me on the stand straight after him, I can cement that loathing well and truly. That's what I do every day: put people in touch with their feelings and the basic values that underpin them. If you put that shrivelled-up bastard *and* the poisonous ex-wife on the stand before me, I might as well not say anything. The jurors' emotions'll be too conflicted. They won't know which way to go and there goes your "beyond reasonable doubt". Fucked to Christmas, sir, with all due respect.'

Peter Yun glanced across at his boss like a frightened rabbit, never having heard anyone stand up to the senior partner before.

'Let's face it, Graham,' the widower went on. 'The little bastard's hardly a menace to society, is he? A totally clean record up 'til now, and the only person he's likely to go after is me. And...'

He turned first to Kierney and then to his manager. 'I'm sorry, guys, but you know this already. To be perfectly honest, I'd be glad if he shot me, 'cause he's already ruined my life. Sure, I want to see him brought to justice for Lynn's sake, and for our children and for my in-laws. But up until a few weeks ago, this bloke was no better or worse than you or me. In fact, I said to Kizzy earlier today to remind me to tell her about how prejudice can influence a trial unfairly, and here we are discussing the very topic right now.'

Gerry leant back in his chair. It had been several months since he had seen Jeff Diamond in action for real, and he had forgotten how formidable he was when in full flight.

'You may have a point,' Winton sighed, as if the wind had been knocked out of his sails.

'I may have a point,' the widower repeated, wiping tears from his eyes. 'Thanks. That's kind of you, Graham. I'm not sure what you and your buddy, Greenshaw, hope to get out of this grotesque piece of theatre, but you've already got him. I can see it in the way you guys are playing lawyers and judges with your playmate, Rosemary. You know García's a goner, don't you?'

The barrister nodded, unusually solemn. 'Yes. We are confident.'

'So what's to be gained from humiliating this bitter and twisted woman?' Jeff asked, his sweeping gaze alighting on each person in turn. 'She should just divorce him quietly and get on with her life. Can you imagine how hard it'll be for her to hook up with a new partner after dishing the dirt to the world's press about her husband?

'You guys should be acting in her interest too. She hasn't been charged with any crime. She's just hacked off she married the guy who shot this gorgeous girl's mother. She's had her day in the sun and made some money selling her story. Leave it at that. She doesn't know any better and she's hurting right now. I hope you don't take advantage of her, particularly when the Queen's case doesn't need her testimony.'

The statuesque orator sat down and finished the last few drops of his wine. Kierney reached out her hand, which he took and wrapped his around affectionately.

Gerry got to his feet. 'I'm starving,' he declared, rubbing his stomach. 'Let's get something to eat and touch base again later on, or in the morning. That way, we'll all have had a chance to digest what's been said.'

'Good idea,' Graham agreed. 'Let's agree to meet tomorrow at eight. Here again, if that's OK with you?'

Jeff nodded. 'Yep, sure. That works, thanks. We'll be here. Bring some more wine.' Everyone laughed.

'You think he's joking!' his manager mocked.

'He *is* joking,' Kierney contradicted without a smile, not wishing the prosecution team to think their star witness was likely to turn up at court under the influence.

A THOROUGH EDUCATION

Jeff rested his left arm around his daughter's shoulders while he shook Graham and Peter warmly by the hand. They went their separate ways in the lift lobby at the bottom of the building; the solicitors benefitting from a car park underneath. Once out on the street, the exhausted celebrity let out a huge roar.

'You were amazing, *papá*,' Kierney praised, hugging him. 'I don't think they'll call Mrs García now, do you?'

'Don't know, baby. They've handled one or two more murder trials than I have, and probably won most of them. The Queen doesn't prosecute lightly. I expect the majority'd be open-and-shut cases, just like this one.'

The threesome strolled towards Circular Quay in search of dinner and distraction. Members of the public, tourists and homeward-bound city slickers waved in respectful deference to the tall superstar and his companions, the trial of their departed loved one at the forefront of everyone's mind.

'Where are we going?' Gerry asked. 'I don't even know where you guys are staying? With my folks?'

'No,' Jeff shook his head. 'We're booked into some new place on The Rocks. I gave Cath the challenge of finding us somewhere soulless and character-free, and I think she succeeded.'

His old friend laughed aloud. 'You *were* amazing, mate, by the way. Kizzy's right. I had no idea what your argument would be.'

'Lucky I didn't throw to you then,' the musician teased. 'Cheers, mate. I just don't think we need to go in so heavy. It won't help in the long run.'

'They, not we,' the older man corrected his client. 'It's their case, Jeff.'

'Yep. You're right,' the dejected husband nodded. 'And Lynn's their wife and mother too, I know.'

'*Papá*,' Kierney scolded her dad's mean streak. 'That's not what Gerry meant.'

'It's fine,' the affable accountant assured with a wide smile. 'I'm a big boy. I can handle your old man's wayward backhands. Let's get a drink, shall we?'

The threesome picked a restaurant on The Rocks, overlooking the Sydney Opera House and with the dark, menacing girders of the Harbour Bridge extending northwards above them. Jeff opened his packet of cigarettes and offered it to Gerry, who was keen to grab one.

'So much for the nicotine chewing gum,' the older man laughed. 'Your face was a picture, Kiz, when I got it out in the court. Did you think it was cake?'

'Yes, I did! I was glad it wasn't, but it was revolting though. That stuff wouldn't help me quit smoking.'

'Here you go,' her father invited, through pursed lips which were hanging on to two cigarettes he was lighting simultaneously.

His daughter accepted with a smile. 'Are you sure?' she checked, looking around them for fellow *al fresco* patrons who might also be reporters.

'No secret squirrel necessary, *pequeñita*,' Jeff reminded her. 'I just didn't want to prejudice the Queen against you earlier.'

'There's that word again! I know, *papá*. That's why I turned it down. So tell me about prejudice then.'

Their friend groaned. 'I can't believe you two. Don't you want to shut off after today?'

'It's my fault, sorry,' the young woman smiled. 'I want to understand all the subtleties, so I don't get surprised when the case twists and turns.'

'But aren't you tired?' Gerry asked.

'Yes, really tired. Are you, *papá*? Would you rather do this tomorrow instead?'

'Yes and no,' the comic answered, scratching his head. 'No time like the present. I want you to understand everything too, angel. I want you to understand why I say the things I'm going to say.'

'Oh? And what *are* you going to say, pray?' his manager queried, stubbing out his cigarette and asking a passing waiter for some menus.

'How should I know?' Jeff sighed. 'It depends when they call me and how much damage Wonderful Wendy's done by then.'

Kierney giggled. 'Wonderful Wendy? Is that García's wife?'

Her dad nodded. 'Wonderful Wendy and the weasel. Sounds like a kids' movie... And now I've prejudiced you against her. Or towards her, depending on how you interpret the word "wonderful".'

The dark-haired gipsy girl was confused, staring at her father's expressionless face. '*Papá*,' she said in exasperation. 'What do you mean?'

'What do you mean, what do I mean?' Jeff flashed back. 'You understood perfectly when we were on Level Three. Now, down here on the ground, you don't understand? My life, already, *pequeñita*! What am I going to do with you?'

Kierney laughed freely for the first time all day, watching a pair of half-Jewish hands rise towards the heavens in amazement at her apparent ignorance. A "Laura's Light" moment, her mother would have called it. She struggled to recall the intense conversation with the two lawyers.

'When I have an idea in my head beforehand about how someone behaves or who they are, so I don't look at the evidence objectively?'

Gerry clapped his hands, nodding in appreciation for his long-time friends' grasp of human nature.

'Nah,' Jeff shook his head, scowling. 'Not even close. Go to your room.'

'I *am* right,' the eighteen-year-old insisted, whining in frustration. 'Tell me I am, please.'

The passionate celebrity stood up and invited Kierney to do the same. They met in the middle, above the table, for him to plant a kiss on her forehead before both returning to their seats to an undercurrent of appreciative sighs from their fellow patrons.

'Of course you're right, angel. You're always right. The danger of prejudice means there's a real risk that a jury might misuse the evidence in some way, or even be misled into doing so. I need you to have the courage of your convictions. Trust your gut. Reserve any hesitation for things that really require extra thought.'

The businessman opposite clapped his hands again. 'You are a genius, mate. No wonder you've got such clever kids. It's masterful, the way you teach. Shall we order dinner?'

Jeff smiled at his daughter, eyes hungry for more of her father's attention. He opened his mouth to say something and then shut it again, making her giggle once more at his staged indecision, but also communicating a subtle message which she immediately understood. And he knew she had understood because tears instantly formed in the corners of her eyes.

'Gez,' he requested, 'would you mind if Kizzo and I had dinner on our own, please?'

'Tonight? Oh, right,' the accountant replied, initially surprised but knowing the determined man far too well to be offended. 'No, mate. Of course not. No worries. I'll shoot off to Mum and Dad's then, before it gets too late for a free feed. I'll see you tomorrow.'

'Thanks, Gerry,' Kierney smiled, as her pseudo-uncle bent down to kiss her cheek. 'And thank you for flying up today too. It's good to have you here. See you in the morning. Please say hello to Celia and Gerald for me. Goodnight'

'I will, darling,' Gerry replied, squeezing his mate's shoulder. 'Night-night, you bastard. Look after this precious one. Don't teach her too much too soon.'

'Jesus,' Jeff murmured, taken aback by a rare insightful comment from his rambunctious business partner. 'That's a bloody nice thing to say, mate. Have a good night and say hello to your folks from u too, please. Drive carefully.'

'*Sayonara*,' his manager saluted them both and walked out of the restaurant, along the promenade towards Circular Quay and his rental car.

'*Muchas gracias, papá*,' Kierney said, her eyes following the lone figure as it disappeared out of sight. 'You didn't have to do that, but I'm really grateful.'

Father and daughter placed an order for their food and a second bottle of Shiraz. They divided the remainder of their first bottle between two glasses. Jeff switched into the chair Gerry had vacated, to sit next to his dinner partner and toast their dearly departed.

Gazing out towards the river, tears in their eyes, the matching pair lost themselves in their own thoughts of the day. The forty-three-year-old put his hand on the youngster's shoulder, and she leant her head over to kiss the back of it. It was moments like this which gave him hope, and he regretted voicing his death-wish in front of his gorgeous girl.

'Thanks for loving me so much, baby. I'm sorry I'm giving you such a hard time.'

'No worries. I should thank *you*, *papá*. I'm glad you're giving me a hard time. You wouldn't be being honest if you didn't. Jet and I know how much *mamá* means to you, and I know it's going to be impossible for you to be happy without her. I really do understand that. I just want to monopolise you as much as I can while I can.'

Their entrées arrived, and the dark-haired Diamonds tucked into their food, both having worked up quite an appetite. Now left to their own devices and as yet undisturbed by other diners, they talked non-stop over dinner about their day in court.

The doting dad was pleased to see how eager the fresh-faced lawyer-in-waiting was to understand each shade and implication and apply her burgeoning intellect to weigh up each point. He marvelled at how alike they were, interested in everything and impatient to make their mark on the world.

'So, *papá*...?' the teenager began, placing her knife and fork across her empty plate. 'If I'd committed some heinous crime, would you be able to admit I'm guilty?'

Jeff leant back in his chair and held his glass up to the light, pretending he hadn't heard her. 'Nice wine this,' he contemplated, slotting the stem between his fingers and swirling the deep red liquid in slow circles.

'Ahem,' Kierney coughed. 'I asked you a question. You have to answer truthfully. What's "under oath" in Spanish?'

'*Sí*, Your Honour,' he replied, leaning forward again. 'My apologies. "Under oath"? I have no clue. I've never been to a Spanish trial. "*Juramento*", probably. Something like that. *La verdad, la verdad entera y nada exceptúa la verdad, que Díos me ayuda.* Now, what was the question again?'

'If you knew I was guilty of a crime, could you convict me?' Kierney asked again, laughing. 'And be serious!'

'I guess it would depend on what you'd done,' her dad responded with a wide grin. 'What have you done?'

The eighteen-year-old giggled again. 'Serious, *papá*.'

'I *am* being serious,' her teacher insisted, looking her straight in the eyes. 'Are you a danger to society? Are you likely to do it again? Are you sorry? Was it a *crime de passion* that I would've committed in your place? Have you done this ten times before and never been caught? Have you ruined anyone's life as a result of your heinous crime?'

The young woman sighed. 'OK, OK! I get it. It's complicated. Too much to hope to get a yes or no, I suppose.'

'*Exactamente, pequeñita*,' Jeff nodded, pouring some more wine into her glass. 'Life's very colourful. Very few things are completely black or white.'

'Do you think García committed a *crime de passion?*'

'*Mais non!*' came the grieving man's sharp retort. 'He committed a crime of spite; of jealousy. It's close, but more than splitting hairs, as you said earlier. A crime of passion is committed by your heart. His wasn't. It was committed by his mixed-up head.'

'Do you really not care if he gets convicted or not?' Kierney asked again, her voice temporarily lowered for the waiter's approach, about to deliver their main courses.

The widower paused while the task was competed, his response delayed further when the young man asked the stars to autograph his order pad. 'Well... For justice to be done to the letter of the law, and speaking as a citizen of the Commonwealth, yes, I care, *pequeñita*,' he answered. 'He deserves to be punished for what he did. But do *I* care, personally? Nope. What difference would it make whether he's in prison or not?'

'He might come after you,' Kierney suggested. 'And before you say you'd be glad, I know you wouldn't want to see me and Jet suffer.'

She immediately felt guilty as tears welled up in the great man's eyes. 'Believe me, gorgeous...' he sighed. 'That poor bloke'll never come after me now. Not after what's happened to him, and with the public shellacking he's received.'

'But why not?' his daughter persisted, relieved to hear a rational response. 'Surely he would've expected the reaction to what he did to be pretty extreme?'

Jeff shook his head. 'No, baby. I doubt if he ever gave it one serious thought. People with this kind of obsession seldom consider the consequences. They're not thinking like you and I are now, endlessly analysing things from different angles. I know 'cause I've been there. You get consumed by one thing, to the exclusion of all else.'

'So do you think he's insane?'

'Insane?' her father repeated, disapproval causing an upward inflexion in his deep voice. 'That's a very damning word. Prejudicial, I could say even... Where's your artist's palette now?'

'Sorry, *papá*. I mean diminished mental capacity,' Kierney corrected.

'Better,' the philanthropist smiled, finishing a mouthful of steak. 'But don't back down so quickly. I might agree with you. I'm just pushing you a little further each time. Testing you out. You're safe, Kizzo. You can say anything to me, OK?'

'Yes, OK. I love you, *papá. Gracias.*'

'I love you too. And you don't have to thank me. You're teaching me too, y'know. It's very gratifying for me, hearing you debate like this. It shows me how ready you are for the world.'

'You know what?' Kierney said, her eyes full of mischief. 'I think you're prejudiced *for* García because you can understand his position *and* you feel sorry for him. You've crossed the empathy-sympathy line. I think that's dangerous for tomorrow.'

Jeff lay down his cutlery and raised both hands in front of his face, palms towards his daughter. 'Hey, steady!' he cried. 'I said "Don't back down," not "Feel free to attack me." Where the hell did that come from?'

'You're under oath, sir, remember... I think it's the same risk as putting Wonderful Wendy on the stand.'

'And you'd be perfectly correct, *pequeñita*,' he assented, 'if I were going to talk as freely in court as I am now. But I shan't be.'

The teenager pointed her left index finger at her father's face as if to say "Gotcha!" 'But isn't that what "the whole truth" means?'

'Absolutely. Yes, it bloody well is, baby. Welcome to the real world. Try this one for size: it's all about constituency.'

'Constituency?' his daughter echoed. 'What does constituency mean in this context?'

'It means that when I'm talking to you here, I'm representing only myself. When I'm on the stand tomorrow, I'll represent you and Jet, Grandma and Grandpa and pretty much the whole of Australia who loved your *mamá*. So the whole truth as myself, sitting here with you, is that I don't need to see that bastard behind bars, and yes, I do feel sorry for him in the cold light of his morning after. However, Crown witness Jeff Diamond's whole truth needs to match everyone else's need to see a guilty man behind bars for a length of time befitting his crimes. Tomorrow my constituency demands are different.'

'Wow!' Kierney exclaimed. 'I love that so much! The politics of justice. Shit!'

'*¿Perdóneme?*' her dad chuckled. 'Who gave you permission to use language like that in front of me?'

'That's the consequence of treating me like a grown-up,' the youngster smiled, picking up her glass full of adult beverage and finishing it. 'Now I understand the difference between local, national and international government too. Your constituency demands different things. But why can't you just represent yourself on the witness stand, instead of all of us?'

'I could. There's nothing to stop me from doing so, but the result might not be what the rest of Australia needs.'

'I.e. he might get off?'

'Bingo! Principle Number Three, *genia*,' the master communicator nodded. 'Otherwise, they'd have to put each and everyone else on the stand too. On this occasion, it's my duty to represent the larger constituency, in the interest of time and money and for the greater good. As Gerry keeps reminding me, it's not our case. It's the Queen's case. And Her Majesty liked your *mamá*, so she probably wants to see García behind bars.'

'*Papá*, that's a really sad joke,' the child in the young woman rued, her grin vanishing. 'When do you have your say?'

'Now, baby,' Jeff reassured her, reaching over and stroking his daughter's cheek. 'Now, with you, in this fantastic conversation that I don't want to end. But I know you're tired, so we should call it a day.'

Kierney shook her head, wondering if she should request the dessert menu. 'Oh, no. Not yet. I'm just getting started. I want to hear about Granddad.'

'Granddad? Tonight?'

'Yes.'

'But won't that risk me tipping further over your magical empathy-sympathy line?' the arrogant teacher smiled, knowing he had hung the youngster on a technicality.

'Damn!' she whined, hitting the table with her fists. 'As soon as I said it, I knew that's what you'd come back with. Damn, damn, damn!'

Jeff attracted the attention of the waiter and signalled for their bill. 'Let's get out of here,' he suggested. 'I think we should go back to the hotel and continue this conversation over a cup of coffee and *un petit cognac* or two. Sound good?'

'Yes, *papá*. Good idea. *Fantastico*, in fact. Do they breathalyse people before they take the stand?'

Her father looked surprised at yet another question without notice. 'Don't think so, but I'm not going to take the stand with anything in my system,' he responded. 'That'd be irresponsible and extremely disrespectful to my constituents. Anyway... I might not get on stage tomorrow at all.'

The two sultry gems walked out of the restaurant unnoticed and strolled hand-in-hand towards their hotel at the very end of the short peninsula known as The Rocks. The illuminated Opera House shone against the pale, cloudy dusk, and they leant over the railings for a few minutes to take in the view, smoking a cigarette and watching the endless stream of ferries pulling in and out of Circular Quay.

'There's one thing your *mamá* helped me rationalise very early on,' Jeff stated, turning around to face his daughter and settling back on the metal barrier.

'What's that?'

'The recognition of statistical significance.'

'Is that principle Number Four?' Kierney chuckled. 'How am I going to remember all this?'

'Ah, you will. Since when did you start to forget anything?'

The young woman shrugged. 'What's the principle of statistical significance then? Sounds more like maths than justice.'

'Clever girl. Hold that thought. *Mamá* and I used to have long, long, long discussions about supporting the rights of minorities. Shall we go?'

Within five minutes, the conversationalists were back at their hotel, entering a lift full of inquisitive people. Everyone knew the trial of Lynn Diamond's murderer was taking place this week, with every paper and television new show covering the build-up. Their fellow guests were excited to see the famous pair walking among them.

'I hope he goes away for twenty-five or thirty years,' one man said, reaching forward to shake Jeff's hand.

'I don't,' said another. 'If this was back home in the US, he'd be going to the electric chair for what he did.'

The grieving husband silenced these opinions as quickly as he could. 'I can't discuss anything, I'm sorry. I'm on the stand later in the week, so let's just see what happens. Thanks for your support. We appreciate it.'

Kierney let themselves into her room, and her dad picked up the telephone to order some coffee and a bottle of brandy from Room Service. They sat on the small balcony and stared out underneath the bridge, across the river towards the gaping mouth of Luna Park.

'What were you going to say about statistical significance?'

The tall superstar crossed his legs and took a long drag on yet another cigarette. 'Jesus Christ, you don't waste much time, do you? Ah, yeah. Statistical significance... When does a minority become so statistically insignificant that the cost of giving them what they need represents an opportunity cost to greater society that's larger than the benefit received by the minority?'

'*¿Qué?* Say that again, more slowly.'

The wise man smiled. 'D'you know what the term "opportunity cost" means?'

'What else you could've bought with money you spent on something,' she answered. 'That wasn't a very elegant explanation, was it?'

'Good enough,' her dad praised. 'Don't doubt yourself either. It's the concept that you need to understand, not necessarily the precise definition. I don't know if I could do any better. When *mamá* was studying economics, we used to argue for ages over the best use of money, or rather "scarce resources", to use the correct terminology. Her teacher at MA gave the class the argument that opportunity cost was the relationship between scarce resources and how they could've been used if you hadn't already spent them.'

'So why did you argue?' Kierney asked, eager to uncover extra morsels of information about the mother she missed so much.

''Cause I took a much more philosophical approach. For *mamá*, resources always had a quantifiable number associated with them... dollars spent or saved, hours taken or saved, points won or lost, *et cetera*... but I don't see it that way. D'you know what "utility" is in economic terms?'

'No,' the student admitted.

There was a knock at the door. The gracious guest went to answer it, returning with a tray of drinks and placing it on the balcony table. He looped a starched white napkin over his right wrist and waving his left hand over the array of wares on offer.

'What can I get you for, *mademoiselle?*'

'Please could I have some brandy in my coffee?'

'*Du cognac dedans?*' the comic translated. '*Mais bien sûr, mademoiselle. Avec du lait aussi?*'

The teenager giggled. '*Oui, merci. Vous êtes très gentil, monsieur.*'

'*Oui,*' her father agreed in mock arrogance. '*J'en sais. Et vous êtes très charmante.*'

'*Merci,*' Kierney sighed, watching the tall, handsome gentleman slump down into his chair and begin to cry. 'But I'm not *mamá*, am I?'

Jeff stared out across the water, clenching his jaws to stem the tears. He didn't want his daughter to know how right she was. He shouldn't even be putting her in this position. Kierney was not here as some perverse substitute for Lynn on one of the famous couple's many overnight business trips to Sydney. She was here to attend the trial of the man who killed her mother.

'I'm sorry, Kizzo,' he said, ashamed. 'I am having a great time with you, and sometimes I manage to kid myself that I don't miss your *mamá*. It's unfair of me to pretend you're her. In fact, it disgusts me, if I'm perfectly honest. You're going to make someone, or a whole bunch of lucky someone's, a very sexy, sophisticated and exquisite partner one day. But here and now, you're my daughter, and I have to stop this ridiculous charade.'

The young woman blanched, unsure how to respond. 'No, you don't. You'd behave exactly the same way if Jet were here, and if *mamá* were here too. This is fun. We've always behaved this way, and I love you oodles for it. You're making me feel very special.'

The widower sniffed and took a gulp of neat brandy. 'I saw you freeze that security guard this afternoon,' he smiled, wiping his eyes, 'and I saw your *mamá* in you then.'

'I know. I could see you out of the corner of my eye.'

'Jeez, Kizzy, I miss her so much,' he admitted, putting his head in his hands. 'I can't begin to tell you how much.'

Kierney raised her coffee cup. 'To *mamá* and everything she's made us into,' she toasted. 'We love you, *mamá*.'

Jeff lifted his brandy glass in response and let out a deep sigh. 'Yes, indeed. Your *mamá* gave good utility,' he said, taking another deep breath, determined to continue their conversation.

'Utility,' the compassionate youngster remembered where their discussion had been interrupted. 'Tell me.'

'Sure thing, *pequeñita*. Utility is the value that something brings to its consumer, whether that be usefulness or satisfaction or even happiness. *Mamá* often tried to measure utility in numeric terms, 'cause it's simpler to compare relative utility that way. Hence me telling you to hold the thought about maths earlier...'

'Oh, yes. I forgot. Sorry, *papá*.'

'No matter. I used to tease her that just because something had a large number written on its price-tag, it didn't mean it was better appreciated.'

'But what does this have to do with the statistical significance of minorities?' the youngster asked, looking lost.

Her mentor poured a fresh round of coffee and took another large mouthful of the rich, smooth liqueur. 'Because of opportunity cost,' he answered, bringing them back to where they had left off in their encounter with the fervent lift passengers. 'When does the utility of satisfying a tiny minority become too low, in terms of the relative utility of a majority?'

The dark-haired student continued to draw a blank.

'Here's a clue, *pequeñita*: it comes down to constituency again. Take the example of education... If you spend a few thousand dollars educating a child with a severe intellectual disability, the utility that child gains is immeasurable for him- or herself, since it provides stimulation and excitement and all the other things that intellectually able kids take for granted.'

Kierney nodded. 'But that same few thousand dollars spent on an able child might be money better spent for society as a whole?'

'Yeah, precisely. Perhaps not morally, but as far as the impact on the rest of society. You've got it. That able child may go on to be a research scientist like your Auntie Anna, who potentially discovers the cure for cancer.'

'But why couldn't the intellectually-disabled kid find the cure for cancer?'

'No reason. It could happen,' her father acknowledged without hesitation, 'and I wish it would happen, 'cause it'd do wonders for changing perceptions...'

'Prejudice even!' the dark-haired gipsy girl yelped.

'Yep. Prejudice even,' he laughed at the sudden impetuosity. 'You see how it's all interlaced? With the right programs in place, the child with the disability might well go on to find the cure for cancer, but on top of people's prejudice holding her or him back, it's statistically improbable.

'If you look at utility in terms of potential return on investment, which is the better bet?'

'The able kid.'

'Sure. However, if you look at utility in terms of whether you've done something ethically right, it's line ball, isn't it? It's shouldn't just be about the quantitative benefits. Take the example of feeding famine victims in Africa, then...'

'OK,' Kierney smiled, knowing this was one of her father's highest-priority passions. 'Ten thousand dollars' worth of seed and farming equipment versus a ten thousand dollar donation to an Australian charity like The Smith Family.'

'Great,' Jeff said, slapping the table with his fingers. 'Perfect. If a village community in Eritrea or Ethiopia were to put that money into cultivating and irrigating their land, they'd be able to feed themselves for many years to come. But if we gave ten thousand dollars to The Smith Family to pass on to a particular community of disadvantaged families in Melbourne or Sydney, it'd get lost very quickly in the higher cost of living, the bureaucracy of our systems and the sheer enormity of the problem. Therefore, which group gets the greater utility in that example?'

'The Africans,' the teenager replied, sitting taller in her chair.

'Correct. The minority. But are they statistically insignificant?'

'Depends if other villages learn from them and get the same opportunity to adopt the new methods.'

The proud father winked. 'Precisely, you amazing creature! They widen their constituency, deliver more utility than can be measured monetarily and become statistically significant.'

'Cool!' Kierney beamed. 'I see now. So what does this have to do with García's trial?'

'Nothing whatsoever!'

'Liar! This whole thing started with you in the witness box. Come on, papá!'

'OK, Your Honour! Jesus, you're hard on me... I have the choice of being statistically significant or not tomorrow,' the forty-three-year-old answered, suddenly sapped of enthusiasm. 'Like you said, when do I have my say? When I saw García sitting there in the dock today, it started me thinking about just how many minorities there actually are.'

'At the end of the day, aren't we all a minority of one?' the eighteen-year-old offered.

The philanthropist nodded. 'Pretty much. Exactly my point, pequeñita. Who's to say that someone else with a particular set of needs is less deserving than bloody Juan Antonio is? I was comparing him to me and to your granddad; all three of us being men who came into this world in pretty meagre circumstances. We can all choose to make something of our life by taking advantage of services that society offers us...'

'Or not.'

'Or not,' Jeff agreed. 'Spot on. But is it his fault if he didn't? Many people aren't aware of what exists to help them. Maybe their particular bespoke situation isn't catered for. But regardless, everyone has a choice to do the right thing or the wrong thing. The question for me tomorrow is, did García know he was doing the wrong thing?'

'Killing *mamá*?' his indignant daughter exclaimed. 'Under which circumstances would that be doing the right thing?'

'Yeah, I hear ya. Hang tight, baby. In isolation, and to the wider constituency of the Commonwealth, I agree with you a hundred percent, and that's what I'll take the stand with,' her father said, calming the young woman down by stroking her glossy, dark hair. 'But when that spaniel walked into the hotel foyer that morning intending to kill me, did he, as Juan Antonio García alone, believe he was doing the right thing or the wrong thing?'

'Does that even matter though?' the teenager asked, flagging a little. 'The law says you don't kill people without just cause. He broke the law.'

'Yes. But the law also says you can't drive faster than a hundred kilometres per hour on the freeway. Have you broken the speed limit yet?'

Kierney frowned. 'Of course I have.'

'Did you cause any harm to anyone or anything while you were speeding? Do you think you did something wrong?'

'No,' she sighed. 'Just something against the law.'

Jeff reached across the table and took the teenager's hand. 'Sorry,' he sighed, seeing how deflated she had become. 'Tough, isn't it? We all take risks every day. Well calculated risks, if you're smart. Poorly calculated risks, if you're not. You weigh up the opportunity cost of sticking to the speed limit and decide that the statistical likelihoods of crashing the car, injuring someone, injuring yourself or copping a ticket are all low, therefore the combined probable opportunity cost of taking the risk is outweighed by the exhilarating utility you'll get from driving at a hundred and twenty kilometres per hour.'

Kierney nodded. 'And it's probably only perceived utility too. Is that extra twenty kilometres an hour really going to give me that much more exhilarating utility?'

The speed-demon laughed, lifting his hands to the ceiling. '*¡Excelente!* I like that angle a lot. That's your *mamá* talking again. I would always answer yes to that question.'

'Because we're all in a minority of one,' the dark-haired woman sighed, walking round to the other side of the table and hugging her father around the shoulders.

'Yep. Damned straight, angel,' he said, kissing her hands as they interlocked across his chest. 'If García truly believed that I presented some danger to the perceived or real utility of his little constituency, then perhaps he didn't believe he was doing anything wrong by eliminating me. Even though he knew he was breaking the law, maybe he didn't think the law was right for his particular situation, and it was a risk he was willing to take.'

His daughter yawned. 'It's tiring, this business of humanity. Do you want to go to sleep?'

'We should,' Jeff nodded. 'Although the perceived utility of sleep is much less for me than the real utility will be. We can talk about Granddad tomorrow night, if you like.'

'García still shot at *mamá* four times,' Kierney reminded her exhausted witness, as they brought the tray of drinks back into the room and closed the sliding door to the balcony. 'He killed her intentionally, so he's guilty of murder.'

The world-changer embraced his daughter and kissed her forehead hard. 'He did, gorgeous,' he replied, crying at her gentle forthrightness. 'I'll be statistically significant tomorrow, don't you worry. He's going to prison because you and Jet don't have a *mamá* anymore. I promise you that.'

'Are you going to your room?'

'Yeah. Do you believe me?'

'Not sure,' the young woman admitted. 'It's none of my business anyway. I'm sorry.'

'It's not, but I'm glad you care,' Jeff smiled. 'I'll watch TV for a while. Who knows? *Mamá* may come and visit me.'

His daughter rolled her eyes and thumped his chest playfully. 'Shut up, p*apá*.'

'OK,' he smirked. 'So you don't want me to wake you then, if she turns up? I'll tell you all about it at breakfast time. Oh, but I might be late for breakfast.'

'If you're late for breakfast, I hope it's for that reason,' the sympathetic teenager told him. 'Don't answer the phone if you're having sex. I don't want to hear your heavy breathing first thing in the morning.'

'Now *you'd* better shut up,' the widower smiled, smarting at the image she had put in his mind. 'That's highly unlikely now, isn't it?'

'G'night, *papá*. Thanks for the conversation tonight. It's fascinating learning about this stuff, and I hope we can do it again tomorrow night.'

'We shall, *pequeñita*. Many times. Sleep well.'

Finally alone in his hotel room, having kissed Kierney goodnight one final time and content to have heard the thud of a deadbolt behind him, Jeff found himself mulling over Gerry's parting comment. *Don't teach her too much too soon.* The simple but powerful sentence weighed on his mind, and within a few minutes, the tattoo on his chest stung again.

'Jeez, angel, that's a welcome feeling. Thanks for dropping in,' he said into the air. 'Or have you been here all night? Quite the little miracle, our daughter, isn't she?'

The mournful celebrity first removed his shoes and then the tie, which he had lowered to half-mast around his neck since leaving the courts. He lay down on top of the bed and pulled his belt clear of his waistband, dropping it onto the floor to his left.

Reaching for the remote control, he surfed across the many channels, searching for something to divert his mind sufficiently to induce sleep. The red digits on the clock-radio marked eleven-thirty, renewing his guilt at keeping Kierney up so late.

Jeff settled on a recorded football match from the English Premier League. His thoughts turned to his son in Cambridge, and he wished the larrikin had been in Sydney to participate in this evening's conversation. He now had sole responsibility for the two teenagers; he could screw them up royally or deliver them to adulthood as two grounded and well-rounded individuals. It was now all up to him, yet Lynn's sporadic but edifying messages showed she was with him all the way.

Levering himself to a sitting position, the philosopher picked up the telephone receiver and dialled his son's number.

'Hello. This is Jet,' he heard the cheerful voice say.

'Mate, it's Dad,' the caller began, tears springing forth yet again. 'How're you going?'

'Hey, Dad. Sorry, I didn't recognise this number. I'm fine, thanks. What about you?'

'Ah, OK, I guess, thanks. I'm ringing from our hotel in Sydney. Today was the first day of your mum's trial. Kizzy's just gone to bed after a long, robust dinner conversation. She exhausted me.'

His elder child sniggered. 'Oh, yeah? Dubious. The other way around, more like, old man. What was it like? Have you been in the witness box yet?'

'Nope. Tomorrow maybe,' Jeff answered, loosening up on hearing his son's sunny disposition. 'It's a slow process. Ridiculous amount of checking and re-checking of facts. Asking the same question over and over.'

'Trying to trip people up?'

'A bit of that, but more a deliberate effort to make the jury understands and remembers the right info'. I wish you were here to see it, rather than hearing about it second hand. Kizzo's glad she came. It's going to give her some closure, I reckon.'

'Hmm... You too, I hope. I have been thinking about it,' Jet admitted, 'but I'd rather not miss more uni' or the pre-season. The bastard's not going to get off, is he?'

The widower inhaled and held his breath while a wave of sorrow engulfed him. He wasn't prepared to risk exposing Jet to a re-run of his and Kierney's critical dissection of the day over the telephone. From this distance, he couldn't guarantee the young man's emotional safety net would catch him, since he was less mature than his sister when it came to shades of grey.

'No, mate. He's going down. I'll bore you senseless with all the gory details when we're biking around the countryside in the summer.'

'OK, cool. Sounds great. Does García look sorry?'

'He's beginning to. To start with, he just sat there expressionless. But as the day went on, he began to look a bit more uncomfortable. Y'know, there's a whole heap of support for us out here, mate.'

'I bet,' the student replied. 'Here too. I still get stopped all the time by total strangers wanting to hug me and shake my hand.'

The father chuckled. 'Cool. We are too. People've been shouting, "Lock 'im up!" from the public gallery where we're sitting. And an American bloke in the hotel tonight told us he's recommending the electric chair.'

'Oh, shit!' Jet exclaimed. 'He's not on the jury, is he?'

'Thankfully not. But García's first up tomorrow morning for questioning, which'll be interesting. Just before me. Although they want to put his wife on the stand too...'

'Really?' the disgruntled young man interrupted. 'What's the deal with her? I didn't think spouses had to testify.'

'No deal, with any luck. They can't be forced to testify, but apparently she's more than willing. Has she been in the papers over there?'

'No. Why? What's she done?'

'Mate, it's actually a pretty unpalatable situation,' the empath explained in a more serious tone. 'Some tabloid or magazine's convinced her to speak out, and it's bloody humiliating.'

'Right. Is she being paid for her story? Humiliating for whom?'

'For her. Wendy, her name is... She's divorcing him, for a start. And now she wants to appear as a witness against him. I don't want it to happen, but it's up to the prosecution barristers.'

'Sounds cheap and nasty,' his son offered. 'I'm with you.'

'Cheers, mate,' the grieving husband replied. 'I agree. Mum doesn't deserve a bloody circus. We just want to see a conviction based on evidence and a fair sentence. Case closed, move on.'

'The lawyers have obviously been watching too many Grisham movies,' Jet chuckled. 'Are they looking for fame and fortune out of this?'

'Yep. I think you're right. That's what I said, but they didn't bite. Turns out Blake-san went to school with the Defence Counsel.'

'Bloody hell! Is that a problem?'

'No. They didn't know each other well. Gerry was kidding around how the various Supreme Court legal eagles are all best friends out of court but arch-rivals in court. It's a bit too theatrical for my liking.'

'Wow. I never thought I'd hear you say that,' the larrikin chided, 'Mr Larger-than-Life!'

'Hey! Fuck you, mate. That's enough of that. How's the workload going?'

'Pretty well, thanks. I still find it hard to concentrate sometimes, but it's much better than I expected.'

This news heartened the older man, 'Great. Kizzy's doing all right too. We have our moments, and she's been fantastic. I'm still leaning on her way too much. Have you talked to her lately?'

'Only over e-mail,' Jet confessed. 'I'll ring her at the weekend. When do you think the trial'll be over?'

'Don't know, mate. They allocate two weeks, but I don't think it'll go that long. It depends how many blind alleys we go down for the sake of a good front-page spread.'

The student groaned. 'I'm glad I'm not there in that case.'

'Well, anyway... I'm stoked I got to speak to you. I need to try and get some sleep so I'm on song for tomorrow.'

'Sure, Dad,' the young man replied. 'Just yell "Lock 'im up!" a few times. That'll do it.'

'Right. Thanks for the advice, coach,' the star witness laughed. 'I'll let you know how I go.'

'Cheers. Good luck.'

'You too, mate. Work hard and play harder.'

'Always, *maiastra*. Bye.'

Jeff replaced the receiver and went into the bathroom, slain by an acute pang of jealousy at his son embarking on a long and successful journey filled with learning, leisure and ladies. He cursed his uncharitable reaction, knowing full well that he had enjoyed more than his fair share of all three in his time.

While he undressed, the billionaire stared at his "JL" tattoo in the mirror and wondered what his beautiful best friend made of his interactions with the children this evening. He didn't begrudge the teenagers a single second of his time, but he missed the ability to halve the load with their mother.

'Are you coming for a shower?' he asked, scanning the ceiling. 'It's been a shit of a day. I'll treat you well, angel. Very well.'

The single man stood under hot jets of water, feeling thoroughly disenchanted. Had he tried to take more from life than he was entitled? He had so many things to be grateful for whenever he cast his mind back over their life singular, and yet the only image dominating his tired brain tonight showed him slamming headlong into a solid brick wall.

How life had changed for the family best known for making the most of everything... How could he have been so reckless as to let Lynn slip away and take all that was worth having with her, bringing their plans and ambitions to a crashing halt? Even the air-cooled brakes on his brand new Aston Martin couldn't have taken him from a hundred down to zero any faster.

Weren't they the couple with the Midas touch? This wasn't supposed to happen to them. As Gerry had mentioned only days earlier, they had taken every precaution against such a disaster: engaging professional security consultants; taking part in endless risk assessments; and diligently adhering to every recommendation.

After the exorbitant amounts of time and money spent over two decades on protecting their interests, an insignificant, all-beige singleton had derailed the entire Diamond train without even appearing to know what he was doing.

'Fuck you, Miss Irony,' the desperate man harked back to the imaginary tormenter from his past. 'Ain't that right, angel? That bitch got us in the end.'

Jeff thumped the tiled wall with both fists. Ideas of abandoning the trial altogether plagued his lonely conscience. What if he couldn't withstand the interrogation Stephen Greenshaw would direct at him? He had already given the prosecution team reason to doubt his desire to see García convicted. The weight of evidence and public opinion alone should be enough to put this man behind bars, so perhaps they were better off without his contribution?

'Am I that strong, angel?' he implored. 'D'you trust me to represent you well enough? Truly? Please be there and keep us company.'

IN THE DOCK

Jeff woke not long afterwards in a cold sweat. He had been visited in his sleep by his father and Juan Antonio García together, taunting him from the public gallery as he stood in the witness box answering a barrage of questions from lawyers and judge alike. Kierney and Gerry were nowhere to be seen, and neither was Lynn, driving the stirring dreamer into a blind panic, convinced he would never see anyone he loved ever again.

It was five-thirty, and sunlight streamed in through the balcony window. The tormented man sat bolt upright and reached for the receiver before pulling his hand back under the sheet. *Stop leaning on her*, he chastised himself. His daughter didn't need to hear about his nightmares.

Twisting each wedding ring in turn, he tried his hardest to visualise the day ahead. A few hours' sleep after last night's educational discussion had solidified his argument, with the span of his constituency now fully resolved in his mind: a cold-blooded murder had been committed, and someone universally adored had been taken from her family, friends and fans.

To the prosecution witness' great relief, the telephone rang beside his head less than ten minutes later. He smiled, pulling on the coiled wire and catching the receiver as it flew towards his face.

'*Bonjour, mademoiselle.* Sleep well?'

'*Bonjour, papá.* Yes, thanks. Shall we go for a run?'

'Sure thing, baby,' he agreed, feigning enthusiasm. 'Five minutes?'

Father and daughter sprinted up the steep hill behind The Rocks to avoid the droves of commuters making their way into the city on early morning ferries and trains. The runners twisted and turned through the streets of Pyrmont and on towards Darling Harbour, around the wharves and following the river as closely as possible to prevent themselves from losing their way. When they reached the Western Distributor Road, they doubled back to the hotel, spurred on by visions of a hearty breakfast.

In the dining room, the young woman had an announcement to make. 'I'm going to change my course for next year.'

'Ah, yeah? Let me guess...'

'Human Rights Law,' his daughter's response aligned with his prediction. 'It's much more useful than International Law and Politics.'

'They'd cross over, I'm sure,' he told her. 'Not sure about more useful, but definitely more you.'

'So you're OK with it? You don't think it's a bad move?'

Jeff shook his head. 'Absolutely not. Follow your dreams, *pequeñita*. And you have the right temperament for that sort of work. Jet couldn't do it, but you'll excel.'

'Thanks, *papá*,' the teenager was delighted with her father's reaction. 'Are you ready for today?'

Her father nodded, raising his eyebrows. 'Jesus! No way! Are you?'

'No, not really,' she laughed.

'I spoke to Jetto last night, after I left you. He wishes us luck.'

'Good. Thanks, bro',' Kierney cast into the airwaves.

'His instructions were to shout "Lock 'im up!" a few times from the witness box, which compares not too favourably with the intellectual content of our conversation, don't ya think?'

The competitive younger sibling giggled. 'That's hilarious. I'm sure you put him up to it though.'

'Yeah, well... I might've. Oh, and I've come up with a new question for you, if you're up for it tonight, Ms Human Rights Lawyer.'

'Awesome!' she replied. 'Do I get advanced notice, or are you going to spring it on me?'

'Darwin.'

'Northern Territory or Charles?'

'Charles, of course,' came the billionaire's amused retort. 'It's not possible to have an intellectual conversation about the Top End.'

His daughter wagged a scolding finger. 'Ooh! That's a bit pretentious, isn't it?'

'Ha! Walked into that one,' the amateur professor shrugged in agreement. 'Don't make me think in the mornings before I've had a cigarette.'

'You'd better inform Mr Winton of that fact too then, just in case you don't get called 'til tomorrow.'

Jeff scowled. 'Shit! Don't tell me I have to endure another twenty-four hours' waiting.'

'Did you sleep?' the youngster asked, sensing some tension building.

'Not too much,' the widower shook his head. 'But I'll be fine. Stop worrying about me.'

Taking the hint, Kierney left her seat for seconds from the breakfast buffet. Her dad could hear her interacting with concerned guests while she loaded her plate and was awed by the polite positivity in her answers.

'*Papá?*' the bright-eyed eighteen-year-old changed the subject, sitting down and tucking into her food. 'Can the Accused be forced to take the stand if he doesn't want to?'

'That I don't know,' her father answered, watching her take a bite of toast. 'Probably not, but they'd lean on him pretty hard. Why d'you ask?'

Kierney put her hand in front of her mouth while she chewed, appearing so cute and childlike that Jeff once again succumbed to his jangling emotions.

'What's the matter?' she asked, concerned. 'What did I say?'

The great man sighed and forced a smile. '*Nada.* You look like a girl but you act like a woman,' he said. 'You're full of grace and dignity these days, just how your *mamá* was when we first met. It's exquisitely painful for me to watch and listen to you, knowing you've got everything ahead of you.

'It was the same with Jet last night. I was raging with jealousy after I got off the phone, thinking of him going to classes with other students and partying all night. It's not that I'm not bitter that you've got all these opportunities ahead of you guys, but it kills me to know Lynn's and mine are over.'

'Hold that thought,' the kind teenager mimicked the rock legend. 'That's what you need to say on the stand. That's your Victim Impact Statement in a nutshell.'

Jeff's eyes lit up. 'Jesus, baby! You're right. That's actually brilliant. Thanks heaps.'

'*De nada, papá.* I asked about whether the Accused has the choice to be a witness in his own trial because I was thinking how easy it would be for a nervous person to really incriminate him- or herself if they weren't careful. Especially someone not too smart.'

The confident performer frowned. 'Yeah, I guess it's possible. The Defence'd coach them pretty comprehensively, I'm sure. I imagine it must be in their best interest to take the stand in the overwhelming majority of cases, 'cause even though the judge might tell the jury that silence doesn't equal guilt, they're probably going to subliminally believe it does. They're gonna think, "If he's innocent, why doesn't he stand up for himself and say so?"'

'S'pose so,' Kierney said. 'But all those technicalities and all the details they have to remember... They can hardly say, "Hang on a minute. I need to check my script." It'd be a nightmare, even if you *were* innocent.'

Her father chuckled. 'I agree. And another weird thing I read is that if a witness lied in an earlier appearance, and the Accused contradicts him or her with what's actually the truth, the jury has to disregard the Accused's testimony until there's a chance to recall the Witness and ask them if they lied.'

'Really? How confusing for the jury. It's only true because I said it first? I'm definitely not going to break any laws ever again. Not even speeding. I can't stand the thought of all this stress.'

'Wise move, gorgeous,' Jeff smiled, 'because, on top of that, you've already established that if I were your witness, I may feel obliged to help convict you, depending on what you've done.'

'Argh!' the teenager laughed, reaching forward to rub her father's shirt over his tattoo. '*Mamá*, help! Save me from this confusion!'

After breakfast, the pair of dark-haired Diamonds walked back into Sydney's CBD, towards the Supreme Court building. Jeff rang Gerry's number to find out if he wanted a coffee before their meeting with the prosecution team at eight o'clock. There was no response, so he directed Kierney into a small café on Castlereagh Street and bought three take-aways, hot, sweet and strong.

Before the morning chill had a chance to cool the aromatic brews, their third amigo was spotted jogging towards them. 'Morning, guys,' he crowed. 'How are we this fine day?'

'G'day! You're awfully chipper about something, old bean,' his friend countered, shaking an outstretched hand and proffering the spare *caffè latte*.

'Superb, thanks,' the Mosman native replied. 'I've had my proposal accepted.'

'By Fiona?' Kierney asked. 'Fantastic! Congratulations!'

Jeff's wounded heart sank, and his daughter watched on as he embraced his best buddy and passed on his best wishes too. News of someone else with exciting opportunities ahead of him was the last thing her father needed to hear this morning, although all good fuel for his testimony.

'That's great news, mate,' the widower tapped his manager on the shoulder. 'What's Fiona's phone number? I'm going to ring her right now and tell her what a mistake she's making.'

The accountant read out a string of digits, which the celebrity dialled straightaway, while they stood drinking their coffee and soaking in the morning sunshine.

'Fiona, it's Jeff,' he announced, hearing the woman's businesslike Toorak accent. 'Good morning. Pretty good, thanks. You? Day Two. Yes. You make it sound like a test match. Yeah. That's OK. We should get them out by tea time. I'm joking. I'm *joking!*'

Kierney and Gerry exchanged glances, imagining the sophisticated solicitor's responses to the false merriment purveyed by their handsome companion, who raised his eyebrows at their reaction and continued.

'Hey, listen... Someone's just told me you've agreed to make an honest man out of a certain filthy-rich executive. Ha! You're not wrong. A tall order indeed. Congratulations, Fiona. I'm really pleased for you. Scared, but pleased. We should. Kierney sends congrats too. Yeah, she's with us. It's hardly a bundle of laughs, but we'll get through it.

'Will you let us... me or whomever... take you guys out to dinner when we get back, to celebrate? Pick somewhere you'd like to go. Thanks. Have a good day and pick a very expensive ring. He can afford it. He's avoided shelling out for way too long. Now it's your duty to make him pay. Thanks again. See you soon. *Adiós*.'

Gerry slapped his best friend on the back as the call terminated. While Jeff had been talking, his daughter had requested their manager go easy on her father today, leaving the Irishman embarrassed and ashamed.

'Sorry, mate,' he said. 'Poor timing on my part. Should've perhaps left it 'til this evening.'

'What? No way! I asked *you*, remember? You're not wearing your poker face this morning. Blindingly obvious something was up. Has my minder been bending your ear?'

Kierney turned her back, trying to avoid the inseparable friends' matching accusatory demeanours. The VIP client grasped his daughter's shoulder and hugged her in close while they walked into the lobby of the Supreme Court building and ascended the escalators to the first floor.

They were issued with a replacement set of temporary passes, shown through the security barrier and directed back to their wood-panelled hideaway on Level Three. Graham Winton and Peter Yun already sat waiting for them, spruced up and ready for another day in gown and wig.

'Apologies, gents,' the tall celebrity said. 'Mr Blake here's just got engaged, so I had to do my bit to put his fiancée off before she makes a colossal mistake.'

Graham stood up and offered his hearty congratulations to the Diamonds' right-hand man, followed by his young apprentice.

'If I need a pre-nup', I'll give you a call,' Gerry joked, endeavouring to downplay their effusiveness. 'Now... What's the order of service for today, gentlemen?'

The group sat down, and Peter passed copies of a printed timetable across to his boss while Winton talked them through the new running sheet.

'Jeff, we discussed your impassioned plea last night on our way back to the office, and you've convinced us to keep the sequence as per the original plan this morning.'

The celebrity nodded. 'Cheers. I'm pleased.'

'Just so you know...' Graham added. 'We're still keeping Mrs García as a potential witness, whom we may call if we think there's value later in the proceedings.'

'Again, thanks. So that means I'm up before García or after?'

'After,' the senior barrister clarified, pointing to the piece of paper. 'That way, there's a touch less likelihood of remembering exactly what was said yesterday before we broke, and neither will he be able to feed off anything you say.'

Jeff shook his head, sneaking a glance at Kierney. She had assumed Gerry's poker face today, and it made him shiver inside.

'Fair enough,' he replied, raising his hands. 'Your battle, your tactics, Graham. I'll just wait to be called. We're sitting about six rows from the front. I decided we were a bit too prominent yesterday morning, which is why we moved back for the rest of the day. We don't want to be disruptive to anyone.'

Graham nodded. 'That's fine. We'll request a recess between the Accused's and your own testimony, and I'll send Peter here to accompany you below stairs. Defence Counsel and I met with Her Honour last night, and she warned us she's going to be much tougher on keeping the noise down from the public gallery today.'

'Good luck with that!' the businessman chimed in, to a row of resigned expressions. 'They're a fired-up bunch. I'm sure they're prepared to be thrown out just to get their point across. I only hope the jury doesn't somehow think my client's whipped them up into a frenzy on purpose.'

'Can't be helped, Gerry,' Winton responded in no uncertain terms. 'Once you go on the stand, Jeff, especially. Greenshaw told me yesterday that he's been receiving death threats for agreeing to represent García. And he also told me he was at Sydney Grammar with you.'

The former Head Boy nodded. 'It's a small world, Graham. He's a few years older.'

'Is the fact that Defence Counsel's receiving death threats privileged information?' Jeff interjected, with a glint in his eye.

'No. Why?' the barrister asked, perplexed.

''Cause I could use it to our advantage when he asks me to go through that horrendous list of security risks that Cathy from our management company put together for him.'

Graham turned to his junior associate and issued a directive. 'Could you just make a quick enquiry of the court officer? Just to be on the safe side.'

Peter assented. 'Certainly. We'd better go, Counsel. It's eight-thirty.'

Everyone clambered to their feet and wished each other well for the day. The black gowns whisked their animated mannequins out of the room and down the corridor. The previous day's security guards were now stationed outside the meeting room door, entering as soon as the lawyers had departed.

Jeff, Gerry and Kierney made their way back to the public area. They passed lines of people cheering and clapping, all hopeful of securing a place in the audience for the latest episode of Sydney's hot, new, real-life drama.

While waiting for the court officials to arrive, the Irishman described the coverage he and his parents had seen on last night's television news. Apparently, there had been violent scenes between groups of female and male fans, fighting in the street outside a pub close to the courts.

'So is that what you were talking about?' the rock star shook his head. 'I wondered where you were going with the comment about me whipping people into a frenzy. Christ Almighty! It *is* a fucking circus, and today's only going to make it worse.'

As the trio made themselves comfortable on the hard, plastic, flip-up seats, Gerry turned to his long-time friend. 'You know, mate... We were also talking last night,' he began, 'about what a pointless act Lynn's murder really was.'

'And you're telling me this why exactly?' the widower asked, smiling in mock bewilderment.

'Because after all your concerns about someone in your family being killed by an organised crime syndicate associated with your pa, she ends up as the victim of some bitter, lovesick crackpot.'

Kierney frowned, not knowing what to make of these latest observations.

'That's spooky,' Jeff squeezed his daughter's shoulder. '*Mamá* and I were discussing the very same thing.'

'*Papá*,' the teenager warned. 'Don't say that.'

'Sorry, baby,' her dad cocked his head. 'Although, mate, it'd be bloody hard to convince me that a better organised murder would make Lynn's death less pointless. And anyway, be careful what you say about bitter, lovesick crackpots. There's a lot of them about. I was that soldier, once upon a time, remember?'

Gerry scoffed. 'True enough, mate.'

The young woman sighed, wishing the day was nearly over rather than only beginning. They watched the jury file in and take their seats, followed by the Defendant and his two accompanying officers. Both teams of lawyers were already in place, scrambling to their feet as soon as the rear door opened and the court officials entered. Judge Milne flipped her gown out behind her, preparing to be seated, and invited everyone to follow suit.

She reminded the solemn dozen that their duty was to consider evidence presented to them in the courtroom itself, and not to take into account any comment made from the public gallery. She also referred them to television and radio bulletins from the previous night, insisting they disregard any news reporting on the trial. Finally, she asked Graham Winton, for the Queen, whether he was ready to summon his next witness.

'Yes, Your Honour. The Prosecution calls the Accused, Juan Antonio García Ruelas.'

A buzz of excitement was quick to circulate in the steep rows of seating, and Jeff watched twelve pairs of eyes dart upwards from the jurors' benches.

Kierney nudged him. 'They didn't listen,' she smiled. 'You were right.'

'Bitch fight in the Supreme Court,' her father whispered, drawing an imaginary newspaper headline in the air in front of his daughter, who giggled.

'Quiet, you two,' Gerry scolded.

'The Prosecution calls the Accused, Juan Antonio García Ruelas,' the court officer repeated.

García was installed in the witness box, barely tall enough to see over the lectern. The same official gave him a copy of the Holy Bible, and he read his oath in a feeble, heavily accented voice. The judge spoke to him in a gentle tone, suggesting that he speak as loudly and clearly as he was able, to ensure the jury could hear his responses to questioning. The small, moustached man nodded.

'Mr García,' Graham Winton began. 'Can you please confirm to the court that you are Juan Antonio García Ruelas of three hundred and thirty-nine Parkes Street, Parramatta in New South Wales?'

'Yes. I am Juan Antonio García Ruelas.'

Listening to the owner of this pathetic, croaky voice utter his name, Kierney looked up into her father's eyes, aware that his body had tensed up next to her. 'Poor bastard?' she whispered.

'No. Just bastard.'

'*Muy bien.* Keep it that way.'

'Yes, boss.'

Winton continued. 'Thank you. Mr García, could you please tell the court where you were between nine-twenty and ten o'clock on the morning of the sixteenth of February this year?'

'I was at The Pensione 'otel,' García responded in a flat, weary tone.

'For clarification, was that The Pensione Hotel on George Street in Sydney's Central Business District?' Graham asked. 'And if you please, Mr García, address the bench as "Your Honour".'

'Yes, Your Honour.'

'And why were you at The Pensione Hotel that morning?' the barrister went on, his tone hardening slightly, either caused by an increased level of adrenalin or fuelled by the apparent compliance of his witness.

'I was there because I knew Jeff Diamond goin' to be there,' came the simple but telling reply.

The guttural "J" escaping from the Spaniard's mouth sent more shivers down Jeff's spine, reminding him of the way his maternal grandfather and uncles used to address him as a boy. It had always made him think they were spitting on him, which they were, metaphorically. He closed his eyes as the first tear of the day rolled down his cheek at the sickening childhood memory.

'Prejudice in action,' he murmured, in response to Kierney's concerned air. 'Tell you later.'

'Mr García, why did you go to the hotel that Mr Diamond was visiting?' the Prosecution asked.

'Because I was very angry and I want to kill him,' the Accused answered, as plainly as any prosecuting barrister could have wished for. 'Your Honour.'

Again, the jury's collective gaze shot upwards to the public gallery, unable to block out the many jeers and shouts. They were searching for the Defendant's original target in the rows of faces.

'Because you were angry and wanted to kill Jeff Diamond,' the pompous lawyer repeated for good measure.

'Yes, Your Honour.'

'Why were you angry? And why did you want to kill Mr Diamond?' the prosecutor continued, measured and self-assured.

'Lot o' reasons,' the small Spaniard answered, with the first sign of resistance.

'Are you able to describe two or three of those reasons to the court, please, Mr García?' Graham pressed him.

'Because is rich and famous, from an immigrant family, and my wife always tell me must be more like 'im. I get sick to 'ear 'ow 'e come from nothin' and make so much money and 'ave such a good life, with 'is beautiful wife and kids. I...'

The shaking, sallow-skinned man stopped himself from issuing another damning sentence, probably in response to a signal from the Defence bench which was hidden from the public gallery's view.

Again, the Spanish habitual prefixing of words beginning with "s" with an extra syllable and the series of missing aitches struck a chord deep within the widower, not only dragging back more painful memories of his mother's family but also reminding him of the many silly skits he used to enact with his dream girl.

How many times had he put on a comic Spanish accent when they were clowning around? Lynn's smiling face flashed before his mind's eye, leaving as fast as it had arrived.

'Thank you, Mr García. And can you take us through your actions while you were inside The Pensione Hotel and looking for Mr Diamond?'

'I wait in the lobby for 'im to arrive, Your Honour,' García responded. 'Then I seen Lynn Diamond get out of Mercedes sport and come into the 'otel. I make a call on my mobile to the Reception so I could find where Jeff Diamond will go, but they didn't understand me.'

'Didn't understand you?' Winton interrupted, stifling a chuckle. 'What did you ask the hotel reception staff when you telephoned them?'

'Where is Mr Jeff Diamond?' the Defendant confirmed, a pronounced lisp typical of native Spanish speakers, coupled with the guttural "J", indeed making his words difficult to discern.

'And then what happened, Mr García?'

'I see Lynn Diamond walk to other side and sit down. She pick up the phone, and I realise she was connected to me.'

The widower froze. These were the missing pieces in his puzzle, and the thrall of morbid fascination gripped him, refusing to let him breathe. Nausea frothed inside with the anticipation of finding out the extent of this horrible man's "connection" with his wife.

Gerry's arm wove behind Kierney's neck and came to rest on his friend's shoulder. He could feel Jeff's heartbeat through his clothes, and the muscles of his upper back were twitching wildly. The teenager in between gripped her dad's hand, also pondering the Accused's next answer.

Winton pressed on. 'When you realised that Ms Diamond was connected to you via the telephone, what did you do?'

The Defendant hesitated, anxious eyes fluttering to and fro between the judge, the jury and Greenshaw's team. Silence in the public gallery was absolute as everyone waited for the witness' reply. From their high vantage point, they were again unable to see the communication between client and lawyers.

'Don't clam up now, you bastard,' Jeff hissed. 'You're walking right into our hands. Keep going.'

'*Papá*, shhh,' Kierney begged.

García coughed. 'I panic because I don't know where Jeff Diamond is. I say to her, "Where is your 'usband?"'

The rock star stifled a laugh, bordering on manic.

'Shhh,' his anxious daughter urged again. 'Let the words wash over you.'

The widower tried desperately to assume control of his physical reactions, feeling his stomach turn over and wondering if he were about to be sick. Hysteria was setting in, with his mind conjuring with the number of times he had played with a silent aitch of the word "husband" to make Lynn and the children laugh.

'Did Ms Diamond answer your question?' Graham invited.

'No,' García shook his head. 'She say, "This Lynn Diamond. Can I 'elp you instead?"'

Jeff's heart beat so fast that the blood vessels around his ears and eyes were pulsating and his vision became blurred. He willed himself to stay conscious, not wishing to miss a word of the weasel's confession. With deliberately slow, deep breaths, he leant into Gerry's arm and held his daughter's hands.

'We love you, Jeff,' a man behind him spoke in a calm voice. 'Hang on in there.'

The collateral victim didn't turn around. 'Thanks, mate,' he said instead, summoning a voice from somewhere.

'Mr García,' Winton carried on. 'What did you do once you had exchanged these words with Ms Diamond?'

'I panic. I shoot 'er. I don't know what to do. I shoot 'er and run away in the 'otel.'

'You beauty!' another male voice shouted out from several rows behind the celebrities, causing the public gallery to erupt into taunts of abuse at the apparent confession.

Jeff shook his head, still not prepared to turn around. Blood drained from his brain, and his legs began to shake violently. Kierney's head still rested on his shoulder, and he wrapped his arm around her.

'It's not "You beauty" at all,' he uttered a soft groan. 'He said, "I don't know what to do." He didn't say he killed her intentionally. He said he didn't know what to do. They told him not to say "I killed her." Just "I shot her," And he didn't let 'em down.'

Losing her cool, Judge Milne almost yelled into the cheap seats for silence. She made her request three or four times before the drop in volume was sufficient for proceedings to continue and to enable her to address the jury.

'Ladies and gentlemen, you have just heard much commentary, noise and unrest coming from the public area up to your left. I urge you again to concentrate on what's said down here by the Accused, the prosecution and Defence teams, and by the court officials. Please disregard any comments coming from members of the public.'

The jury shuffled in their seats and focussed back on Graham Winton, who was standing ready to resume his interrogation.

'Thank you, Your Honour,' the attorney said. 'Mr García, you said you panicked and shot Ms Diamond.'

'Yes, Your Honour.'

'How many times did you shoot Ms Diamond?'

'Three or four time, I think.'

'You're not sure how many times you shot Ms Diamond?' Graham persisted. 'But you pointed the gun at Ms Diamond and you pulled the trigger.'

'Yes. No. I panic. I just fire a few time and run away.'

'Sorry to say this, mate,' Gerry hazarded, tapping his friend on the knee, 'but he sounds like a character from a bad spaghetti western.'

Kierney slapped her pseudo-uncle's right thigh hard in return. 'For fuck's sake!' she hissed, loud enough for the surrounding people to hear.

The youngster's response to an adult's tactless comment caused several people nearby to laugh, and the whispered account between neighbours in each row spread like ripples in a pond, radiating out from where she had dropped her priceless stone.

'Well done, Kizzo,' Jeff kissed her right temple. 'I'm proud of you.'

His daughter wept into her hands, and their manager apologised for his crass comment.

'Leave it, mate. Just leave it.'

Winton left it too. Making no progress in establishing whether the Accused had intended to kill his victim, he changed his line of questioning.

'Mr García, did you ever write any threatening letters to Mr or Ms Diamond, or to any of their family?'

'No, Your Honour.'

The attorney held up a cream-coloured document wallet to show the court. 'Ladies and gentlemen of the jury, these are the letters circulated to you yesterday while Detective Inspector Fisher was giving evidence,' he articulated, fanning out the various handwritten notes which the police had found in the Accused's house, before turning back to address the man in the dock. 'Mr García, did you write the letters contained in this folder?'

'Yes, Your Honour. But I never send them.'

'You are aware that these letters contain threatening language?' Winton asked. 'Please will you read the note marked with the number three in the top right-hand corner, Mr García?'

The Defendant stiffened up, becoming nervous and shuffling his feet. He picked up the sheet of paper handed to him by the court officer and scanned the lines for a few seconds. In a faltering voice, he read aloud.

'"I want kill Jeff Diamond because you are in love with 'im and is only an immigrant murderer's son. I work 'ard for you and 'e do nothin' for you."'

Winton's eyes surveyed the people in the jury, then the public gallery where the noise level was again on the increase. His eyes travelled over the judge and finally the Accused once more. 'Please could you confirm for the court that you wrote this note?'

'Yes, Your Honour. I write it.'

'Thank you, Mr García. And to whom did you write that letter?'

'My wife,' he responded.

'And did your wife ever inform the Diamonds or the police that you had written these notes?'

'No, Your Honour. I don't know. Don't think so.'

'For how long had you intended to kill Jeff Diamond, Mr García?'

'Ten years. Fifteen years. Maybe more.'

Again the public gallery stirred, gasping their surprise at such a frank admission. It was perhaps an accidental choice in his question, the intellectual thought, but the Prosecution's veteran counsel had successfully supplanted the word "intended" into the Accused's brain, where strictly he ought to have used the word "wanted", as García had read from his note. Led by the nose into a trap, the poorly educated Spanish native had accepted intent. And so, albeit subconsciously, had the jury.

'What gave you the impression your wife was in love with Jeff Diamond?' Winton continued, with a hint of mischief in his voice.

'Because she tell me 'ow good-looking is and 'ow talented at singing and dancing, and that 'e do many good things. Raising money for charity and stuff.'

'Mr García, are these reasons you mention good reasons to want to kill someone?'

Jeff's gaze locked onto Kierney's wide eyes, reminded of their conversation the previous night. Her smile in return was so sweet that he kissed her hair in abject gratitude, feeling his tattoo twinge a moment later.

'Yes, I think so,' García answered, sounding somewhat pathetic.

People were once again on their feet in the public gallery, hurling insults and becoming incensed. Two bailiffs marched down each aisle, issuing warnings that any further disturbance would result in ejection from the building. The volume subsided gradually, and the judge signalled for the prosecution team to continue.

'Mr García, it is against the law to kill someone in Australia, as it is in Spain and most other countries with a mature legal system,' Winton explained. 'You are aware of that, aren't you?'

'Yes, Your Honour.'

'Why then do you think being good-looking, a good singer and dancer and raising money for charity are good reasons for killing Jeff Diamond?'

'Because 'e not deserve so successful life,' García's response was unusually fierce. ''Is father in prison for murder, and 'is mother were a whore. He only do it to make up for this.'

Gerry and Kierney felt the man sitting with them expel the contents of his lungs as his own anger grew inside. It had been many years since the hard-working billionaire had heard his mother referred to as a whore. All around him were stunned, their gasps and moans playing the offbeat of his heart and raising his blood pressure still higher. More than he cared to admit, he was discomfited by the realisation that there was more than a trace of *idiot savant* about this rat-like man.

García hadn't finished. 'Diamond come to Australia a poor boy like me, wi' nothin', and now is multi-millionaire with all the women scream at 'im. Make you look at 'is face. His wife very beautiful. His kids very beautiful. Big 'ouse and awards and friends in big business. Is no' fair 'ow he 'ave that from who 'e were.'

The senior barrister seemed somewhat taken aback by the spray of information the Accused was volunteering, stopping short of looking upwards into the public gallery. Instead, the Diamonds saw his eyes fix on something out of their sight. The Defence team, at best guess.

'Mr García,' he continued. 'Surely if you and Mr Diamond started out in similar situations, you also had the same opportunities to do well?'

A ripple of laughter emanated from the public area, and the widower observed the twelve random citizens intently.

'No, I don't think so.'

'He's right,' Kierney whispered to her dad. 'He's a minority of one, and so are you.'

'Correct. But don't tell him, gorgeous,' Jeff smiled, having regained some control over his tortured mind.

Winton began yet another new line of enquiry, focussing on the jury as he spoke. 'Mr García, how did you find out that the Diamonds would be staying at The Pensione Hotel on the sixteenth of February this year?'

'My sister-in-law friend work there and she 'ear people talkin' about,' the Accused replied. 'They stay there two or three time before. I think is their favourite place to stay in Sydney.'

'It was,' Jeff muttered, 'until you showed up, you fuckin' rodent.'

'While you were waiting to shoot Mr Diamond,' the barrister changed tack again, 'did you have the intention of killing him, just as you described in your letter?'

'He was not there,' the ignorant man responded.

'Yes. I understand that,' the patient prosecution lawyer acknowledged, reinforcing the point. 'Humour me, please, Mr García. You told the court you came to the hotel to kill Mr Diamond. And so when you realised that Ms Diamond was there in his place, did you intend to kill her?'

'I panic. I don't know what to do.'

The hunter was closing in on his prey. Jeff gave the senior counsel his due; he was damned good.

'Why didn't you leave the hotel and plan another attack on Mr Diamond? Why, if you didn't know what to do, didn't you leave without shooting Ms Diamond?'

'Because then I think 'e suffer more if I take away 'is wife, Your Honour. If I kill 'im, 'e no suffer anymore, and maybe I do. So if I kill 'is wife, 'e suffer like me.'

'You arsehole!' came a cry from the left-hand side of the public gallery, soon endorsed by several other people calling the Accused by similar names.

The judge pleaded for quiet, and everyone calmed down once their latest stock of expletives had been purged.

'Do you remember, Mr García,' Graham asked, 'during Detective Inspector Fisher's testimony, he read out a sentence in Spanish which Mr Diamond is reported to have heard you say when he encountered you outside the hotel entrance?'

'Yes, Your Honour.'

'Can you recall what you said to Mr Diamond at that time?'

'Yes, I say in my language I want to kill 'im but what I did was better,' the timid man answered with some hesitation.

'Good man,' Jeff murmured. 'Hang yourself nice and slow. Go on, you bastard. Tell 'em again how you intended to kill my guardian angel.'

Kierney leant into her father's arm again and was surprised how far his body temperature had risen. She remembered her mother describing the way he used to boil up in the early days, before he had conquered his instinctive fury. Looking up into his furrowed face, she saw beads of sweat on his brow, and his eyes were bloodshot.

'Are you alright, *papá*? Do you want to leave for a while?'

The widower shook his head. 'I'm OK, thanks. Let him finish, and we'll get a break anyway. I can't miss this.'

'This is the sentence in question...' Winton took another sheet of paper from an associate on the bench behind him. 'For the benefit of the jury, as you heard Detective Inspector Fisher read out yesterday... I apologise for my atrocious Spanish pronunciation.'

There was polite laughter from around the courtroom as Winton cleared his throat. 'You were reported as having said, "*Quería matarlo Ustéd, pero es mejor así.*" Is that right?'

'Not bad for an Aussie,' Jeff dealt his daughter a playful prod.

The Defendant nodded. '*Sí*. Yes, Your Honour.'

'And can you please translate this phrase for the court?' the barrister requested.

'It mean, "I want to kill you, but this way is better,"' the Accused did as he was asked.

Winton's bulging blue eyes fixed a dramatic stare in the jury's direction for a number of seconds. 'Whom, in this case, did you want to kill, Mr García?' he asked.

'Jeff Diamond,' the Spaniard answered.

'And whom did you want to kill when Mr Diamond was not available at the time when you had made your decision to kill him?'

García chose not to furnish the court with an answer, so the Queen's representative asked again. Still no response, but the lawyer did not press a third time, turning back to his bench after a long pause.

'Lynn Diamond,' the witness whispered with a frightened look towards his bench.

'Mr García,' the judge rebounded. 'Please could you repeat your answer a little louder? Whom did you intend to kill when Mr Diamond was not available?'

'Lynn Diamond,' the Accused sneered.

Jeff noted the expert but questionable ethics on show again, as did his wife's ghost. Taking advantage of the witness' obstinacy to effect an almost imperceptible word substitution, Rosemary Milne had planted the seed on the Crown's behalf. Was this prejudice on her part, or simply another case of middle-classed bias?

He closed his eyes while the disquiet surrounding him became unbearable. It was as if he were cast adrift on a sea of fired-up concert fans chanting his name as the band left the stage and the lights went out. The strident choir almost raised him to his feet to take a bow.

'Jesus Christ,' he moaned. 'Jesus fucking Christ. What the hell's happening?'

'They love you, *papá*,' Kierney answered. 'And *mamá*. They wish she was still alive, just like we do.'

The court officer thumped the table several times with an empty water glass, attempting to calm the courtroom down. Judge Milne spoke in a loud voice.

'Ladies and gentlemen, please remain silent during the proceedings. I understand that you're agitated by what you've just heard, but please remember that this is the Supreme Court. We have a process to follow to ensure this trial arrives at the right outcome. Be patient with us while we go through this process, I beg you.

'Ladies and gentlemen of the jury, I'm calling a half-hour recess now. The Prosecution has no further questions for this witness, and the court will resume at eleven o'clock with the Defence's cross-examination. Thank you, everyone.'

The security guards sitting on either side of the well-known trio ordered it to its feet, hastening them up the steps and through the exit doors. When they reached their usual meeting room, Jeff requested that one stay behind to look after his daughter while he and Gerry detoured to the restroom. The teenager was grateful that her father had the presence of mind to pick the meat-head who hadn't tried to chat her up the previous day.

'Are you OK, *papá*?'

The anxious man gave her a thumbs-up sign and disappeared from view, pursued by his faithful manager. Once inside the bright, chrome-adorned bathroom, he ran into a cubicle, slamming the door behind him. The older man stood at a urinal, listening to his old friend's violent vomiting.

'Mate, you got a result,' Gerry shouted through the door.

'Not yet, we haven't,' the widower retorted, coughing hard. 'He hasn't been cross-examined yet, and neither has he confirmed he was fairly treated. We're a long way from a result, mate.'

'But look at the weight of public opinion,' the accountant insisted, seeing the superstar reappear, his face as white as a sheet. 'Fuck! You look terrible.'

'I need to get back to Kizzy,' Jeff muttered, splashing water on his face and scooping handfuls into his mouth to rinse away the acrid taste. 'Sorry you had to live through that, mate. You ready?'

Gerry put his arm around the star's shoulder and led him back down the corridor to their room. Kierney looked concerned as the pair walked in, so the billionaire lifted a chair from his daughter's right, moved it up close to hers and sat down. He held out his left hand, and she took it, kissing his fingers one by one.

'You OK, *pequeñita*?'

'Not sure,' the young woman answered. 'He definitely did it. There's no doubt about it, but I'm all over the place. Nervous, scared, confused, pissed off... And happy I heard him confess. But oh, my God, *papá*, what about you? All that noise in there. It was completely deafening!'

The songwriter leant forwards with his elbows on the large mahogany table, resting his head in his hands. 'I don't know what to feel either, *pequeñita*,' he agreed. 'I want to cry, shout, cheer and shrivel up into a ball, all at the same time. She spoke to him. Your *mamá* spoke to that fucking bastard before he shot her. Her last words should've been to one of us, not to that piece-of-shit wanker.'

Jeff's instincts chose his next course of action without his brain's adjudication, and he found himself crying uncontrollably. 'She asked him if she could help him,' he sobbed. 'The man who put a bullet in her skull. You should've sent him next-door to find me, angel. Sent him to find me in the bloody car park.'

'Do you think she could see him?' the tearful teenager asked. 'He can't have been far away, can he?'

The great man gulped, raising his eyes to the ceiling. 'Jesus, Kizzy, I don't know. Maybe. Did you see the gun pointing at you, Regala? What a god-awful thing to see just before you die. I'm so sorry, angel. I'm so fucking sorry it wasn't me.'

'Calm down, mate,' Gerry got to his feet, putting one hand on his friend's shoulder and slid a full coffee cup and saucer towards the widower's left elbow with the other. 'Drink some of this and have a ciggie.'

'We can't smoke in here,' Kierney said, pointing to a sign on the opposite wall.

'Stuff that,' Gerry cursed, reaching into the inside pocket of his jacket for his cigarettes.

'No, mate,' the superstar challenged, sitting back and smiling at his daughter. 'The lady's right. We need to behave like model citizens right at this minute, no matter how anarchic we might feel.'

Jeff opted to spend the rest of the break with the eighteen-year-old while his business manager went downstairs to take in sufficient nicotine for the three of them to last until lunchtime. He warned her not to be too worried when the Defence pushed hard to prove that García had not intended to kill her mother.

'They're going to do their damnedest to make the jury believe the bastard wasn't already thinking of killing *mamá* before he pulled the trigger.'

'And perhaps he wasn't,' the teenager interjected in a melancholy tone. 'That's what you were going to say next, wasn't it?'

'Yep. The more I hear his voice and look into his face, in all honesty, I don't think he had any real intent to kill her. Much as it pains me to utter these words, he should be on trial for manslaughter, not murder. I'm willing to bet big money it didn't occur to him that killing Lynn was better than killing me until after he killed her.'

His daughter's eyes betrayed the fact that she had come to the same conclusion. 'Probably not until he confronted you in the entrance,' she let out a deep sigh, sinking down into her chair.

Her father nodded. 'I think so, baby.'

Kierney's enquiring mind was bristling with energy, yet her sadness held her back. Jeff's heartrate soared off the chart, on the verge of exploding, as he watched the intelligent youngster wrestle with the complex adult emotions coming at her thick and fast.

'He definitely intended to kill you, *papá*, didn't he?' she continued, hoping this would help them deal with the conundrum her dad had presented. 'He wrote that note and said so to the court.'

Jeff smiled. 'Yes, he did, at that time. I don't think he would've gone through with it though. Don't think he had it in him.'

The young woman sighed, still more perplexed. 'Oh. Why not? He pulled the trigger on *mamá* when it was you he'd wanted to kill for all those years. Why wouldn't he have gone through with it if you'd been in the lobby?'

''Cause he would've chickened out, I reckon. And because he's a simple man who doesn't seem to have taken a single chance in his whole life until recently,' the empathetic man outlined his theory. 'Faced with having to redefine himself after living for so long with this chip on his shoulder about me, he probably would've concluded he wasn't up to it.'

'No!' Kierney shook her head, swallowing down the last of her glassful of water. 'I can't believe you're giving him the benefit of the doubt. What's this about, *papá*? Do you want *mamá*'s killer to walk free now?'

'No, I don't,' the widower persisted, despite his instinct to rescue his gorgeous gipsy girl from her anguish. 'I absolutely don't want him to walk free. I'd be more than happy to see him rot in hell, but I don't believe in scapegoats, *pequeñita*.

'Y'know, I used to dream about killing my dad almost every day. Probably multiple times a day actually... But I didn't want to spend the rest of my life in jail, so I never would've gone through with it. I didn't intend to kill him, but I sure as hell wanted to. I know what it's like to hate someone that much. It eats you up.'

'But you had good reasons to hate your dad,' his daughter snapped back. 'García doesn't.'

'He does,' the kind teacher smiled. 'At least, he thinks he does. He said so just a few minutes ago, didn't he? He was asked that specific question.'

Kierney groaned, knowing her father was right. 'Yes. Alright, he did. But wouldn't you have said your reasons for wanting to kill Granddad were good too, if you'd been asked by a court back then?'

The philosopher took a few seconds to consider her hypothetical. It was a good one under pressure, and it impressed him.

'No, Your Smartarseness. I don't think I would've. Constituency again, as it happens. My reasons were great for me and my family because I was fucking sick of him screwing with our lives. But as a citizen of Australia who wanted to make something of myself and who wanted to meet your *mamá*, they weren't good enough reasons to keep me out of prison.'

Kierney was laughing through her tears. 'Your Smartarseness? Thanks heaps!'

'Come on! Allow me some poetic licence for once, won't you?' her dad shrugged, before turning around to see Gerry returning, followed by one of the security guards.

'We're on, guys,' his manager announced. 'Time to see the little runt squirm some more.'

'Thanks, mate. Can we have five more minutes, please? We'll be right there.'

The door closed behind the Irishman, and father and daughter were once again on their own with their serious conversation. Jeff smiled at his sultry adolescent with aching, dark-ringed eyes.

'Gerry said something interesting earlier...' he continued. 'That García likely stalked me many times over the years and didn't kill me. So firstly, how close did he get to pulling the trigger on any of those occasions? And secondly, what was different about this time?'

'*Mamá* was a soft target, Kizzo. She was easier to kill than I would've been. That was her misfortune, I'm sorry to say. He hated her far less, if at all, but she was easier to kill.'

Kierney looked up and locked eyes with her beloved *papá* for a few moments. Both questions sent shivers down her spine, and she felt suddenly lightheaded. Taking a deep breath and reaching for the water jug to refill her glass, she saw him scratch his chest and heard him whistle under his breath.

'What does *mamá* think?' she asked.

Jeff sniffed, brushing new tears off his cheeks. 'She doesn't know either, baby.'

'He said *mamá* was beautiful, but you make people look at your face. What a weird thing to say! Don't you think? He hated you because people look at you and not at him. That's like narcissism, isn't it?'

'Maybe. It'll be interesting to hear the psych' reports when we get that far. We'd better get going soon.'

'So what are you going to do when you're called later on?'

'Another good question,' Jeff nodded, standing up and hugging her close. 'What should I do for my constituency? Should I allude to the miscarriage of justice that might occur if he gets convicted of Lynn's murder, on the basis that he intended to kill me intentionally but got her instead unintentionally? Or are the two crimes together the equivalent of one murder? Should I just let him go down because that's what our fans want?'

The student looked up into her father's eyes. 'If I'm in your constituency, I don't know yet. And we should ask Jet too, I suppose. Can we?'

'There'll be time if I get called after lunch, but we need to hope he's near his phone,' the father responded, glad that this openhearted young lady was thinking of herself a little. 'And what about "G" and "G"? And everyone else who's thirsty for his blood? What would it look like to them if I start barracking for the other side? I'd sound pretty ungrateful after all their support earlier this morning.'

'Can I ask you one more thing?' the thoughtful teenager asked.

'Sure,' the handsome man nodded, standing up and threading his arms into the sleeves of his suit jacket.

'Is that why you didn't go to any of *mamá*'s Sydney concerts before you knew her?'

Jeff paused with a mouthful of water, staring his living legacy right in the eyes. She had his measure, well and truly, as had her mother at the same age. Feeling suddenly vulnerable, he placed the empty glass on the table and growled.

'OK! Carve me wide open, why don't you? You already know the answer, based on what we were just talking about.'

Kierney nodded apprehensively.

'I didn't trust myself, *pequeñita*,' her father confessed. 'You're very perceptive. I was in a bad, bad place back then. I was scared I would've rushed the stage and done something extremely stupid. Plain and simple, baby, and I rest my case. *Vamanos*.'

The eighteen-year-old held her hand out to the man she adored, and the pair left the room in a hurry. Gerry and the two uniformed men, who had been waiting outside the meeting room door, fell into formation around the Diamonds as they made their way down the wide corridor and took their seats back in the public gallery. People heckled messages of support from all sides, and the dark-haired pair did their best to acknowledge them without encouraging any further uproar.

Kierney was anxious, grabbing her father's hand. 'But you have to stay true to your beliefs, *papá*,' she whined. 'And if you believe he didn't intend to kill *mamá* and wouldn't have been able to kill you, then you have to say so.'

'Jesus, Kizzo. I need to talk to Winton,' Jeff said, the courtroom's oppressive atmosphere engulfing him as soon as he sat down. 'He's going to be the one committing murder. He thinks I'm going to clinch his deal, but how can I?'

The compassionate sage smacked her dejected dad on the knee. 'The jury decides, *papá*. Not you. Your job's to say what you believe, just like any other witness. You don't have to take the blame for the jury finding for the Defence if you speak with integrity. You don't have to take the blame for anything, OK?'

The widower bent forward and cried into his hands. Gerry rolled his eyes in frustration that the half-hour break hadn't seemed to have done his friend any good, searching the youngster's eyes for answers.

'You should've come downstairs for a smoke and talked shit for a few minutes, mate,' he hissed.

'Doubtless,' the superstar replied, 'but sometimes there are more important things to do, mate. Kizzy, you sound just like *mamá*, when I made my confession to her in the Intercontinental all those years ago. She was the first person to tell me all the shit that happened around me wasn't my fault. I know it isn't, angel, but it sure as all hell feels like it.'

Kierney straightened up and kissed her father's cheek, saying nothing. The court officials were back in their places, and García stood downcast in the witness box.

CONSTITUENCY

'Ladies and gentlemen,' Rosemary Milne opened the session. 'Thank you for your patience. May I please remind you to keep as quiet as you can during the trial? We shall continue with the cross-examination of the Accused. Counsel for the Defence, are you ready?'

'I am, Your Honour,' the flamboyant barrister affirmed, his gown lifting him to his feet. 'Mr García, good afternoon. The court has heard you say that you had wanted to kill Mr Jeff Diamond for a long time. Do you understand that intentionally taking another person's life is wrong and constitutes murder?'

'Yes, Your Honour,' García replied without hesitation.

'Do you believe you committed a murder on the sixteenth of February, nineteen-ninety-six,' Greenshaw asked.

'I don't know,' the Accused answered.

'Interesting tactic,' Jeff turned to the others, feeling a little calmer at last. 'It's got to be a set piece. *Ignorantia juris non excusat.*'

His business partner slipped the cuff on his suit jacket aside and turned the face of his watch towards his client. 'Half-past three,' he sniggered, 'and twice on Sundays.'

The closet intellectual smiled and shook his head at his old friend's sarcasm, pushing his arm away. It was his own fault for being so pompous. Meanwhile, Greenshaw paused for effect before redirecting the witness, for the benefit of the jury.

'Were you at The Pensione Hotel on George Street in Sydney on the morning of the sixteenth of February this year?'

'Yes, Your Honour.'

'What was the purpose of your visit to this hotel?'

García remained silent.

'Have you visited this hotel before?' Greenshaw continued, without waiting for an answer to the previous question.

'Yes, Your Honour.'

Defence Counsel nodded. 'When was that, Mr García?'

'The week before.'

'And what was the purpose of this visit?'

Silence again.

'Mr García, would you say that you were in control of your emotions on the days when you visited The Pensione Hotel?' Greenshaw asked, putting on a kindlier tone.

'No, Your Honour,' the Accused replied. 'I was angry because my wife talkin' about Jeff Diamond come to Sydney again, and I seen it in the paper.'

The Defence's strategy was revealing reveal itself to the astute onlookers sitting six rows back in the dress circle. 'Were you provoked by anyone to commit the act with which you're charged?' the wily solicitor asked the Accused.

'Yes, Your Honour. My wife, and all the television coverage of Diamonds,' García responded, as if by rote.

Jeff shook his head again. 'We *are* at the theatre after all,' he whispered to the others. 'He's memorised his lines. There's no way he'd use the words "television coverage" of his own accord.'

'And this television coverage made you very angry?' Greenshaw continued, his tone becoming more menacing, no doubt intent on raising the Accused's blood pressure.

'Yes, and my wife make me very angry,' García nodded. 'She never stop tellin' me why not be more like Jeff Diamond.'

Kierney leant into her father's arm again, and he kissed the side of her head. The barrister made no deviation from his plan this time.

'Mr García, were you seeing a doctor or psychologist regarding your feelings of extreme jealousy and anger towards the Diamonds?'

'No, Your Honour.'

'Did you ever visit a doctor or psychologist for these reasons prior to the sixteenth of February, nineteen-ninety-six?'

'No, Your Honour.'

'Did anyone advise you to?'

'My wife want me to,' the crestfallen prisoner told the court, holding his right hand up to his forehead.

Greenshaw turned to the jury and summarised for them. 'So, Mr García... You had experienced feelings of jealousy and anger for many years, including a strong desire to kill a man, and your anxiety had gone untreated for all this time. Is that right?'

'Yes, Your Honour.'

'Did any other person ask you or put pressure on you to commit this act?' Greenshaw asked next, reaching for a bundle of paperwork from the bench behind him.

'No, Your Honour.'

The Defence barrister held a collection of exhibits aloft for the benefit of the jury. 'Ladies and gentlemen, this folder contains the notes and letters found at the Accused's house when the police searched it. They are the same documents that the Prosecution circulated earlier.'

He passed the collection to the man in the dock who leafed through them one by one, but without reading them for a second time. Several occupants of the public area shuffled in their seats and murmured to each other at the Defence's insistence on going over old ground.

'Mr García, did you write the notes being shown to you now?'

'Yes, Your Honour.'

'Tell me, Mr García,' the lawyer went on. 'Had you ever seen the Diamonds in person prior to the sixteenth of February this year?'

'Yes, Your Honour.'

This time, the noise from the gallery was laced with anticipation. Jeff exchanged a silent message with Gerry, reminded of his earlier observation about stalking.

'Where was that?'

García did not hesitate. 'In Parramatta parade when 'is father die and in two concert. I go with my wife.'

'You saw the Diamonds in person on three occasions,' Defence Counsel repeated for the jury's benefit. 'Including being in the audience at two Jeff Diamond concerts. Have you ever spoken to Mr Diamond or another member of his family?'

'No, Your Honour.'

Greenshaw kept up the quick-fire questioning. 'How did you feel on the occasions when you saw Jeff Diamond? In the parade or at the concerts?'

'Same,' the small, pathetic man answered. 'Angry that 'e come from Parramatta and 'is father in prison for murder, 'cause 'e make so much money and become famous.'

Greenshaw again paraphrased for the jury. 'You experienced the same feelings of jealousy and anger at these times also, because you considered Mr Diamond's background made him unworthy of his success.'

'Yes, Your Honour.'

'Objection!' Winton sprang to his feet.

'Counsel?' Rosemary Milne allowed him to interrupt.

'Your Honour, Counsel for the Defence has already established the Accused has not received medical help for his emotional state. The Prosecution seeks to understand the honourable gentleman's objectives in repeating these questions.'

'Mr Greenshaw?' the judge turned to the opposing bench.

'Your Honour, the Defence seeks to explain to the court how deeply these feelings of resentment ran in the Accused's psyche, and that he was driven to commit the crime out of extreme pressure that his mental state could not support.'

'I'll allow it,' the judge overruled Winton, who sat down obediently.

'Love, one,' Kierney's humour was gentle, gazing up into her father's face.

Jeff smiled but said nothing. He was more interested in what the central character had to say rather than any devious and distracting subplots architected by these supporting actors.

'Mr García, was Mr Diamond's father known to you?' Greenshaw changed tack again.

'No, Your Honour,' the Accused replied. 'Only what in the papers.'

Judge Milne raised a hand to the Defence bench and turned to the banks of seating to her left. 'Members of the jury, remember that the information you will hear in the following questions relates to crimes that were committed many years ago and bear no relevance to this case or to the Accused. Not to any of the Witnesses, in fact.'

A renewed round of whispers ran around the public gallery, and the celebrity noticed several jurors turn to each other and exchange a few words. He knew the judge's comments bore reference to him and wondered how many of the dozen had already made this connection.

'Did you know of Pavel Diament, or Paul Diamond as he was better known, prior to his conviction in nineteen-sixty-four?' Defence Counsel asked the Accused.

'No, Your Honour.'

'And how did you come to know that Jeff Diamond's father was serving a prison sentence for murder?'

García was again word-perfect. 'Through newspaper reports when 'e die.'

Greenshaw nodded and smiled to encourage his witness, who was holding up well to his examination. 'When was this, please, Mr García?'

'I don't remember. Early 'eighties, I think.'

The barrister's voice became louder and more excitable. 'Did this provide you with further motive to harm Mr Diamond?'

'Yes. I think so,' replied the Accused, sighing with relief that he had reached this point.

'Objection!' Winton shouted again, springing to his feet. 'The Defence is leading the Witness.'

'Too late,' Jeff scoffed under his breath. 'Very clever, Graham, old boy.'

The judge sustained the Prosecution's interruption and asked the jury to disregard the Accused's answer, forcing Greenshaw to ask a different question.

'Mr García,' he asked, 'how did finding out Jeff Diamond's father was in prison for murder make you feel?'

'I 'ate 'im more,' the witness answered, nervous that he had no script for these lines but with enough awareness to know he shouldn't say he had intended to commit the crime.

The billionaire watched members of the jury turn to each other in confusion, hoping the judge would make some sort of clarification. She did not. The Defence lawyer was on a roll however.

'Why, Mr García, if you hated Jeff Diamond more after hearing about his father's situation, didn't you attempt to kill him at this time?'

The widower tapped Kierney's knee, who nodded in acknowledgement.

'You were right,' she whispered.

Gerry gave the pair a quizzical stare, but neither offered any further clues. García shuffled from foot to foot in the witness box and stared up to the ceiling for a few moments before responding.

'Don't know,' he answered. 'I want to kill him, but I didn't do it.'

'What was your mental state at the time you heard about Mr Diamond's father's criminal history?' Greenshaw asked, again adopting the gentler tone.

'I was very angry,' García replied, 'and jealous that Jeff Diamond could be rich and successful and get a beautiful woman if 'ave a father who a murderer.'

'Would you say you were more or less angry and jealous at this time, back in the early 'eighties, than you were when you came to The Pensione Hotel on the sixteenth of February this year?'

'Less angry, Your Honour,' the Accused answered straightaway. 'My wife not givin' me 'ard time then. I 'ad a job, and my kids were young. She busy with them.'

Greenshaw paused for a few seconds, patently not expecting this answer.

'Where's he going to go now?' Kierney asked her dad.

Jeff shrugged. 'He's got to get him to blame someone or something for his diminished mental capacity.'

'But without leading him,' the young woman guessed.

'Yep.'

'So, Mr García,' Greenshaw asked, 'please could you tell the court which were the factors that caused you to get so angry that you came to The Pensione Hotel on the sixteenth of February this year with the desire to kill Mr Jeff Diamond?'

The intelligent superstar gave his daughter a wry smile, as if to say, "That'd do it". The witness paused again and looked up towards the public gallery. The target of his gaze stared down at his own shoes, not seeking to make eye contact with his wife's killer and thereby influence his response. García's eyes returned to the judge, to whom he replied.

'Jeff Diamond life get easier, and my life get worse,' he answered with more vehemence than any prior question had educed. 'They 'ad twenty years anniversary. He act like a king, and my wife keep tellin' me I useless and look at Jeff Diamond and learn somethin'.'

The mesmerised audience above, having curbed its outrage until this point, now broke into loud remonstrations of anger.

One woman stood up and shouted at the top of her voice. 'That's because he was trying to make the world a better place, you horrible little man. When did you ever try to do that?'

The court officer banged the heel of her hand down several times to reclaim some decorum in the courtroom, but an enthusiastic round of applause had now erupted in the gallery.

'That's not Wonderful Wendy, is it?' Kierney nudged her father, who remained intent on avoiding eye contact with anyone.

'Don't know,' he replied, leaning back in his seat with his eyes closed as the clapping washed over him. 'Mate, have you got any more of that gum?'

Gerry reached into the inside pocket of his jacket and pulled out a brand new pack, breaking it open and distributing two little sachets. 'Take a double dose,' the accountant suggested, slapping his friend's left knee. 'Looks like you need it.'

'Cheers, mate,' the superstar smiled, unwrapping one piece and offering the second to his daughter. 'This is an absolute trip. I can't believe I'm here listening to this stuff. It's totally surreal.'

Kierney turned down the offer, screwing her face up in disgust. Greenshaw was ready to carry on with his questioning, glaring up into the public gallery. The judge appealed again for calm, which took its time to settle.

'Mr García,' Defence Counsel resumed, 'when you were initially detained by the New South Wales Police at The Pensione Hotel, what reason did they give for detaining you?'

García gazed down at his feet to gather his thoughts, thankful that the subject had been changed after the outburst. 'They told me there was a shootin' and they need to talk to everyone who seen anythin',' he replied, apparently back on script.

'Thank you,' Greenshaw responded, 'and did you ask if you could leave the hotel at this point?'

'I ask security, and 'e say I must wait for police.'

'Did you try to leave the hotel?'

'No, Your Honour.'

'Why was that?' Counsel for the Defence pressed his witness.

'I was standin' next to Jeff Diamond, and 'e look at me like he stop me leavin',' García told the court.

The celebrity frowned. 'What does that mean?' he asked Gerry. 'That can't be a rehearsed line.'

His manager shrugged, while his old school chum changed tack again.

'How long do you think it took the police to arrive, Mr García?'

'A few minutes,' the Spaniard replied. 'There was big fuss where Lynn sitting. We lookin' at the fuss, and then hear noise of police cars arrive.'

'Don't you dare speak her name, you arsehole,' the grieving husband snarled through gritted teeth. 'Since when did you earn the right to do that?'

'What did the police do when they saw you with Mr Diamond and the security guard?' the Defence lawyer asked.

'Jeff Diamond not there no more,' García blurted out. 'Only security man.'

Stephen Greenshaw and the judge exchanged a quick glance before the Accused's comment was examined further. 'Please could you clarify where Mr Diamond was at this time, according to your recollection, Mr García?'

'He go to see 'is wife body,' the witness' demeanour was unmoved, and his tone matter-of-fact.

'I see,' Greenshaw sighed, turning round to his associates on the bench behind him.

'This is getting very confusing,' Kierney whispered to her dad and their friend.

'Shhh,' Jeff warned, smiling. 'Let them mess it up for themselves, gorgeous.'

The team rushed to exchange a few pieces of paper, and Greenshaw turned back to face the Accused again. 'Mr García,' he said, now sounding a little fed up, 'were you put under any duress... any pressure... by police officers or any member of the Prosecution or Defence prior to this trial?'

'No, Your Honour.'

'You stated earlier that you were manhandled by Mr Diamond when you tried to leave the building prior to your arrest. Is this true?'

'Yes, Your Honour.'

The smile returned to Greenshaw's face. 'Thank you, Mr García. Please could you describe for the court how Mr Diamond manhandled you at this time?'

'Did you?' Kierney whispered.

'I don't remember,' her dad frowned. 'It happened so quickly. I don't know if I touched him, steered him round or just spoke to him.'

García again lifted his gaze to the public gallery and scanned the rows. 'He say, "Do you 'ear a man shoutin' to stay in the buildin'?" Then 'e stand in my way and walk up to me.'

'Did Mr Diamond touch you or use force to encourage you to go back into the hotel?' Greenshaw urged the witness.

'He shout at me and make me turn around,' the Accused answered. 'Is a big man.'

'Did Mr Diamond touch you or push you back into the hotel?' the Defence barrister laboured his point, probably expecting a different response.

'He walk towards me and make me turn around,' the diminutive Spaniard repeated, appearing confused.

'How did he make you turn around, Mr García?'

'He is a big man.'

'Objection!' Graham Winton jumped to his feet, receiving approval to articulate his issue without delay. 'The Defence has used the term "manhandle", Your Honour, but we now hear that Mr Diamond did not touch the Accused. It is not possible to allege "manhandling" solely because Mr Diamond is a big man.'

Muted laughter rippled around the public gallery.

'Sustained, Mr Winton,' Judge Milne sighed. 'Mr Greenshaw, would you please obtain a clarification from the Accused?'

'Certainly, Your Honour,' Counsel for the Defence agreed, unperturbed. 'Mr García, please could you tell the court what you experienced when Mr Diamond requested you go back into the hotel?'

García shuffled again. 'I was scared of 'im.'

'You were scared of him?' the lawyer repeated. 'Because you thought he would hurt you?'

'Yes, Your Honour,' García replied, relieved, 'and because I shoot his wife.'

'Objection!' Winton cried out again.

'Counsel for the Prosecution?' the judge requested again.

'Thank you, Your Honour,' Graham answered in a confident tone. 'The Accused claims he re-entered the hotel without being touched or pushed by Mr Diamond because he was scared of him, and the Accused was scared of him because he had recently pointed a gun at Mr Diamond's wife and opened fire.'

'Yes, Counsel,' the judge nodded. 'What is your point?'

Winton continued. 'My point is, Your Honour, that Mr Diamond had no idea before he entered the hotel through those revolving doors that his wife had been shot. Mr Diamond was responding to a request from the hotel manager to prevent anyone from leaving the hotel. If the Defence is intending to allege entrapment or somehow that Mr Diamond was taking the law into his own hands, Your Honour, the jury needs to understand that Mr Diamond was not aware that a serious crime had been committed at this time.'

'Objection sustained,' the judge declared, turning once more to the twelve attentive citizens. 'Ladies and gentlemen, the Prosecution is entitled to object in this instance. I ask you to discount the Defence's claim that Mr Diamond had either manhandled the Accused prior to his arrest or attempted to detain a person without authority because he knew his wife had been shot. The sequence of events demonstrates that Mr Diamond could not have known the fate of his wife at the time he encountered the Accused.'

Several jury members nodded, and others ran their eyes along the rows of faces in the public gallery, keen to catch a glimpse of the well-regarded personality linked so inextricably to this trial. The judge requested the Defence continue with its cross-examination of the Witness without delay.

'Thank you, Your Honour,' Greenshaw said. 'Mr García, you said you were scared of Mr Diamond. Why was that?'

'Just because is Jeff Diamond,' he answered without thinking.

People in the public gallery laughed with derision, and the judge once again sought silence.

The barrister branched off with a new and unrelated question. 'Mr García, are you aware that you've been charged with illegally being in possession of a firearm?'

'Yes, Your Honour.'

'And you pleaded "not guilty" to this charge,' Greenshaw continued, being passed a handgun and silencer in separate clear evidence bags by his colleagues.

'Yes, Your Honour.'

The solicitor briefly held up the plastic bag containing the weapon, before it was collected by the court officer and transferred to the dock. 'Do you recognise this firearm, Mr García?'

'Yes, Your Honour.'

'To whom does it belong?'

'To me.'

'From where did you purchase it?'

'I don't remember,' García replied. 'From Victoria. I buy it in Mildura, Victoria.'

Greenshaw nodded. 'Thank you. And for how long have you had this firearm in your possession?'

'About two years.'

'Did any member of your family know you possessed a firearm prior to the sixteenth of February this year?' the lawyer asked.

'No,' answered the Accused.

'How many times have you fired this gun?'

'Many time,' García admitted readily.

'Where have you fired this gun?'

'At a gun range in Parramatta,' the Spaniard opened up. 'I'm a member of the club there.'

Still Greenshaw persisted with his questions. 'Do you have a licence for this firearm?'

'Yes, Your Honour.'

'You are positive you applied for and were granted a firearms permit for this gun?'

'Yes, Your Honour.'

'Are you aware that the New South Wales Police have not been able to find records pertaining to a firearms permit in your name in Victoria or New South Wales?'

'Yes. But I got one two years ago.'

Greenshaw backed off a little. 'Where did you apply for your firearms permit, Mr García?'

The small man relaxed. 'From the shop I buy the gun. In Mildura, Victoria.'

The Defence barrister did not alter his tone of voice or attempt to draw the jury's attention towards his next redirection. 'Mr García, once you realised it was Ms Diamond at whom you were pointing this handgun, were you intending to shoot her?'

'I don't know,' he replied. 'I was confused.'

This time, Greenshaw spoke more slowly and reduced the volume of his voice to put his client further at ease. Kierney and her father exchanged appreciative nods at the subtle way in which the Defendant was being influenced into talking more freely.

'Mr García, did you fire the weapon by accident?'

'Yes, Your Honour.'

'Objection!' Winton shouted again.

Judge Milne indicated for him to speak up.

'Leading, Your Honour,' the prosecution lawyer suggested to the court. 'Plus, Your Honour, the gun had four rounds missing from its chamber when it came into police custody. There were four rounds found at the crime scene. The first one may have been fired accidentally, but what about Numbers Two, Three and Four?'

'Objection sustained,' the judge allowed, almost smirking at the dramatic way the experienced barrister counted on his fingers. 'Mr García, is it your opinion that you fired all four bullets unintentionally? By accident, rather?'

'Shit,' the widower cursed under his breath.

'What?' Gerry replied, surprised by his friend's mild expletive.

'The post-mortem states it was the first bullet that killed her,' Jeff sighed. 'The fourth may have, but the second and third definitely didn't. What does it matter about Numbers Two, Three and Four, woman? Concentrate on your own evidence.'

Down below, García answered on cue. 'I don't know.'

'Winton's fucked up his own case,' the rock star whispered in disbelief, clutching Kierney's hand. 'Jesus Christ.'

'The jury might not notice, *papá*,' she said, squeezing his hand tight. 'And *they* have to believe the first one was accidental.'

The judge addressed the Defendant again. 'Mr García, after you fired the first bullet at Ms Diamond, did you intend to keep pulling the trigger and release three more bullets?'

'I don't know, Your Honour.'

An uncharacteristic stillness descended on the public gallery, extending equally to the twelve people on the judge's left. Stephen Greenshaw turned to face the jury in triumph before swirling his gown around the other way, towards the presiding officials and opposing counsel.

'Your Honour, the Defence has no further questions for this witness.'

Winton piped up. 'Your Honour, the Prosecution wishes to re-examine the Accused for a short time.'

Judge Milne stifled a yawn, much to Kierney's amusement, before signalling him to proceed. 'Counsel for the Prosecution will redirect.'

'Thank you, Your Honour. Mr García, earlier this morning you helped the court with a translation of the Spanish phrase you uttered to Mr Diamond when you encountered him in the hotel entrance, after you had fired the gun four times.'

The portly lawyer waited for García to confirm his recollection and for the jury to hear his acceptance of the whole series of events strung together.

'Yes, Your Honour.'

'Thank you,' the lawyer continued. 'Can I please ask for the transcript of this portion of the trial to be read back to the court, from when I remember the Accused admitting to intending to kill both Mr Jeff and Ms Lynn Diamond.'

There was a flurry of activity from the court recorder, seated in front of the prosecution associates beneath the judge's bench. She took a few minutes to locate the part of the recording to which the barrister referred, coughing to clear her throat.

'Prosecution asks, "You were reported as having said, "*Quería matarlo Ustéd, pero es mejor así*". Is that right?" The Accused replies, "*Sí*. Yes, Your Honour." Prosecution asks, "And can you please translate that phrase for the court?" The Accused translates the phrase as "I want to kill you, but it's better this way." Prosecution asks, "Whom, in this case, did you want to kill, Mr García?" The Accused answers, "Jeff Diamond." Prosecution asks, "And whom did you want to kill when Mr Diamond was not available at the time when you had decided to kill him?" Question repeated. The Accused answers, "Lynn Diamond."'

Winton paused again to let the jury finish taking in for a second time the responses which had been given earlier that morning.

'Thank you, madam,' the solicitor followed on. 'Mr García, is that how you remember your testimony?'

'Yes, Your Honour.'

Masterful, Jeff acknowledged. The Queen could rightly be proud of her main man. With this one simple request, he rescued his earlier *faux pas* and had now redirected the focus exactly where he needed it to be.

'Ladies and gentlemen of the jury,' Senior Counsel for the Prosecution addressed them. 'As you heard from the transcript, this morning the Accused was very clear about his intention to kill both Mr Jeff Diamond and Ms Lynn Diamond. However, a few minutes ago he indicated that he didn't know whether he had fired the bullets which killed Ms Diamond intentionally. The Prosecution will call two expert witnesses later in this trial who will testify that it is not possible that the Accused fired accidentally or unintentionally at the Victim.'

The Diamonds watched the jurors nod their heads. Surprisingly, Judge Milne moved to diffuse the Prosecution's statement, much to the pair's disappointment.

'Thank you, ladies and gentlemen. The Accused appears to have contradicted himself during his time on the witness stand. However, please understand the different context in which he was being questioned by the Prosecution and the Defence. The Prosecution's initial questions caused the Accused to admit that he wanted to kill Ms Diamond, however the Defence's questions caused him to focus on the *actual act* of killing Ms Diamond. In the second context, he claims not to know whether he fired the gun accidentally or intentionally. This is a subtle difference, but a difference nonetheless.'

The jurors stared back at the judge, some offering bewildered nods again. Others checked their watches, as if wondering when they might be offered sustenance and a comfort break. Sure enough, the lunch recess was called, and the officials and jury filed out of the court below the public gallery.

The volume of chatter increased, and the Diamonds' security guards were quickly on their feet, ready to convey their famous charges back to their wood-panelled sanctuary. As they waited for a gap in the stream of people heading up towards the exit, Jeff watched García being escorted back to wherever they stored him during lunch. He sighed deeply, and Kierney put her hand in his.

'Come on, *papá*,' she encouraged. 'Let's get some food. I'm starving.'

Gerry climbed the steps behind the celebrities. 'He recovered well, Winton,' he said, referring to the Prosecution's perceived gaffe. 'Don't you think?'

'Ah, yeah. Pretty well,' his friend nodded, deflecting a pat on the back launched from across the aisle by an over-enthusiastic member of the public. 'The judge is saving the day. She's on the money.'

The Diamonds and their loyal attachés found themselves in the usual room, replete with a repeat serving of the previous day's fare. An hour's recess had been granted after the Accused's ordeal, and Jeff suggested their security contingent might take a forty-five minute break too. This idea was met with unanimous approval.

Mindful of everyone's stress levels, the tired songwriter attempted to avoid the topic of the trial while they ate their sandwiches and drank copious quantities of water and orange juice.

'What shall we do tonight?' he asked, pouring three cups of coffee and shunting them across the table. 'I think we should do something diverting and non-brain-taxing, like a harbour cruise.'

'Sounds nice,' Kierney agreed. 'Relaxing. We mustn't forget to phone Jet before we go back in, *papá*. We'll run out of time.'

'Now?' Gerry asked. 'Why? It's still the middle of the night for him.'

Jeff sighed. 'Yeah, mate. I know. Kizzy's right. We've got something to discuss with him before I go on the stand. And it's even more important now, after the things the judge's said in summing up before lunch. Winton'll be sending for me before long, so you're right to hurry us, *pequeñita*. Let's grab a ciggie and something to eat, then we can try and get hold of him for a few minutes.'

Seeing Kierney beaming at her father, keen to resolve their dilemma, the accountant stood up and stretched. 'I'm guessing I should make myself scarce.'

'Not at all, mate,' his friend replied. 'Unless you want to. Let's all go downstairs for a quick smoke first.'

Fortunately, the corridors in the Supreme Court building were almost deserted when the threesome headed for the lift down to the designated smoking area. Jeff dialled his son's mobile telephone while they were having their first cigarette, and the voicemail system intercepted. He then selected the alternate number in his directory, the switchboard for Jet's hall of residence. It was hardly surprising, given the time difference, that no-one answered this either.

Jeff rang the first number again and left a message for Jet to return their call as soon as he received it, leaving a brief *précis* and the fact that only forty minutes remained before his latest live appearance.

'Do we ask for a postponement?' Gerry asked, as they made their way back up to Level Three. 'Or ask them to call another witness instead?'

'Nope. Let's start without him, and if he rings back, we'll do our best to catch him up. Is that OK, Kizzo?'

Kierney nodded. They filled their plates and sat down in their customary places, surprised at how hungry they were. After a few quiet moments, Jeff leant back in his chair and took a deep breath.

'OK, guys. Here's where we are... I won't back-track over last night's conversation, Gerry, if you don't mind, because we haven't got much time.'

'Whatever,' their manager agreed. 'I'm not sure I'm going to get this anyway, whether you back-track or not.'

'Thanks, mate,' the impressive celebrity replied. 'What we have here is the establishment of *mens rea* as opposed to *actus reus*.'

'Men's what?' the accountant guffawed. 'I'm lost on the first sentence. You had me at "Thanks, mate," but now I'm screwed.'

Kierney giggled. 'Me too, Gerry, and I was there for last night's conversation! What are you talking about, *papá*?'

Jeff continued, smiling at his humorous companions. 'Keep up, you imbeciles! I remember reading quite a few law books years ago, and it all came back to me in the early hours of this morning. And then even more so when the judge started explaining about the context of questioning.'

'I like the sound of this already,' the young woman said, leaning forward and resting her arms on the table's polished surface.

The father's mobile telephone buzzed in his trouser pocket. 'Oh, wait... Fantastic,' he murmured, his eyes bright for the first time that day. 'Jetto! Thanks for ringing back.'

The sportsman sounded groggy on the other end of the line, and Jeff handed the handset to his daughter while he moved the conference telephone into the middle of the table.

'*Papá*'s going to ring you back with this mushroom phone thingo,' Kierney told her brother, 'so we can all hear each other. Talk soon.'

She ended the call, and the nineteen-year-old's middle-of-the-night voice croaked over the speakers loud and clear. 'What's happened?' he asked his father. 'Something about who you represent when you're on the witness stand.'

'Yeah, mate. Exactly that,' Jeff affirmed. 'Your sister and I were talking earlier about constituency; who'll be counting on me for what when I'm being questioned. I have some opinions about this bastard, García, and whether I think he's guilty of the crimes he's being charged with, and I want to know what you think.'

'Have you gone stark raving mad?' Gerry interrupted. 'After all this, you're going to turn round and support his "not guilty" plea?'

'No, not necessarily, mate. Let's have the discussion before you start accusing me of anything, please.'

His manager raised his hands in front of his face. 'Sure. Yes. I'm sorry.'

'Dad?'

'Yes, son?'

'I'm happy with whatever you do. Aren't you, Kizzo?'

'Mostly,' Kierney told her brother, 'but it's important we all get to air our views. It's complicated, bro'. Unbelievably complicated. There are so many different angles. I came here thinking I already knew everything that was likely to happen, but there are surprises all the time.'

'OK,' Jet acknowledged. 'Let's get on with it then, or you'll run out of time.'

'Cheers, son,' Jeff agreed. 'Before you rang, I was just saying to these guys that the real crux of this case comes down to *mens rea* versus *actus reus*, which are basic legal terms I remember learning ages ago. Today, the Accused changed his tune between being questioned by the Prosecution and the Defence, and the judge told the jury that it all depended on context.'

He paused, looking at his daughter to see if she was comfortable. A non-committal "Mmm..." came from the Cambridge night-time.

'*Bueno.* So the way I see it, we... they have to establish whether, at the time when that bastard had your *mamá*'s beautiful face in his gun's sight, he truly intended to shoot her. The Defence says he did it accidentally 'cause he was confused at seeing her and not me. But beforehand, the Prosecution got him to admit he wanted to kill both of us. Now, wanting to kill and actually killing are not the same thing, are they? You okay with that concept to start with?'

All three agreed they were comfortable so far. Jeff leant forward into the telephone, feeling his heart rate increase as he gathered his thoughts. His eyes so needed to cry, but there wasn't time.

'Mate, last night Kizzy and I were debating why this bastard should be convicted, and of what. I told her I didn't give a fuck if he goes to prison or not, since nothing's going to bring ma*má* back. Murder or manslaughter makes little difference to me. He's unlikely to kill anyone else. But that's speaking for myself only. A constituency of one.

'That'd be an incredibly selfish way to conduct myself this afternoon, given all the support I've been given by you guys, and you, Gerry, and the Dysons. All our friends, everyone we work with, *et cetera*, *et cetera*. And even the people with us in the gallery here, Jetto. It's amazing to hear them calling out around us, interrupting proceedings and risking being launched by the bailiffs. They all want to see this guy go down, don't they, guys?'

Gerry and Kierney both nodded before following up with an audible response for the benefit of the man on the other side of the planet. Jeff laughed and carried on.

'Did you get that, son?'

'Yes, Dad.'

'So, as I said to Kizzy yesterday, what does my constituency want me to do with my opportunity in the witness box?'

'So what's this *mens rea, actus reus* thing then?' Jet interjected. 'Guilty mind, guilty act? Is that what it means? You have to have both to be done for murder?'

'Spot on, mate,' Jeff confirmed, suitably impressed. 'Concurrence. They must be contemporaneous. You guys are awesome. Your education has not been wasted after all. It's so gratifying to hear you come to your own well-formed opinions. It means you're equipped for your own life, which is all a parent really has to do.'

Kierney reached out and grabbed her father's hand while he continued.

'*Mens rea* is guilty mind, as Jet says, or I suppose more like evil mind. That's the basis upon which convictions are made. People can commit *acti rei*...I don't know my Latin plurals, so forgive me; i.e. evil acts. The Accused commits an evil act, either intentionally or unintentionally.'

'And if it's unintentionally, he doesn't have a *mens rea*,' the young man's voice boomed through the speakers.

'Exactly, mate. Or more pedantically, it doesn't prove *mens rea*. Is that kosher with you too, Kizzy? Gerry?'

His daughter nodded energetically, and the successful Melbourne executive smiled and raised his right hand. The average punter committing tax fraud would never be judged in terms of an evil mind, in his many years of experience representing clients in court cases. Perhaps he ought to look upon them differently from now on.

'Works for me, mate. Concurring with his contemporary anus sounds about right.'

A muffled laugh came from the telephone speaker.

'Therefore,' Jeff carried on, rolling his eyes at his old friend's predictable flippancy, 'a murder has been committed if the jury decide *actus reus* and *mens rea* have both been proven, but if it's only *actus reus*, it's only manslaughter. So by García saying he doesn't know if he killed *mamá* by accident, I'm not convinced he's guilty of murder.

'But you don't have to be convinced, *papá*,' Kierney repeated her argument from earlier. 'Jet, tell *papá* he's not responsible for what the jury decides.'

'You're not,' her brother obliged. 'What difference does constituency make, Dad? You're on the stand to tell the truth, the whole truth and nothing but the truth, aren't you? Not to say if you think he's guilty or not.'

Gerry pointed towards the telephone. 'The brat hath spake well, my lord. You're taking on too much. Leave it to the barristers to sort out. You just have to answer their questions.'

There was a knock on the door, and in walked Graham Winton and Peter Yun.

'Speak of the devil,' the family's manager laughed, standing up to shake their hands. 'Good afternoon, gents. You've come to take him away?'

'Good afternoon, Gerry,' the effusive man replied. 'Good afternoon, Jeff and Kierney.'

'And Jet,' the youngster added, pointing to the conference telephone on the table, with its flashing green light.

'My son's on the line from the UK,' the superstar explained, frustrated to be running out of time. 'We were just talking about my testimony and how I'm best to represent the interests of my family and friends.'

Graham indicated to his associate to take a seat. 'Good afternoon, Jet,' he shouted into the microphone. 'It must be very early for you. I'm Senior Counsel for the Prosecution, Graham Winton, and also here is my colleague, Peter Yun. How are you?'

'I'm fine, thanks, Mr Winton,' the nineteen-year-old replied. 'Actually, it's late. I'm a uni' student. Dad, I know what you're trying to say. People are influenced by what you say and how you say it, and the jury will definitely be. But that's a good thing, isn't it?'

The widower sighed. 'It's a good thing as long as what I say and how I say it reflect you guys' wishes and not just mine.'

Winton interrupted. 'If this discussion is about murder versus manslaughter, I'm glad you're having it. The judge called Greenshaw and me into her chambers just now and gave us a serve because she believes we should have sorted out the charges before trial.'

'Fuck,' Jeff cursed under his breath. 'What does that mean? Mis-trial?'

'No,' Winton laughed, a little too loud for the celebrity's liking. 'It means we have to be very tight in making sure we can tie the remaining witness' answers to the Accused's admission of intent during my questioning. He told the jury directly that he wanted to kill Ms Diamond. Apologies, young man, for my bluntness. We heard the public gallery's indignation. Everyone wants him convicted of murder because of the damage he's done. The jury will come to this conclusion too.'

'Right,' the handsome world-changer snapped, frowning in dissatisfaction. 'Isn't this country's justice system meant to prevent wrongful convictions? We've got some poor, pathetic bastard who's a pushover on the stand, and we're damned well going to make sure we're seen to avenge the crime. That's a fucking travesty, Graham.

You're making him a scapegoat so you and your colleagues look good on the six o'clock news.'

'Jeff, hold on,' Gerry urged. 'That's a bit rich.'

Winton was quick to retaliate. 'With respect, I resent that remark, Mr Diamond. The Prosecution's working hard to convict your wife's killer. The Accused has admitted to the intent. He pulled the trigger four times.'

'Yes,' the great man nodded, attempting to calm down. 'I agree with all that. I apologise if I offended you, Graham, and I appreciate all your efforts, but I don't want to be part of something that sends a bloke to prison for the rest of his useful life for something he didn't intend to do. García's not a lifelong criminal. He's not a member of some organised crime gang. He's a fuckwit from the western suburbs who's annoyed with how his life turned out. If someone had run Lynn over and killed her in a genuine traffic accident, we wouldn't be twisting and turning our stories to make it look like the driver did it on purpose, even if it was an extremely careless or negligent act. Would we?'

'*Papá*,' the eighteen-year-old piped up. 'Please could I ask Mr Winton a question?'

'Of course you can,' her father replied, releasing her hand from his nervous grip. 'Ask.'

'If, through the rest of the trial, it looks as though manslaughter's the right charge, can it be changed?'

'Yes, indeed,' Graham confirmed to the young woman who was so anxious to keep the peace. 'Murder can be downgraded to manslaughter, but not the other way around.'

'No upgrades,' the Cambridge comedian's voice spluttered through the telephone. 'Sounds like Qantas.'

Everyone groaned, and Jeff shook his head. 'Thanks for that, Mr Hilarious. Sometimes I wonder why we bother...'

'Well then,' the sister continued. 'Jetto, are you concentrating?'

'Yes.'

'*Papá*, my opinion is you need to use your powers of influence to get the longest manslaughter charge you can for *mamá*'s killer. He killed her. There's no doubt about that. So he deserves to go to prison for that.'

'Yeah,' Jet echoed his sibling's comments. 'I agree, sis'. And if it really looks like it was an unintentional evil act by someone who isn't really evil at his core, then the jury'll find him guilty of manslaughter. He'll go to prison, learn his lesson and might even come out of prison happier with who he is.'

Winton stood staring at the space-age contraption in the middle of the table, straining to hear the young man at the other end. 'You have very mature children, Jeff,' he smiled, looking to Peter for confirmation. 'Greenshaw would love to have you two working for him, I can tell you!'

Sycophantic bastard, the widower cursed inside, casting a polite smile back at the barrister.

'Thanks, Graham. They would make good lawyers, I agree. We've been arguing all our life. And thanks to you too, kids. That's exactly what I needed to hear. I'm not sure Grandma and Grandpa would agree though. I have to think of them too. Gez?'

'Mate, anyone with a conscience would agree in principle,' the businessman replied. 'It'll come down to how emotional the jury is, I guess. The Dysons aren't unrealistic people. They're not seeking revenge for Lynn's death any more than you are. And you're right; it's not going to bring her back. The general public's a whole 'nother matter, but they're not the ones you should be seeking to represent, mate. That's the Queen's job, and this man's here...'

'Jeff, we have to get downstairs,' Winton said, tapping his wrist and then pointing to the telephone. 'Are you finished with your call?'

The Crown's next witness looked at his own watch. 'Yeah, Jetto. Ten past one. We'll have to go. Are you alright with all this?'

'Sure, Dad. Go for it. I love you guys. Just do what you need to do. *Bon courage.*'

'Cheers, *hijo mío*,' the father signed off, reaching out towards the star-shaped unit as if he could touch his son through it. 'Thanks for everything, and I love you too.'

'See ya, Kizzo. I wish I was there with you now.'

His father shrugged. 'Up to you, mate. We'd love to have you here.'

'Go to bed, bro',' Kierney shouted. 'Love you.'

'Thanks. I'll think about it, Dad. Bye.'

'*Adiós*, son.'

The Prosecution's star turn pressed the red button on the telephone's keypad. A single, continuous tone sounded, and the line went dead. He sighed and dealt his daughter a half-hearted flash of his wise, dark-ringed eyes.

'Here we go,' he declared, getting to his feet. 'Do I have time for a ciggie?'

'Yes, of course,' Winton replied. 'I'll join you. Peter?'

The young lawyer shook his head.

'Would you like some coffee?' Kierney asked the junior solicitor, steeling herself for a reaction from her father.

'Oh, yes. Thanks,' Peter answered with a wide smile.

Jeff's hand brushed his daughter's back as he left with Graham and Gerry. He didn't have to say anything. His children's lives were continuing along nicely after hitting a substantial bump in the road. It was a bittersweet feeling for both of them.

'Good luck, *papá*,' the pretty teenager said, standing up and giving him a kiss. 'I love you too.'

'Thanks, gorgeous. Enjoy. And remember, no cheering and clapping.'

Kierney whined. '*Papá*! As if?'

The three men left the youngsters to their fifteen minutes of light entertainment, ducking down a staircase that Winton directed them to.

'Yes!' the proud father rejoiced with his old friend as they made their way to the arboretum, pumping his fist in the air. 'I was hoping that might happen.'

'You're incorrigible,' the executive laughed, slapping his mate on the back. 'They'd better not divulge any doctor-patient confidentiality in their pillow talk.'

Winton turned around with a quizzical air, and Jeff's eyes cautioned his manager to be quiet. The smokers assuaged their cravings in double-quick time before Gerry left them to retrieve Kierney and find their seats in the public gallery.

The superstar followed the Queen's barrister into the inner sanctum of the court, into what looked like one of the hundreds of nondescript dressing rooms he had used at concert venues around the world. But instead of guitars, keyboards and spangly clothing strewn everywhere, there were lockers with gowns and wigs hanging on the handles, a few desks, and boxes and boxes of paperwork.

Prosecuting Counsel motioned to the intelligent and compassionate celebrity to sit down, handing him a running sheet of the questions he was planning to ask. 'You've made my job much easier,' he confessed to the widower. 'I've been wrestling with the whole intent topic myself. You can't imagine how relieved I was when I came into your phone call halfway through and realised you weren't looking to crucify the Accused.'

Jeff smiled. 'So why did you pounce on me then? For Peter's benefit?'

The senior partner gave a furtive laugh. 'Yes, I suppose so. The young lawyers aren't aggressive enough. They need to have certain examples set. I'm sorry to have gone off like that.'

'Don't be,' the great man responded, crossing his legs and leaning back in his chair. 'I do the same for my kids. I try not to be too hypocritical, but it's a fine line sometimes. By the way, for the record, I thought the way you used your objection to reinforce García's contradiction was a stroke of genius. A free cross-exam.'

'Many thanks,' the barrister replied, chuffed to receive the positive feedback. 'Astute of you to notice my tactic. It's an old trick. Stephen would've seen it coming.'

The collaborator smiled at the competitiveness in the older man. Boys were still boys, no matter how long in the tooth they were. Greenshaw and Winton were adversaries during the day and best buddies in their downtime; no different from his father-in-law and his various international Olympic counterparts. Jeff could live with that.

'How do you want me to play the "Did you attempt to detain the suspect?" question, when Greenshaw asks?'

'You didn't detain him. He didn't say you did.'

'He didn't say I didn't either,' the tall musician smirked. 'He couldn't have got past me. I wouldn't have let him.'

'But you didn't touch him. And besides, you didn't even know who he was or what he was supposed to have done by that point,' the rotund, red-faced man insisted.

'True,' the witness acquiesced. 'OK. You've convinced me. In truth, I have no good memory of that period. I'm a pretty instinctive person at the best of times. Lynn's the one who remembers each precise step and which sequence she executed them in. As for me, I'm your worst nightmare, Graham, 'cause I use and abuse words for sport. I can't help it. It drives my staff crazy. But I'll keep to the story, don't worry.'

'You're a smart man, Jeff,' Winton praised.

'Yeah. Too smart for my own good,' the widower nodded, rubbing his left pectoral muscle, which hadn't sent him a message for a long time. 'It cost my beautiful best friend her life.'

'Well, don't be saying that on the stand,' Graham responded, chancing a smile at the tragic irony oozing out of the infamous lothario. 'It's nonsense, by the way. If it were so, any number of people would have come after you by now.'

A court officer entered the room to inform them the judge was ready to resume in five minutes. The barrister gathered up his papers and wig, stuffing them under his arm as he did several times each day. He held his hand out for Jeff to return the running sheet.

'I'm afraid I can't leave that with you,' he said. 'A witness can't be seen to be prompted for his responses.'

The great man nodded, handing back the piece of paper. 'Fair enough. Advise to keep it spontaneous. It's not a good look to put the jury to sleep, is it?'

Winton chuckled, inviting the handsome celebrity to go ahead of him through the door. A court official moved to take charge of her next witness, awkwardly refusing to make eye contact with her idol.

'See you in court,' Jeff called back with a grin, before quickly stepping into line with the diligent, uniformed marshal.

The barrister headed in the opposite direction to enter the courtroom through another door, finding Peter and Moira already at the bench. He placed his pile of papers next to them and drank half a glass of water, rolling his shoulders.

Let battle commence.

The barrister was looking forward to the next hour or so with fervid impatience. He had fought and won many high-profile cases in his career, but somehow this one excited him the most. There was something mysterious yet curiously likeable about Jeff Diamond, and the unprecedented level of public support behind this charismatic icon lent still further gravitas to his role as Crown Prosecutor.

FACE TO FACE

Up in the public gallery, Jeff Diamond's fiercest supporters held their breath. They were watching Winton prepare to question his star witness. Gerry extended his right hand to the dark-haired gipsy girl he had known since birth, and she took it willingly.

'He'll be fine,' her father's oldest friend reassured her. 'You know your dad. He always pulls rabbits out of hats when he most needs to.'

'Thanks. Yeah, I know. It's still horrible though. I can imagine how he's feeling. What's the point of going through all this if it doesn't change anything?'

Their manager squeezed her delicate hand. 'Justice will be done,' he whispered, as the court officer announced the arrival of Judge Rosemary Milne.'

'All rise.'

Everyone stood up and waited for the dignified woman to be seated. She immediately addressed the jury, who appeared considerably more animated by the prospect of the grieving Australian hero's testimony.

'Ladies and gentlemen, I trust you all had a pleasant lunch. This afternoon I make another extra special request to you and to the members of the public up there...'

The judge's eyes lifted to the dress circle and found Kierney's straightaway. The youngster didn't look away, and the two women smiled at each other ever so slightly for a fleeting few seconds. Once her attention had reverted to the business at hand, the presiding QC issued several specific instructions regarding the coming session.

'We are about to call the next witness for the Prosecution, and this will be Mr Jeff Diamond, the Victim's husband.'

A gasp whipped up from around the courtroom.

'Now, I know many of you identify strongly with Mr Diamond and his family. They have been part of our everyday lives for many years. I know you all understand they're still in mourning for their loss, and you have been supportive of them during the first couple of days of this trial. Regardless of your affinity with Mr Diamond and his deceased wife, I have to ask you now though to remain completely still and quiet during his testimony.'

Judge Milne scanned from left to right along the rows of public seating, hoping her words were being understood. Silence greeted her for now, and she continued with greater force.

'The court cannot allow comments from the gallery to interrupt proceedings and the jury must be able to concentrate on what's said by the witness in response to questions from the Prosecution and Defence teams. If the trial is disrupted, we risk having to abandon it altogether and declare a mis-trial. I'm sure you would rather see this case arrive at a verdict, as we all would. Ladies and gentlemen of the jury, do you understand this obligation on you?'

Most jurors signalled their agreement, and the judge seemed satisfied. She turned to the Queen's bench and invited it to call its next witness.

'Thank you, Your Honour,' Winton responded in a loud voice. 'The Prosecution calls Mr Jeffrey Moreno Diamond.'

A ripple of avid chatter burst irresistibly from the public gallery as soon as the statuesque figure entered the courtroom through a side door, accompanied by the star-struck official. They watched their idol survey the scene as if arriving on stage during the overture of another sell-out concert. He gave Graham Winton a courteous nod before turning to the judge to acknowledge her similarly. The court officer swooned as she swore in her new witness.

Kierney heard nothing but voices whispering around her. Remarks about how thin her father was, how tired he looked, and how sad their situation must be. Tears pricked at the back of her eyes as she watched him being shown into the small wooden box on the opposite side from the Accused.

'Good luck, *papá*.'

Jeff stood tall and gazed up to where his daughter and Gerry sat. He flashed his eyes at them, but resisted the temptation to wink. He felt alright, he reckoned. Not nervous, not too angry and relatively well in control of his emotions. This was unlikely to last, however...

'Mr Diamond,' Graham began, looking towards the stand and then across to the jury. 'We are all very sorry for your loss.'

'Thank you, Senior Counsel and Your Honour,' the witness nodded with a melancholy half-smile and a brief flick of his hand.

Winton was a born actor, hamming it up for the occasion. Responding in kind, the seasoned campaigner did his best to project his public persona's usual largesse. He hoped the packed courtroom couldn't tell his suit was now two sizes too big, before concluding that it was actually an apt metaphor for the way he felt. He vowed to use the fact that he was now drowning in his own clothes to the Queen's advantage. "A shadow of his former self," many journalists had written over the last few weeks, gloating in their perceived originality.

It was true. The remaining half of Australia's most enduring celebrity partnership no longer fitted his gargantuan image, and yet this afternoon he would have to wing it like never before. He owed it to Lynn to give his finest ever performance right now. Despite twelve hours' growth since this morning's shave, his neck moved with uncharacteristic ease inside his stiff shirt collar as he turned his head to focus on the prosecuting counsel.

What a complete contrast for the jury to come to terms with, between one witness and the next. From the shy and awkward García, dressed in a shapeless, light grey jacket and black trousers which were saggy and over-washed and barely tall enough to be seen over the barrier, to the imposing presence of Jeff Diamond, in a charcoal, subtly-pinstriped Italian suit worn over a tailored Savile Row shirt and a silk tie of the darkest green with a fine gold thread woven through it to catch the light and draw attention to its wearer. His thick, dark hair had been freshly cut before leaving Melbourne, revealing a touch more grey than before, adding to the distinguished countenance his soul-mate had loved so much.

From a man so instantly forgettable to the rock star admired and adored by millions. On the outside, Jeff looked every one of his three-point-two billion dollars, at last count; a far cry from the worthless little man who had vacated the same enclosure prior to the luncheon recess.

The widower stood straight and firm, making eye contact with each juror. He needed to give the impression of being ready for anything, even though on the inside he feared caving in at any moment.

Regulating deliberate, slow breaths, the witness dropped heavy hands down onto the wooden rail in front of him, his three rings clattering against the varnished surface to reinforce the trial's significance. On his right hand, the four-stoned, black family ring, and on his left hand, his own and Lynn's wedding bands, sitting side-by-side on adjacent fingers.

Without looking up, he could sense the jurors registering these shining symbols from the far side of the courtroom, safe in the knowledge that the extravagant gesture had served its purpose. It had reminded everyone why they were here.

'Mr Diamond,' Winton started again. 'Can you please tell the court if you see the man you apprehended at The Pensione Hotel on the sixteenth of February, nineteen-ninety-six, after you heard the call for people to remain in the building?'

'Yes, I can, Your Honour,' the witness answered in a deep, smoky voice that educed a hushed reverence throughout the assembled crowd.

The victim's husband stared at the dejected Spaniard in the dock, raising his left index finger towards him and pointing to the exact spot on his forehead where the first bullet had struck his dream girl.

'The Accused.'

Several people in the public gallery clapped their hands. Judge Milne issued a stern rebuke and another request for total silence, warning that she would not hesitate to instruct the bailiffs to remove anyone causing further disruption.

Winton fixed at the jury in a stern stare. 'Ladies and gentlemen, the Witness has identified the Accused, Juan Antonio García, as the man who was attempting to leave the scene of the crime that morning. Mr Diamond, please could you tell us what you were doing at that time?'

The celebrity cleared his throat, fighting against the tension as it tried to close his windpipe. 'Yes, Your Honour. I was entering the hotel after parking our hired car in the car park next-door,' he recounted flatly. 'Lynn and I had flown up from Melbourne that morning.'

'And please could you describe the scene when you arrived at the hotel entrance?' the barrister's tone was unusually respectful.

The great man sighed. So this was what it was like to be involved in a murder trial. Peculiarly like a chat show, he mused, in an effort to keep his mood light.

'Certainly, Your Honour,' he addressed the judge, before turning back to the prosecution bench and Winton's patient air. 'When I reached the doors, I could hear quite a lot of noise coming from inside the hotel, and a few people were running across the foyer. I then heard the manager shouting for people not to leave the building.'

Winton interrupted. 'What did you think had happened, Mr Diamond?'

'I had no knowledge of anything having happened, Your Honour. I was focussed on meeting Lynn at the check-in desk. It felt like something unusual was going on, that's all.'

'Something unusual?' the lawyer repeated. 'Please could you explain your comment?'

'Yes, Your Honour,' the star witness gave a slight sniff of derision. 'I spend way too much time in hotels but don't often see people running in an entrance lobby, and it's not common to hear staff yelling at their guests to stay inside.'

Jeff smiled at the jury and saw recognition spread across some faces. *Cool it*, he thought to himself. *Just answer the questions.*

Winton smiled too. Game on!

'Yes, of course. Mr Diamond, when you saw the Accused trying to leave the hotel, what did you do?'

The witness took a deep breath, organising his thoughts. 'I stood in his path as he exited the revolving doors and asked him whether he'd heard the manager's instruction. I think I also asked him if he knew what was going on, but I can't be sure. I know I wanted to at the time, but I might've got distracted by the activity inside. He stared at me for a couple of seconds and then said something which I didn't hear properly but thought was Spanish.'

'Spanish?' Winton echoed with his typical theatrics. 'And how did you recognise that this man spoke to you in Spanish?'

'Spanish is my first language, Your Honour,' the formidable, exotic-looking star repeated information that the court had already heard.

'I see,' Graham nodded. 'Thank you. But you couldn't hear him clearly?'

'No, Your Honour. He mumbled something, and the revolving doors were quite noisy, so I asked him in Spanish to repeat himself.'

'What did you say to him precisely, Mr Diamond?' the Prosecution asked.

The witness chuckled, thinking what an overly minute detail this was. 'I said, "*¿Qué dices, hombre?*" which means, "What did you say, mate?"'

Another wave of subdued gossip flowed round the room. Jeff Diamond fans around the world would have recognised such a phrase as his normal conversational style, always friendly and informal with ordinary people. Judge Milne gave Winton a stern glare, warning him not to let his witness run the show.

The barrister coughed. 'Thank you, Mr Diamond. Did the Accused repeat what he had said?'

'I assume so, Your Honour,' the handsome man replied. 'I didn't hear him the first time, so can't be sure if he repeated it word-for-word.'

This throwaway line made the dress circle laugh, along with the actors down below, including the judge. She shook her head at the Defence bench, who shrugged back. Jeff felt sorry for Winton, who had been made to look a fool.

'Yes. I see. What did you understand the Accused's words to mean the second time?'

Feeling guilty, the star witness kept a straight face as he replied. 'He said in Spanish, "*Quería matarlo Ustéd, pero es mejor así.*"'

But it was Winton's turn to laugh. 'Thank you, Mr Diamond. A much better accent than mine. And what did you take this to mean?'

Again, the question elicited a low volume of interest in the courtroom, and the widower waited for it to die down. A sudden bout of distress took him by surprise.

'Thank you, sir,' he answered, his throat tightening. 'It means, "I wanted to kill you, but it's better this way."'

'Thank you,' Winton said. 'I am sorry if this is difficult for you. You may pause at any point. Please could you tell the court what you understood by this comment?'

'At the time, I had no idea what he meant. I didn't know who this man was. I assumed he was working, maybe making a delivery to the hotel. He looked afraid, and I'd already guessed there was something going on in the lobby. I remember wondering why he looked so scared.'

The grieving husband's resilience was on the slide. Needing to arrest his tumbling mood, he moved to capitalise on the fear he supposed García would also be revisiting at this moment, facing off with his captor at his own trial. Imbibing energy from the electrified atmosphere, the victim's husband stared directly at the Accused from across the wide hall and watched the small man's gaze plummet towards the floor.

Jeff turned back to the jury and checked if they had observed the Defendant's behaviour. Content with their level of engagement, he then glanced up to where Kierney was sitting, finding she too was focussed on the jurors. Before returning his attention to his inquisitor, the witness momentarily made eye contact with Gerry, who gave him a subtle wave.

Winton carried on. 'Mr Diamond, what did you do once you had heard the Accused's words?'

'Nothing in response to his words, Your Honour,' he answered. 'I walked towards him and into the revolving doors. He turned around and went back into the hotel ahead of me. There was a doorman on the other side who was watching us coming in.'

'Did you touch the Accused?' Counsel for the Prosecution asked.

'No, Your Honour.'

'Did you say or do anything else to the Accused?'

'No. Nothing else, Your Honour,' the witness responded, taking his time. 'As soon as I got into the hotel and saw panic all around, I lost interest in this man, more concerned about the chaos and the fact that I didn't know where my wife had disappeared to. I began to ask around for someone to tell me what was going on.'

'And how would you describe this panic and chaos all around you?' Senior Counsel asked.

Jeff's eyes welled up with tears as he forced his mind to present the circumstances back to him in sequence. He fought to suppress the extent of his sadness, not wishing these latest traumatic flashbacks to influence the jury.

'People were running around everywhere like headless chooks; staff and guests. Not the normal leisurely pace, I guess, and everybody looked worried and upset. The hotel's manager, Chris Nichols, was shouting instructions to his people. On the opposite side to the desk, receptionists and guests were screaming and pointing across the lobby, where other staff were putting up some sort of barrier.'

'I'm sorry again, Mr Diamond,' Graham said, with more compassion than the widower expected. 'Please, could you tell the court what you were told had happened?'

Now lightheaded, the celebrity steadied himself by resting his hands on the rail in front of him. His warped mind pictured himself as a priest about to give a sermon, and he smiled involuntarily. Looking up into the public gallery, Kierney's apprehensive face righted his equilibrium.

'No-one told me anything to begin with, Your Honour,' Jeff recalled, staring into space. 'I asked where my wife was, and no-one could or would tell me. I had a sixth sense that something terrible had happened to her, so I ran over to where they were assembling a makeshift screen. People tried to stop me, but somehow I knew Lynn was behind there, so I pushed past and saw her...'

He put his left hand up to his eyes and squeezed his thumbs into his temples to lessen the pounding in his head. 'I'm sorry, Your Honour,' he said, sniffing back tears and straightening his stance.

'Please, Mr Diamond,' Judge Milne replied. 'Take your time. This must be a horrific memory for you.'

From deep inside, the temper of a teenaged boy from the western suburbs flared up in anger at this patronising woman's slap-in-the-face comment. Jeff struggled not to react with one of the uncontrolled outbursts which had defined his childhood.

Of course it is, you stupid, bloody woman.

'Thank you, Your Honour,' the forty-three-year-old man of the world responded, forcing a benign smile to thank the judge for her concern. 'It is.'

At this precise moment, looking up again to seek solace in his daughter's eyes, the celebrity picked the single, defining difference between himself and the man on trial: he had conquered the bitterness. The chip on his shoulder was long gone and only reappeared in the worst of his memories. García had not made this transition. He was still stuck amid his anger, never having learnt how to separate the two worlds; exactly as his own father had claimed shortly before he died.

Winton coughed, ready to resume. 'Are you good to carry on, Mr Diamond?' he asked.

Jeff nodded. 'Yes. All good, thanks.'

'Can you please tell the court if you saw the Accused again after you crossed the foyer to inspect the screening?'

'No, Your Honour,' the witness replied, a little calmer. 'After a few minutes, I heard sirens, and the police arrived while I was sitting in front of Lynn. I was told afterwards that they'd questioned him and he'd been arrested, but I'd pretty much forgotten about him at this stage.'

The question-master backtracked a little, which the celebrity was expecting. 'You may have heard earlier in this trial, ladies and gentlemen of the jury, that the Defence maintains Mr Diamond manhandled the Accused when he encountered him outside the hotel entrance.'

The word "manhandled" was spoken slowly and deliberately, with a hint of comedy in the barrister's delivery. 'Mr Diamond, please could you confirm to the court that you did not manhandle the Accused into the hotel?'

'Absolutely not, Your Honour,' Jeff insisted, his mind presenting a clear memory in the nick of time. 'Coming in from the car-park, I was carrying two suitcases, one in each hand, and my jacket. I didn't touch the Accused, or even say anything to him, except to ask if he'd heard the request not to leave the building. Later, when he'd spoken to me, I asked him to repeat the phrase I didn't hear properly. I didn't have to ask him to go back in. He made that decision himself. Maybe he decided he didn't have a choice?'

The judge was quick to pounce on the last sentence, requesting the jury disregard it since it contained conjecture on the witness' part. 'Please ignore Mr Diamond's last remark,' she instructed. 'The Accused was not compelled or pushed by Mr Diamond to turn and go back into the hotel. He turned around of his own free will.'

Jeff nodded an apology. He took Rosemary Milne's lack of feedback as a sign to stop playing to the crowd, which both amused and annoyed him. It was acceptable for counsel and judge to have their in-jokes and banter, yet clearly unacceptable for key witnesses. He returned his attention to Graham Winton, who was preparing his next question.

'Thank you, Your Honour. Mr Diamond, had you ever met the Accused before the sixteenth of February, nineteen-ninety-six?'

'No, Your Honour.'

'Did you recognise him at all, either his appearance or his voice?'

'No, Your Honour.'

'Were you aware he had attended two of your concerts, or that he was present at the parade you held after your father passed away?'

'No, Your Honour. Not until earlier today, that is.'

What a ridiculous question, Kierney thought, imagining her father to be exercising considerable restraint. How many people did he meet every week? Each time he went on stage, as she well knew from her own experience, crowds were mostly a rolling sea of bobbing heads and swaying arms. It was nigh on impossible to pick out particular faces, let alone commit them to memory.

Down in the witness box, Jeff again took time to examine García's body language. After over three decades of bitterness and disgust, he was finally gaining insight into his father's bargain with the legal system. From ten metres away, he substituted García for his old man, facing his accusers with freedom hanging in the balance.

He wondered if the man he detested so vehemently would have been remorseful in court. He doubted it. The only son of Polish immigrants had become a hardened criminal at an early age, with no compassion for those whose lives he destroyed. The prisoner hadn't even been sorry on his death-bed, and his billionaire son shuddered as he pictured him in the old Supreme Court building, lying through his teeth in front of the authorities he despised.

Well, if Paul Diamond had lied under oath, it obviously didn't do him any favours, the star witness decided. He still went down. At least García had the bearing of one lost and dejected, incapable of putting on a potent performance for the court.

Jeff wondered whether his father had been supported by anyone in the public gallery during his trial. He had read in this morning's newspaper that García's family had disowned him. This was a sad indictment on their fellow humans, punishing the poor man before they had even heard his case. Surely they could have stood by him until they knew for sure he was a criminal.

'Mr Diamond,' the witness' overactive mind heard, breaking him out of his daydream.

Winton was addressing him again. 'Please could you tell the court how you felt when you discovered the man whom you encountered in the hotel entrance had fatally shot your wife?'

Jeff shook his head, leaning forward onto the front panel of the enclosure again.

'How did I feel?' he repeated, blowing stale air out through pursed lips. 'It'd take me a week to describe how I felt. "Devastated" is a word that's been used to excess to describe me in recent weeks. And furious that he'd been able to get to her in such a public place. That about sums it up, Your Honour.'

He saw the Queen's representative make eye contact with the judge and backed off, not wishing to be blamed for provoking an undue sympathetic reaction from the jury or the public gallery. As an advocate for his vibrant and precious constituency, neither did he wish to divulge that he didn't much care if García was convicted or not. Lynn was gone. He would be no more or less devastated if her killer had been caught through an ensuing investigation than if he were still at large.

'I certainly wished it was me who'd been killed instead,' the widower explained. 'That was another primary emotion, I suppose. But our daughter, up there, and our son studying in the UK weren't ready to lose either parent. In fact, I remember the police congratulating me for my part in catching my wife's alleged killer. The comment sickened me, because I would far rather have stopped him *before* he shot her. This would've been worth their congratulations.'

While the fans in the public gallery gasped, Jeff stared into the judge's eyes, challenging her to issue him with a warning. No, he justified such an explicit answer. Why should he provide a lukewarm account of his feelings? He was a witness in the Supreme Court, asked to describe how he felt when he discovered his beautiful best friend had died a violent death. What did she expect him to say? Disappointed?

Judge Milne responded to the intensity of the billionaire's eyes with a knowing smile. She was an intelligent woman, and he was left in no doubt that she understood his *modus operandi*.

She addressed the prosecution barrister without drama. 'Counsel for the Prosecution, do you have any further questions for this witness?'

'One more, Your Honour,' the prosecutor replied, closing his file and walking up to his witness, who towered above him. 'Mr Diamond, I read somewhere that you give fifty percent of your earnings to charity, particularly organisations devoted to mental health issues. Is this true?'

Jeff smiled, knowing this to be Winton's final salvo. 'In theory, yes, Your Honour,' he opened.

He looked up into the gallery, resisting a wink at Kierney as the courtroom once more became animated. In any other circumstances, he would have given his customary "Yes and no" answer, the preface for any question prompting a naïve, binary response. As anyone who knew him would be aware, nothing was ever this simple in his mind.

'Fifty-fifty was the model Gerry, my manager, and I started out with when I released my first single and started earning decent money from recording and performing. I had learned to survive on very little during my student years and was blown away with the ridiculous amounts of money that began to flow in.

'I always dreamed of being able to make a difference to ordinary people's lives if I ever made something of myself, so I asked that we halve whatever came in and put it into a separate fund that could be allocated to charities and other worthy causes.'

Although the jury seemed fascinated and the fans seated above were enjoying this trip down Memory Lane, the billionaire imagined he oughtn't to labour the point beyond Winton's purpose.

'These days, it's way more complex though,' he continued, eyes lifting to Gerry, who raised his hands with seven digits extended. 'I'd say the percentage is even higher these days. About seventy, the financial wizard's telling us... thanks, Mr Blake... if we count the venture capital that goes to medical research and biotechnology which aims to help alleviate suffering, along with the Diamond Celebration Foundation, which is mainly about improving people's ability to repair their own mental health.'

'Objection,' Stephen Greenshaw injected, lacking some of his usual dynamism. 'What is the relevance of these laudable facts and figures, please?'

Before Judge Milne could refer to opposing counsel, Graham was already posing a follow-up question. 'Of course, Your Honour, these details speak to the missed opportunity for the Accused to have benefitted from the Witness' generosity. Am I right in saying, Mr Diamond, that you and your wife targeted the area of Sydney where Mr García lives for specific investment in mental health services, since this was where you also grew up and struggled as a child.'

'That's true, Your Honour,' Jeff nodded. 'Lynn and I were committed to reversing the trend in adverse outcomes for children in the south-western suburbs. In fact, it was Lynn's idea to hold a parade through the streets after my dad passed away, to encourage young people to invest in themselves and build a more successful future.'

'Not to resort to violent crime born out of envy and despondence,' Counsel for the Prosecution added, taking a leaf out of the great man's book, 'which must make the Accused's crime against your beautiful wife seem like an even more bitter irony.'

The widower sighed, seeing most jurors wiping their eyes. 'Indeed, Your Honour. It certainly feels that way. Lynn was as dedicated as I was to creating a fairer world, where everyone has access to the same opportunities. She didn't deserve to die because someone considered himself hard-done-by in comparison to her husband.'

'Thank you, Mr Diamond,' Winton declined, giving the charismatic celebrity a brief nod. 'That concludes the Prosecution's questions for this witness, Your Honour.'

'Counsel for the Defence...' the judge turned to the opposing bench without delay. 'Your witness.'

While the guard changed in front of his wooden playpen, the superstar took a moment to reconnect with Kierney. He could see her leaning against Gerry's arm, their hands entwined, and another grudging stab disturbed his concentration. Why was his mate filling his place so naturally? He hoped the lecherous bastard wasn't getting his jollies at the expense of the young woman's heightened emotional state.

The Defence barrister was on his feet, a taller and slimmer man than Winton. The songwriter could now see why the man's gown seemed to waft constantly: he never stood still, like a jogger swapping from foot to foot to prevent his muscles from tightening up while waiting at traffic lights.

'Mr Diamond,' Stephen Greenshaw began. 'First, let me pass on our condolences too, on behalf of us all on the Defence bench.'

Jeff nodded, shooting a few more daggers García's way to encourage the jurors to pay keen attention. 'Thank you, Senior Counsel.'

'Mr Diamond,' the lawyer boomed again, this time directed at the jury. 'How tall are you, please?'

'Six foot four, Your Honour,' the witness answered, bemused. 'A hundred and ninety-five centimetres.'

'And how tall would you think the Accused is?' the Defence barrister continued.

'About five-nine. One-seventy centimetres or so.'

'How much do you weigh, Mr Diamond?'

Predictable, the intellectual figured, realising where this line of questioning was heading. 'Now or on the sixteenth of February?' he toyed with this new inquisitor.

A couple of the jury members nodded to each other, appreciating the clever response. Greeted by muted laughter from those up above, Jeff was reminded of the many magazine articles and television reports which described his weight loss and gaunt appearance, and it pleased him to see the irony in the Defence's tactic was not lost on the court.

Greenshaw clarified, frustrated at the witness' ability to garner sympathy from virtually every question. 'On the sixteenth of February, sir,' he snapped.

'Just over a hundred kilos, Your Honour.'

'One hundred kilograms,' Counsel for the Defence repeated for the benefit of the jury. 'And would you be so kind as to estimate the Accused's weight, Mr Diamond? On the sixteenth of February, that is.'

'Seventy kilos or so.'

'Seventy. Seven, zero. Yes. Thank you. Are you aware that your size and perceived strength can appear threatening to a smaller man?'

'Of course, Your Honour,' the forty-three-year-old replied, intrigued as to how Greenshaw planned to make his point.

'Thank you, Mr Diamond. If you're faced with a situation where you want to make a person do as you wish, would you consider your size to be an advantage?'

Jeff shot a glance to Winton, who had a sly grin on his face. 'Sometimes, Your Honour,' he answered somewhat dismissively, 'but not always.'

The witness' non-committal response momentarily floored the lean, fidgety man. 'Very well. So are you able to give me an example of a situation where your size would not be an advantage in making people do as you wish, Mr Diamond?'

'Certainly, Your Honour. If I wanted to gain their confidence or if I needed them to feel safe,' the experienced negotiator answered.

Counsel for the Defence was losing both ground and face, and he became defensive as a result. The witness sympathised with him but let him struggle on, watching Winton's amusement growing out of sight from the public gallery.

'Yes. Thank you. And similarly, if you wish to prevent someone from doing something he wants to do, is your size an advantage in that case?'

'The same answer applies,' Jeff responded, extending a metaphorical olive branch ever so slightly. 'It depends why he wants to do it and why it's a bad idea. If it's because he's scared, then it's not an advantage. But if he's being belligerent, it could be.'

Up in the gallery, Kierney laughed with her dad's closest friend. 'That's enough rope to hang himself with. He can't help playing with people, can he?'

Greenshaw grasped the delicate bough. 'Mr Diamond, you told the court you thought the Accused looked terrified when you met him leaving the hotel.'

'Yes, Your Honour. I did.'

'And you're also on record as saying that the Accused turned around and headed back into the hotel when you walked towards him,' Defence Counsel reiterated.

'Yes, Your Honour. He did.'

Greenshaw's opposite number emitted a stifled giggle, leading the judge to launch another steely glare in his direction. The questioner persisted in contempt for his learned colleague, this hypnotic star's timing and delivery proving as exquisite as they were infuriating.

'Are you of the opinion, Mr Diamond, that the Accused felt threatened by you in this situation?'

'Objection!' Winton sprang to his feet, right on cue.

'Counsel?' Judge Milne addressed the prosecuting solicitor.

'Thank you, Your Honour. The Witness is being asked to give an opinion about how the Accused felt at that moment. He was not in a position to know how the Accused felt. Mr Diamond did not know what had happened inside the hotel to cause the Accused to leave despite the manager's instructions.'

'Objection sustained. The Witness is not required to answer the question.'

Prosecuting Counsel and his mesmerising co-star gave each other an invisible high-five, and several whoops of joy were overheard from the public gallery. Greenshaw was only moderately affronted, no doubt half expecting to receive such a ruling. He shuffled his papers around for a few seconds while deciding upon his next question.

'Was it your intention to threaten the Accused back into the hotel, Mr Diamond?'

'No, Your Honour,' Jeff answered. 'It just happened that way. People tend to do what I ask. I don't know why, but they mostly do. I must just have the knack, but it's not meant as a threat or any sort of order.'

Greenshaw retired hurt, conferring with his associates briefly before returning to the front line. The celebrity took a sip of water and stared past the Accused to the jury. One woman in the front row gave him a surreptitious wave, only to receive an adroit telling-off from the man to her right. Jeff turned away, not wishing to get the poor woman into trouble. Evidently, he still had that aforementioned knack and vowed to use it wisely from now on.

'Mr Diamond,' the restless solicitor began again with renewed vigour, 'please could you explain to the court how it came about that you and your wife had separated that morning, your wife going into the hotel ahead of you?'

Separated? A well-chosen word from the experienced lawyer, the witness realised. Was he hoping to tease out a rift between husband and wife? Perhaps a blazing row in the car on the way from the airport? A row that had broken out due to the tension he might be exuding, knowing he had planned Lynn's assassination for that very morning? A well-chosen word, but unfounded.

'Certainly, Your Honour,' the oft-lauded lover prepared to account for the sequence of events which represented his greatest ever regret. 'We usually separate, as you say, when we arrive at hotels, especially when we've rented a car. Also, sometimes if we arrive in a taxi or limo'. It was our normal "MO". One of us parks the car first, or collects the luggage from the boot if we've been picked up, while the other checks in and goes up to our room.'

Again, Jeff systematically made eye contact with members of the jury, this time those occupying the back row. His heart was beating fast, and he could feel sweat forming in his palms as he tried not to reveal how reliant he had become on the handrail.

'Not only was this an expedient use of time, but it was also a bit of a romantic tradition of ours, to meet each other in a hotel room,' he explained, doling out one of his most disarming smiles at the two men and two women sitting in a line. 'Twenty years is a long time. We learned how to keep it real.'

All four smiled back, the whole courtroom melting like fine Belgian chocolate on a summer's day. The handsome celebrity was reeling everyone in on an invisible hook, and the power went to his head in exactly the way he had anticipated.

'Just a private thing we both enjoyed, if you know what I mean,' the smile turned into a genuine sob.

The afternoon's star witness dare not look up into the dress circle, for fear of his reaction alarming his daughter. In response to the Defence barrister's enquiring eyes, he composed himself, and the patented rock-star smile returned. Winton stepped forward as if he were about to request a short interval.

'If there was luggage involved,' Jeff continued, the tattoo on his chest now also rendering assistance, 'I usually took care of the car and brought the bags in, even though Lynn was more than capable of carrying them. It's just not a good look, and the papers always have a field day with things like that. She didn't like it, but it complied with our publicists' wishes and assuaged my protective tendencies.'

Judge Milne was the next to show concern, as tears flowed once more and remorse rang in the bereaved man's ears. Australia's only benevolent lion threw back his mane of black hair flecked with grey and issued a silent roar to his wife's ghost before continuing his testimony in a voice as rich and resonant as he could summon.

'I apologise, Your Honour. I'm fine. It's so hard to come to terms with how different things might have been if only we'd switched roles... There were plenty of times when I checked in and Lynn parked the car. Many, many times. Who knows? She might well have been standing here today instead of me,' he hesitated, seeking undeserved permission from his gorgeous daughter.

Or was he begging forgiveness? *Previously voiced opinions notwithstanding*, the father appended through the telepathic airwaves for the eighteen-year-old's benefit. The crowd caught its breath and murmured, and to his delight, Kierney gave him a sly thumbs-up.

'Your Honour, I did not send my wife in to cover for me, if that's what Counsel for the Defence is intimating,' he explained. 'No way would I have done that. This was a transition year for us, and we'd never been happier. This particular weekend was a treat for us. A few days away from the kids with no training, and no work obligations after the Childlight fundraiser lunch. Lynn was only recently retired from the professional tennis circuit, since the Open at the end of January, so she was all mine for the whole weekend. I cannot begin to tell you how inviting a prospect this was...'

The superstar's voice cracked again, and he noticed how silent the cavernous space had become. He turned a few degrees to his right and faced off against the Accused, who was cowering in the dock. Was that regret on his face too?

'Neither of us is on tour at the moment, and Jet and Kierney are self-propelled these days, so we were having a weekend off. Y'know, like normal people,' Jeff inhaled. 'Drink some wine, play golf with friends and enjoy each other's company. Simple pleasures...'

Greenshaw had had enough. There were only so many heartstrings a witness should pull, and Jeff Diamond had taken full advantage of his quota. No doubt about it. The defiant barrister stepped forward until he stood less than a metre from the witness box, raising his hand and bringing the plaintive interlude to a close.

'You are an empathetic man, it appears, Mr Diamond,' he changed the subject.

'So I'm told, yes,' the forty-three-year-old nodded without expression, swallowing another slug of water.

'When the Accused described his feelings of jealousy and anger concerning your similar backgrounds and the large gap in your respective levels of success, do you understand how he might harbour ill feelings towards you?'

'Absolutely. Yes, Your Honour,' Jeff answered, hearing a muffled rebound from those present.

'Thank you. In that case, can you understand how those ill feelings might be magnified over the years, when your life seemed to go from strength to strength while the Accused's life stayed static or in some ways deteriorated?'

'Yes, Your Honour. I can definitely understand it,' the witness' clear voice affirmed. 'I receive plenty of hate-mail full of the same ill feelings. But there are several inaccuracies in the Accused's account of how similar our backgrounds were. He could've checked these out a long time ago and realised he was comparing us unfavourably.'

Winton became nervous. Too much information.

'Which inaccuracies are these?' Greenshaw sought clarification.

'Well, Your Honour... Firstly, I'm not an immigrant,' Jeff relayed to the jury, his inflexion staid and succinct. 'My mother, my sister and I were all born in Sydney's south-west. Only my father was born outside Australia. Mr García would've been better off comparing himself to my father, and we're all now aware of his situation.'

A huge roar erupted around Kierney and Gerry. Their eyes darted around before focussing back on the judge below. The Diamonds' tireless advocacy for those dealt a raw deal in life was a significant factor contributing to the respect they enjoyed from the public.

'Ladies and gentlemen,' Rosemary Milne sounded tired. 'Please remain silent during the questioning of this Witness. And Mr Winton, please advise your witness not to lure my court with concert reportage.'

The superstar nodded, appreciating her point. 'I apologise, Your Honour.'

Defence Counsel grinned. 'What other inaccuracies were there in the Accused's testimony concerning yourself, Mr Diamond?'

'Objection!' Graham Winton piped up, seeking and obtaining the judge's permission to explain. 'Irrelevant to the case, Your Honour. Mr Diamond is not the one on trial here. He should not have to rectify misconceptions the Accused may have of him or his family.'

'Mr Greenshaw,' the judge asked the bouncing barrister, 'of what relevance is your question to this case?'

'It speaks to the level of anger and jealousy which the Defendant has for the Witness, Your Honour,' came the justification.

'I'll allow it, for now,' Rosemary Milne told both lawyers. 'Carry on, Mr Diamond. The other inaccuracies?'

Jeff took a deep breath, remembering how liberating it had been to open up to Lynn about his painful childhood and adolescence; the sense of empowerment she gave him simply by listening without prejudice. He had funnelled every ounce of energy into breaking the invisible shackles that chained him to his lowly origins, allowing his guardian angel to hold the gates open into her star-crossed world.

'Thank you, Your Honour. I'm happy to answer this question because I think it's absolutely relevant to this case. The Accused spoke as if he and I had the same opportunities to make something of our lives, based on the type of family we come from and where we grew up. And on the face of it, that's true,' he told the court, his delivery moderated and patient. 'But I'm what's known as a statistical anomaly. The exception to prove the rule, if you like... People like me didn't often turn out this way back then, it's true. But a few did, and it was seldom by accident.'

The billionaire philanthropist engaged the jurors in earnest, knowing he had them in the palm of his hand. This was an excellent speech to be making on behalf of his constituency, especially for the droves of young people who took advantage of Childlight's services, desperate to break out of the dead-end lives of which García complained.

'I learned as much as I could, I worked hard, I got lucky and liked what happened as a result. So I learned some more, worked harder and got even luckier,' the boy from Canley Vale continued, glancing up at the ever-loyal Gerry Blake in the dress circle. 'And I used a few people along the way. That's how I chose to break out of the life I was born into. There's nothing stopping any of us... even Mr García... from doing the same.

'People don't always live in poverty because they want to, but more because they don't know how to change things. Or they don't want to make the effort to change things. I wasn't going to let that happen to me. I hunted down opportunities when others in my school and neighbourhood did not, because I knew these opportunities would never, ever come looking for someone like me.'

Stephen Greenshaw was ready to burst, red in the face and dying for the chance to draw the star witness' impassioned soliloquy to a close. On the prosecution bench, Winton was frowning. It was the closest he came to admiration for a fellow human being.

Jeff wound things up, again focussing directly on the jury. 'And consequently, when Lynn and I became parents, we gave our kids the education and life experiences that I'd always wanted. Those from which she'd benefitted. You better believe we did! But we wouldn't have wasted it on them if they hadn't wanted it or didn't deserve it.

'It's not about money or fame. It's about attitude and ambition. Anyone can be me, or whomever they want to be. They just have to make their opportunities happen. That's where Mr García's argument falls down, Your Honour, and why he should've channelled his jealousy into improving his own lot rather than killing the mother of my children.'

The inked emblem on the widower's chest stung so intensely that he winced and exhaled. Spellbound, the people in the gallery began to clap, scrambling to their feet to support their dispossessed hero. They interpreted his reaction as being overcome with emotion, even though at this moment, the front-end of the Diamond pantomime lion felt wonderfully serene and content. His counterpart was here, watching over him and their daughter, whom he could see on her feet and applauding with the rest.

Judge Milne waved both hands in a downward motion to request those in the gallery to keep their opinions to themselves. She was fighting a losing battle.

'We love you, Jeff!' came another cry from a woman high up in the left corner. 'You're amazing!'

The inspired witness stood still, waiting for the crowd to calm down. It did so as soon as the superstar raised his left hand, again to Greenshaw's intense annoyance. The Supreme Court had been transformed into a Big Top for the time being. The right man had become the ringmaster, all things considered.

Through the initials etched into the orator's chest, Lynn echoed the fans' sentiments. *There, angel*, he transmitted through the airwaves. *I've turned your trial into a circus. I knew I would. I promised I wouldn't, but I did.*

Juan Antonio García was in tears in the witness box, prompting the modern-day Pied Piper to turn his eyes from him to the jury and back again, assuming they would follow his gaze and catch the Accused's reaction fair and square.

Up in the dress circle, Gerry watched his VIP client in full flight, awestruck and delighted. This must truly be his finest hour. He had seen the great man in action on his feet countless times before. The years of stirring speeches and subtle tricks to put people in touch with life's most important choices had made him into a force even the Supreme Court couldn't better.

'Your dad is a most remarkable man,' he said to Kierney, who had tears streaming down her face. 'Isn't he?'

The teenager nodded. 'Yes, and the saddest. Why did García have to kill *mamá*? Look how much good there is left in him, that's now going to be lost to all of us. I hate that man down there. I really hate him, even if he didn't mean to kill her.'

The Diamond family's manager signalled to the security guard next to him that they should leave. Both bodyguards stood up together.

'Come on, Kizzy,' Gerry urged. 'Let's get out of here for a while. I'm sure the judge'll call a recess to let everyone calm down. Come on, darling. You need a break.'

Reluctant to abandon her father, Kierney resisted. 'No. I want to stay to find out what's happening. I'm good. Please, can we stay a bit longer?'

The accountant sat down again, with the two security men following suit. Jeff watched this tiny sub-plot play out from the witness box, sensing something was amiss. He beckoned to Winton, who attracted the attention of Judge Milne and the Defence team.

'May we approach the bench, please, Your Honour?' Counsel for the Prosecution requested.

Both senior counsels stood side-by-side, looking up to the middle-aged woman like two naughty schoolboys receiving a dressing-down from their teacher. She nodded, and the two men turned and walked back to their respective benches.

'Ladies and gentlemen, I'm calling a thirty-minute recess. Please have your conversations in this next half-hour and be ready to resume in silence, with due respect for the proceedings. Thank you.'

The court officer clenched her fist and banged the desk in front of her as hard as she could. 'All rise.'

Those who were not already risen did so, waiting while the officials filed out through the rear door. Barristers and witness followed thereafter, along with the jury, who exited on the other side of the courtroom. Last to leave was the Accused, flanked by his two custody officers.

Kierney also rose, watching the dejected little Spaniard trudge out of sight, somehow looking smaller after each session. 'Sorry, Gerry,' she said. 'I'm ready now.'

Jeff was the first to arrive at the familiar meeting room, already sipping on a cup of fresh coffee when the others burst through the door. His daughter rushed into his arms, sobbing.

'*Papá!* You were so fantastic,' she wept on his shoulder. 'I love you so much. You were incredible.'

'Thanks, gorgeous,' her father said, stroking her hair and kissing her forehead. 'Are you alright? I saw you crying up there, and you were so far away. I couldn't help you and I'm really sorry.'

'I hate that man for taking *mamá* away,' the teenager repeated, wiping the tears away and slumping down onto a chair. 'He's ruined your life and made you desperately sad. I hate him, *papá*. I really do.'

'*Mamá* and I hate him too, baby,' Jeff said, his tattoo itching furiously under his shirt, 'for the same reasons as you do. He'll get what he deserves, don't worry. Let's go and have a cigarette downstairs, just you and me, huh?'

Kierney nodded and smiled. Gerry poured himself a coffee and set about listening to his messages, waving cheerfully to the pair. Down in the smokers' zone, father and daughter sat on their own but in full view of several groups of onlookers who kept a polite distance.

'Do you have to go back down there?' she asked.

'Yep. 'Fraid so,' the widower replied. 'Not for too much longer, but I know they're going to ask me more questions about the death-threat letters. Cath provided them with everything we had, so they're bound to be looking for some way of linking García with one or more of them. They have to do their best by him, Kizzo. You understand, don't you?'

'Of course I understand,' the teenager answered, stamping her foot. 'It's just that I miss you up there with us. It's nice looking down on them and making comments to each other. It's not the same with Gerry.'

'I know,' her father smiled. 'He's not a people person, is he? Never has been, never will be. He cares though; wants us to be happy. He just doesn't know how to make it so. Hopefully, Fiona'll teach him.'

The pair of Diamonds marched back across the Supreme Court lobby, through a swing door and into the stairwell. The area surrounding the lifts was crowded, and they didn't want to be mobbed by a crowd under strict instructions to calm down and prepare to show due respect. They ran up the stairs and were still panting when they reached the meeting room.

'What the hell have you two been doing?' Gerry laughed, seeing them lunge for glasses of water. 'Winton's been here, mate. You've to go downstairs again. They're waiting for you.'

'Can I sit on your knee this time, papá?' Kierney joked. 'I want to be down there with you.'

'Yeah, OK,' Jeff chuckled. 'Why not? You can be my ventriloquist's dummy.'

'I ain't nobody's dummy,' the young woman proclaimed, hands on haughty hips. 'I'll stay here with Uncle Gerry then. Hope it goes well, papá.'

The witness gave his daughter a farewell cuddle. 'Gracias, pequeñita. Don't let Uncle Gerry hold your hand too tightly. It makes me think his mind's elsewhere when he does it.'

'Mate, objection! Don't be so disgusting. Is that what I get for helping you out?'

'Only kidding, mate,' his client lied, slapping the Irishman's back. 'I'll see you guys afterwards. We can go for a long, slow dinner somewhere off the beaten track. What about Coogee or somewhere like that? Italian or Mexican. Some place that does flavour.'

Proceedings resumed for the last session of the day. The public gallery was more subdued after their break, and the jury seemed relaxed. Jeff noticed how much more regularly they were interacting with each other than on the first day, which augured well for all concerned. By the time they needed to make their three important decisions, all natural wariness and uncertainty among a group of strangers should have been eroded and therefore far less of a barrier to free-flowing conversation. How he would love to be a fly on the wall during their deliberations; to be privy to the pathways traversed on their way to a verdict!

Guilt still plagued the doting father for bringing his gorgeous gipsy girl to Sydney this week. Was it a mistake? The trial was harder on her than either had expected. She was in such a hurry to grow up, anxious to catch her big brother and join him in full-blown adulthood. Jeff vowed to slow her down once this ordeal was over.

The officer announced that the court was in session by banging a gavel with great aplomb, an heirloom most likely reserved for rowdy cases in a cabinet of historical artefacts. The judge posted yet another series of warning shots into the public gallery and urged the bank of jurors to concentrate on the facts rather than the ideas used by the witness to convey them.

Said witness nodded in compliance with Rosemary Milne's wishes, thereby agreeing to temper his signature brand of expressive language. He had said his piece anyway, the atmosphere in the courtroom now altered as a result. People were engaged. The case meant something real to them now. His job was almost done.

His chest constricting from a swift reality check, Jeff spied the distinctive logo of his music publishing company in the top corner of an envelope lifted by the Defence attorney. After the committal hearing only a few weeks ago, the Defence team had issued Paragon Holdings, Stonebridge Music and Blake & Partners each with a subpoena to produce all documented threats to the celebrities' safety and any other unusual correspondence which had ever been received for the couple, any member of their family or close friends. Fortunately, both Gerry and Cathy were fastidious at record-keeping and had taken legal advice early in the rock star's amazing career. Between the various offices, they had supplied three full archive boxes of photocopied and printed evidence.

Not one piece of vindictive correspondence could be linked to García however, clearing the Diamonds' management machine of taking inadequate precautions against an event planned in Sydney for that particular February weekend. The Defence's first question to Jeff as the trial continued related to the handful of documentary evidence provided by the Dyson family in response to a further subpoena.

'Mr Diamond,' Stephen Greenshaw opened, his confidence restored during the recess with a strong cup of tea and some sweet biscuits. 'Are you aware that your parents-in-law, Mr Bart and Mrs Marianna Dyson, have supplied the court with eighteen threatening letters relating to your late wife?'

'Yes, I am, Your Honour,' the star responded, biting his tongue at the loathsome "late" reference.

'Please could you tell the court what measures you and your management took to minimise the risk presented by these letters?'

'Certainly, Your Honour. They would've gone through exactly the same process as any we receive directly. Copies go to Victoria Police and to the Australian Federal Police, another copy goes to our contracted security firm, and our admin' staff keep their own records. The security guys liaise with the police independently and do whatever they need to do. There's a weekly combined management meeting chaired by my esteemed business manager, Gerry Blake, up there...'

Jeff's eyes lifted to the public gallery, taking the jurors' attention with them. They saw him point towards his old friend, who sat with the pretty, dark-haired teenager. A brief frisson of pleasure shot through the courtroom when she gave him a quick wave.

'A representative from the security company attends those meetings if anything important has been received or has taken place. They discuss a strategy and put it into action. Lynn and I receive updates after this, including information about anything we need to do or be aware of. And in those specific instances you're referring to there, the Dysons would also've been given an update.'

'Thank you, Mr Diamond,' Greenshaw said. 'Do you employ bodyguards on a full-time basis to protect yourself and your family?'

'No, Your Honour,' the superstar replied. 'We use the services of our security firm when we need them, for certain trips or events that warrant them. There are two gentlemen in the public gallery now, for example, looking after us very well.'

After another momentary pause, during which the witness confirmed the jury was now following his gaze every which way, the barrister threw in a curveball, appearing especially pleased with himself. 'Is it true your children were kidnapped in nineteen-eighty-six?'

'Objection!' Winton shouted, leaping up out of his chair in total surprise and was seized by a coughing fit.

'Counsel for the Prosecution?' Rosemary Milne redirected her attention.

'Thank you, Your Honour,' the lawyer responded, having whipped out a bright, white handkerchief to wipe his imperious jowls. 'The question is irrelevant to this case.'

Her Eminence shook her head. 'I believe the Defence is asking a question about the Diamonds being able to protect themselves from threats. I'm going to overrule you on this occasion, Senior Counsel.'

The Queen's representative sat down, leaving his opponent to bask triumphant in the moment. The public gallery had come to life again, excited to hear about this latest revelation. The cast of this latest Gilbert and Sullivan comic opera must be up for Academy Awards, the musician chuckled to himself, standing firm and waiting for the solicitor to pose his question again.

'Thank you, Your Honour. Mr Diamond, please could you confirm to the court that your children were kidnapped in 1986?'

Kierney held her breath for her father's response. Gerry had completely forgotten about this chapter in their eventful life and straightened up in expectation. Jeff turned to the twelve responsible citizens and breathed deeply.

'Yes, Your Honour. It is true.'

Several jurors gasped and looked away, not wanting to believe this impressive man capable of allowing the lives of his adored offspring to be put in danger. With his own collection of motion picture gongs safely locked away in Escondido's vault, the witness' face flashed through a range of emotions to prolong the suspense.

'Lynn and I arranged for Jet and Kierney to be kidnapped by members of the Australian SAS forces. They were nine and seven years old at the time. Lynn'd been sent to self-Defence classes as a child, and we did the same for our children.

'They needed to learn how to protect themselves when we weren't around, so we gave them a few tests over the years. They were abducted from school and taken to a building in Melbourne's CBD. Then they had to negotiate with their captors and communicate back to us where they were. It worked a treat.'

Greenshaw's expression was a picture. Now reminded of the episode, Gerry laughed so loud that his client could hear him from downstairs in his little wooden box. The public gallery was alive with chatter, but this time nobody burst into applause. Guessing he was skating on thin ice with Her Honour, the outspoken witness glanced over, ready to receive another warning for holding her court in contempt.

Seeing only wry amusement on the woman's face, Jeff made a mental note to thank whoever had thought to leave this somewhat misleading piece of information on file; Cathy, no doubt, simply being her usual thorough and helpful self. He too tried to hide a smile as he imagined the Defence team pouncing with glee on this priceless piece of evidence, eager to prove his negligence.

The tormented soul ought to have known his pleasure would be short-lived, given his current location and the reason he was there. Sure enough, the indefatigable Miss Irony soon reminded him that he had failed to protect Lynn when it mattered, and a combination of fierce, negative emotions washed through him instead.

'I'm sorry, angel,' he muttered under his breath, wiping his eyes.

Counsel for the Defence had regrouped again, his gown now flapping wildly in the witness' direction. 'Thank you, Mr Diamond,' he said through gritted teeth. 'I expect you now wish your children had chosen the sixteenth of February to get their own back on their parents.'

An awkward silence descended on the courtroom, no-one quite able to believe what they had heard. Winton instantly raised an objection to the Defence lawyer's tactless remark, and the sympathetic judge turned to address the insulted witness, about to issue a warning to her learned friend, only to be met with another unexpected reply.

'That's very good, Senior Counsel,' the statuesque star dealt them a half-smile and raised one eyebrow. 'Something I might well have said myself... You're right. Not an hour goes by that I don't hope to see Lynn jump out from behind the scenes to tell us it's all a big joke.'

Up above, Kierney turned to her dad's manager, who had cringed at his former school-friend's hurtful jibe before chuckling at the great man's admirable retort under pressure.

'That weird sense of humour finally came in handy,' she sounded relieved. 'Mr Floaty's got a mean streak.'

The executive nudged his young charge. 'Shhh! You're just like your dad, my girl,' he pretended to scold her. 'Mr Floaty indeed!'

'Sorry. The Honourable Mr Floaty. My mistake.'

Gerry laughed, looking back down at his friend patiently waiting on his feet for Greenshaw's next salvo. Once the public gallery had recovered from this latest loop in the rollercoaster, the judge gave a nod to the opposing bench.

'Mr Diamond, you mentioned earlier in your testimony that your relationship with your wife was in transition,' the barrister asked, drawing quotation marks in mid-air around the last two words. 'Would you please explain to the court what you meant by this?'

The witness drew breath, blindsided by another question that was open to interpretation. 'I'm not sure what you're referring to, Counsel. I mentioned that our life was in transition. I wasn't referring to our relationship *per se*.'

The barrister scowled. 'Please explain what you mean by "in transition", Mr Diamond.'

His tattoo irritated so suddenly and so severely that it caught the widower by surprise. He couldn't help reaching his right hand up and scratching the front of his shirt, behind his open suit jacket. Lynn had second-guessed Greenshaw's motive accurately too, and he allowed himself a gloating smile.

'Our life was in transition,' he said, repeating the lawyer's hand movements, 'because our daughter had finished school and was heading off to university, which meant we were free to pursue activities that didn't need one of us to be home most of the time.

'As any parent of teenagers must agree, to have both children achieve independence presents chances for greater freedom for the parents too. What I meant is that we were exploring how our life might change.'

Greenshaw rubbed his chin, his guile working overtime. 'Did it concern you that you might lose your dominance in this transition?' he said, emphasising the word again. 'Is it fair to say you're a man who enjoys being the centre of attention, Mr Diamond?'

Takes one to know one, Jeff thought, determined not to bite.

'Not at all, Your Honour,' he responded. 'I would've been only too pleased to see Lynn branch out and find fulfilment in ways that don't wreak havoc on her physically. There'd be many around us who'd say Lynn's the dominant force in our partnership anyway, and I never had a problem with that. If you're going to suggest I had her rubbed out because I was worried she'd steal my thunder, you cannot be more wrong, sir.'

Winton rose to his feet. 'Objection!'

His cry was drowned out, however, by whistles and remonstrations erupting from the gallery, where men and women alike were keen to support their hero. While the court officer attempted to quieten them down again, the showman cast his mind back to the number of times he had invited his wife, his children or his friends on stage. It was actually a welcome relief to have the spotlight turned on someone else for a change.

'Counsel for the Prosecution,' the judge shouted above the din. 'Ladies and gentlemen, please be silent and allow Counsel to state the Crown's objection.'

'Thank you, Your Honour. I was about to remind my learned colleague that this Witness is not on trial. The police investigation into his wife's murder has cleared him of any involvement.'

Rosemary Milne hesitated for a moment. 'Sustained, Mr Winton,' she said. 'I hope, Mr Greenshaw, that your line of questioning will lead us back to the Defendant.'

'It does, Your Honour.'

'Excellent. Then please proceed.'

Gerry caught his client's gaze and shook his head. The intellectual responded with a subtle shrug and a half-smile, as if to bid his manager not to worry. A momentary lapse of control had allowed Graham to reinforce the word "murder" in the jury's psyche, and he was inclined to trust the power of innuendo over statements of the bleeding obvious in present company.

'Do you own a gun, Mr Diamond?' Counsel for the Defence rounded on his witness once more.

'No, I don't, Your Honour.'

The courtroom had been drawn in again. This new angle was most intriguing, and Jeff reassessed the jury's level of attention. They were on the edges of their seats.

'Have you ever owned a firearm?'

'No, Your Honour.'

'Did your wife ever own any type of firearm?'

'No, she does not,' the widower stressed, still unable to accept references to Lynn in the past tense. 'She's still a legal entity as far as her assets are concerned, and neither of us owns weapons of any sort.'

Quite apart from this outlandish suggestion, the world-renowned peacemaker was perplexed as to the point of this follow-up question. Was the Defence team proposing the victim might have taken action to defend herself? Outdraw García in some sort of freakish shoot-out? Why not? One good gun deserved another, or some such preposterous gun-lobby notion. And then perhaps he could have burst heroically through the revolving doors and put a slug into Juan Antonio's back, in true Clint Eastwood style. The affable Irishman had been right to compare the scene to a spaghetti western after all...

Jeff's afflicted mind filled with the strains of "The Sun Won't Shine", and he struggled to extricate himself from this disturbing daydream. His *regala* was not amused, and she was correct. He apologised once more with a deep sigh.

Greenshaw's disgust at receiving yet another put-down was plainly audible and in perfect contrast to the clasped hands of a friendly woman in the front row of the jury. Again, Rosemary Milne cast a stern shadow on her Defence Counsel, confirming the witness' earlier antics had been forgiven. He had worked his magic on the presiding judge, with a little help from the hapless solicitor, which went some way to counteracting the sadness now permeating through his mind.

'My error, Mr Diamond.'

'And nor do our kids own guns,' the celebrity added, dismissing the lawyer's apology.

You're clutching at straws, mate, he heard Gravity's familiar sneer inside his head. Regardless, his point had been well made, if the shuffling of bodies on seats and the sympathetic murmuring in the courtroom were anything to go by.

'Please could you tell the court, Mr Diamond, why you do not employ bodyguards to protect you and your wife from potential threats, like other well-known showbusiness personalities?'

Jeff nodded. This was a better question.

'Of course, Your Honour. Mainly because we want to lead as normal a life as we can, within reason obviously... We took the view that we didn't want to always be hidden away behind tinted windows or surrounded by a force-field of security guards on the off-chance some madman would take us out. We took calculated risks, and we paid the highest price. Was it a mistake? Who knows? We lived a very happy and wide-open life for over twenty years, but eventually the laws of probability caught up with us.'

'So,' the Defence lawyer asked with a renewed glint in his eye, 'are you saying you share the blame for your wife's death?'

'Objection!' Winton blurted out again. 'The witness is not to blame for the Accused's actions.'

Kierney inhaled, knowing how much these words would cut into her dad's heart. She gripped Gerry's hand, waiting for his reply.

'Overruled,' the judge agreed. 'I'll allow your question, Mr Greenshaw.'

Jeff raised his hand, indicating he was prepared to answer this question too. 'Yes, Your Honour. I'm saying we took calculated risks,' he replied, outwardly unmoved but inwardly imploding. 'I share the blame for her death but I don't share the blame for her being killed. Many of us, including me and Lynn herself, failed to keep her alive. But we didn't kill her.'

Another huge gasp echoed around the room as its congregation deciphered the celebrity's crystal clear message.

'Mr Diamond,' Judge Milne redirected, sensing the intelligent man's distinction warranted repeating, 'please could you repeat your answer for the jury?'

'Yes, certainly, Your Honour,' Jeff agreed, his voice cracking as he endeavoured to contain his grief. 'I said I share the blame for my wife's death but not for her being killed. By this I mean that anyone who knowingly takes a risk must share the blame for what they're risking. We're all accountable for the consequences of our actions, aren't we? It's the fundamental duty that comes with the privilege of being alive.'

The renowned world-changer paused to let the jury process his last few sentences while Winton and Greenshaw exchanged respectful shrugs. 'Lynn and I... Either of us could've died in any number of ways, and we risked this every day. We all do, don't we? A plane crash could orphan our children, or a head-on collision between two cars... I could easily have died a few years ago in an ambush in eastern Africa, in fact. Our house might've caught fire while we were asleep. I'm prepared to say I share the blame for Lynn's death, and so does she. But I had no part in her killing.'

The lonely figure stared toward the jury through tearful eyes. All twelve were nodding, some weeping and some resolutely expressionless. All twelve had understood his point.

'Oh, *papá*,' Kierney cried too. 'Don't do it to yourself. You don't have to take the blame. It was beyond your control.'

Gerry put a reassuring arm around his friend's daughter and cuddled her into his side. This time, the public gallery applauded their idol again, and he drew much-needed strength from their adoration. His nerves were fraying, his tattoo hadn't stung in ages, and he was reaching the limit of his composure. He longed to be back in the wood-panelled meeting room with the ones he loved. Perhaps Lynn might be in there waiting for him too?

Jeff sniffed and stared down at his shoes, breathing slowly, desperate for a sign his wife's spirit was still in the vicinity. He heard Greenshaw's voice, now subdued.

'Your Honour, I have no further questions for the Witness.'

The judge nodded and checked if the prosecution team wished to redirect. Her request was declined, so the court officer took her cue, declaring an end to proceedings until nine o'clock the following morning.

The atmosphere in the courtroom remained electrified as the stunned crowd rose to its feet and waited for the officials to leave their respective benches. Winton approached the witness box and extended his hand to the celebrity, who was reeling from the last hour's emotional upheaval.

'Thank you, sir,' the seasoned barrister said. 'That was one of the most effective witness examinations I've seen. You were absolutely right about using and abusing words for sport! A gold medal performance, sir.'

Jeff smirked, turning away from an embarrassed, tear-stained clerk who was having trouble unbolting the gate to his enclosure. 'You're welcome, Graham. And thank you too. Is that it? I'm spent. Can I re-join my daughter, who's probably at her wits' end right now?'

Stepping in to help the struggling young fan, the prosecution lawyer freed the tall, dark superstar and motioned for him to walk ahead of him through the side door. 'By all means. You're free to return to the audience for the rest of the show.'

'Very funny,' the entertainer responded with a bitter laugh, immediately heading for the arboretum and pulling out his telephone to ask Gerry and Kierney to meet him there.

'Mr Diamond?' Graham called after him.

'Ah, yeah?'

'Would you and your party do us the honour of having dinner with me and my colleagues tonight?'

'My party? An odd choice of words from you too, under the circumstances,' the widower smiled. 'Is it kosher?'

'Absolutely. You're my Witness, and the Defence has deemed testimony to be complete. I could use some of your wordsmithing ideas for how to sum up for the jury. I'd love to pick your brain a little more on your everyman philosophy, because the jury will lap it up.'

Jeff frowned, remembering his promise to Gerry and Kierney that they would share a flavoursome and relaxing meal somewhere off the beaten track. 'Let me ask the others, if you don't mind. We'd sort of hoped to take it easy tonight. We were wondering about Coogee Beach for some hearty peasant fodder.'

'Excellent choice,' Graham approved. 'I'll wait to hear from you. I get the feeling tomorrow night will be too late.'

'Really?' the widower exclaimed. 'Over so soon? I was just starting to enjoy myself. D'you seriously think it'll wrap up tomorrow?'

'Can't say for certain, obviously, but we only have expert witnesses left. They don't normally take very long, and the jury's already made up their minds, I can tell.'

'I s'pose you can,' the sarcastic showman feigned respect. 'Let me ring Gerry now. Are Peter and Moira invited?'

'Yes, they will be. Most grateful. Thanks, Jeff.'

'Hey, mate. It's me,' the exhausted man announced on hearing his friend's voice. 'Where are you? You guys coming down for a ciggie? Yep. You bet I want to get out o'' here! I need to ask you and Kizzy something about tonight though. I've had a proposition from the Prosecution. Cheers, mate. See you in a minute.'

Jeff ended the call, laughing at yet another base comment from his manager. 'Blake-san's on song,' he told the puzzled barrister. 'He asked if the Prosecution's proposition involves prostitution.'

'It can,' Winton nodded with a smile, 'if that's his thing. He did go to school with Greenshaw after all, so not atypical behaviour.'

Senior Counsel and star witness parted company, the grieving husband striding briskly towards the smoking zone, deep in thought. Several people shouted out to him, and he dismissed them with the barest of acknowledgements.

'Did you hear that, angel? Only one day to go, maybe,' he said into the smoky air, lighting up and ingest a long hit of nicotine. 'You don't have long to wait 'til you find out the little bastard's fate. I hope it goes the way you want.'

With no return message received, Jeff perched on the low wall and waited for the others to arrive. He reflected on his performance in the witness box, wondering whether he was right to pursue such direct engagement with the jury members. It wasn't his case, as Miss Irony never failed to remind him, yet if he hadn't represented those he loved, who would have?

Winton and company weren't paid to push the victim's barrow. Their mission was to convict on behalf of the Commonwealth. Who benefitted from this? The theory proffered safer streets for the average person, he supposed, which was all well and good for the broadest of all constituencies...

The automatic glass doors to the segregated area slid open to allow his daughter to run at him as if she had lost ten of her years. The handsome man stood up, and she tore straight into his arms, crying with relief that they had reached the end of another day.

'*Papá*, I'm so glad to see you,' Kierney yelped, kissing him on the lips. 'Are they finished with you now?'

Jeff laughed aloud, fending off her wild attempts to embrace him. 'Yes, indeed. They're finished with me. Well and truly. Greenshaw never wants to lay eyes on me ever again.'

'Mr Floaty, you mean,' Gerry interjected.

'Who?'

Kierney smiled. 'I call Mr Greenshaw "Mr Floaty" because of the way his gown looks like wings levitating him.'

'I see,' her father impersonated Graham Winton's pompous tone. 'Of course, Miss Diamond. Quite so.'

'How are you going?' his manager asked, offering an opened packet of cigarettes to the pair and their trusty bodyguards. 'That was quite a show you put on.'

'Jesus, mate,' the witness moaned. 'What was I s'posed to do? I wasn't going to let Mr Floaty trample all over me. Did they ring you about that kidnapping file?'

'No!' Gerry chuckled, shaking his head. 'What a classic! I'd forgotten all about it and was initially as shocked as the rest of the gallery. He must've been mighty pissed off when you had an answer for everything. So what's this proposition, mate?'

'Ah, yeah... Winton wants to have dinner with us,' Jeff began, 'to pick my brain about how to sum up. He reckons the trial's going to finish tomorrow.'

'Tomorrow?' Kierney exclaimed. 'That fast? Wow! That'd be so good.'

'It would,' the tired widower agreed. 'Anyway... I told him we'd planned to go somewhere quiet to veg' out, and he wants to bring the whole crew. Peter and Moira, I mean. It'd be good for you to have somebody to talk to who's not a geriatric, Kizzo.'

Gerry took umbrage. 'Speak for yourself, you bastard! Geriatric? I've just got engaged. I'm in my prime, I'll have you know. What a bloody insult.'

'Was Peter good company earlier?' Jeff asked his daughter, winking.

'*Papá*, I'm going out with someone,' the young woman objected. 'Yes, he was friendly enough. Do *you* want to have dinner with Graham though? Aren't you sick of thinking about the trial?'

'Damned straight, I am,' the celebrity confirmed, squeezing his daughter's shoulder, 'but if we've only got one day left and I can help them with their closing arguments, it's worth doing. We'll have more of a chance of getting the outcome we want for *mamá*. Graham thinks the jury's already made up its mind, and there are only the expert witnesses left to call.'

The eighteen-year-old nodded. 'Alright. That sounds OK. I'll allow it.'

'You are in high spirits tonight,' her father remarked, saluting his daughter. 'Permission to call Counsel for the Prostitution, Your Honour?'

Kierney smacked her father across the chest. 'Permission granted.'

The superstar dialled Winton's number and prepared to leave a voicemail. 'Graham, it's Jeff Diamond. We're on for dinner, if you guys are. Let's meet at "*La Spiaggia*" on Arden Street in Coogee, across from the hotel. I think that's what it's called. We'll make a booking for six people, so let me know if that's not OK. Seven o'clock. Or earlier if you're drinking. Give me a ring when you get there. We'll be in the beer garden over the road, I expect.'

Jeff slotted his mobile telephone into his trouser pocket and lunged forward towards Kierney. He lifted her into the air and spun her round.

'Let's get out of here before my head explodes, gorgeous,' he roared. 'I need to buy you a Coca-Cola and this young buck here a few beers.'

EVERYMAN PHILOSOPHY

A summer storm hit Sydney's playground bays just after six o'clock, sending holidaymakers and evening swimmers scattering for shelter. The sky had borne down dark and ominous as the jaded trio caught a taxi back to their hotel from the Supreme Court. Heavy subtropical rain was falling steadily by the time they reached The Rocks.

After making sure Kierney was safe in her room next-door, Jeff stood under the shower and cried like a baby, letting the cool water rinse off the day and mix with his acrid, salty tears. He unthreaded his black jet-stone ring from the middle finger of his right hand and ran his thumb over its four dull stones, wondering what the following day might bring. Thinking beyond the next day only made him cry harder.

'What am I going to do once this dramatic diversion's over, Lynn?' he asked. 'Go home and wait? Why don't you come back? Everyone'll forgive you. They won't mind. I'm ready to have you back. So fucking ready, baby. Just tell me where you are, and I'll come and get you.'

Towelling himself dry, the widower picked up his watch to find that it was already six-thirty. No time for self-pity. They had to dine with the devil tonight. The telephone jangled on his bedside table.

'Hello?'

'*Papá*, are you OK?' came his daughter's sweet, caring voice.

'Yeah, gorgeous,' he hoped his positive sham wasn't too transparent. 'Ready for dinner? We'll have to go soon.'

'You didn't answer my question,' Kierney challenged. 'The truth, the whole truth and nothing but the truth, *papá*.'

'So help me, God,' Jeff completed the well-known saying, elongating each syllable.

'Thanks,' the youngster paused before she spoke, sounding painfully like her mother. 'That tells me how you're feeling quite nicely. May I come to your room, please?'

'Sure, baby. Give me two minutes to get some clothes on.'

She giggled. 'Oh, right! Sorry. I can wait.'

'No. We need to hurry anyway. See you shortly.'

This afternoon's star witness dressed in jeans and a clean shirt, selecting a pair of worn thongs that had flown so many times around the world that his feet slid straight into their indentations. He combed a few wayward strands of wet hair back from his face, checking the mirror-image of his sunken eyes and jutting cheekbones. Kierney would keep a close eye on him tonight, making sure he didn't merely push his food from one side of the plate to the other. He had to find an appetite from somewhere.

Gerry stood downstairs in the lobby, waiting for the pair as they stepped out of the lift. He was busy on the telephone, deep in conversation and catching up on the day's business. Also dressed casually, he raised a highball glass of golden nectar.

'Good-oh,' he said, swallowing down the rest of his beer as soon as he spotted the Diamonds. 'I'm glad we had the same idea about dressing down. I expect the others'll still be suited up, but what the hell.'

The celebrity shook his friend's hand. 'Yeah. I'm with you, mate. We're on holiday this evening, for what it's worth.'

'*Papá*,' the teenager said in a warning tone, 'please don't get too dark and sarcastic with them.'

'I won't, Kizzo. *On y va.*'

'*Qui mal y pense*,' she chimed, never tiring of the family's enduring nonsensical sayings.

'*Honnête soit qui parle de la dance*,' Jeff finished, grabbing his daughter's hand and twirling her in a circle.

He kissed the pretty young woman's forehead, sharing a high-five for good luck, and the threesome set off to flag down another taxi. Outside the hotel entrance, the widower broke into a cold sweat as he re-lived the encounter with García yet again.

His panic attack was swiftly brought under control however, when a group of journalists ran towards him from an unmarked station wagon which had pulled up in the driveway. Once more, he found himself surrounded by microphones and being bombarded with questions.

Their manager did his best to disperse the mob, but there were too many of them. Changing tack, he grabbed the door of the first empty taxi to appear from around the corner, ushered Kierney inside and leant into the open passenger window to give the driver some directions.

After a selection of non-committal, throwaway lines, the superstar convinced the enthusiastic reporters that he was serious about having no comment to make. Breaking away at the first opportunity, he jogged to the waiting car, jumped into the rear seat next to his daughter and slammed the door, grumbling at his soaked shirt and slippery feet.

'Mr D,' the Irishman joked from the front, using his most accurate Defence Counsel impression, 'do you normally employ bodyguards to assure the safety of your family and your esteemed manager?'

'Fuck you, Mr Bloaty,' his client answered through gritted teeth. 'If you can see your way clear to getting us to dinner, I'd be obliged.'

The businessman chortled, supervising the taxi's path as it wove its way through the busy Oxford Street traffic, weaving its way towards Randwick and the coast. He made small-talk with the driver, who was new to Australia and had no idea where Coogee Bay was. Fortunately, the new arrival didn't realise he was carrying Jeff and Kierney Diamond in his cab either; a blessed relief for all three passengers.

The songwriter tipped his head back and held a hand out to his pretty travelling companion. Tears rolled down his cheeks, but neither spoke until Gerry asked for Winton's telephone number.

'Hello. Is that Graham? Gerry Blake here. Very good, thanks. You? Apologies, but we're running a bit late. Yes. See you in there. Great. Thanks, Graham.'

The anonymous white vehicle pulled up outside an Italian restaurant not far from the beach. While his manager paid the fare, Jeff stood in the rain, holding the door open while Kierney shuffled across from the far side.

'Go in, *papá*. You're getting wet again,' she shouted. 'I'm fine.'

Her father didn't move, instead crooking his arm to escort the eighteen-year-old to dinner. She giggled and shook her head in mock frustration, slotting her hand through the gap and clinging to his side.

The prosecution team had already ordered their drinks and were seated at a circular table in the back section of the crowded establishment. Jeff steered Kierney subtly into the vacant chair to the left of Peter Yun, who stood up as the young woman took her seat.

'Sorry we're late,' the songwriter said, shaking each hand before sitting down next to Gerry. 'I was sick of the suit and tie. Hope you don't mind.'

'Not at all,' Graham replied, signalling for some service. 'I'd have done the same in your position.'

A waitress arrived with menus, blushing crimson as she carefully wrote a drinks order for the famous newcomers. The teenager played it safe in the company of legal eagles and ordered an orange juice. She smiled as her father put on a sad face. Placing their food orders soon afterwards, they were left alone to set about winding down after a long, stressful day.

'So, who do you barrack for, Peter?' the billionaire asked, shouting across the table. 'Are you a footy fan?'

'Yes, definitely,' the young man confirmed. 'I go for the Roosters but also like AFL. I was born in Adelaide.'

'Adelaide?' Gerry parrotted. 'Poor you! You're a Crows man, then?'

Junior Counsel nodded. 'Yes. But we didn't even make the finals last year.'

'I know,' Jeff chuckled. 'I'm a Richmond supporter. We put you out. And the Roosters missed the finals this year, too. Bad year for you, mate.'

'You can talk!' Gerry teased his old friend. 'Where did the Eels come, pray? Second from bottom, I do believe.'

'More beer?' the avid sports fan quipped, turning around and waving to the waitress, who came running straight over.

'Do you follow AFL, Kierney?' Peter asked.

'I like it,' the dark-haired gipsy girl replied, 'but I don't really barrack for anyone. We're supposed to support Melbourne and my uncle, but they didn't do too well last year either. I like Essendon, but that's mostly 'cause I like Matthew Lloyd.'

Everyone laughed. Moira, who had hardly said a word up to this point, suddenly came alive in wholehearted agreement with the youngest Diamond. Jeff shot Gerry a relieved glance. Mission accomplished, he thought. It was a relief to see their ruminative companion relax and focus on something other than her dad for once.

Their entrées arrived, replacing conversation with desultory sounds of appreciation. The three solicitors were famished after their day in court. Graham seemed especially tired, content to take a back seat while the friendly banter floated along. Jeff found himself hungrier than he expected, receiving a grin from Kierney when he exaggerated the clatter of his fork onto an empty plate.

'So, sir...' the well-spoken senior partner began, picking up the wine bottle and passing it round for everyone to refill their glasses, 'where in Sydney did you grow up?'

'Me? Canley Vale on Sea,' the billionaire replied to a row of quizzical looks. 'It's a well-kept secret. Paradise of the west.'

Kierney frowned at the first piece of quirky sarcasm for the evening. Her father flashed impish eyes to tell her not to worry. Moira and Peter laughed, never in their lives having set foot in such a run-down neighbourhood.

'But your songs say you were born in New York,' the Scotswoman piped up. 'I always thought you were.'

'No, ma'am,' Jeff shook his head, putting on the east-coast drawl. 'Poetic licence, I'm afraid. My dad was born in New York, but that has no bearing on anything. What about you? Scottish parents?'

'Yes. I'm an immigrant,' the flushed redhead demurred. 'I was only two when we moved out from Glasgow. I don't remember living in Scotland at all. Only from photos.'

'Haven't you been back since?' Kierney asked.

'No. My parents really love Australia and they've pretty much left Scotland behind,' Moira explained. 'My grandparents love to come out here for holidays, and my aunts, uncles and cousins too, so they'd far rather visit us in the sunshine than have us travel to the cold and wet. I do want to visit though, in the next few years...'

Jeff nodded. 'You should. Glasgow's a great city these days. How about you, Graham? Where's your family from?'

'Sixth generation Australian. New South Wales through and through. Some farmers, a couple of doctors. Nothing remotely exciting. English originally, of course, way back.'

'And now a lawyer,' the teenager added. 'That's exciting. I'm fascinated by the legal process. Do you always represent the Queen?'

'Exclusively, yes,' Senior Counsel answered the well-mannered starlet. 'Two of my brothers are also lawyers, and two of my children. My daughter's just started working for Greenshaw's firm actually, which is a touch awkward at the moment.'

The peacemaker laughed. 'I bet. Interesting dinner conversations. Are all their staff issued with gowns that defy gravity?'

Kierney swallowed down a mouthful of water, trying not to spit it everywhere. Her dad winked at her, which only made matters worse.

'Gowns that defy gravity? What do you mean?' Graham asked, perplexed by the mirth around the table.

'We've nicknamed him Mr Floaty,' Gerry joined in. 'Haven't you noticed he's constantly on the move? So far we've had Mr Fruity and Mr Floaty. Who've we got tomorrow?'

'Mr Fruity?' Peter exclaimed. 'Who was that?'

'Karl Fruchtmann, the doorman at The Pensione,' the showman clarified. 'We have to do something to break the monotony up in the public gallery, y'know. You guys need to include a few song and dance routines into your show to entertain us better.'

'Yes, well...' the older solicitor scoffed. 'You certainly livened things up this afternoon, I must say.'

Jeff raised his hand to the weary barrister. 'Yeah. Sorry about that. I have a certain propensity to create havoc.'

'And you do it so well,' Counsel for the Prosecution admitted. 'As someone whose whole career depends on getting an argument across to a wide cross-section of the community, I've never met anyone who can work a crowd quite like you can.'

'Cheers,' the modest star sighed. 'I have to admit it's served me well.'

Their main courses were delivered to the table, and they ordered two extra bottles of wine. As conversation lulled again, the widower's appetite deserted him with the thought of how his success had not always served him well. Sometimes it was a double-edged sword, and the very reason why they sat in this restaurant this evening.

He wondered how many more jealous working-class men there were out there, dissatisfied with their lives and picked on by their wives, over whom he had unknowingly woven his magic spell. A tragic spell, he corrected himself, allowing himself a smile at the pun he couldn't repeat for fear of upsetting his daughter.

His dignified pride and joy appeared cheerful. Every now and again, she looked over to make sure he was still eating, but it had been a good move to seat her with the junior prosecutors. Such role models should be taken advantage of whenever possible, given the level of ambition she held at this impressionable stage in her life.

Jet had never been impressionable, the father recognised. He was dedicated and single-minded, with a strong sense of self inherited from his mother. Kierney, on the other hand, was a sponge, keen to soak up any and every new experience, without fear and sometimes without regard for the boundaries normally imposed on minors. This was entirely his fault.

Graham Winton cleared his throat and fixed today's witness with a firm stare. *Here we go*, the intellectual mused. The brain-picking season was about to be declared open.

'Has this trial been more-or-less what you expected?'

The world-changer frowned, pausing for a moment to think of a sensible response to such a closed but open-ended question.

'Yes and no,' the confident teenager interrupted, giggling. 'That's what he'd normally say in answer to that question.'

Her dad pointed a menacing index finger at the young comedian, and she feigned shame, picking up her napkin and wiping her mouth.

'That's enough, young lady,' he scolded, before taking a deep breath. 'Yes and no.'

Laughter erupted right around the table, except from Kierney, who cringed at the predictability of his response.

'See what I mean?' the barrister chuckled. 'That's a skill not many of us possess. Timing, I suppose, but it's more than that.'

'Enough, already,' Jeff replied, anxious to deflect this blatant attempt at massaging his ego. 'It is "Yes and no" actually. The trial process and the format, and the aspect of the courtroom... that's all pretty standard. But being in the witness box was a huge trip. At one point, my mind was doing its best to convince me you were Michael Parkinson, and I was there to promote my latest album, slash book, slash concert tour.'

The whole table burst out laughing again.

'At least you didn't break into song,' Gerry teased. 'That's what I was waiting for.'

Moira agreed. 'Yes! And half the gallery. And the jury, probably.'

'A bit like "Sister Act",' Kierney added. 'Although you're not quite Whoopi Goldberg.'

'Gee, thanks, Kizzo,' her dad whined. 'Not sure if that's a compliment or not.'

Graham sat with his knife and fork resting on each side of his plate, keen to bring the discussion back to the trial. The grieving husband had hardly touched his main course, and the affable accountant noticed the youngster's frequent sideways glances.

'Oi, Whoopi,' Gerry commanded, pointing at the full bowl of pasta. 'Shut up and eat your dinner. You need your strength for tomorrow.'

'Thank you, Gerry,' Kierney smiled from across the table. 'Well said.'

'Thanks, Dad. Thanks, Mum,' the songwriter griped, loading a large mound of food onto his fork, shoving it into his mouth and swallowing it down without even tasting it. 'How's it all going from your perspective, Graham?'

Peter and Moira turned to their boss, inquisitive for his impressions now they were almost off-duty.

'Well... It was always going to be interesting,' Winton began. 'It's one of those cases you know will be overly complicated by public opinion.'

'Welcome to our life,' the celebrity scoffed.

'Yes. I don't doubt that,' Senior Counsel acknowledged. 'When our firm was appointed, we held a partners' meeting to decide who we'd put on the team. I was in two minds whether to volunteer, but in the end I was glad to take it. I selected Moira because she was the only female who didn't come begging to me, so I thought she would be the most impartial, but she called my bluff soon afterwards.'

'By saying she deliberately hung back?' Jeff asked, smiling at the flame-haired lawyer.

'Exactly,' Graham confirmed. 'And Peter'd just come off a long fraud case which was dry and tedious, so I thought this would be more straightforward for him.'

'And is it?' Kierney asked the young man to her right.

'No! It's turned out to be heaps more involved than I originally thought,' the confident junior shook his head and smiled. 'A man had confessed to a murder, and the police recovered a weapon with his fingerprints on it from the scene. What could be more straightforward than that?'

Wine glass in hand, Gerry guffawed. 'Did you know who the victim was at this time?'

'Watch it, mate,' said victim's husband cautioned.

'Sorry,' the businessman frowned, the alcohol going to his head a little. 'Go on, Senior Counsel, please.'

Graham continued. 'Yes. We knew which case it was alright. Not many come to us direct from the Attorney General's office. And we knew the circumstances of the murder from all the publicity. Our whole office was numb for a week after your wife passed away, Jeff. She was a wonderful woman.'

The great man leant back in his chair, shaking his napkin. 'That she was,' he said, looking at his daughter in sympathy. 'Still is. More than you know.'

'It was clearly going to be an emotionally charged trial, and we didn't know if you'd want to testify, so we were very pleased when you agreed to. The other partners and I took the view that we couldn't do any harm by...'

The portly man paused to select the most appropriate words.

'By jumping on the bandwagon?' Jeff finished his sentence.

Winton shrugged, embarrassed. 'Yes. I suppose so. It was a case that would generate almost exclusively ill feeling towards the Defendant, which is fairly rare.'

The widower didn't much care to humiliate the senior partner in front of his protégés after the arduous day they had all endured. 'I guess the Queen needs good publicity too. At least the court heard the Victim Impact Statement early,' he recalled. 'That was good. Taking the stand was not an opportunity to feel sorry for myself, as far as I was concerned. I've lost my best friend and the only woman to have shared my bed for more than twenty years. My kids have lost their mother and teacher extraordinaire too. But they're not the only reasons why I was in the witness box today. I was actually glad to be called for more technical reasons, i.e. to establish how García had been apprehended.'

Kierney reached her left hand past the empty setting between herself and her father. He took it gladly, brimming with emotion again.

'Thanks, gorgeous,' he croaked.

'Of course,' Graham insisted. 'But it was important that you had the opportunity to show what Lynn's loss means to you. People genuinely want to know how you are. My wife asks after you constantly: "How's he coping? How are the children? It must be awful."'

Jeff smiled. 'Yep. I get it. Thank her for us, please.'

'Certainly,' the barrister nodded. 'Today the jury had the chance to see your face and share your grief. The trial means much more to them now.'

'Yeah. That was exactly my plan,' the talented negotiator agreed. 'Having me and García facing off in opposing boxes must've been pretty confronting for them. Do they get the chance to talk to anyone about that?'

'They can request time with either representation,' Counsel confirmed. 'It hasn't been requested yet. We normally get called in for clarification of detail rather than for psychological support.'

'For you, Jeff,' Peter asked out of the blue, 'what's the nub of the argument? Is it the fact that the Accused claims he didn't know what he was doing when he pulled the trigger?'

His boss glared at the young man's impudence, but their witness was ready to answer any question, no matter how tricky. He was willing to bare his soul if it helped the Queen's team gain a better understanding of the crime.

'Absolutely, mate,' he responded, leaning forward and putting his elbows on the table either side of his half-eaten dinner. 'The before... the years of hate and jealousy... and the after... the outpouring of grief, the witnesses' testimonies and all the evidence being presented in this trial... All that's only useful background info', isn't it? The way I see it, your job in this trial is to determine beyond doubt what happened between the before and the after. The act itself. Was there intent at that precise moment in time?'

Newly energised, Jeff pinched his thumb and index finger together in front of his face, relishing the sensation of friction on his fingertips. 'It's in that tiny slither of time when the principal offence García's charged with actually took place. The rest is filler. Elevator music. Did he intend to kill Lynn when he pulled the trigger? Yes or no? Not before and not after.'

Peter nodded in furious admiration of the direct way his point was being validated. The skilled orator turned to the senior partner, fired up by the liberating experience of talking about the trial from his viewpoint. And from the victim's, hopefully.

'Lynn used to say that knowledge is the what, who, when and where, whereas wisdom is the how and why. Wisdom gained about the before and after can give us insight into the how and why, but that's pretty much redundant for trial purposes, isn't it? We need to focus solely on our knowledge of the facts; i.e. the who, what, where and when of her murder.

'No amount of acquired wisdom can have any bearing on securing a conviction. The machinations of a wise mind can help us, but it's also dangerous to stray from what the evidence is telling us and into conjecture. The judge pulled me up on it this afternoon, did you hear?'

Lines of intense concentration etched into Graham's face gave Jeff the distinct impression that he was about to earn his supper.

'Am I making sense?' he asked the table. 'In other words, the witnesses have fed the jury some of the hows and whys, so your closing statements should cement all that by focussing them back on the irrefutable facts. In my opinion, that is.'

'Understood,' the older lawyer acknowledged. 'Carry on, please.'

Seldom had encouragement been needed for the mesmeric intellectual to air his theories, and he smiled at his own affrontery. 'At the precise moment when he went to pull the trigger, we all heard the little bastard tell us he didn't know what to do. No point trying to understand why. Only he can know why, and it appears he's not smart enough to figure it out. He had the choice to do nothing or something. I wish he'd chosen to do nothing, but he didn't. Unfortunately for everyone, including himself, he chose to do something.'

The man at the centre of everyone's attention caught his breath and winced. 'Excuse me, please, guys. I have to go.'

He gave a sly thumbs-up sign to Kierney, who watched her father's tall frame straighten up above the other diners. He threw his napkin down roughly onto his chair and strode towards the back of the restaurant.

'Should I follow him?' Gerry asked the wide-eyed teenager.

'No. He's OK, thanks,' she reassured the table of startled onlookers. 'He just needs to get rid of the pent-up emotion. He wants to talk but he's sick of crying in front of people.'

Thankfully, the gents' toilets were empty when Jeff reached them, and he stood at the urinal, dizzy and desperately unhappy.

Why were they even having this discussion?

The love of his life wasn't meant to be the victim in a Supreme Court murder trial, and Australia's top-selling rock musician sure as hell didn't plan on being a widower at forty-three.

He hadn't signed up for this gut-wrenching heartache when he moved his small world from Sydney to Melbourne at the tail-end of 1971, a nineteen-year-old university student chasing a hot, blonde tennis champion who sang as if she gave a damn.

Not even what he had envisaged when the iconic Jeff Diamond brand joined forces with Lynn Dyson's gold-plated career in London three years later, taking the entire globe by storm and catapulting their growing family into so many halls of fame.

And not now either, after the country's favourite couple had worked so hard and accomplished so much, on the cusp of a significant and alluring change of direction.

What had happened two years ago to make this run-of-the-mill citizen drive to Mildura and buy a gun? The start of the "Live on Earth" tour? He and Lynn had dominated the headlines regularly around that time. Looking back, it was difficult to remember a time when they weren't in the news for something or other... Perhaps there was no rhyme or reason behind García's decision.

Remembering the vibrant future human rights lawyer and United Nations diplomat he had selfishly abandoned in the restaurant, Jeff washed his hands and splashed cold water on his face, before walking out through the back door, into the laneway behind the restaurant kitchen. He lit a cigarette and stood under the eaves of a nearby building, staring into columns of steady rainfall.

His tattoo twinged again under what had been a crisp white shirt, unleashing another involuntary sob from the solitary smoker.

'Hey, angel. Welcome back,' he sniffed, blowing out a suggestive plume of smoke. 'Where've you been? I miss you so much.'

The billionaire cast his mind back to García's appearance in the witness box. The inconsiderable, pathetic man had told the court that, to his mind, envy was reason enough to kill.

Winton had a wife at home. Could he, as the bereaved husband, beg licence to kill either or both of them because they would at some point be in bed together, enjoying exquisite pleasures now denied to him? Skin against skin, lips against lips...

The door to the master bedroom in their North Shore mansion would soon be closed to muffle the excitement of mutual orgasms from the rest of the household. The kids, the dog, the cat... Whomever. Jeff was definitely envious of this. Almost envious enough to...

Snap out of it, the songwriter cursed under his breath, feeling familiar anger building up inside.

Yes, he understood perfectly what might drive someone to kill out of envy, but how could murder ever solve the problem at its root? Killing Winton or his wife wouldn't bring Lynn back, just as killing Lynn or even her husband wouldn't have turned García's life around. Such an act was futile; utterly pointless for all stakeholders except the legal firms and media magnates, as so often was the case.

Jeff folded his cigarette butt against the brick wall behind him and dropped it into a nearby rubbish bin. Walking back into the restaurant, he paused while a waitress cleared the plates from their table. Gerry had positioned his hand on her lower back, doubtless on the slippery pretext of requesting the dessert menu or more drinks. The sight turned the sad man's stomach again. Once the coast was clear, he sat down and emptied his half-full wineglass down his throat in a single gulp.

'Better?' the accountant asked.

'Yep. Guess so, thanks. Did I miss anything?'

'Just a lot of gossip behind your back,' Kierney smiled.

Her father shrugged. 'That's the chance one takes by disappearing, as your grandma'd say. Sorry, Graham. Where were we?'

'You're fine, Jeff,' Senior Counsel replied, unaware of the evil thoughts that had been given life in the laneway. 'We don't have to talk about the trial.'

'No way! I want to,' he objected. 'Unless it's not helping.'

'Oh, it is helping,' Peter insisted.

'OK, cool,' the celebrity drummed the table with the fingers of both hands. 'In that case... The other interesting thing García said was that, in his opinion, it was right to kill for the reasons he had. Envy, jealousy... Bitterness that my life was better than his... So, is he guilty of the crimes if he didn't believe what he did was wrong? Of course, on the surface, because the law's the law. But is he really? We all know a person can be morally wrong but legally right. Can it work the other way too?'

'*Crime de passion*, you mean?' Gerry interjected in his best Inspector Clouseau accent. 'That's the stuff of romantic songwriters and intellectual philosophers who like hanging out in Paris cafés.'

'Whatever, mate,' the superstar dismissed his manager's teasing with a friendly smile. 'But it's a complex dilemma, and the court's obliged to find the simplest of answers. Did he or didn't he? Yes or no? On or off? Black or white?'

Counsel for the Prosecution was already leaning forward, a question on the tip of his tongue. Jeff took another large sip of wine and cocked his head in the barrister's direction, bidding him to ask it.

'So yes, thanks. What I must ask you, if I may, is if you have this much compassion for the man who shot your wife, does this mean you can forgive him?'

'Forgive?' the lonely man echoed, somewhat taken aback. 'I'm not sure if I even know what the word "forgive" means, to tell you the truth.'

The rest of the table sat in silence, watching the great man's eyes raise up to the ceiling, as if summoning inspiration. '*Perdonar*,' he rolled around the Spanish side of his tongue. 'To pardon. Do I pardon his sins? Yeah. Maybe I might from a confessional point of view. He's not going to do it again in a hurry. But I couldn't forgive him in that sense until I heard genuine remorse. What's forgiveness in legal terms, Graham?'

The older man frowned and paused. 'You have me there, sir. I suppose I was more thinking in the religious sense than a legal sense too.'

'That's right,' the peacemaker chuckled. 'Emotions or spirituality don't figure in the law... Forgiveness in a legal sense would be more like being absolved, I'm guessing. No. Acquitted, rather. To be borne no malice. I can't do that, no. Every time I look into my little girl's eyes, I bear that bastard infinite malice.'

His daughter smiled in sympathy, wondering how comfortable her dad was to be pressed to pass judgement in public on the man who did away with the most important person in his life. She received a wink in return.

'In a religious sense, to me it means, "Are you prepared to let God take care of his sinning, punishment and repentance?" Maybe. I'm confident his conscience'll see to that.'

'Interesting...' Winton mused, fascination plastered all over his face.

The gaunt superstar's eyes filled with tears. 'Is it? I'm glad you think so. I won't forget though. That much I do know for sure. Depends on what I can be sure I'm forgiving him for... Do we really know what he did? And why? I'm not sure we have the right to forgive or not forgive without knowing the full story. And I'm not sure anyone but García can ever know the whole truth. Long answer to a short question, and it's not really an answer at all. Just a whole bunch more questions in the end. Sorry, guys.'

The charitable group all laughed, and Kierney reached for her father's hand again, recalling the conversation they had shared the previous evening.

'I see what you mean,' Peter filled the sudden silence. 'It's all relative. It depends on the context. Like rich or poor, for example. What's rich? A million dollars? A billion dollars? It depends what you want to use the money for. And what's poor? The difference between getting a guaranteed dole payment of two hundred dollars a week or having to beg for your next cup of soup.'

'Spot on, mate,' Jeff praised, lifting his glass to the Adelaide native. 'Also, what's an immigrant, for that matter? Someone who arrives here with just the clothes on his or her back, unable to speak the language? Or professional people from Glasgow?'

The widower's eyes filled with tears again, smiling at the redhead opposite. '"Wet weather refugees", as my gorgeous wife used to call them. Or someone who's been educated in a school that teaches English in Cambodia or Pakistan, a middle-class citizen who wants to live in a freer society? Everyone's situation is different, but our legal system'd go broke if we assessed each case on its individual merits.'

'Yes, I agree,' his daughter chimed in. 'As devastating as it is for us to lose *mamá*, García only killed one person. What about persecution and genocide of entire populations? Or a rogue gunman shooting indiscriminately in an American school? Who's the most guilty?'

'They're all guilty,' Graham informed the teenager in a patronising tone. 'The law can't be taken relatively, Kierney. It's absolute. Did they commit an act that contravenes a law? As your dad said, it's not about how or why? Did they or didn't they? Notwithstanding anything else happening around them that they may consider a worse act.'

Jeff's anger reignited at how the barrister shut his daughter down while she was learning how to interact in this type of company. 'We all know life isn't that simple, Counsel,' he sighed, casting a sympathetic wink towards Kierney. 'But I agree it's what you guys have to do in the next day or so. Guilty or not guilty. Has the Queen been wronged. No matter how much we want to, we can't focus on telling the jury why the act was so unnecessary and how pointless it was.

'For the purposes of this trial, you can't afford to give a shit about what the arsehole hoped to gain out of killing Lynn? Or even from making the rest of us suffer? One person's misfortune doesn't translate into another's happiness. All the stuff that life's really about... You can't. It's too much of a distraction. You just want a "Yes or not yes" decision. Not even "Yes or no," since the Queen's not interested in the shades in between. Beyond reasonable doubt. Black or not black.'

'Exactly,' Graham affirmed, holding so tightly onto his wine glass that it was in danger of shattering in his hands. 'But don't get me wrong, good people... Back in the office, we spend hours and hours asking philosophical questions about each case, so we get things clearer in our own minds on how we want to shape the prosecution. For example, if I may, Jeff...'

Accepting that they had restored him to a figurative witness box for the sake of Winton's role-play, the widower acknowledged the ruddy-faced lawyer in anticipation.

'Did you meet or correspond with the Accused prior to the sixteenth of February?' the wigless barrister posed.

'No, Your Honour. Not to my knowledge,' he answered with a half-smile. 'Not surprising, but authors of the crank letters we receive don't tend to identify themselves too readily.'

Everyone around the table chuckled at the unexpected light relief.

'Objection!' Kierney cried out, appealing to the young man to her right for assistance.

Her neighbour played along, although not quite to her liking. 'Objection overruled.'

'Why?' she asked, disappointed. 'I haven't even told you what it is yet!'

'The witness is not on trial here,' Peter deferred, embarrassed by his over-exuberance.

Winton pointed a finger at his associate. 'No, but...'

The trainee barrister tensed up, under considerable pressure from both boss and father to provide a courageous answer. 'Because Counsel asked... and the Witness answered... in the context of having prior knowledge that the Accused planned to kill him.'

The pretty teenager nodded, looking sideways at her dad. He could tell she was annoyed with herself that she hadn't understood this angle and dealt her a kind smile. Cruel lessons were the easiest to learn, but quite the hardest to watch.

'Were you pissed off at Greenshaw for taking a stab at you about blaming yourself?' Gerry changed the subject.

'Damned straight I was!' the proud man laughed. 'The bastard. But it could've been much worse. He hadn't asked the question philosophically back to his team, had he? Otherwise he might not have asked it at all.'

'Unless they assumed the jury wouldn't make the leap as to the difference between dying and being killed,' Winton surmised. 'Most people wouldn't, especially in a murder trial. Someone has died as a result of being killed. It's the same event from where they sit.'

Jeff nodded. 'The question I was more afraid of was, "Are you sure your sixth sense didn't inform you that something had happened to your wife when you first encountered the Accused?"'

'*Papá!*' Kierney exclaimed. 'Don't say something like that. It's worse than blaming yourself.'

'I know, baby,' her father agreed. 'That's what I mean. I wouldn't have had a good answer for that one, and I left myself wide open during your initial questioning, Graham.'

'You did,' the barrister confirmed, his previous hypothetical abandoned. 'It's always dangerous to presume you know something you can't reasonably know.'

'Can't reasonably know?' the poet echoed with an inquisitive look on his face. 'What does that mean? Surely your average juror understands the concept of instinct on some level? People understand gut feel, experience, judgement, or however you want to name the things we *just know*.'

He painted quotation marks in the air around the last two words.

'You can't prove you *just know* beyond reasonable doubt, I s'pose,' the bright student countered, copying her dad's gesture. 'At least, not someone else's reasonable doubt, because they don't know what you feel.'

'OK, sure. I can accept that. But does it mean courts shouldn't advise juries to accept that people trust their own instincts?'

'Yes. They ask the jury to focus on the indisputable facts,' Peter answered.

'Whoa!' Jeff feigned alarm, leaning back in his chair and twisting his wineglass up to the light. 'It's worse than I thought. There really is no room for the how and why. No wisdom required. So when you ask the jury to deliberate at the end of a trial, you expect them not to use their own judgement on the grey areas? If that were the case, you'd hardly ever get a unanimous verdict. What if there aren't sufficient indisputable facts?'

'We get unanimous verdicts because some people are more easily persuaded than others,' Graham replied.

'Or more persuasive,' Gerry added, pointing at his mate. 'I can just imagine you on a jury. Everyone'd just fall in line. You'd have them so bamboozled.'

'Grotesquely unfair, Blake-san,' the celebrity moaned, raising his glass to his loyal manager. 'Well... If that's the case, there's no justice in the justice system whatsoever. If twelve good men and true... twelve good persons and true, sorry ladies... don't represent twelve genuinely independent decisions, then as my learnt friend says, we're always at the mercy of dominant people.'

'So, *papá*... Here's a hypothetical for you,' Kierney offered, sitting up straight.

Jeff smiled. 'Oh, yeah? Go on then, Geoffrey Robertson.'

'What if you were the jury *Foreman* for García's trial...'

'As me or as someone else?'

'As Joe Bloggs,' the teenager clarified.

'Cool. OK, go for it, *pequeñita*.'

'And what if there were two jurors who had a gut feel that Jeff Diamond had conspired with Juan Antonio García to kill his wife?'

'Do you seriously want me to answer this question objectively?' the widower asked, not too comfortable with his daughter's newfound courage.

'Yes and no,' Kierney answered, as firm and compassionate as her beloved role model. 'Not if you don't want to.'

'Go on,' Jeff replied, sceptical and more nervous than he ought to be.

'Thanks. How would Joe Bloggs, i.e. you, try to come to a unanimous verdict without dominating?'

The great man countered with yet another question. 'Did Jeff Diamond really conspire to kill his wife?'

Gerry and Graham looked at each other, both keen to watch the pair go head to head.

'Of what relevance is this, please?' the young woman asked, giggling.

''Cause I want to know if the majority or the minority is right in your hypothetical.'

'But we never know that in advance,' Peter interjected.

'You do, mate,' Jeff contradicted him with a wry smile. 'You said so yourself earlier. You had a confession. He was wearing a holster, they found a weapon at the scene covered in his prints. It's a straightforward case.'

The young man shrugged in defeat and sat back.

'The majority is right,' Kierney answered, 'for the benefit of this exercise.'

'But even though we think we know the truth when the trial starts, we can't guarantee it'll still be true at the end,' Peter butted in again.

The father could sense the young woman becoming frustrated by her inability to control her own game. 'Geoffrey Robertson says the majority is right on this occasion,' he called everyone to order, 'in which case I'd ask my fellow jurors to re-examine the evidence bit by bit, and at each point vote "Guilty" or "Not guilty". As soon as there's a point of difference, they should stop to find out why.'

'That has the potential to take a bloody long time,' his manager interrupted.

'And?' came an abrupt retort. 'Does a twenty-five-year sentence wrongly handed down outweigh another day of the jury's time?'

'Unfortunately, therein lays another big issue with Australia's judicial system,' Winton lamented, breaking out of his tacit thrall. 'As I told you before, a murder trial is usually allotted two weeks. We're often under quite a bit of pressure to complete within the timeframe.'

'KLF, I hope you're listening to this,' Jeff addressed his daughter and waved his hand around the table. 'When you're changing the world, you'd better add this to the list. They'd have never dissolved minority rule in South Africa if we'd said, "Hurry up, guys. You need to make this decision by Tuesday, 'cause we need the room for Northern Ireland."'

The group laughed again. Gerry attracted the attention of the waiter and requested another bottle of wine and a round of coffees.

'Dessert?' he asked. 'Or is everyone too full?'

Moira and Kierney agreed the dessert menu would make for good reading.

'So, Jeff...' Graham prompted. 'What if your point-by-point deliberation still doesn't produce a unanimous verdict? You've been in there for a week, and there's been no ground gained on either side.'

'On either side, it would be a non-verdict, I s'pose,' the widower replied. 'Sad to say, García and Diamond walk free, Bloggs goes home furious and disillusioned, hoping he never gets called for jury service again. And you guys go home feeling frustrated, only to be subsumed into next week's case and forget all about it. You can go for a majority verdict when there's only one juror in dispute, can't you?'

'In certain circumstances we can, yes,' Prosecuting Counsel confirmed. 'It'd be up to the judge.'

'So what if the one remaining juror who still believes there was a conspiracy is actually right?' Kierney asked the table.

'It happens,' Peter admitted, grinning. 'Sometimes. Especially in the movies.'

The eighteen-year-old gave him an exasperated look and raised her hands. She couldn't be bothered to debate any longer, dismayed that the young Asian-Australian appeared destined to become as condescending as his boss. Their drinks and desserts arrived, and Gerry poured wine for those who were still drinking, predictably only himself and his VIP client. The prosecution team were due back at work early in the morning, and it was already ten o'clock.

'Art imitating life or life imitating art,' the accountant quipped. 'Take your pick.'

'So what was it like to be kidnapped?' Moira asked the famous teenager, changing the subject while tackling a large bowl of tiramisu.

'Very scary,' Kierney answered. 'We thought it was real, no doubt about that. The men had guns and ordered us around. Although, if we'd thought about it more... in hindsight, you know... there had been quite a lot of build-up to it. We just hadn't put two and two together.'

'Didn't you hate your parents for putting you through it?' Peter asked.

'No,' the youngster laughed, beaming at her dad. 'It was frightening at the time, and we didn't know if we'd ever see them again. But it gave us a huge high when we were reunited. Didn't it, *papá*?'

'Sure did, gorgeous,' Jeff replied. 'It was pretty scary for us too 'cause we weren't allowed to call it off if you didn't figure things out. We'd agreed to give ourselves a maximum of five days before we'd come and get you. It was incredibly stressful on us too! The guns weren't loaded, by the way... In case one of you'd got hold of one and taken matters into your own hands, Rambo-style.'

'Oh, my God!' Kierney cried. 'Does Jet know that? We wouldn't have had the guts to do it, anyway!'

It was the senior counsel's turn to ask a hypothetical. 'So, back to the trial for a second, please... If Greenshaw had pressed the issue of your having conspired with the Accused to have Lynn killed, how would you have defended yourself, out of interest?'

'Does this help you determine how you're going to sum up?' the suspicious man asked. 'It's an insinuation I'm not happy with, I have to say. It was bad enough from my daughter, but it's pretty offensive coming from you.'

'Apologies, Jeff,' Graham said. 'No offence intended. I'm interested to see how you'd approach convincing the jury there's no basis of truth to his supposition.'

'Alright. For the sake of hypotheticals, I can't resist,' the showman assented. 'I'd have to try, but there aren't any facts to call upon. It's purely my word against his, isn't it?'

'Indeed,' the barrister nodded, rubbing his hands together. 'Exactly. Thank you. Thanks very much.'

'I guess I'd be looking for prejudice to help me,' the handsome intellectual began, again taking Kierney back to the previous night's discussion. 'I'd be banking on the jury already *just knowing* I'm the type of bloke who does everything with the utmost sincerity and intensity. And Lynn too. If one or both of us no longer felt the same way about our relationship, we would've called it quits. I wouldn't have had her killed.'

Moira's mouth fell open, and her spoon stopped halfway between lips and bowl. All present were struck by the very sincerity and intensity that the star foreshadowed.

Fully expecting this reaction, he continued. 'And I'm a hundred percent sure Lynn didn't correspond with García with a view to having me killed either, by the way. But we can't ask her, so that's a fact that'll never be substantiated right there...'

'Jeff, can I interrupt you?' Graham requested, reaching for the jacket hanging on the back of his chair and delving into the inside pocket. 'Would you mind if we record you? I think there's a lot of mileage in hearing you speak like this. For the how and why, as you said.'

'Sure,' the great man agreed, 'if you think the inside view's helpful. Didn't we already conclude the how's and why's are pointless? It won't surprise you I'm as often misquoted as quoted, so why should this be any different? Hey, d'you remember the time, *pequeñita*, when someone wrote in a magazine that I de-oxygenate and then re-oxygenate my blood once a month to stay healthy and energetic?'

The young woman nodded, wondering where this old memory had come from.

'Now, I smoke between thirty and forty cigarettes a day and drink more alcohol and caffeine than water,' her father scoffed. 'D'you honestly think I'd put myself through that rigmarole when I top up my bloodstream with crap voluntarily every day?'

As the others frowned, the tattoo on Jeff's chest twitched again, and he smiled, rubbing his shirt to let Kierney share in the divine communication. He saw tears flood into her eyes and vowed to give Winton's hypothetical his best shot, for all their sakes.

'So, Counsel, my argument would be this: if Lynn's and my marriage had broken down, I'm certain we'd have had the maturity to honour each other's right to continue living, whether we'd want to or not.'

'Jesus, mate,' Gerry muttered, extending his right arm and resting it on the celebrity's shoulder. 'Nobody thinks that.'

'It's a hypothetical, Gez,' his client replied, beginning to cry again. 'We celebrated our twentieth wedding anniversary on New Year's Day this year; the happiest we'd ever been. How much more hypothetical does it get? We had another hectic year ahead of us, travelling heaps and building our various business and charitable interests. You know all this already, Kizzy.

'But more importantly, the Atlanta Olympics are on later this year, and they were to be Lynn's swansong as far as her professional sporting career's concerned. She was going to retire from competitive sports altogether after the Olympics, and we'd planned one hell of a holiday in October with the kids and some friends...'

Jeff put his head in his hands and took a few deep breaths. 'Sorry, everyone,' he said, pressing the heel of his hand into his pectoral muscle. 'A huge and extravagant vacation before we focused on launching the next chapter in our life. Jesus, we had a whole heap of awesome stuff left to do together, until that fucking spaniel arsehole, García, put a stop to everything.

'Lynn was contemplating going into politics; into the Senate to begin with. Even Australia's first president in a few years' time? Who knows? I was going to be immeasurably proud of her, that's all I know for sure.'

Gerry flipped open his packet of cigarettes, and the widower accepted one. Lighting it and blowing a plume of smoke upwards, he carried on.

'Y'see, guys, we never set ourselves any limits. That's what people like García will never understand. It was my turn to take the back seat after all these years in the limelight, with the kids all grown-up. Lynn now had the scope to do more. So much more. We always likened ourselves to the two halves of a pantomime horse, and she was keen to swap ends. It was my turn to be the arse-end.'

Peter and Moira checked with their boss for permission to laugh at this peculiar image. Graham was grinning, so they relaxed too. The emotional celebrity stirred three spoonful's of sugar into his coffee and took a gulp, eyes red and watery.

'For the last twenty years, I've been the front-man, luxuriating in glorious acclaim, while she'd been doing all the hard *yakka* behind the scenes. It was time to swap places. I was really looking forward to the change.'

Kierney slipped across into the vacant chair next to her *papá* and wrapped her arms around him like a small child. He pushed her away a little and reached his much longer wingspan round her instead, cuddling in close.

'I'm effing tired, guys,' he wept. 'I just wanted to play golf and mind the phones. I didn't want her dead. She'd been my steadfast lighthouse while I churned around in the stormy waters for all that time. I loved our life. I can't even begin to tell you how much I loved it. It was absolutely damned perfect. Same with our amazing kids. We were all practised in balancing challenge and reward, which makes for a very happy family, and we wanted it to continue forever, didn't we, Kizzo?'

'So what would you like to see as the trial outcome?' the shy, red-haired Scot ventured.

The celebrity's mouth broke into a grin, sniffing his tears back and kissing his daughter's upturned forehead. This was the best question of the evening, yet still somewhat hypothetical since two witness testimonies remained to be heard. Both sides' summing up and the jury's deliberation stood between them and any verdict.

'Moira, this trial's not about Lynn not being alive anymore,' the widower answered, looking the attorney-in-waiting straight in the eyes. 'She's only a prop in this play. The jury's here to decide the fate of the man who shot her, and you guys are here to help it do that. And notice I didn't say the man who killed her. There's the difference that's key to the outcome of this trial.'

Graham Winton's ears pricked up like a dog tuning into a high frequency sound. His star witness opened both hands as if to say, "You're welcome to it."

'The Accused pulled the trigger, but it was the bullet that killed her. Think about it for a while... God knows, I have! It's that infinitesimally short interval of time; that second or two when García was allegedly thinking he didn't know what to do. For me, having listened to the evidence so far, that's the crux of this case.'

A sob broke forth from the songwriter's mouth, halting his heartfelt oration. 'When that fucking bastard saw my beautiful best friend at the far end of his silencer, did he pull the trigger intending to kill her or not? Murder or manslaughter? That's charge Number One. At this point, either one works for me because the end result's the same, regardless of intent.'

As he spat the last few words through bitter lips, Jeff held up his right index finger, then extending a second finger and gripping both hard with his left hand. 'Charge Number Two... Intent to kill me? There's probably a whole host of people out there with this wish, lurking in the shadows, and with a bunch of much more worthy motives, no doubt. García didn't kill me, and quite frankly, I don't believe he ever would've. He doesn't have the balls. He couldn't even walk past me in the hotel entrance.'

Tears subsiding for now, the victim's husband paused to afford his words maximum impact before continuing. 'As Kierney and I were saying last night, if he killed me, he'd lose the basis for his existence, I reckon. That's a very confronting thing for a simple man. So then it comes down to owning a gun without a licence...'

Jeff's left hand now grabbed three straight and supple, piano-playing fingers and held them up in the air. 'The dumbass tells us he had one but can't produce it, so maybe he's innocent of that too. Maybe the bloody shopkeeper should be arrested for extorting stupid people's money and not applying for the permits on his customers' behalf.'

The ring of bewitched faces smiled and nodded. It could happen. The philosopher placed both palms on the table and pushed his chair back before leaning into it and crossing his long legs.

'A good outcome for me, and I hope us,' he concluded, looking to his daughter for confirmation, 'would be guilty of manslaughter. Or woman's laughter... Lynn's laughter, to be more precise. Not guilty of intent to kill me, because I don't think he'd ever have gone through with it, and who cares about the bloody firearms licence? It has no bearing on the rest of the case. What sentence would someone get for this as a sole offence?'

'Non-custodial,' Graham answered, shrugging. 'It really is an also-ran. I'm not entirely sure why the police persisted with it, given he confessed to the higher-order charges. It's not as if they didn't have anything else to keep him with.'

'That's what I thought,' Jeff sniffed. 'So there you have it... That's the result we'd like. Kiz, am I right?'

'Yes, *papá*. Sounds good.'

'Can I ask why you don't want a guilty verdict for intent to kill you?' Peter hazarded. 'He hasn't made his intentions a secret during the trial. Of the three, that's the charge I'd put money on.'

'Steady, Pete. Don't do that! I'm not saying I don't *want* a guilty verdict. Just that I don't *need* it,' the widower replied, pitching his voice much lower to match the level of scrutiny he sensed from other diners nearby. 'And also because I wanted to kill my father and the people he hung around with for my whole childhood. Again, I'd never have gone through with it, but I was damned well hanging out for him to die.'

'Oh, my God! Why?' both junior solicitors were horrified.

Their witness smiled. 'That I'm not prepared to tell, even if you do represent Her Majesty. I'm not having that juicy information stored on your Dictaphone and risking it falling into the wrong hands. There are limits to my openness. Suffice to say, I understand the emotions García lives with. My perfect wife was too easy to kill, and killing me would've been like killing his own soul. He'd no longer have recognised himself.'

Moira gasped. 'Heavens! I never thought about it that way. He's a scared little man with a big grudge. He's hardly Ivan Milat or Slobodan Milosevic.'

Emptying the last dregs from the wine bottle, Jeff laughed. 'You're not wrong there! They'd be comparisons he doesn't deserve. Graham, can I ask *you* a question, please?'

'Certainly. We owe you quite a few,' the senior partner replied. 'What is it?'

'Are you still intending to call Wendy García?'

'No. Greenshaw referred it to the judge. Apologies. I should've told you earlier. Judge Milne ruled that because Mrs García was a former spouse likely to denigrate her husband out of bitterness, rather than a loving spouse trying to stop her husband from going to jail, her testimony would be unfairly biased.'

The spent celebrity shook his head. 'That disappoints me greatly.'

'Mate!' Gerry exclaimed. 'You were the one who raised the objection first!'

'I know, mate, but not for those reasons,' the great man frowned. 'The judge is unfairly biased, as far as I'm concerned. She allowed me to take the stand. No-one more unfairly biased than me, eh? I'm hardly going to give the little worm a good character reference.'

The barrister chuckled. 'That was exactly my point at the briefing, but they overruled me.'

'For the record,' Jeff added, 'my reasoning was different, in that it may be seen as polarising the jury unnecessarily to either end of the spectrum. Either she'd make the jury feel unnecessarily sorry for him, in which case he might get off scot free. Sorry, Moira... Y'know what I mean.'

The female junior counsel giggled, accepting the star's apology for such a lame pun.

Their enigmatic dinner guest continued. 'They'd think, "Poor bastard, his wife's turned against him." Or, at the other end of the spectrum, she might paint the Accused as an absolute monster. We already have enough passion surrounding this trial, without adding an ex-wife into the mix.'

Graham switched off his voice-recording device and wound it back for a few seconds to make sure it had captured the conversation. It had. He nodded to Peter and Moira, who both looked exhausted.

'On that thought-provoking note, I'd better drop you two home,' he announced. 'We're back in court at eight to brief the Coroner. You met Dr Ron Hanson before, I believe, Jeff. He was at the hotel when they transported Lynn's body.'

Jeff remembered this man alright; he was the one who told him Lynn's clothing wouldn't need to be disturbed in order for her to be pronounced dead. He chose not to put this memory into words in front of his flagging daughter.

'Yeah. I know who you mean. And the psychiatrist appearing for the Defence. Are they the only two witnesses left?'

'Yes,' Graham confirmed. 'I'll cross-examine her very closely. We've had some advice of our own with regard to such cases of extreme jealousy. This lady's not someone I've met in court before, so I'm not sure of her credentials.'

'Probably less credentialed than you, mate,' Gerry sniggered, referring to his friend's extensive back catalogue on the subject of mental illness. 'You should get back in the box.'

'No, thanks,' Jeff shook his head, inviting Kierney to stand up. 'Get back in your own box! I've done my bit. I'm going back to the dress circle to see the final act unfold and applaud at the curtain calls. I've already written the song.'

'Oh, really?' Moira's soft brogue asked. 'A song about the trial?'

'Yep. But it'll never see the light of day because it'll be too dark to be allowed out.'

'Is that right? Who censors your music?' Graham enquired, incredulous.

'My brother and I do,' the teenager interjected with a smile. 'We mark them with red pen and get him to have a good, hard think about it.'

Jeff cuffed the top of the precocious student's head. 'Get thee to bed, young thing. Who's paying?'

'On us,' the senior partner jumped up, sliding a credit card out of his wallet. 'It was my honour. It's been a very entertaining evening indeed.'

Gerry disappeared out of the front of the restaurant to find a taxi, following the normal protocol for evenings out in public with his most important charges.

'We're going to make a run for it,' the superstar declared, noticing neighbouring patrons staring and pointing. 'Just in case García's brother's here waiting for me.'

'Papá!' Kierney whacked her father hard on the arm. 'You did so well up until then.'

Her dad grinned, seeing Gerry waving from the doorway. He shook each lawyer by the hand and gave Moira a quick kiss on the cheek. She blushed and held her hand against her face without thinking, making the superstar smile. He had the same effect on women wherever he went, even as a shadow of his former self.

'Come on, gorgeous,' he invited, taking the eighteen-year-old's hand.

'Does he have a brother?' the barrister yelled after them.

'Yes,' Jeff shouted back. 'Two. Your learned friend said so.'

Father and daughter propelled themselves into the back of the idling taxi, which soon sped off, listing violently round the corner and accelerating along the beach promenade. The rain had abated, but there was hardly a soul on the streets at this time of night.

As they drove back towards the city, the lonely man mulled over the Prosecution's last-minute question. Why had Juan Antonio become jealous and angry at the disparity between their lives, where his brothers presumably had not? Or maybe they were all alike? Did the others have happier marriages? Were they abused as children? Were his brothers still around? Had García killed them too?

'Christ, I'm tired,' Jeff groaned to his fellow passengers. 'You wouldn't believe what my mind's churning over.'

'What?' Kierney asked.

'Nothing for you to worry about, *pequeñita*. Just more questions for myself, that's all.'

TOWARDS A VERDICT

The next morning, Jeff awoke at six-forty-five to the sound of the telephone ringing. Still dressed in last night's shirt and jeans, he found himself stretched out on top of undisturbed bedclothes as usual. His head ached from too much wine and nicotine and too little water and sleep. He reached for the receiver as the noise reverberated between his ears.

'Hello?'

'*Papá*, are you coming for a run?'

'D'you want to go for a run?' he played his normal trick.

'Not really, but I'll go if you want to.'

'No, I don't want to either. What about a swim?'

'Oh, yes! Great idea!' the teenager exclaimed. 'Why didn't I think of that? I'd love to. Did you bring bathers?'

'I did,' her father affirmed in mock disgust. 'D'you really think I'd suggest going skinny dipping in a Sydney hotel with my daughter?'

She laughed. 'No. But we never discussed going swimming before we left home.'

'Life is full of surprises, baby,' the sad man rued. 'Meet you at your door in five?'

'Cool. *Adiós*.'

Only a brace of fellow early-birds graced the hotel pool, each swallowing a fair amount of water at the shock of seeing Jeff and Kierney Diamond arrive through the glass door. Shedding their bathrobes and slipping off their thongs, the stars dived straight in and swam underwater to the deep end of the twelve-metre length, executed expert tumble-turns and motored down again. They exercised for a solid fifteen minutes, matching each other stroke for stroke.

'How's your head?' Kierney asked when they eventually stopped for a breather.

'Better now. Pretty fuzzy when the phone rang.'

'Did you sleep in your clothes again?'

'Do you want breakfast?' Jeff countered, receiving a dunking for his obstinacy.

Jeff fought the spirited youngster off and sprinted back towards the shallow end. The lithe teenager ducked under to kick herself off the wall in hot pursuit. His extra length and power prevented her from catching up, and he was up and out of the water before she touched the tiles. They towelled themselves off sufficiently to don their robes and make their way back to their rooms in relative decency.

At breakfast, the buffet was heaving with business people on their way to meetings, conferences and court cases in Sydney's CBD. Jeff directed Kierney to a table in a remote corner, far away from the professional diners, and explained his revised game-plan.

'I'd rather not be in court for the closing arguments,' he confessed.

'Really? Why not?' she asked. 'Because you don't want to hear how the lawyers interpret you from last night?'

'Partly, yes, but primarily because I don't want Winton to feel under pressure, like I'm checking up on him from above while he's trying to deliver a respectable performance.'

'Oh, OK.'

'And also because I don't want the judge and jury looking up at us all the time. I'd rather not distract anybody when they need to concentrate on the facts.'

'So do you want to see the experts at least?' the youngster asked. 'I do.'

'Ah, yeah. Absolutely. In fact, I'm especially interested in the psych' assessment. I've got a feeling something bad happened to García before his family came to Australia.'

'A gut feel?' teased the dark-haired gipsy. 'Sorry. Not allowed. Stick to the facts, please.'

'Yes, Your Honour,' her father smiled. 'Where did his *mamá* disappear to? I wonder why she didn't move to Sydney with the rest of them?'

'Perhaps she died?' Kierney offered, a shiver running up her spine.

'Yep. Perhaps he killed her?' the story-teller nodded, his blood-curdling tone making her giggle. 'Winton hasn't given me any details of the psychiatrist's report that's been submitted as evidence, but he hasn't hinted at anything untoward either. He might not understand enough to be able to interpret it fully. He didn't sound as though he had much confidence in the Defence's expert witness, but he's paid to say that.'

The young woman inhaled. 'Oh, my God! This is turning into something way more convoluted than I ever expected,' she admitted. 'I'm going to be glad to get home. Do you think it'll finish today?'

'Don't know, angel. Gerry's going home tomorrow, anyway. I asked him to, 'cause Fiona shouldn't be on her own when they've just got engaged. He'll have been here for all the juicy bits, and the rest'll be in the papers pretty soon anyway.'

'So what do you want to do? Leave before the summing up?'

Her father nodded, shrugging.

'Both sides'?'

'Yeah, I think so. Though I am curious to hear how Floaty goes. He better have a good set of associates working with him 'cause he didn't seem much of a lateral thinker to me. Do you have a nickname for Winton?'

'No,' the clever student replied. 'He's like a teacher who doesn't give his students any credit for working things out for themselves. Peter was telling me he checks absolutely everything they do. He's looking for another job actually.'

The great man laughed. 'He shouldn't have told you that. Not very professional.'

'We're not his clients,' Kierney reminded him. 'I doubt if he's told the Queen.'

'Fair point,' Jeff conceded, placing a kiss on his fingertips and transferring it onto the bridge of the teenager's nose. 'Does he want to come to Melbourne? You could dump David for him.'

'*Papá*, I don't fancy him,' she whined. 'Stop trying to matchmake me. I'm quite happy, thank you. Don't you like David anymore?'

'Yeah. Sure I do. Ignore me. I'm only jealous. Did you speak to Jet last night?'

'No. I went straight to sleep. I could hardly keep my eyes open to clean my teeth. Did you?'

'Left a message. Clearly otherwise engaged. We'll ring him tonight if we have any news. I wonder how long the jury'll take to come to a decision. Less than twenty-five years, I hope.'

'Jeez!' Kierney groaned. 'That's a long time to wait to find out your sentence. He'll be sentenced and immediately freed!'

Her father nodded. 'It happens. More for short sentences though. Some suspects spend so long in custody awaiting trial that they've been detained for longer than their sentence, and the Queen has to pay them compensation.'

'Really?' Kierney sounded surprised. 'How much do you get for losing a day of freedom?'

'Minimum wage, I guess, depending on who your lawyer is,' he answered. 'Not much for your average petty criminal on Legal Aid. Much more for these top-end-of-town executives who embezzle to feed their gambling habit.'

'Embezzle,' the teenager wound the sizzling syllables around her tongue. 'That's such a funny word. Where did it come from?'

'It's got to be French, or even Latin,' Jeff shrugged. 'So are you happy with that plan?'

'I am, Senior Counsel.'

By the time Gerry turned up at court, the Diamonds were installed in the public gallery alongside their dutiful security guards. They hadn't caught up with the prosecution team prior to the trial resuming, and the judge had already entered and taken her seat.

The door panel opened at the rear of the hall, and the bailiff led García back to his usual spot. He sat down meekly, without even looking around.

'*Papá?*'

'*Sí,*' Jeff answered, suspicious.

'Will you tell me later what happened at Granddad's trial ?'

'*Cierto,*' her father agreed. 'If you really want to know, *pequeñita.*'

'I do. *Gracias,*' Kierney nodded, squeezing his knee and focussing on the next character to be introduced into the play's absorbing plot.

The widower watched the balding, bearded figure of Dr Hanson being sworn in. He looked exactly how an expert witness should: grey suit, conservative shirt and tie and a face weathered by experience; like a favourite teacher one meets every ten years at the high school reunion and who still remembers everything about each student.

'Ladies and gentlemen of the jury,' Rosemary Milne commenced her latest set of instructions. 'You are about to hear from a senior physician from the Coroner's Office. The Coroner's Office is responsible for carrying out post-mortem examinations, or autopsies, on the deceased victims of violent crimes. This witness is a recognised expert in his field. Unlike the other witnesses we've heard from so far, who are restricted to relaying the facts as they saw or heard them, this witness' expertise allows him to enter a professional opinion as evidence, in this case based on scientific knowledge and qualifications.'

The jurors all nodded, attentive and eager to discover more. As she called Prosecuting Counsel forward, those in the public gallery settled back to hear what the Coroner's representative had to say.

'Good morning, Dr Hanson,' Graham Winton prepared to launch the battle's first exchange. 'You were called to attend a fatal shooting at The Pensione Hotel on George Street here in Sydney, on the morning of the sixteenth of February, nineteen-ninety-six. Is that right?'

'Yes, Your Honour.'

'Can you please describe the scene when you arrived at the hotel?'

'Certainly, Your Honour. I arrived a few minutes after half-past ten in the morning. The Coroner had been informed of the shooting by the New South Wales Police at nine-forty-five. When I reached the hotel, the crime scene had been cordoned off, and the deceased's body was still *in situ*. The police had completed their initial forensic survey of the scene.'

Up in the dress circle, Jeff leant towards his old friend and whispered. 'Are you OK with hearing this stuff, mate? Please don't hang around if you don't want to. I'm not too sure how I'm going to go, to be honest.'

Gerry nodded. 'Play it by ear. Cheers, mate.'

'In your professional opinion, Doctor,' Winton continued, 'had Ms Diamond's body suffered any degradation during the police search at the scene?'

'No, Your Honour,' the bearded man answered without hesitation. 'There was a significant amount of blood on the furniture, excreted through wounds to Mrs Diamond's head and torso. This was analysed at the scene and matched with samples from her body later in the laboratory. Otherwise, the deceased's body remained in the same condition.'

'Does he know you sat with *mamá* for a while?' Kierney panicked suddenly, nudging her father.

'That won't matter,' he smiled, nauseated as he relived these appalling memories. 'They've eliminated me from their enquiries, thank Christ. D'you notice Winton's asked him to use *mamá*'s name instead of saying "the Victim" too? That's a very good tactic. Keep reminding the jury that they're hearing about a real person; someone they knew and loved. I bet the Defence doesn't do that when their time comes.'

Counsel for the Prosecution fired off another question without delay, not wishing the jurors to dwell on any single piece of information. 'Dr Hanson, how did you identify the Victim?'

The grey-haired medic gave a small cough, slightly incredulous as to the pertinence of this detail.

'I had no trouble identifying the Victim as Lynn Dyson Diamond, Your Honour,' he told the court. 'Hers is an instantly recognisable face, and I had been introduced to her husband just a few minutes earlier in the hotel lobby.'

'Is there any way you could have been mistaken, Mr, I mean, Dr Hanson?' Winton asked.

'Fuck!' Gerry sneered. 'That's ridiculous. As if they're going to now come out and say it wasn't her body and that someone's hiding Lynn somewhere. Are they serious?'

The teenager was confused. 'They're not going to say that, are they? Of course it was *mamá*. Doesn't the jury think we might've noticed if it was someone else's body?'

Her dad sighed. 'Yes, gorgeous,' he consoled her, glaring at the clown at his other shoulder. 'Ignore this wise-crack here. The Defence may be planning to claim I know where she is, and we faked her death for some reason. Insurance claim or something bizarre. Don't take his words too seriously. He's trying to get ahead of the game, that's all.'

'It's a nice idea though,' the youngster smiled, leaning against her favourite rock. 'Forget bodyguards. Just take body doubles wherever you go, so they can get shot instead of you.'

'World leaders do that all the time,' the patient man grinned. 'The oldest trick in the book. I wish we had. Though, there's another good question... Which unlucky schmuck would you pick to take a bullet for you?'

'Shhh,' Kierney grimaced. 'Stop with all the complications. Just listen.'

Graham Winton picked up a number of sheets of paper which were stapled together in one corner. He gave them to a court officer, who passed them over to the jury *Foreman*.

'Ladies and gentlemen of the jury, the exhibit that's being circulated now is a copy of the Coroner's report into the Victim's untimely death. The autopsy performed on Ms Diamond. I must warn you, it contains some detail you may find distressing. Dr Hanson, please could you describe the injuries which the Victim sustained and your findings as to the cause of death.'

The barrister's latest move taking him by surprise, Jeff made an executive decision. 'Come on, Kizzy,' he instructed. 'I don't want you sitting through this.'

'But everyone'll look up at us,' Kierney replied, startled. 'It'll be disruptive.'

'Yeah. I know. I should've thought of it earlier, but tough shit. Let's go and grab a coffee. I'll bring you one back if you're staying, mate.'

The celebrity stood up, as did the two security men around them, leaving his manager behind while the pair was escorted out. He watched García's eyes follow them up the steps and then noticed the judge raising her hand to Winton, presumably to bid his witness pause until the Diamonds were out of the courtroom before answering the question.

'Thank you, Your Honour,' Senior Counsel said, turning round and seeing last night's dinner guests disappearing from the gallery. 'Please continue, Doctor. Ms Diamond's injuries, if you will.'

'Yes, of course,' Hanson replied. 'Three bullets from a point-two-two calibre handgun and through a silencer, consistent with the weapon found at the scene. The first round penetrated the Victim's skull, about three centimetres to the right of the centre of her forehead, at the junction of the frontal and anterior diploic veins. It became lodged at the back of the brain, having passed through the temporal artery. We conclude that this bullet would have caused Mrs Diamond's death within two to five seconds.'

There was a loud gasp from the public area. Even though Gerry had read the Coroner's report in full some weeks ago, hearing this beatified woman's condition described by medical jargon in such a clinical and unemotional way affected him more than he was prepared for.

His old friend's revelations about the plans he and his exquisite wife had for the coming years had been rolling around his mind overnight, and consequently the accountant hadn't slept well at all.

The injustice of Lynn's murder was only just beginning to hit home to the self-confessed good-time guy, now that his duties for the funeral, memorial service and trial were mostly discharged. Here was he, looking forward to focussing on his new life with Fiona, while his best mate was facing into to a significant number of unfulfilled dreams.

Hanson resumed after a few seconds, as the whispers died down. 'When the first bullet punctured the Victim's frontal bone, it caused extensive damage to the top- and mid-sections of the deceased's brain and the higher vertebræ of her spinal cord, before coming to rest at the back of the skull. Severe internal bleeding would have given rise to heart failure and asphyxiation almost immediately.'

From his elevated position, Gerry saw several jury members become discomforted, jabbering to each other and putting their hands to their mouths. The Accused sat motionless in the dock, hands on his knees and staring at the floor, while the doctor continued speaking.

'The second and third rounds were discharged in rapid succession, with a fourth round fired three to five seconds afterwards. The second bullet penetrated the Victim's shoulder, a relatively superficial wound, and the third bullet missed Mrs Diamond's body and was found buried in the back of the sofa on which she had been sitting. The fourth bullet penetrated the Victim's rib cage, impacting the heart and the liver, and would have had a sixty to seventy percent chance of causing death in its own right.'

A muffled scream went up in the jury's benches. One of the male jurors had passed out, falling sideways onto the woman next to him. Another female juror stood up and was attempting to leave the courtroom in a hurry, making for the restroom with a hand cupped over her mouth.

'Ladies and gentlemen,' the judge called out. 'We'll take a thirty-minute recess. We shall resume at twenty past ten. Thank you.'

Everyone scrambled to their feet, and the officials quickly filed out of the door at the back. The Accused was escorted from the hall while the jury sorted itself out, some helping the stricken man to his feet. The executive watched this latest development with mixed feelings, wondering where the Diamonds had gone for their coffee. He skipped up the steps towards the exit, dialling Jeff's mobile number.

'Mate, where are you?' he asked as soon as the line connected. 'They called a recess. A bloke fainted in the jury. No, I'm not kidding! Others were chucking up. The Coroner's report. Lynn's like family to us too, mate. You should've been here. *Bon courage*, and all that. Where are you? The judge called a recess 'til ten-twenty. Yes. Great. See you in five.'

Gerry's coffee was sitting waiting for him when he strode into the café. He could tell by his friend's expression that the topics of their brief telephone call and the reason for the unexpected break were off limits in front of Kierney, leaving the conversation to drift to other subjects. Jeff had rung Celia to see if she was free to accompany the youngster shopping and take her mind off the trial, and the ever-caring grandmother had been only too happy to drop everything.

'Excellent,' the businessman said, looking forward to his first sip. 'Thanks for this. What are you going to do while the ladies are spending?'

'Coming back in with you. I want to hear the cross-exam'.'

The threesome chatted about trivial matters for another ten minutes or so before parting company. One security guard walked with Kierney back to the hotel, where she would meet Gerry's mother, and the other turned back to the Supreme Court with the two tall, handsome amigos. They smoked a quick cigarette while fending off a group of fans who had spotted the celebrity and followed him into the building, then jogged towards the lifts to reclaim their spot in the audience.

By the time Jeff and Gerry returned to the public area, the officials and the expert witness were already installed in their usual places. Several well-wishers pushed their way to the end of their rows, attempting to shake the revered songwriter's hand as the stately pair paced down the aisle towards their seats. He noticed the area seemed more densely populated today, as if the concièrge had released a batch of unsold tickets.

The victim's husband observed the hunched Spaniard. The two officers who ferried him back and forth from the holding cell were all but superfluous, so compliant was their prisoner. He must have given up on the prospect of being free. What must that feel like? The widower pondered his father's situation. Had he remained mutinous right until the verdict was pronounced? Or did he too reach a point in his trial when he no longer held out any hope of the jury finding for him?

Somewhat like knowing one's wife wasn't coming back, wasn't it? At some stage he would pass this point, Jeff concluded with mixed emotions. Despite how far into denial both men might venture as the hours and days went by, their respective desperate glimpses of a happy ending were fading fast.

Judge Milne addressed the jury. 'Ladies and gentlemen, thank you for your patience and fortitude through this witness' difficult testimony. I trust you're feeling better after the recess. We will do our best to get through Dr Hanson's report as quickly as possible. It's very important you feel well enough to pay it your fullest attention. If you need to leave the courtroom again, please notify the *Foreman*, and we'll call another recess if necessary. Counsel for the Prosecution, please continue with your questions.'

'Thank you, Your Honour,' Winton replied, turning to face the expert witness anew. 'Doctor, you've told us that two of the four bullets fired by the Accused at the Victim would certainly have caused her death. Is that correct?'

'I expect so, Your Honour,' Hanson answered, 'but I cannot categorically confirm that. The first bullet, yes, certainly. The fourth, as I said, a sixty to seventy percent chance of causing fatal injury. If the fourth bullet had been the only one to enter Mrs Diamond's body, life support may have prolonged her life if she had been admitted to hospital rapidly, but the chances of survival would be low due to the serious trauma her internal organs would have sustained. This means that a full recovery would have been very unlikely.'

'Thank you, Doctor,' the barrister said, checking the jury was comfortable with this detail. 'And the second and third bullets, Dr Hanson?'

'Not life-threatening, Your Honour,' he answered with greater conviction but far less vigour. 'The third did not make contact with Mrs Diamond at all. It was found buried in the couch, on a trajectory some twenty centimetres to the right of the Victim's upper arm. And the second bullet entered the top of the biceps muscle of the Victim's left arm, passing straight through into the chair behind her. It resulted in a minor injury.'

'I see,' Winton nodded. 'Thank you. Dr Hanson, please could you tell the court, in your professional experience, is it likely that a person firing the type of handgun used in this crime could shoot four times without being fully aware that he has fired four rounds?'

'No, Your Honour,' the medic told the jury. 'The trigger on this particular handgun is fairly stiff. Our firearms specialists tested the weapon found at the scene in our range and reported that it was difficult to fire multiple rounds in quick succession. The firearm used for this crime is not one on which the trigger can be held down to fire multiple rounds. The mechanism loads each round separately.'

'Thank you, sir,' Counsel for the Prosecution replied with a satisfied grin, expecting but not receiving any objection from the Defence bench. 'So can I ask you again to confirm for the court whether it was possible for the Accused to have fired four rounds from this firearm in an accidental fashion?'

'Your Honour, in my opinion, the only way the Accused would have been able to fire this weapon accidentally would be if it had malfunctioned.'

'And was the firearm in good working order when your people examined it, Doctor?'

'Yes, it was, Your Honour.'

Graham Winton stood tall, turning to the jury and then back to the witness. The crowd in the public gallery took a valuable opportunity to breathe, so quiet had they fallen during the Coroner's gruesome account.

'One last question, Doctor, before I hand you over to the Defence for cross-examination,' the lawyer almost chuckled. 'Please could you confirm to the court that, prior to the horrific and fatal injuries the Victim sustained as a result of the Accused's actions on the sixteenth of February this year, Ms Diamond was in good health?'

Jeff sighed, thinking back to the argument which had arisen between himself and his children on this subject while they had been opening Lynn's letters. If only the weapon had malfunctioned... If it had failed to fire, or if García had been a poor shot, none of this drama would have been necessary and everything would be as it should be. Ms Diamond, hopefully with an equally robust Mr Diamond by her side, would have remained in good health for another fifty or sixty years. If only, if only, if only...

'Indeed, Your Honour,' Hanson replied. 'Mrs Diamond was in perfect health prior to the incident, as we would expect.'

A ripple of excitement ran around the public gallery. A lone positive piece of news about their cherished superstar was most welcome after the catalogue of injuries the Coroner's representative had described.

'Thank you, Dr Hanson,' Winton nodded. 'I have no further questions, Your Honour.'

Judge Milne addressed the jury. 'Ladies and gentlemen, can I please verify that you feel well enough to move straight on to the Defence's cross-examination of this witness?'

The *Foreman* gave a cursory scan around his eleven colleagues and issued an emphatic nod. Evidently, the initial shock of being forced to imagine the aftermath of the shooting had dispersed, the jury now able to focus on the details in relative comfort.

'Thank you,' the judge acknowledged, turning to Stephen Greenshaw. 'Counsel for the Defence, are you ready to proceed with your cross-examination?'

'We are, Your Honour,' the gangly solicitor responded, already on his feet. 'Dr Hanson, good morning.'

'I'm looking forward to finally meeting up with him again after this is over,' Gerry grinned at his pallid companion. 'Mr Floaty! It suits him well. He always was an officious bastard, even back in high school.'

Jeff smiled. 'All in good time, mate. For now, let's see how many holes he can pick in the Coroner's report.'

'Good morning, Mr Greenshaw,' Hanson responded.

'Hmm,' the celebrity frowned. 'They obviously know each other very well. There was none of this familiarity with Winton. Did he go to your silver spoon school too, by any chance?'

Gerry nodded, shrugging. 'True, mate. Perhaps. He's a bit long in the tooth for me to remember. He'd have been long gone by the time I got there. Floaty's been doing this for a while, you know. They'll have crossed swords in here before.'

The bouncing barrister laid down his first challenge. 'Dr Hanson, you told us earlier, in response to a question from my learned colleague on opposition counsel, that the Victim's body had already been examined at the scene of the crime by the time you reached the hotel.'

'Yes, Your Honour. It had. The scene was cordoned off to the public, and the police had marked items of evidence and taken photographs.'

'Was the body moved at all during this process?'

'No, Your Honour.'

'Thank you. On whose instructions were you called to attend the hotel, Doctor?'

'The detective in charge, I assume.'

'Detective Inspector Fisher?' Greenshaw persisted.

'Yes, Your Honour.'

'Could you please describe what was going on when you arrived at the scene?' Counsel for the Defence asked.

'I was told the deceased, Mrs Lynn Diamond, was located inside the screened section of the hotel's foyer. The hotel manager had requested a barrier to be put up, to dampen the hysteria that had developed after the incident,' Hanson told the court. 'A large number of people were milling around the crime scene; many crying and very distressed. He was attempting to restore calm, I believe.'

'Here we go,' Jeff hissed, anticipating the Defence's plan of attack.

'Doctor, were you notified who, apart from the police, had access to the Victim's body before you and your team arrived?' Greenshaw enquired.

'Your Honour, I was informed that Mrs Diamond's husband had rushed over to the scene and that he had sat with her for some time,' the solemn, grey-haired man answered. 'The police requested him to withdraw, but it was understandably difficult for him to leave her side.'

Another collective intake of breath echoed through the public gallery, and the celebrity saw several jurors looking up in his direction before turning to each other to pass a comment. The lawyer continued.

'Are you certain the Victim was deceased before Mr Diamond rushed over and sat with his wife, Dr Hanson? And touched her face and hands, as I gather.'

Again, the undercurrent of whispers in the upper-level seating was disconcerting, and Rosemary Milne raised her hands towards it. 'Ladies and gentlemen, please refrain from speaking while the Witness answers the Defence's questions,' she implored.

'You know... This court could make do with a librarian instead of a judge,' Gerry quipped. 'All she seems to do is say "Quiet, please" every now and again.'

'Shut up,' Jeff said through clenched jaws. 'This is important.'

'Yes, Your Honour,' Hanson replied. 'There was no possibility of the Victim still being alive by the time Mr Diamond reached the scene. Mrs Diamond would have been deceased for at least five minutes, I would estimate from the police reports. It may even have been ten minutes. And I'm satisfied that no contamination of evidence occurred during this period, Your Honour.'

The tiered ranks of fans and well-wishers heaved a sigh of relief along with the victim's husband. He could feel all eyes upon him as he stared down to check the jury's reaction. They were all looking at him too, so he turned his gaze to the floor.

'Thank you, Dr Hanson,' Greenshaw moved on. 'Can you articulate for the court the various ways in which a recently deceased person's body may become contaminated when your team transports it, in such a way as to compromise your subsequent examination and the results of the autopsy?'

Again Jeff tensed up, waiting for the witness' response.

'I could, Your Honour, but the information would not have relevance to this case. Coronial case officers followed the same standard procedure for Mrs Diamond as they would employ for any other person. Photographs were taken of the installation prior to removal and were submitted to my office as part of the case documentation later that day. The furniture and other exhibits affected at the crime scene were removed from the lobby shortly afterwards and were taken to a locked storeroom for further forensic investigation.'

Jeff felt momentarily sickened but said nothing, reflecting on the older man's terminology. He had never thought of his beautiful best friend as an installation before, but this odd characterisation was entirely apt for the Crown's purposes. Exhibit One, Your Honour. It was hardly the Natural History Museum, nor even the Guggenheim, but he appreciated the materiality of this impersonal descriptor.

The barrister sounded frustrated again. 'Thank you, Doctor, for your comprehensive answer to my question. Can I please ask you to clarify for the court whether the Victim's body could have been tampered with before you and your team arrived to examine it?'

Ron Hanson stood taller in the witness box, as if to assert himself further against the barrage. 'There is always a risk of contamination, Your Honour,' he stated in a more forthright tone. 'Airborne bacteria or other particles may alight on the skin, for example. Atmospheric conditions may change over time, as another.

'However, in this case, our examination found nothing irregular on Mrs Diamond's body that might have complicated the autopsy. The three bullets had already passed through her body and into the wall or chairs, and the cause of death was abundantly clear.'

'Jesus Christ,' Jeff moaned. 'I'm so glad Kiz isn't here to listen to this. Installations, bullets passing through, irregular particles... It's all too disgusting for words.'

'Nearly over, mate,' Gerry reached behind his friend and patted him on the back.

Red in the face and annoyed that the doctor was not rising to his bait, Defence Counsel pivoted towards the jury. 'Is it possible, sir, with all your years of experience in this field, that anyone could have tampered with the Victim's body prior to your examination?'

Gerry whistled under his breath. 'Bloody hell, Stevie. Leave it alone, for God's sake.'

'He's just doing his job,' the celebrity said, massaging his eye sockets in an attempt to dislodge the pain in his head. 'He doesn't have anywhere to go with this anyway, mate. Does he think Hanson's going to suddenly admit to finding strangulation marks on Lynn's neck?'

The Coroner's man shook his head. 'No, Your Honour. We found no evidence that Mrs Diamond's body had been tampered with. She died as a result of bullet wounds, as I have already stated for the court.'

Unperturbed, Grimshaw took an exaggerated step back as if seeking to provide a visual alert that he was about to change tack. 'Dr Hanson,' he boomed. 'Your assessment of the Victim's health prior to the shooting, how was this established?'

'First, through an examination of the Victim's vital organs, Your Honour,' the older man responded, 'to look for tumours, for example, and blockages in the heart valves, major veins and arteries that might signal cardiac infarction or arrest. Mrs Diamond's brain showed no sign of stroke, and her lungs were healthy and clear, indicating that she was not a regular smoker, drinker or drug-taker...'

Jeff chuckled. 'Lucky he didn't have to slice me up in that case, otherwise it would've been touch and go whether they'd rule I'd contributed to my own demise.'

Gerry nodded and smiled while Hanson supplied another verbose answer.

'There was no evidence of influenza or other respiratory conditions. Second, subsequent to our own post-mortem procedures, the Victim's usual physician provided my office with complete medical records. Mrs Diamond had no pre-existing health concerns whatsoever.'

'Thank you, Doctor,' Greenshaw said, more subdued again. 'Clearly a clean bill of health then.'

'Yes, Your Honour,' Hanson nodded. 'Very clean, as we would expect.'

'Indeed, indeed. That brings me to my last set of questions, Doctor,' Defence Counsel announced in a distinctly disinterested tone. 'Regarding the firearm used to shoot the Victim, you told the court the only circumstance that would result in the Accused firing the weapon four times accidentally is if it had malfunctioned. Is that right?'

'Yes, Your Honour. That is my office's professional opinion.'

'In that case, in your office's professional opinion,' the lawyer mocked, 'what is the likelihood of the weapon malfunctioning intermittently? By this I mean it was in good working order when your experts tested it, but it may not have functioned correctly when my client held it in his hand. Can you give the court your opinion on this, please?'

The doctor scratched his head inadvertently, taking a moment to think about the question. Jeff noted it was the first time the witness had hesitated during his whole testimony.

'Yes, Your Honour. It is possible for the weapon to develop an intermittent fault,' he admitted, eliciting a gasp from certain areas of the dress circle.

'Objection!' Graham Winton sprang up.

The judge focussed her attention on the Queen's bench. 'Counsel for the Prosecution?' she invited.

'Thank you, Your Honour,' he replied. 'The Accused has told the court, during his time on the witness stand, that he had fired this weapon many times at his gun club. He did not indicate the weapon had any type of intermittent fault.'

Jeff could hear quiet laughter behind him and cringed at the Prosecution's somewhat weak suggestion.

'Objection!' Greenshaw countered. 'This specific question was not asked of the Accused, Your Honour.'

The judge clicked the button on the end of her pen a few times before pointing it at each lawyer in turn. 'Perhaps an omission, gentlemen? Counsel?' she invited the opposing bench to respond.

'The Prosecution is asking the Witness to make an assumption. Dr Hanson was not present to hear the Accused's account of his use of the weapon.'

'Objection sustained, Mr Greenshaw, and objection overruled, Mr Winton. Mr Greenshaw, please ask your question again.'

'Thank you, Your Honour,' the Defence lawyer rejoiced, well into objection deficit in terms of this trial. 'Doctor, in your opinion, is it possible the weapon used to shoot the Victim could have malfunctioned intermittently?'

Hanson nodded. 'Yes, it is possible, Your Honour. The firearm belonging to the Accused has been thoroughly tested at the Coroner's facility and did not display an intermittent fault of any kind. I would say therefore not likely, but a slim possibility.'

'Thank you, Dr Hanson,' the pompous barrister said.

'Fuck,' Jeff muttered. 'What a remarkable coincidence! He didn't know whether to shoot her or not, and the gun chose that exact same moment to go off in his hand four times? Jesus Christ, I don't think so.'

'You said you'd be content with manslaughter, mate,' came Gerry's gentle reminder. 'It's the first hint of a slide so far, isn't it?'

The celebrity gave a heavy sigh, 'I suppose, yeah, but it's still wrong. The gun didn't malfunction that day. I'd give away my entire fortune if they could prove it to me.'

'Careful. A large slice of my income depends on your fortune,' the accountant chuckled. 'I'd advise against such a rash move.'

His friend's self-interested quip amused Jeff, but he didn't let on. 'D'you think it's possible?' he asked instead. 'Honestly?'

'You heard the good doctor,' his bombastic friend responded. 'He said it was a slim possibility, though unlikely. But seriously, mate, no. I don't believe it happened in Lynn's case.'

'Not likely, but possible,' Greenshaw repeated to the jury. 'Ladies and gentlemen, you have listened to the doctor's professional opinions. There is a possibility that the weapon malfunctioned in the Accused's hand on the sixteenth of February, nineteen-ninety-six at The Pensione Hotel, causing four rounds to be discharged in quick succession at the Victim. Only one of those bullets would have been enough to cause the Victim's accidental death.'

'Bullshit!' came a loud voice from the first few rows of the public gallery.

'Yeah!' another person yelled out, and the courtroom once more erupted in hysterical chatter.

Rosemary Milne stood up, signalling for the court officer to call for order. 'Ladies and gentlemen, quiet, please,' she urged, in true librarian style. 'I'm calling another thirty-minute recess, after which we shall resume with further questions for this witness. Dr Hanson, you are not yet released.'

The Coroner's representative acknowledged the judge, who was already making her way out of the court. Everyone followed suit, gathering up their coats and other belongings. Jeff, Gerry and the remaining security detail made their way downstairs for a cigarette, soon surrounded by people eager to show support for their idol.

Unconstrained by the need to protect his daughter's sensibilities, the patient star listened to the many theories on offer, nodding and shaking his head at random. Sorely tempted to join in with their disquiet at the allegations they had all heard, the typically outspoken celebrity avoided expressing any opinion.

There was a message on Jeff's mobile from Cathy, asking how the trial was going. He pressed the button to return her call and walked away from the crowd, politely excusing himself. After he had spoken to his faithful office manager for a few minutes, he picked Kierney's number from the list. It went to voicemail, which was a good sign. She was either trying on some new clothes or enjoying a quiet coffee and cake with her pseudo-grandmother in a chic café where it was right and proper to mute one's telephone.

'Kizzy, *soy yo*,' he said after the tone. '*¿Qué tal?* We're just on another break, so don't worry about ringing back. Nothing particularly interesting to tell you. I'll ring again at lunchtime to find out where you are and if you're having lunch with Celia or with us. Send me a text or leave me a message. Whichever's fine by me, but the psychiatrist's up next. I know you want to listen to their report. *Te amo, pequeñita. Adiós.*'

Back in the courtroom, the man from the Coroner's Office was once more under the pump from Defence Counsel, the supplementary shot of coffee taken during the impromptu recess having injected extra venom.

'Dr Hanson, my client maintains he made an honest and excusable mistake by shooting the Victim accidentally that morning, because he was confused by not seeing Mr Diamond, his intended target.'

Immediately, the most vocal and highly caffeinated members of the public were up in arms again. The judge took no prisoners this time and instructed the bailiffs to remove those who had stood up to hurl abuse at the Defence attorney.

Greenshaw's demeanour was unaffected however, and he continued as soon as he received the go-ahead. 'In your medical opinion, Doctor, is it possible for a reflex action to cause the Accused to pull the trigger instead of releasing it?'

Hanson answered, 'Well, Your Honour... A reflex action or spasm is not voluntary...'

'Objection!' the prosecution barrister shouted. 'Point of law, Your Honour.'

The judge allowed Winton to outline his issue.

'The Defence is alluding to an accidental squeeze of the trigger not being *actus reus*, Your Honour, whereas you and I know it's the act of presenting the weapon which is the *actus reus*. If the firearm had been in the process of being raised towards the Victim and it had suddenly gone off and delivered a fatal wound, this would not necessarily be construed as *actus reus*. However, on this occasion, the Accused has testified that he took aim at Ms Diamond.'

'Good man,' Jeff murmured. 'Nice work.'

The judge turned to the jury. 'Ladies and gentlemen, the Prosecution raises a valid point. The actual moment where the Accused can be said to have taken aim at the Victim is not absolutely clear in this case. However, the gun was raised at the Victim and several bullets were fired into her body, resulting in her death.

'The legal term "*actus reus*", which the Prosecution has used here, means an act committed knowing it was against the law. An evil deed, if you like. If the Accused raised the gun and took aim at the Victim, one could reasonably assume intent at that time. But if the Accused changed his mind after this moment and no longer intended to shoot the Victim, and yet the firearm still discharged, this does not excuse him from the crime of murder.

'Ladies and gentlemen of the jury, it is up to you to decide whether the intent to shoot to kill Mrs Diamond existed from the time the weapon was trained on her, up to and including the time it took for the Accused to pull the trigger. I hope this is clear to you. Objection sustained, Mr Winton.'

Jeff saw various jurors appear confused and even agitated at the judge's complicated explanation. Even to him, with an above-average fluency in legalese, it had come across vague and garbled. If the Accused himself claimed he didn't know, what chance did the jury have?

'Mr Greenshaw,' the patient woman said, 'please continue with your cross-examination.'

'I have no further questions, Your Honour,' the Defence barrister admitted, retreating to his bench.

Judge Milne dismissed the witness and checked the clock hanging on the balcony wall below the gallery balustrade. She called an early lunch recess and instructed everyone to return at one o'clock.

'She's just thrown the kitchen into chaos,' Gerry groaned, rising from his seat and stretching his spine, first one side and then the other. 'I'm getting too old to sit in one place for this long.'

'Know what you mean,' his friend agreed, downhearted and feeling his own body aching and cramped. 'Let's see what's in the sandwiches today. My concern now is that we've watched our friend the librarian open the door a little too far. Reasonable doubt's creeping in.'

'Do you think so?' the accountant asked, sounding surprised. 'Jesus! What the hell do you mean?'

'The good lady Rosemary said one could reasonably assume intent if he'd aimed the gun. But then again, it'd also be perfectly reasonable to assume the bastard may've just wanted to scare her or issue some sort of threat.'

Gerry frowned and nodded, walking along the familiar corridor towards the lifts, trying to keep the well-wishers at a sensible distance from his valuable charge. 'That's true, mate. You never miss a trick.'

'It's a vain hope to think no-one else'll come to this realisation. Especially Defence Counsel,' Jeff sighed.

He shuddered at the mental image of his wife sitting lifeless on the couch in the hotel foyer that awful morning, as relaxed as if she had been talking to her mother or to one of the children. Nothing about this memory suggested an impulse to flee.

'Scaring or threatening Lynn would only have been an option if she could see him, and I'm pretty sure she wasn't able to. She'd have moved. You know how lightning fast her reactions were, mate.'

Again Gerry nodded, putting his hand on his client's shoulder as the tears flowed again.

'She'd have only needed to move a few centimetres in either direction and that first bullet would've missed her. Fuck. If only you had, angel. I need to talk to our esteemed friend.'

The widower stopped in the stairwell, leaning into a corner on a mid-level landing, and dialled Winton's number. There was no hint of recognition coming from his tattoo, but he refused to let it bother him. His *regala* knew he was onto it.

'Yes, hi. I'm fine, thanks, Graham. You?'

Breathing deeply to steady his nerves, Jeff explained his angle on Judge Milne's parting comment to the jury. Winton paid due attention and promised he would ask his associates to research the likelihood of García being in Lynn's line of sight when he had taken aim. Symbiosis in action, the two men fed off each other again: this deep thinker who was not the barrister's client was proving most helpful; and the case which was not Jeff's fell further under his influence.

'What did he have to say?' Gerry asked when his friend ended the call.

'They're going to try and figure out how well Lynn and García could see each other, if at all,' the songwriter recounted, with his hand poised on the door handle of their third-floor sanctuary. 'If there's a chance they'd made eye contact, he's going to move to have García take the stand again. If not, he'll include some commentary in his summing up about a range of things the bastard could've been intending to do when he raised the gun.'

Kierney and her kindly chaperone were waiting in the wood-panelled meeting room when the men entered. Jeff was pleased to see her looking so composed, giving both women an impetuous hug.

'Thanks so much, Celia,' he said, kissing the elegant woman on the cheek. 'I'm very grateful. Did you have a nice morning?'

'We did, *papá*,' the youngster replied, pointing to three bags left on a nearby chair.

'Your credit card bill will show how nice a morning they had,' Gerry chided, eliciting a hard stare from his mother.

'Who cares?' Jeff retorted, helping himself to a handful of sandwiches from a platter on the large table.

'How are you, dear?' Celia asked. 'You look exhausted.'

'Perpetual state these days. Thanks, though. I can't remember not being exhausted. That last session was bloody tough, but the next one should be better. It's the psychiatrist who assessed García for diminished mental capacity.'

His friend's mother nodded. 'And that's the last witness?'

'As far as we know. There was talk of putting his ex-wife on the stand, but she's feral. I don't think she'd be a credible witness. The jury's confused as it is.'

'Are they? How come?' Kierney sounded perturbed. 'I thought Mr Winton told you they'd already made up their mind.'

'Today's testimony was confusing,' the celebrity explained. 'The Defence threw some curve-balls at the Coroner's man. About the gun and the spaniel malfunctioning at the same time... And then the judge gave them a long-winded explanation of intent that made things worse rather than better, in my opinion. I still think it could go either way.'

'So it'll depend on the closing statements,' Celia surmised, having received a full briefing from the knowledgeable teenager. 'Good thing you went for dinner with them last night.'

'Perhaps,' Jeff nodded. 'The gallery's pretty fired-up. The jury'll be hard-pressed to ignore them.'

'Do you think it would've been different if we hadn't been here?' Kierney asked.

'No,' Gerry replied. 'While you were away this morning, there was still plenty of muttering and oohs and ahhs. People are very angry about this case. Lynn was very important to all of us, Kizzo. Everyone wants to see García get what he deserves.'

'Definitely,' his mother agreed. 'Anyway, I should be off. I hope this afternoon's not too distressing for you, dears. Come over this evening. We're just at home on our own.'

'Thanks, Celia,' her favourite house-guest replied, getting to his feet to bid her farewell. 'Thanks again. I'll give you a ring later on. Don't plan anything for us. We'll probably stay in the city and get an early night. Either way, I'll ring you.'

'You're very thoughtful, Jeff,' Celia stood on tip-toe to kiss him on the cheek. 'You always have been.'

The superstar smiled his three-billion dollar smile, and the grandmother swooned yet again. It had been so for the last thirty years.

'Flattery will get you everywhere, Mrs Blake.'

Kisses and goodbyes exchanged all round, Celia left the room, accompanied by one of the security guards. Father and daughter hugged each other tight.

'Was it horrible this morning?' the teenager asked.

'Yes, bloody horrible, but interesting all the same. Greenshaw thought he had a bit of a win with the malfunctioning gun, but he lost it again at the last minute with the judge's sermon on intent. His gown lost its floatiness.'

'Oh, no!' Gerry laughed. 'He's become Mr Saggy now.'

Kierney giggled too. 'Excelente. I'll look forward to watching him question the psychobabble expert.'

With a precipitous groan, Jeff closed his eyes as tears welled up without warning. He leant forwards and sobbed into his hands, leaving Gerry and Kierney exchanging glances in dismay.

'Papá, what's wrong? What did I say?'

'Nothing, gorgeous,' he croaked. 'It's just that term: "psychobabble". It was one of the first made-up words mamá and I shared. Way back. It was a shock to hear it come out of your mouth, out of the blue, that's all.'

The young woman hugged her father's shoulders. 'Sorry, papá.'

'Whoa,' Jeff sighed, regaining his composure and longing for a sympathetic sign from his wife's ghost. 'That came from somewhere deep. Sorry, guys. Shall we slip downstairs and have a ciggie before we get called back in?'

Cigarettes smoked, they were soon sitting in their familiar spot, six rows back against the centre aisle. It had begun to feel normal for their fellow spectators to share the public area with these critical observers. The Accused was led into his box, and the jury filed back into their three banks of four seats. They seemed calm and collected enough, the superstar thought.

'The Defence calls Dr Philippa Moroney,' announced the court officer.

A plump woman in her early forties and with a cheerful, glowing face entered the witness box and took her oath. She stood no higher above the railing than García had. Jeff saw her nod towards the dock from across the courtroom, and the pitiful man returned the gesture. Paradoxically, the widower was pleased to see some rapport between psychiatrist and patient, since it meant her testimony was more likely to contain some practical reality along with the usual sprinkling of theoretical suggestion.

'Dr Moroney, good afternoon,' Stephen Greenshaw began, sprightly again after his lunch. 'Can you please describe to the court the qualifications you hold in the field of psychiatry and any work you've done that may be relevant to this case?'

'Yes, Your Honour,' Philippa Moroney answered in a high-pitched, softly spoken voice with a definite North American accent. 'I have a degree in Clinical Psychiatry from the University of Vancouver, Canada, and I'm a fellow of the Canadian Psychiatry Association. For my doctorate, I specialised in the rehabilitation of serious criminals, and I've spoken at conferences all over the world on this topic. I'm currently on a three-year professorial assignment with the Australian Federal Police, where I work on particular cases alongside local psychiatrists.'

Father and daughter stared at each other in amazement. The Defence had selected a Canadian psychiatrist as the expert witness who would undoubtedly be aware of Jeff Diamond's collaboration with another eminent consultant psychiatrist from the same country by the name of Sarah Friedman. These two women were likely to have appeared together on the North American speaker circuit many times.

This was also the celebrity's area of expertise. He, more than most present at this trial, understood both theory and practice of mental illness and the effect it had on one's ability to lead a normal life. Either Winton had omitted to mention this to the Defence team, or they hadn't researched too hard into his bibliography. Only his discography. It had always irked the gifted academic that the most impactful products of his career were the ones about which his huge fan-base knew the least.

'This world is way too small,' Jeff whispered. 'How unbelievable is that? I wonder if she declared any sort of conflict of interest.'

'Perhaps she volunteered?' the youngster posited. 'She might've wanted to work on this case, if she knows Sarah.'

Kierney was right. This was a more plausible scenario. Would it be an advantage or disadvantage if the witness were to reveal this second degree of separation? She ought to be unbiased, as a professional, but if a link between her and the victim's husband surfaced during questioning, how would the jury interpret it?

'¿Le preocupas?' the eighteen-year-old asked her pensive father.

'Sí. Un poco,' Jeff nodded, reaching for his mobile telephone to send the prosecution team a text message.

'I thought so. That's why you're cutting off the circulation in my hand,' Kierney chuckled, shaking their interlocked fingers to arrest the tingling sensation.

Her father smiled, releasing his grip. 'Sorry, pequeñita.'

'Dr Moroney,' Greenshaw continued. 'Did you know, or know of, the Accused prior to being assigned as an expert witness to this case?'

'Only from the publicity surrounding the death of Ms Diamond, Your Honour,' she replied.

'You had never met the Accused prior to him being arrested for these crimes?'

'That's correct, Your Honour,' the psychiatrist answered. 'I had not.'

'Thank you, Doctor. How many times have you met with the Accused, and for how long?'

The overweight woman rocked back and forth a little in the witness box, beginning to perspire. 'The Defendant and I have had four meetings altogether, two lasting one hour each and the other two for three hours each,' she answered. 'A total of eight hours of consultation time, Your Honour.'

'And please could you tell the court what information you were given about the Accused and about the case when your engagement began?'

Dr Moroney's eyes lifted to the ceiling while she decided how to answer this question. 'Officially, I met with a consultant psychiatrist from the New South Wales Police who was initially assigned to the case, and then also with a consultant from the Federal Police. They provided me with their notes from interviews with the Accused, and copies of the letters and other papers taken from his home after the shooting.'

'And unofficially?' Greenshaw asked, working up to something pre-arranged.

'Unofficially, I was bombarded by media coverage, on television, in the newspapers and magazines,' the psychiatrist told the jury. 'Like everyone else, I was deeply affected by Ms Diamond's passing. It was impossible to avoid reading or hearing about it, and it was sometimes difficult to know what was based on fact and what was pure fantasy.'

'Weird,' Jeff turned to his friend. 'Greenshaw should be objecting to the credibility of his own witness. She's admitting to prejudice.'

'No more than anyone else,' Gerry replied with a shrug.

'True, but she's an expert witness,' the celebrity persisted. 'She's here for her individual opinion, not to substantiate indisputable facts.'

'The Crown should ask her if she owns any of Lynn's CDs,' the executive quipped.

His VIP client chuckled, shaking his head. 'OK, OK. I get it. They should ask everyone. Yes. Point taken, Blake-san.'

On the other side of the humble musician, his daughter was smiling. 'I wonder if Mr Floaty owns any of mamá's CDs? He should disqualify himself.'

'So why isn't Graham objecting?' the Diamond family's manager asked, serious again. 'Do you think he's asleep after our long night?'

'No. I expect he's struggling to stifle his laughter,' Jeff suggested. 'If this woman was so deeply affected by Lynn's murder, how could she have a bias towards the man who shot her?'

'Because she's a professional,' Kierney interjected. 'Just like you. How can you sit there and say...'

The teenager stopped herself from uttering the word "manslaughter", in case she was overheard.

'I hear ya,' her dad smiled. 'Well saved, baby. I'd like to think you're right. But is any one of us truly unbiased? Ever?'

'Probably not,' the young woman whispered.

'So...' Counsel for the Defence went on. 'Doctor, how did you approach your first meeting with the Accused, having absorbed all this unofficial information about him?'

The woman placed her hands side-by-side on top of the lectern, seeming to raise herself up a few centimetres. She had spotted Jeff and Kierney in the public gallery and became more agitated.

'I believe in giving people a fair trial, Your Honour. I went into each meeting prepared to listen to what Mr García had to say, to ask a series of questions and to give him the benefit of the doubt. In other words, to remain impartial.'

'Thank you, Dr Moroney,' Greenshaw said. 'Would you please describe, for the benefit of the court, the mental state of the Accused when you met with him on the first occasion, and how long after the event this was?'

'Yes, Your Honour. The Accused was nervous and lacked self-confidence in our first meeting. There was a complete lack of trust. I asked him only general questions to start with. How was he feeling? And how was he being treated? He answered "Good" to all questions and withdrew into himself further. My professional assessment after the first fifteen minutes was that he was disassociated with what had happened to him and from the remand prison itself. He gave me the impression of being very isolated and inwardly focussed. And fearful.'

Jeff closed his eyes. 'She's pretty good.'

'Please explain, Doctor, what you mean by the term "disassociated"?'

'Oh, yes. I'm so sorry,' the psychiatrist responded, a little flustered. '"Disassociated" means putting a distance between oneself and one's circumstances. It's often also referred to as "depersonalisation". The patient does not want to think of himself as who he is, because he is frightened or because the environment doesn't suit him for whatever reason.

'Once I introduced some questions about the crimes he was charged with, the Accused's behaviour changed to more anxious and talkative, although he remained relatively resigned.'

'In your professional opinion, Dr Moroney,' the Defence barrister asked, 'what did you conclude about the Accused's mental state on or around the sixteenth of February, nineteen-ninety-six?'

'Your Honour, according to the reports from the New South Wales Police and the AFP doctors, the Accused showed significant signs of depression and anxiety. He expressed deep feelings of anger and resentment towards the Victim's husband, both to the other psychiatrists and to myself. He displayed bitterness and envy and spoke of being driven mad by his hateful thoughts.'

Jeff shifted in his chair, the familiarity of the doctor's words jarring his soul. He was reminded how numb and disassociated he too was feeling, given the strain of the present environment. It was insulation against the painful realities of life, and he recognised the definition only too well. García looked no different today, unmoved and staring blankly into space.

'The Defence has made a mistake calling this woman as their expert,' Jeff said to his companions. 'She can't even comment first-hand on what his state of mind was immediately after shooting Lynn, so how on Earth can she accurately assess what drove him to do it?'

'Shame he didn't see a doctor before, like his wife asked him to,' Kierney added. 'Then, even if he or she hadn't been able to help him, at least that doctor would've been better to have here.'

'Whose side are you two on?' Gerry sniggered in disbelief. 'You should be rapt Winton's going to have a crack at her.'

The grieving father glared at his friend. 'For fuck's sake, mate.'

'Sorry,' the affable man responded, bewildered by the Diamonds' unending sibylline charity.

His client let the apology go, intent on listening to the questions but vowing to revisit the tactless comment which overlooked the fact that if García had sought medical help, the mother of his children might still be alive.

Greenshaw pressed on. 'Dr Moroney, did the Accused give you the impression of a man who would commit a murder?'

'No, Your Honour. He did not,' the woman shook her head, caught up in the drama implied in the lawyer's tone. 'He gave me the impression of a meek and mild man who had been driven to distraction. Pushed over the edge, so to say. And by the time I met with him face-to-face, his demeanour had returned to meek and mild.'

'Driven to distraction? Could you expand on this expression, please?'

'Yes, Your Honour. The Accused told me that his feelings of jealousy towards the Diamond family and their lifestyle, coupled with his own poor relationship with his wife and the fact that his job was giving him dissatisfaction, resulted in periods of intense rage, during which he would fantasise about killing Mr Diamond.'

Gerry nudged his old friend. 'Are you OK with hearing this? Did you want to go?'

Jeff shook his head. 'No, mate. I'm fine. Kizzy, what about you?'

The songwriter's daughter definitely looked a little pale, now he had the occasion to check. He felt guilty for allowing himself to become so engrossed in the battleground below him. Kierney gave him a queasy smile but insisted she wanted to stay.

Her father put his arm around her and kissed her temple. 'Thanks, gorgeous,' he whispered. 'I shouldn't have ignored you.'

'Doctor, in your experience, what types of events or circumstances lead meek and mild men to commit violent acts?' Greenshaw enquired.

'Oh... A whole range of things, Your Honour,' Moroney answered. 'If the person is on medication and misses sufficient doses, suppressed behaviour may return that may result in a violent tendency.'

'Psychosis, you mean?' the barrister interrupted, prompting his witness.

'Yes, in some instances, Your Honour,' the witness replied. 'Or severe depression. In some cases, people with normally manageable mental disorders are provoked beyond their tolerance, which can also make them act out of character.'

'Thank you, Doctor. Which of these potential reasons does your professional opinion lead you to favour in this situation?'

Philippa Moroney hesitated for a few moments. Jeff understood why. This woman did not see patients day-in and day-out like an ordinary psychiatrist would. He wondered if she ever had. She was a paid opinion-provider, not a true practitioner. He could tell by her lack of confidence that she was acutely conscious of this fact right now.

'My diagnosis for the Accused is that he is severely clinically depressed, and that his depression and anxiety have gone untreated for many years.'

'For how many years?' the lawyer asked.

'Since he arrived in Australia, I believe. At six years old,' the doctor answered. 'For forty years, therefore, Your Honour.'

'*Excelente*,' Jeff whispered, taking Kierney's hand. 'Now we're getting somewhere. That's the first piece of real data she's given us.'

Plainly, Defence Counsel disagreed with the philomath in the dress circle. He looked frantic, as though he wanted to reach into his witness' mouth and extract the information he sought.

'Not before this?'

'No, Your Honour,' Moroney affirmed. 'The Accused, his father and his two older brothers arrived in Sydney without their mother. It's my opinion, and that of my colleagues, that his depression and anxiety stem from having left his mother behind in Spain at such a young age.'

An associate from the Defence bench handed a folder of papers to the court official, who passed it to the *Foreman*. It was the psychiatrist's report, and the jury was asked to read the summary on the first page.

Kierney squeezed her dad's hand. 'We're all in a minority of one.'

Jeff sighed, uttering a low groan as he began to cry again. Desertion, abandonment, betrayal... All the emotions which had plagued him as a child, but for much different reasons. In the dock, García was crying too. Was the jury watching? No. They were all transfixed by the Canadian psychiatrist, which was an element of good fortune for Lynn's constituency.

The world-changer knew he couldn't influence this judicial fissure from his place in the upper reaches. Moreover, in the moment, he found he no longer had a strong inclination to do so.

The circumstances of his own childhood had left him scarred like García, yet he hadn't murdered anyone. He hadn't even shot someone while not knowing what to do. He had never put himself in a position where he might shoot someone dead if his weapon were to malfunction.

'Are you alright, *papá*? What are you thinking?'

'Yeah. All good, *pequeñita*. I'm thinking that diminished mental capacity definitely exists, but it's no excuse for doing what he did,' he whispered, wiping his eyes and looking around to check no-one was listening. 'There are thousands upon thousands of people who might be as depressed and angry as this little runt but who never take another person's life from their loved ones.'

'You, for example?' the eighteen-year-old reinforced her father's concerns, in the same way Lynn would have.

The lonely man shrugged, feeling a dull tingling sensation in his chest. The first for some time, he realised.

'Heaps of people could be labelled with diminished mental capacity, but it's a matter of degrees,' he explained. 'Sure, he wasn't Mr Happy, but he had two arms, two legs and a functioning brain. He was married with children. He had a job. OK, not one he liked, but hey... Does that mean his mental capacity is diminished beyond the point of being accountable for his own actions?'

Counsel for the Defence drew the jury's attention back to the witness, tired of waiting for the material evidence his case required from her testimony. 'So, Doctor, for the court, your diagnosis is that the Accused has suffered severe depression and anxiety for the last forty years, and that because it has gone undiagnosed and untreated, his ability to handle his mental state led him to snap, so to speak, causing him to commit the violent act for which he is on trial, that the Crown alleges to be murder.'

'Yes, Your Honour,' the doctor nodded. 'That is my professional opinion.'

Jeff's body froze in anticipation of the Prosecution's interference, which was not forthcoming. Where was Winton for this most obvious leading question? He exhaled and spoke a little louder, beginning to care less whether others around him overheard.

'So does this infer he was walking around with a loaded gun for forty years without incident, only to snap on that day? Not likely, Your Honour.'

Furtive laughter tittered from the seats surrounding the famous onlookers. Kierney frowned, urging her father to be quiet. However, her warning morphed into a smile of delight when she watched her father clench his left arm into his body. Her *mamá* was calling, and her feedback was edifying.

'You didn't do that on purpose, did you?' the youngster whispered.

He shook his head, crossing his tattooed heart.

'Objection!' came the familiar voice of Graham Winton, drawing the Diamonds back to the proceedings below.

'Counsel for the Prosecution?' Judge Milne croaked, having sat inert for almost an hour.

'Thank you, Your Honour,' the red-faced senior partner replied. 'The court cannot be expected to believe the shooting was unplanned, simply as a result of a "snap" in the Accused's mental state. He had brought a loaded gun into the lobby of the hotel where his nemesis had booked to stay that night.'

'I won't allow the objection, Mr Winton. You'll have to wait until your cross-examination to put your theory to the Witness.'

'Apologies, Your Honour,' he relented, raising both hands amid high drama.

Jeff shook his head and smiled in appreciation, forgiving the barrister's earlier omission. 'Very clever. He gets his point out in the open, buys time so the jury can consider it, and then gets another opportunity to drive it home later. Nice move.'

Greenshaw and Winton exchanged melodramatic glares, two prize-fighters closing in on their moment of truth.

'Dr Moroney,' the Defence barrister addressed his witness. 'One final question. You agreed to my use of the word "snap" to describe a switch in the Accused's behaviour from meek and mild to violent?'

'Yes, I did, Your Honour.'

'Is it therefore possible, in your professional opinion, for the Accused to "snap back" the other way equally quickly, from violent to his usual meek and mild self?'

Again, Philippa Moroney took a few seconds to consider her response. She wrang her hands and became red in the face.

'Yes, Your Honour,' she answered. 'It would be possible if the moment of anger or desperation had passed or if something else had diverted his attention.'

Jeff leant forward, eager to learn how this latest twist would play out.

'So, in your opinion, could the Accused have been training his gun, having snapped into his angry, violent state on the assumption that he was going to see Mr Diamond in his line of sight, and then snapped back again when he realised his weapon was pointing at Mr Diamond's wife instead?'

The celebrity watched the jury perk up at this lateral suggestion. It was a good one, he had to admit.

Kierney dug him in the ribs. 'That's interesting,' she whispered.

The public gallery was mumbling to itself while the psychiatrist considered her reply. Jeff nodded, putting his fingers to his mouth.

'Yes, Your Honour,' the nervous woman replied. 'That's a reasonable theory.'

'By which you mean what exactly, Doctor?'

She sighed. 'I mean that in such a transition, Mr García would have been confused, which may have led him to pull the trigger without true consciousness.'

'Thank you, Dr Moroney. I have no further questions.'

The crowd became agitated again, left in limbo as the witness breathed a sigh of relief and took several sips of water. Looking to deflect opposing counsel's obvious glee at having finished on a note of apparent doubt, Graham Winton leapt out of his chair, clutching several pieces of paper covered with handwritten scrawl.

The judge shook her head, waving to the court officer to prepare for a break.

'Ladies and gentlemen, we shall take a short recess of twenty minutes before carrying on with the Prosecution's cross-examination of Dr Moroney. Please return promptly by three o'clock. Thank you.'

STATE OF MIND

Back in the safety of their meeting room down the corridor from the lifts, with their dogged security staff stationed outside, father and daughter were grateful for the chance at last to speak freely about the psychiatrist's testimony.

'What happens to the minority which gets so small that it's not worth anyone's attention,' Kierney asked, 'because the rest of us have got our hands full and can't do everything?'

'They get nothing,' Jeff answered with resignation.

'Do we just let them become extinct?'

The billionaire shrugged, sipping on an insipid cup of coffee. 'Ugh! That's disgusting,' he moaned. 'Good question, angel. What do you think? Darwinian principles are OK for nature, but are they right for the so-called superior human race? At what stage do we step in and say a minority's worth saving?'

The teenager harked back to the conversation the evening before last, where they had spoken of her parents' debates about utility and statistical significance. She assumed "Survival of the fittest" was what her dad had meant by "Darwinian principles".

'Fittest for what?' she thought out loud. 'Is it about potential utility?'

'You *are* sharp these days,' Jeff chuckled. 'Perceived utility, potential utility. You really get it, don't you?'

'I hope so,' Kierney smiled. 'Sometimes it takes a while for the penny to drop, but I do eventually get there.'

'You're streets ahead of most people, Kizzo,' the proud father reassured her. 'Don't be hard on yourself. You're an introvert who's learned to be extravert. Like me, a thinker, then a doer. That's just who you are. You come to the right conclusion, but it might take you a bit of time. Jet's definitely a doer then a thinker. He forces himself into introversion to give matters sufficient consideration. Either way's fine, as long as you're aware of your strengths and weaknesses.'

'Was *mamá* an introvert or an extravert?'

The handsome philosopher stood up and walked over to the window, staring out over the heritage-listed buildings leading down to the harbour. Lynn's smiling face filled the void behind his eyes, and his heart skipped a beat with short-lived excitement. When would this reflex optimism die down? It was like a potent but fleeting high; a drug dealing him a spike of pleasure before shoving him over the edge into another chasm of darkness. He pressed the palms of his hands on the glass and leant into the windowpane, half hoping it would shatter and tip him out to the pavement below.

Not high enough, Miss Irony cackled from the inner recesses of her host's sick mind.

'Your *mamá* was as close as I've ever known to being right on the line,' he answered. 'Point zero. She was manufactured that way. My guess is she was born like you and me, but her years of Dyson schooling balanced her out. Jet was born on the other side of the line. He's more like your Grandpa and Anna. Definitely a doer.'

The young woman nodded. 'That makes sense. But how are we ever going to help these tiny minorities if we don't have infinite resources to do so on a case-by-case basis? It's impossible.'

'Yeah, gorgeous. It is impossible. Perfection isn't feasible, and neither should it be. If it were, we'd get too complacent and eventually degenerate. The important thing is to understand how to prioritise. Agree on how to prioritise, rather...

'And the other important thing is to educate people well enough to be able to help themselves. García didn't know to get help when he needed it, neither did his father nor presumably his teachers. His wife did, but by then he was too grown-up and stubborn. Men tend to see seeking help as a sign of weakness. We're hopeless that way, *pequeñita*.'

'Will prison help him or make him worse?' Kierney asked, smiling and looking at her watch. 'Wow! We have to go back. Can we talk about Granddad tonight, please, *papá*?'

'We can talk about anything, baby, if you're up for it.'

The teenager clapped her hands in excitement. 'I'm up for it.'

Gerry had already taken his seat when the Diamonds returned to the public gallery. He was chatting to a small group of people who fell silent when the others arrived. The loyal business manager was relieved to see them.

'Good grief! They're so hungry for gossip,' he laughed. 'It's amazing how many ways of saying "No comment" a man can come up with under pressure.'

Jeff smiled. 'Know what you mean, mate. Your silence will be rewarded.'

'Glad to hear it. What's the plan for tonight, by the way? This isn't going to be over, is it?'

'Nope,' his friend agreed. 'We'll have the closing arguments in the morning, and maybe the jury'll have made their decisions by the end of tomorrow. We may get home for the weekend.'

'What about Wendy?' Kierney interrupted. 'Do you know if they're still going to call her? Either side?'

'This morning I'd have said no, but I think there's been a bit of a swing to the Defence today,' the widower conceded. 'Maybe the Prosecution does need to call in her services, but she'd have to be thoroughly briefed and kept in check. It could so easily backfire on them. They've also got their own psych' on standby, remember?'

She nodded, weighing up these options while they watched the actors resume the same positions on the stage as before the intermission: Winton on his feet, Dr Moroney in the left-hand box and García isolated yet prominent in the dock. The jury appeared weary, despite the extra opportunity to stretch their legs and rehydrate.

'Did you want to go to Mum and Dad's tonight?' Gerry asked.

Jeff inhaled, looking at his watch. 'Shit! Thanks for reminding me. I promised to ring Celia and let her know. I'm so bloody self-absorbed these days. It makes me sick.'

'No sweat, mate,' his manager said, slapping his friend's knee hard. 'You know what she's like. We could rock up on the doorstep unannounced at midnight, and she'd still welcome us with open arms. It won't matter. We can call her at the end of this session.'

'Cheers, mate,' the famous man sighed. 'It's still bloody rude though. Not a good example to set my daughter.'

Kierney nudged her father's shoulder playfully, and he returned the favour, pushing her into the bodyguard on the other side. The burly man looked round in surprise, his arm not yielding an inch on impact. She giggled as she bounced back into her dad from the deflection.

'Dr Moroney, good afternoon,' Winton's self-assured voice rang out. 'I trust you are fine to continue?'

'I am, Your Honour. Thank you.'

'Good-oh. Now, in your earlier testimony, you stated the Accused did not give you the impression he was capable of murder, but he has confessed to shooting someone at close range. Could you please inform the court how we can trust your professional opinion?'

'Bloody hell!' the well-groomed executive exclaimed, as did several others within range. 'What was that? He's really going for the jugular. Don't beat about the bush, Winton, old boy.'

The barrister's opening salvo had been a little too direct for comfort, Jeff concurred, choosing to say nothing. Greenshaw was caught napping, one of his associates having to prod him to object, which he did with his gown in full flight. The judge warned the Prosecution to treat the witness with the utmost courtesy, but allowed the question.

The poor woman wobbled a little on her ankles before responding surprisingly well. 'Your Honour, I said Mr García didn't give me the impression during our meetings of being someone who would commit a murder. I believe that was the question from Defence Counsel. This doesn't rule out a different side of his personality manifesting at other times.'

'Very well. Thank you for clarifying. So in that case, you do think the Accused is capable of committing murder at other times?' Winton asked in a less attacking tone.

'It's a possibility. His profile suggests he might be capable of violence when he is at the lowest point of his depressive cycle,' Moroney answered.

'Thank you, Doctor. Are you able to envisage a situation where his rage would drive him to murder someone?'

The plump woman was sweating, redder in the face than the chubby barrister. She took a large gulp of water and prepared to reply.

'Your Honour, there are many documented cases where previously law-abiding people have snapped and committed assaults or even murder. I had not met the Accused prior to Ms Diamond's shooting. Nor did I witness the act. Therefore, I cannot give the court a definitive answer as to how full of rage he was on the day, or whether it was sufficient to cause him to shoot someone. I'm sorry.'

Jeff winced. 'Don't apologise, woman. It's your professional opinion we're after, not retrospective mind-reading.'

The security guard to Kierney's right laughed aloud, as did several others around them. The teenager pulled a childish face, as if to say, "Oh-oh," before grinning at her dad.

Winton was on a roll. 'Was this man psychotic, in your view, Doctor?'

'No, Your Honour. I don't believe so.'

'You don't believe the act he committed on the sixteenth of February this year was a psychotic act?'

'No, Your Honour. The Accused was in touch with reality. He has a clear memory of the day of the shooting. In my opinion, he committed an act out of extreme desperation and anger. Psychosis implies distortions in the brain, such as hearing voices or hallucinations, or imagining one is in a different situation or environment. In my discussions with the Accused, he confirmed complete awareness of where he was and why he had gone to the hotel that morning.'

'Doctor, would this act of desperation and anger have been preventable if the Accused had been receiving appropriate treatment for his mental disorder?'

The words "mental disorder" slipped off the lawyer's tongue as if they tasted foul, causing Jeff's blood to boil with the implied superiority. Did anyone in his family suffer from a mental illness? Did any of his friends? Had he ever bothered to ask, or even think about it?

'Probably, Your Honour,' the witness answered, her confidence growing. 'The majority of patients respond well to treatment. Sometimes it takes a while to find the best treatment, and a few do not respond at all well. Everyone is different, Your Honour.'

Kierney smiled at her father, and he kissed her temple.

'How would you have treated the Accused, Doctor?' the prosecution barrister asked.

The psychiatrist was ready for this question. Again, the celebrity sneaked a look at the Defendant, who remained motionless and disinterested. Was this his natural state the court was seeing during the trial, or had they presented him in a medicated condition? It didn't much matter, but this mouse-like man was possibly the meekest, mildest murderer the world had ever seen.

'I would have prescribed a daily dose of anti-depressants to start with... say twenty or forty milligrams, depending on health issues and whether the patient was on any other medication... with a sustained programme of cognitive therapy to get him comfortable with talking about himself and to acknowledge his problems. If he felt under stress about his work or his family life, I might also prescribe anti-anxiety medication such as beta blockers or similar, and recommend he attend a self-help group of some kind.'

'Assassinators Anonymous,' Gerry sniggered.

To his surprise, the widower laughed too, before delivering a swift kick to his friend's ankle.

The doctor continued. 'If the symptoms persisted or even worsened due to having acknowledged their existence, I would consider increasing the dosage or changing the prescription. Even residential care, if the patient could afford it or if it were available to him some other way.'

'Interesting comment,' Jeff muttered to his daughter, a disheartened finger stabbing the air between himself and the Spaniard. 'If it were available to him? It *is* available to him. That's the other thing that makes me so effin' angry, you pathetic weasel. I wonder if he even bothered to find out how much we put into mental health services in this city.'

Down below, Winton turned to the jury but continued to address the witness. 'So, Doctor, in your professional opinion, was the murder of Ms Diamond avoidable?'

'I cannot be certain either way, Your Honour. But in the large majority of cases, appropriate, sustained treatment of a patient who wishes to feel better will generally yield positive results.'

'In this case, Dr Moroney?'

The celebrity held his breath. 'Crunch time, lady. Did Juan Antonio wish to feel better?'

The woman rocked back and forth again and glanced over to the Defence bench for support, receiving only polite smiles. 'Yes, Your Honour. I believe the Accused would have responded to treatment, and the shooting could have been avoided.'

Prosecuting Counsel glossed over the Defence's expert witness' unhelpful and sympathetic conclusion, brooking the line of enquiry on a tangent to keep the jury's attention just enough to play the Queen's advantage.

'Dr Moroney, have you any idea what percentage of people suffering from severe depression and anxiety end up committing violent acts such as this?'

'Not an exact figure, Your Honour,' she responded. 'Very small, Your Honour.'

Winton persisted. 'Small? How small? Five percent? Ten percent?'

'No. Probably less than one tenth of one percent.'

'Thank you,' a triumphant Graham Winton stated for the jury's benefit. 'One tenth of a percent, ladies and gentlemen. An estimated one in every thousand people with severe depression and anxiety end up committing violent assaults.'

Jeff leant back in his chair and stretched his legs as far as the fixed seating allowed, their relentless restlessness driving him crazy. 'I don't know why he's so smug. It doesn't have any bearing on the case because García never sought treatment. Is Mr Floaty even paying attention? Why isn't he on his feet?'

'He's banking on the jury not making the distinction,' Kierney offered.

A broad grin spread across her dad's face. 'Whoa! That's brilliant, angel. I'm very impressed. You could well be right.'

'So, in your professional experience, Dr Moroney, does the fact the Accused has suffered in the way you describe for many years without committing such a violent act mean his mental capacity was diminished on the sixteenth of February this year, as the Defence would have us believe?'

The psychiatrist again paused for a short while. 'In the sense that he was not feeling positive about his life and was experiencing anger and jealousy, yes, Your Honour. The Diamond family is often in the news over the holiday period. Their visit to Sydney may have exacerbated his negative feelings, reminding him of the difference between their lives and his own.'

Winton pressed her further. 'But, Doctor, I'm sure you're aware that the Diamond family visits Sydney regularly and have been a headline act in Australian festive entertainment for the last twenty years.'

'Yes, I am well aware of this, Your Honour.'

'Thank you. And would you agree that the Accused must also be well accustomed to seeing the Diamonds in the news? During his testimony, he even told us he attended a Jeff Diamond concert!'

Hearing jeers from the public gallery, the psychiatrist's gaze darted to her left, where García appeared lost and dejected. 'Yes, Your Honour.'

'So, Doctor Moroney,' Prosecution Counsel spoke more to the jury than to the Defence witness, 'why this year and not last year? Or any year in the last two decades?'

The woman stood taller and raised her hand. 'I'm unable to answer that, Your Honour, as the court already knows. I had not met the Accused before this year, and there are no medical records available for me to assess his psychiatric history.'

The widower whistled under his breath. 'Jesus. She's standing up to him better than I thought she would.'

Graham mimicked the doctor's actions, increasing the urgency in his tone too. 'Of course. I'm sorry. So let's concentrate ourselves back on the sixteenth of February this year. Would the Accused's exacerbated negative feelings about his life and his periods of anger and jealousy be expected to impair his judgement so far as to commit such an act of violence as murdering someone in cold blood?'

A nervous tremor coursed through the crowd, slithering past the three amigos and their minders on its way around. It had been a while since their last reminder of the stark circumstances surrounding Lynn's demise.

Her husband exhaled, daring to gaze from side to side and engage in direct eye contact with their fellow mourners. Then, capitalising on the energy afforded him by this dangerous game, he leant forward to see if the jurors were affected similarly.

'In some cases, yes, Your Honour,' Dr Moroney replied.

'In most cases?'

'No. Not in most cases, Your Honour.'

'In this case?'

'In this case, probably not,' the psychiatrist muttered.

'Could you repeat your answer for the jury, please, Doctor?' Winton requested. 'Do you think the Accused's mental capacity was diminished to a greater level than usual on the sixteenth of February this year?'

She took a deep breath. 'Probably not.'

'Thank you, Doctor.'

Jeff watched the twelve stoic citizens take in the last few questions and answers. Some straightened up and listened more intently, whereas others shook their heads. The dress circle had become quiet, eerily expectant.

Winton continued after a deliberate pause. 'One final question, Doctor, if I may?' he turned back to the witness. 'The Defence's last question to you centred around a suggestion that the Accused had "snapped", to use my learned colleague's own word, out of the state of rage which had led him to be pointing a gun at a person with the intention of shooting, perhaps fatally, before "snapping back" into his normal state when he realised he was about to shoot someone else. That is, his intended victim's wife, Ms Lynn Diamond.'

'Yes, Your Honour.'

'From a rage to meek and mild, which I believe were your words.'

'Yes, they were, Your Honour.'

'How therefore can you explain, Dr Moroney, the fact the Accused pulled the trigger four times, releasing four rounds at his victim?'

The red-faced woman's breathing became heavier, visibly troubled by this argument. No help came forth from the Defence bench. There was none they could provide. It was a reasonable question.

'No, Your Honour. I cannot explain that.'

'And similarly, Doctor,' Counsel for the Prosecution turned the screws a little further, 'how can you explain the words the Accused uttered to the Victim's husband? The words which roughly translate into "I wanted to kill you, but it's better this way." Does this sound like a man who has had a "reverse snap"?'

Hearing several jury members laugh at this invented term, the Canadian bowed her head. 'The only way I can explain it would be to suggest that he had by then resigned himself to his fate,' she stammered a little. 'The deed was done, and the meek and mild man knew there was no hope of escaping the consequences of his actions.'

Clever answer under duress, Jeff nodded. The nervous psychiatrist had succeeded in maintaining the ambiguity upon which García's Defence depended.

'Oh!' Winton jumped back to the witness, startling her. 'There *was* one other thing, Dr Moroney. When you met with the Accused, did you discuss whether he thought he had achieved his goal that morning at The Pensione Hotel? When he told Mr Diamond, "I wanted to kill you, but it's better this way," did the Accused believe it really was better this way?'

This time, with the doctor still under oath, there was no way of muddying the waters. Philippa Moroney had no choice but to answer the Prosecution's question in a straightforward way. The surviving celebrity spouse stared down at García, both men waiting for the expert's opinion.

'Yes, Your Honour,' she affirmed. 'The Accused was adamant that Mr Diamond deserved the crime that had been perpetrated against Ms Diamond.'

The public gallery, which had shown such collective restraint for the last few hours, suddenly burst into a cacophony of angry shouts and taunts, with many people on their feet and pointing at the small, docile man in the dock.

'You little bastard!' one man yelled.

'Couldn't agree more,' Jeff whispered to Kierney, who was as white as a sheet. 'Say it, beautiful.'

'You little bastard,' the young woman repeated self-consciously, leaning against her father and crying. '*Puta de mierda, Juan Antonio García Ruelas.*'

The father kissed his daughter's hair and pulled her body towards his, tightening his right arm around her shoulder. '*Muy bien, gorgeousita.* Well done.'

A sharp pain seared through the widower's chest for three or four seconds before coming to a sudden stop, making him cry even more. Gerry looked across at his good friends and shook his head in sorrow.

Leaving the Supreme Court at the end of a third long day, Gerry and Kierney parted company with the great man and left him talking to the prosecution team in the downstairs lobby. They walked back with the spoils of this morning's shopping to the car park where the accountant's rental car had been hurriedly abandoned earlier.

'Phew! What a day!' the accountant exclaimed.

Kierney nodded, shaking the colourful bags. 'Worse for you two than me. Mine was quite easy.'

'Can I ask what your dad's thinking of doing when he gets back to Melbourne?' Gerry asked, pleased at last to speak to the young woman alone. 'Have you talked about it?'

'No, not much,' she replied. 'I know he's scared he'll be lost when he doesn't have to focus on anything. Having the funeral and the memorial service, and now the trial, at least he's been busy and forced to go places and get on with stuff. I'm not sure what he'll do when it's over. Moving house'll be his new focus, I suppose.'

'And what are *you* going to be doing?' the kind Irishman asked.

'More of the same,' the youngster shrugged, knowing this wasn't the answer their manager sought. 'I've got a project organised with Melbourne Uni'. A human rights research project that sounds really interesting.'

As expected, the indomitable executive didn't find such work at all appealing and continued to press his own agenda. 'Still living in at home though?'

'Yes. Of course,' Kierney told her pseudo-uncle with a grin. 'Where else would I live? I'm only a child.'

'Yeah, right,' Gerry chortled. 'Only a child indeed... Even more reason for you not to get sucked into all this misery, my girl. You need to start enjoying yourself again and not be so concerned with your *papá*.'

'We're fine,' the teenager insisted. 'It's not all doom and gloom when we're at home, and it's not as if he won't let me go out or see my friends or anything. To be honest, he has to push me out some days.'

'Hmm... That's OK then. Just make sure it doesn't get to you, or I'll have to send Auntie Fiona over to sort you out.'

Kierney giggled. 'I'm glad you two've got engaged. I really like Fiona. When do you think you'll get married? Soon?'

The pair had reached Gerry's hired car, having picked up a following of inquisitive fans along their journey. He opened the doors with the remote control gadget and shielded the teenager from view. The car's indicators flashed to greet them, and they slotted the collection of bags into the rear footwell. Before anyone had time to approach and deter their departure, she dropped into the passenger seat and fastened her seatbelt.

'Don't know yet when we'll do the deed,' Gerry resumed their discussion while starting the engine. 'We'd like to do it soon, but we're concerned about your dad's feelings. It'd be like snubbing our noses at him if we do it too soon.'

'Oh, I don't think so. He'd be really happy for you. Plus, it'll give him something else to work on, providing you give him plenty of jobs to do. Will he be your best man?'

The executive chuckled. 'Well... I don't know that either. What with the huge choice of friends I have, we'll have to run a lottery for that privilege. For sure, I'd love to have him as my best man, but I don't think it'd be fair on him.'

'Why not? He won't see it that way. Ask him.'

'And he'll feel obliged to say yes.'

'I'll ask him,' Kierney suggested, smiling. 'Leave it to me, Uncle Gerry.'

'Right you are, child,' her driver laughed. 'Much appreciated.'

The car turned left into Macquarie Street and pulled up outside the Supreme Court. The slim, dark-haired celebrity jumped out and ran towards the entrance, where she had spotted her dad still talking with Graham Winton. He waved to her through the window and shook the solicitor's hand. They met in the doorway and both ran back to the waiting car.

Jeff opened the rear passenger door to let his daughter slide in. 'Cheers, mate,' he said, jumping into the seat in front and slamming the door hard.

Gerry checked his wing mirror and moved off at speed into the evening traffic, heading for the Harbour Bridge and his parents' home. 'I take it you don't want to do anything in the city first?' he checked, hoping they were committed to crossing the river without detour.

'Nope,' the superstar replied, turning round to confirm with Kierney, who shook her head. 'We'll stop on the way and get some wine and flowers.'

'You don't need to do that,' the North Sydney native scoffed. 'I never do.'

'Yeah, well...' his friend sneered, winking at his daughter. 'By the way, guys, Winton said the jury was told this morning they'll be put up in a hotel tonight, pending closing statements tomorrow morning. The end seems to be in sight, ladies and gentlemen.'

'And no Wonderful Wendy?' Gerry asked.

'No Wonderful Wendy,' the forty-three-year-old confirmed, smirking. 'Mr Floaty's apparently talking about calling a handgun specialist though, so that's a possible delay. But I think Winton's quietly confident they won't be able to get him to say anything convincing enough regarding the ability to shoot four times accidentally with that type of weapon. Then there's the line of sight thingo to prove or disprove intent. We might see García up there again in the morning.'

'It would be good if it did finish tomorrow,' a wistful female voice came from behind the two tall men. '*Ya he tenido suficiente. Estoy harto.*'

'*Yo también, pequeñita,*' her *papá* agreed.

'*¿Qué?*' Gerry asked over his shoulder. 'I'm not wearing my translating trousers today, *gringos*. Help me out here.'

Kierney laughed. 'Translating trousers! Can you get those? They'd come in very handy. Are they available for both sexes?'

'Sure thing,' their chauffeur joked. 'Blue for boys and pink for girls.'

'*Excelente*,' the teenager giggled. 'That means "excellent", by the way.'

'Kizzo, steady!' Jeff rebuked his daughter for her cheeky reply. 'Respect your elders. Are you old for this purpose, mate?'

'Bastard,' Gerry hissed through gritted teeth. 'You can respect your elders too, mate, or you can walk. Take your pick.'

Knowing they were no more than two kilometres from the Blakes' house, the celebrity fumbled for the door handle in jest. 'It means, "I've had enough and I'm fed up," mate, if you're interested.'

Celia had spent all afternoon listing suitable topics of conversation with which to divert the eighteen-year-old, who was happy to help with dinner preparations once they reached the homely Mosman residence. The two women talked about the Blake grandchildren, Tamilla's recent holiday and the fact that Gerald's heart condition was affecting the couple's ability to play golf and enjoy their retirement.

After a shower to wash away the day's legal proceedings, Jeff strode into the kitchen to remove three beer bottles from the fridge, stopping to kiss both women before re-joining the men who were smoking on the deck outside. 'Thanks, Celia. I owe you.'

'No, you don't, silly,' his best friend's mother disputed, patting him on the arm. 'Just relax. Dinner will be ready in a quarter of an hour.'

After Kierney had set the table in the large dining room, she lingered at the far end, in front of the framed pictures on the sideboard. She counted four wedding photographs: one for each daughter; a black and white one of Celia and Gerald, taken in the late nineteen-forties; and the radiant, smiling faces of her own parents. Her *papá* had become like a second son to the Blakes, and she was grateful on his behalf.

These pictorial souvenirs made her think back to the story Dr Moroney had related about García's mother being absent in his life. It must have been horrible for a young child to be without a mother to cuddle into, to wash and dress him and feed him. Even though Kierney and her brother had spent many days and nights supervised by various nannies or being looked after by their fantastic father if their mother had been travelling, she still remembered the extra-special feeling of *mamá*'s love and attention.

It was not so different for an independent eighteen-year-old either, she rued, tears brimming again as she stroked her parents' wedding picture.

'*Te amo, mamá. Te amo, papá.*'

After dinner, Jeff took his daughter up to the bedroom which Celia always allocated to the young lady when she visited, and they sat together on the bed nursing steaming mugs of tea. It was pleasant to be alone again, and the teacher hadn't forgotten her request to talk about her grandfather's trial. However, first there was her other question to debate.

'Do you think incarceration has the power to rehabilitate offenders?' the intellectual asked, watching her face break into a wide smile.

'Oh, cool! Thanks for remembering. Some yes, some no.'

'What was that? "Yes and no?"' he teased. 'How can I let you get away with that?'

Kierney smiled. ''Cause it's my answer, take it or leave it!'

'Well, you're right, *pequeñita*. Tell me why.'

'It'd depend if García wanted to get better, I s'pose. If I were depressed and didn't like my life outside of prison, and then was given a long sentence, I'd probably find it hard to want to feel better.'

Jeff nodded, comparing it to his own situation and the life sentence which García had handed down two months ago. 'Yeah. It'd definitely be tough,' he agreed, 'but the psychs in prison'd work with him. They'd try and make him talk and work on a plan to make his general mood positive, I'm sure. Does he strike you as the type of person who's going to mix with other hardened cons?'

'No. Not at all,' the teenager shook her head. 'I think he'll be too timid and scared to mix with anyone in there. He seems very isolated.'

'Good observation,' Jeff replied, tapping her knee. 'Very good, in fact. That may have quite a lot to do with the fact he's sitting in the dock at his own trial though.'

Kierney giggled, tossing her long hair back over her shoulders. 'Then it's not a good observation!'

'No, it is,' the wise teacher insisted, 'cause I think you're right. He's obviously isolated from his wife, even though up 'til his shooting spree, they were still together on some level. I wonder what his relationship's like with his kids? Not too good, by all accounts. And he doesn't like his job either, so isolated must be pretty damned accurate.'

'Was Granddad isolated from Abuela before he went to prison?' the young woman engineered a deft change in topic.

Jeff leant against the bedroom wall and stared across the room to a painting of horses galloping across a paddock, bought by one of Gerry's sisters at an art fair years ago. As usual, whenever his mind was forced back to his childhood without warning, his first instinct was to clam up. Taking a deep breath, he fixed his daughter's eyes in his.

'Sorry, *papá*. You don't have to answer these questions tonight.'

'I do. I made you a promise, didn't I?'

Kierney nodded, and her father took another deep breath, steeling his mind into co-operating.

'I really don't know.'

'After all the suspense, that's all you can say?' she burst out laughing. 'Was that so hard?'

The billionaire laughed too, reaching for a nearby cushion and hurling it towards the dark-haired gipsy girl whose turn of phrase constantly reminded him of his beautiful best friend.

'Truthfully, I have no memory of my folks getting on or not getting on,' he answered. 'They used to fight and then end up running into the bedroom and slamming the door, making all sorts of noises that Auntie Lena and I didn't understand. Except we knew not to go in, 'cause we'd either get yelled at to get out or something thrown at us.'

Kierney frowned. 'Fight and then have sex?'

'Yeah. Sometimes I wonder if they could even distinguish between the two,' the handsome man shrugged. 'But that's just my memory. I have no real idea. It wasn't healthy, that much I know. *Abuela'd* come out to get a beer from the fridge or their cigarettes, and she'd have a shine on her cheekbone like she'd been slapped. But she always went back in again.'

'Oh, my God,' the teenager gasped, making no attempt to hide her revulsion. 'Why?'

'All she'd ever known, I reckon. Who knows? Maybe they loved each other in some perverse sort of way? I have a sneaking suspicion that my intensity comes from your granddad. I guess he could be very persuasive and dominating. And your *Abuela* was young and swept off her feet, so she just accepted whatever he did. I did the same to your *mamá* for a while, and to every woman before her, but she got wise to me pretty quickly and put a stop to it.'

'Stop to what? You never hit *mamá*, did you?'

'Jesus, no!' Jeff replied, aghast. 'That's not what I meant. I've never hit any woman, and that's the absolute truth, gorgeous, I promise. I was a dominating obsessive-compulsive for the first few years we were together, but never once tried or even wanted to hit her.'

Kierney had tears in her eyes, feeling guilty for her insinuation. 'I never thought you would've, *papá*. I'm sorry for even saying it.'

'Forget it, *pequeñita*. It's not important.'

'So how did you learn how to be so loving, growing up in an environment like that?'

Her dad shrugged. 'Fuck knows... I just knew the way my parents behaved was wrong. From reading, watching TV, seeing my friends' families... One thing I do regret is the fact that Lena never learned to care. She never opened her eyes like I did, so I was lucky.'

The teenager shook her head. 'No, *papá*. You weren't lucky. You were a statistical anomaly.'

'Yeah. That's right,' he chuckled. 'I forgot. So to answer your original question, prison can help people who want to be helped. There's a whole heap of services available. It depends on whether they have the maturity and the desire to break away from who they are when the doors slam on their freedom.'

'OK, here's another one for you...' Kierney went off on a tangent, her brain revitalised now the dark-haired pair were alone. 'What *is* maturity?'

'What's maturity? Whoa! Question without notice! That could take several nights to discuss. Making sound decisions? Having a healthy respect for yourself, and everyone and everything around you? What d'you think it is?'

The precocious youngster smiled. 'Nothing to do with age.'

'It is sometimes, but not always. People we might think of as mature can often do pretty immature things, for one reason or another. Maturity and human nature don't always work harmoniously. Out-of-control emotions can make us do startlingly immature things.'

'Such as killing?'

Jeff nodded. 'Sure. People can do things way out of character if something messes with their emotions. That's when you get *des crimes de passion*. But on the other hand, it may be that they've been faking being mature for all that time, and whatever provoked them unleashed a very natural response.'

'Argh!' the eighteen-year-old groaned, clutching her head in her hands. 'Life is so complicated. Every question I ask has a thousand answers.'

The patient teacher extended a sweeping right arm towards his star pupil, inviting her to cuddle into him. She accepted with enthusiasm, and the two remained still for a moment, enjoying one another's proximity.

'I'm making you grow up too quickly,' her regretful father confessed. 'When we get home, I'm going to use a can-opener to extract your brain and then lock it away in the filing cabinet for a month. That'll force you to relax. Are you OK with that?'

'No,' Kierney giggled. 'I like being confused. Tell me about Granddad's trial, please.'

'OK. If you really want to know, I'll tell you,' Jeff sighed. 'I wasn't there, so it's all hearsay as far as I'm concerned. I'm just going on what the lawyers would tell me.'

'Why didn't you sit in the public gallery, if you wanted to know?' his daughter asked.

'Well, first, because they wouldn't have let me in without an adult. But second, at only twelve, I didn't have much of your aforementioned maturity, so I would've been the one yelling profanities from the cheap seats.'

The youngster laughed. 'That's so funny. I forgot you were only twelve. I can never think of you as that young.'

'Hard to believe, I know, but I was, once upon a time. There's just not much evidence to support my claim.'

'You must've been such a cute little boy. All dark and mysterious, outside and inside.'

'Are you trying to butter me up for something? What's with all the compliments all of a sudden? Do you need to borrow money?'

'No!' the indignant teenager answered. 'I'd love to see a photo of you when you were little, that's all.'

'Good luck,' Jeff replied, with more than a trace of bitterness in his voice. 'I've never seen any. There'd probably be a few lying around somewhere. At my *Abuela*'s place, maybe. There were quite a few of Auntie Lena because she was their only daughter's first grandchild, but they'd lost interest by the time I came along. And anyway... That's enough feeling sorry for myself. Just check out your own kiddie pictures and imagine yourself with short hair. That'd be pretty close.'

The young woman slapped her dad's knee. '*Es ridículo, papá*. Did you wear long, flowery skirts along with your Doc Marten's boots?'

'Yeah. As a matter of fact I did,' the celebrity lied, receiving another sharp slap, 'which is why there are no photographs. They were ashamed of my penchant for cross-dressing. Anyway, anyway... I did manage to convince the police to give me the name of the solicitors assigned to represent my dad. They wouldn't speak to me at all to begin with, so I dragged my mum along in one of her more lucid hours. Very enlightening for an arrogant twelve-year-old actually, 'cause it confirmed that I already understood much more about the world than she did.'

'Wasn't *Abuela* interested in finding out for herself?' Kierney asked in amazement. 'Didn't she want to know what they had Accused her husband of?'

'She did, yeah. But she didn't know how to go about it,' her dad explained. 'You know how Auntie Lena is?'

The teenager nodded, yawning.

'Well, think of someone half as naïve again, and that was my *mamá*,' the great man sighed. 'She just didn't get life. Didn't think she needed to. As far as she was concerned, girls went to school for as long as they could get away without taking a test, then hooked up with a man, got pregnant and spent the rest of their lives looking after children. That's what her mother did, and her sisters-in-law. The only difference was their husbands gave their wives a reasonably good life.'

'Wow... That's really sad,' the young woman muttered. 'That's why there'll always be more of the same kind of people.'

'*Exactamente, pequeñita*,' Jeff agreed. 'And also the main reason why we're working to get girls interested in finding out what else they can do with their lives. Also, this type of kid has no sense of how life changes as you get older. I had friends at school, both boys and girls, who had no concept of the years after sixteen and being able to leave school, even though most of them lived with their parents. I never understood how they couldn't imagine themselves beyond their teens.

'That was my parents' biggest problem too: they never realised it costs money to pay rent and feed themselves and two kids. They thought they could survive on the dole while drinking and going out whenever they wanted. You can't blame them for thinking crime was easy money when that was the only alternative that occurred to them. Impressionable in the extreme; easy prey for gangland recruiters and pimps.'

Kierney shuffled along the bed towards her pillows, struck by a sudden need to look her father in the eyes while he told this story. Her natural childlike reaction of dragging the bedclothes up over her legs caused him to pause and catch his breath.

'You are still so cute,' his voice cracked. 'It's unfair of me to burden you with all this shit when you're so gorgeous.'

A smile spread across the sleepy nymph's face. 'But you were only twelve. I've got five years' more maturity than you had.'

'Oh, really? You think so?'

'Just get on with the story, papá,' she whined. 'What happened at the meeting with Granddad's lawyer?'

'Ha! It was pretty bloody comical, baby. I'd come armed with a list of questions which my mamá was going to ask, but after she'd asked the first one and I'd jumped in about ten times with supplementaries, the woman started to address me directly. She thought I was fifteen or sixteen, I later found out, and she thought my mamá must've had me in her very early teens. That's until it came out that I had an older sister, and then she thought she'd check how old I was!'

'And did she stop speaking to you after that?'

'No, luckily. The police hadn't caught Granddad in the act, or even near the scene, so I asked on what basis they'd arrested him. The solicitor said an informant tipped the police off. I remember asking then if she knew just how unpopular my father was.'

'Did you? Wow! What did she say?'

'I got a whack round the head from my mum,' Jeff answered, rubbing his ear as if the blow still smarted. 'She didn't realise I was trying to defend him and thought I was just corroborating the grass' information. Fortunately though, the solicitor was interested, and I could give her the names of some potential alibis or at least some sort of character reference, for what it was worth.'

'So you helped with your dad's Defence,' Kierney summed up, impressed but not surprised. 'Against the Queen... Did you think he was innocent?'

'I hoped he was,' her father sighed, his eyes asking hers to make a clear distinction.

'Hope for the best but expect the worst,' the young woman recycled another of her father's favourite expressions.

'*Cierto, pequeñita,*' he chuckled. 'I don't know how hard they tried to defend him, to be perfectly honest. Nowhere near as hard as for García, I'm sure. They had a knife that had both brothers' blood on it.'

'Yuck!' Kierney yelped, pulling a face. 'That's a horrible thought. Wouldn't stabbing a second person with the same knife leave the first person's blood on the second body?'

Jeff shot his daughter a sickly frown. 'That *is* a particularly revolting thought. I guess it all got mixed up together. They must've found both blokes' blood on it through forensic analysis, but again, I don't think anyone tried too hard to discredit their findings. The solicitor agreed to meet me outside the Supreme Court after the first day of Granddad's trial to give me an update, but she never turned up. I was mighty pissed off, let me tell you.'

'So how did you find out what happened?'

'Just by making a pain of myself,' the seasoned negotiator scoffed, 'not that you could ever imagine me doing that...'

His innocent girl grinned. 'Of course I can't, *papá*. What was Granddad charged with?'

'Two counts of murder,' he replied under his breath, landed back in their current circumstance. 'One for each Jaworski brother. He was found guilty of both, unanimously. Slam dunk, baby. Close the door and throw away the key.'

'So you didn't see him again, or talk to him, at all until *mamá* arranged it?' the teenager recalled.

'Yep. That's how it was. I asked to see him when he was first convicted, but they refused. And after that I gave up trying. Abandoned him, I guess... I hated his guts anyway, so it wasn't hard to wipe my life clean of him. My sister wanted nothing to do with him either, and my mother's parents made it perfectly clear that he was no longer part of the family. Neither was I, for that matter. It wasn't until quite a few years later that I even stopped to think about how he might've felt. Maturity again, I suppose.'

'Did *Abuela* think he'd committed the murders?'

'She would never answer me,' the abandoned son replied. 'I don't think so. She was always sort of under his spell. After everything he put her through, it was as if it wasn't worth it for her not to go with the flow. Like whenever she used to complain about all the contraband in the house, he'd lash out and yell about doing his best to feed her children.'

'Her children?'

'Yeah. We were always her children. Only his when he was in the mood,' Jeff sneered. 'So eventually, she just started drinking his stock instead!'

Kierney frowned. 'What a completely different environment to how Jet and I grew up... It sounds terrible. I'm sorry you had to go through all that.'

'Thanks, angel. It wasn't so bad while I was in it. Much worse for Auntie Lena. Much, much worse.'

The eighteen-year-old yawned and lay down, sliding down the mattress until her head could settle into the pillow's softness. 'I can understand how you empathise with García, *papá*.'

'Yeah?'

'Yeah. I was thinking earlier of how awful it'd be at six years old not to have a *mamá* to love you. And that's not supposed to make you say, "But now you don't have one either."'

'But you don't,' the grieving husband stressed, with a deep sigh. 'You're a good person, Kierney Lynn Freedom Diamond. Too good, perhaps. The world doesn't deserve people like you, when arseholes like García are roaming around shooting people they're jealous of.'

'People like *us*, *papá*,' the teenager corrected her father. 'People like us.'

'Yeah, OK,' the humble world-changer acknowledged. 'Y'know, that's the one sobering thought *mamá* and I never rationalised properly: unfortunately, no matter how hard people like us work to change things, there are still so many people like García out there; people who want to bring the rest of us down. D'you know the expression "tall poppy syndrome"?'

'Yes. Punishing those who stand out above the crowd.'

'Exactly,' Jeff smiled. 'Especially statistical anomalies with a loud mouth and heaps of money who are often on the telly. But he's the only one who pulled the trigger. I guess I should be grateful we made it as far as we did without such a disaster.'

The songwriter's eyes welled up again, making Kierney cry too. They both knew what the other was thinking. Why my dream girl? Why my *mamá*?

'It would've been so damned easy for me to turn to crime,' the superstar continued, sniffing, 'like Lena did. Christ knows how much I wanted to lay into those bastards who repeatedly raped my mother and sister. Not just a twelve- or thirteen-year-old's punching and kicking, but with a knife or even a gun. And then I'd have been no better than my dad.'

Kierney wiped her eyes. 'Why didn't you mention that to the court today?'

''Cause I'm not the one who's on trial,' the widower reiterated, reaching for her hand. 'And nor's Auntie Lena. We don't have to explain ourselves to anyone apart from those who love us and whom we love.

'Religious people and all the psychologists'll tell you to forgive and forget because that's the only way you'll conquer the effects of trauma. But I don't subscribe to that theory, as you know. I won't forget what those bastards put my family through, and I'm sure as hell not going to forgive them. I can move on, and have moved on, all without forgiving or forgetting.'

'So how did you stop becoming someone like García, who just snaps?'

'Oh, that's the easiest question of all, *pequeñita*. I found your *mamá*, that's how,' Jeff replied, letting go an uncontrollable roar. 'I looked for her and I found her. I didn't sit around and wait 'til she found me, which is what that fucking weasel García should've known. Then you and your brother came along and made me into who I wanted to be. I learned to leave the bitterness behind, and only at times like these do I have to dredge it up again.'

The tired young woman pulled back the sheets and crawled over the quilt on her hands and knees to plant a kiss on her father's lips. 'I'm sorry to make you dredge it up again. Thanks for telling me. You should go downstairs to the others. I'm sure they want to make sure you're alright.'

'Are *you* alright?' the storyteller asked the brave teenager.

'Yes, thanks. I'm tired and want to fast-forward to tomorrow. I want to go home and carry on with our life.'

'Good girl,' the father said, pushing himself off the bed and standing up. 'You're very strong. You'll be fine. And I'm sure Jet will be too. Sleep well.'

JUSTICE IN ACTION

Early the following morning, the threesome waved goodbye to Celia and Gerald and drove back towards Sydney's CBD and Day Four of the trial. Kierney had woken twice in the night crying for her *mamá* but now felt much better after a shower and some breakfast. She knew her *papá* would have cried for her *mamá* too, which made her all the more determined not to mention it.

Jeff had indeed slept fitfully, jumbled nightmares swirling around his head, mixing his past with his present to the point where he had decamped downstairs to watch television in the dark.

'*Papá*?' Kierney began from the back seat of the Commodore.

'*¿Sí?*'

'Shouldn't the Queen have found her own psychiatrist as a witness to say he or she didn't believe García's mental capacity was diminished far enough for it to excuse his actions?'

'They could have,' her father answered, again impressed with the question. 'I talked to Winton about that yesterday too. They had someone lined up apparently, but he's known to take a hard line against immigrants, so given the sentiment in the gallery's pretty left-wing, they pulled him after Day One. At least Moroney sat on the fence. She didn't work out too well as a Defence witness, which is what Graham intimated at the start.'

'Oh,' Kierney said. 'That makes sense, I s'pose. Not enough time to bring another one up to speed.'

The cynic scoffed. 'Trust the experts. I guess if they pit two psychs against each other and their evidence is contradictory, the jury won't be able to decide beyond reasonable doubt. If neither is believable, or if one negates the other, they can't condemn the Accused.'

'Like cricket,' Gerry chirped from the driver's seat. 'If there's no conclusive evidence the batsman edged the ball, he's not out, even if the replay later shows he did hit it. They have to give you the benefit of the doubt and let you stay in.'

'What?' the teenager giggled. 'That reminds me of the funny poem Jet brought home from Lord's the time you two went to The Ashes, *papá*. They're in 'til they're all out, and when they're out, they come in and the next one goes in until he's out.'

Jeff and Gerry both laughed, trying to remember the rest of the famous rhyme.

'What about the batsman who's not out at the end?' the sports-mad accountant added. 'He comes in when everyone else is out, even though he's not out.'

The judge began the morning's proceedings in a sombre tone, explaining the process to be followed now that they had heard from all witnesses. She explained the list of evidentiary exhibits that had been presented, and the court officer re-circulated the various documents and photographs. The jury was instructed on the legal issues at question for each piece of evidence, slowly and methodically, while the crowd in the public gallery practised their patience.

The prosecution team had managed a brief meeting with Jeff and the others before court resumed, ready to explain the implications of Peter and Moira's deliberations on intent. Their results confirmed the celebrity's suspicions that his keen-eyed wife would not have had any idea that a gun was being trained on her as she sat in the lobby, since García had been at least ten metres away and behind a partition obscured by an arrangement of leafy indoor plants. They thought it safe to assume the Accused had staked out a hiding place to launch an ambush rather than a post from which to menace his victim.

Nevertheless, the victim's husband insisted on taking this test a step further. Nothing could persuade him to return to The Pensione, regardless of how much influence it might have on the remaining hours of the trial. Consequently, their best attempt to re-enact the crime had seen Jeff perform a graphic and convincing demonstration of the firearm being used as a threat.

Using Peter as a potential victim, he had retreated a metre at a time and pointed an imaginary weapon at the barrister-in-training to see if it alarmed him. At about an eight-metre distance, and still in direct line of sight, they all agreed there was little weight to any argument of García's intended scare tactics. For the gunman to have stood this close to the victim for up to a minute, he would have needed to be in full view of the concièrge's desk.

The preoccupied celebrity took a good look around the public gallery, trying to discern which types of people took a week out of their lives to attend the trial of Lynn's killer. Around him was a broad cross-section of the community, age-wise, multi-ethnic and gender-balanced. Although this diverse microcosm of the Diamonds' fan-base pleased him, he found it hard to fathom there being this many Sydney residents with nothing better to do.

Or had they seen this as of sufficient import to take leave from their jobs? For the New South Wales native who had defected over the state's southern border a quarter of a century ago, it was humbling to realise his family was held in such high regard by so many ordinary folk.

Yet, as the saying went, there was always one...

Judge Milne raised her voice to signal the closing summaries were about to begin, first the Prosecution and then the Defence. She informed the jury that they were invited to convict the accused if they believed beyond reasonable doubt and without dispute between jurors about the ingredients of the offences, but that it was also up to them to convert the murder charge to a merciful verdict of manslaughter if they saw fit.

'Merciful verdict?' Kierney turned to her father. 'Merciful on whom?'

Jeff didn't reply. He knew he didn't have to, and his daughter added rhetoric to her arsenal.

'Ladies and gentlemen,' Rosemary Milne addressed the jury. 'Owing to the importance of this trial to public interest and also the seriousness of the charges, my office will be available to you during your deliberation process. If you have any questions about the legal points or the evidence, please make them known to my officers, and I shall attend to them in person. Questions you raise will be passed on to both Prosecution and Defence teams, unless it contains a reference to your voting numbers around a potential verdict. Is that clear, ladies and gentlemen?'

The jurors all nodded, anxious to carry on with the show's *dénouement*. Before handing over to Graham Winton, the judge requested he include a chronology of steps leading to the accused's apprehension, arrest, charge and committal. She urged him to make sure the jury recalled the correct sequence of events.

Counsel had clearly been briefed on this request in advance, with the flamboyant barrister producing a typewritten piece of paper from his folder with a flourish, waving it proudly around the courtroom.

'OK,' the celebrity declared, slapping Kierney's knee. 'We're off.'

'Are we?' the young woman said with a hint of disappointment.

'Yep,' he replied, turning to Gerry. 'You staying or coming?'

'What's the alternative?'

'Movies? Hotel? Back to work? Come on. Before they get started.'

Obediently, the Diamond entourage stood up and made their way out of the elevated area, stopping for a cigarette in the deserted arboretum. Their departure caused quite a stir, and they could hear the chief librarian attempting to calm everyone down from the top of the steps as they opened the rear doors.

'Why are we leaving?' the teenager asked, almost running to keep up with the men.

''Cause we've heard everything once already, and the summing up is the lawyers' opportunity to be at their most dramatic,' her father replied. 'I don't want any of us to have to sit through any exaggerated hype. You're welcome to stay if you want to, either of you, but I'd rather not. Winton'll ring us when the jury's sent out.'

'I'm over it, I have to say,' Gerry resigned. 'Good call, mate. I might head to Dad's office for a while. I'm getting a trifle jittery at being away from the in-tray for so long.'

'Fair enough. Kizzo?'

'I was looking forward to hearing how they pull it all together,' she answered, trying not to sound too disgruntled.

'Really? Are you serious?' the widower asked with a sly wink. 'You're not prepared to wait for the DVD to come out?'

The teenager huffed. 'Yes, I'm serious, but I get the feeling I'm going to be overruled. It doesn't matter.'

Jeff closed his eyes, taking a long drag on his cigarette. Lynn would have stuck to her guns, he thought, cursing the macabre pun. He always gave in too easily. Yet how could he deny his daughter the chance to see the trial of her mother's killer come to its natural conclusion?

At eighteen, he would have insisted on sitting through it too. Hadn't they talked about this very need last night, in relation to his own father's trial? Exhaling through his nostrils to calm his nerves, he turned to the older of the two security guards.

'Would you mind taking Kierney back in, please?'

'No, sir. It'd be my pleasure.'

The teenager stared at her father in childlike surprise and rushed into his arms. 'Are you sure?' she checked, hugging him and desperate not to cry. 'I don't have to.'

'Lynn was your *mamá*, *pequeñita*. She gave you life. I owe you this opportunity.'

'*Muchas gracias, papá*,' the young woman gasped. 'I promise I'll leave if it gets too much. I'll ring you.'

'Has your phone got plenty of charge?'

'Of course! Who do you think I am? Jet?'

'Just checkin',' the doting dad shrugged. 'Get in there then, but don't sit where people can see you easily, especially Winton or Greenshaw. Stay well back, guys.'

The uniformed man nodded and beckoned Kierney to follow him. She gave her hero a final peck on the cheek and set off towards the lifts. Jeff gritted his teeth as he watched her go, placing his hands on his head to stretch the tension out of his back and shoulders.

'Shouldn't have done that,' he frowned, turning to Gerry. 'She's too like me for her own good.'

'No comment,' his manager sniffed. 'What do I know about kids? She'll be fine.'

'Let's get coffee,' the celebrity suggested, looking at his watch. 'Too early for a beer. Is it OK if I take up some office space for a while too? Just to check in with Cath, *et cetera*?'

'Of course!' Gerry mimicked Kierney.

'Members of the jury,' Rosemary Milne began, once everyone had taken their seats. 'I've been told you have not been able to reach a verdict so far.'

It was two o'clock on Friday afternoon, and the dozen had been recalled to the courtroom to consult with officials to iron out several differences of opinion. The public gallery had cleared except for about thirty die-hards determined not to miss the verdict. All microphones had been switched off, making it impossible to hear the discussion below.

Judge Milne continued. 'I have the power to discharge you from giving a verdict but shall only do so if it appears there's no likelihood of genuine agreement being reached after further deliberation. I'm very reluctant to discharge you at this point, because experience has shown that most juries can agree if given more time to consider the issues.

'Each of you takes into the jury room your individual experience and wisdom, and we therefore expect you to judge the evidence fairly and impartially. You also have a duty to listen carefully and objectively to the views of every one of your fellow jurors. You should weigh up each other's opinions about the evidence and test them by discussion, from where I trust you'll reach a better understanding of the differing perspectives you may have. This may convince you that your original opinion has a flaw.

'The jury's verdict must be unanimous, or with a majority of eleven to one, if I consider the circumstances to warrant it. That's not, of course, to suggest that you should agree with a verdict if you do not honestly think it's the correct one, because you remain under oath until you're released from jury service.

'And can I please stress that it's immaterial whether you deliberate for eight hours or eighty hours. Each time you come back, I must be convinced you've deliberated diligently enough, given the nature and complexity of this case. For this reason, *Foreman*, will you agree to another four hours of consultation? That would take us to six o'clock or thereabouts.'

The twelve tired citizens nodded in agreement.

Judge Milne concluded her lecture, picking up her glasses' case and ornate fountain pen. 'Take care to re-examine the matters upon which you disagree and make a further attempt to reach a verdict. If not, after this time, I'll make another decision about discharging you. So, in the light of what I've already said, I ask you to retire again and see if you can come to a clear verdict.'

The jurors were shown back out to their room. Graham Winton sat with his associates, all of whom were well and truly ready for the weekend. He sent Jeff a text message with the latest news, suggesting that they would all most likely be returning on Monday morning.

'Shit!' the celebrity cursed when the SMS came through.

'What's the matter?' Kierney asked, looking up from her book.

'Looks like we'll have to wait 'til Monday for any chance of a verdict,' he explained. 'D'you want to go home and fly back on Sunday night or Monday morning?'

The youngster frowned. 'What would we do if we stayed here?'

'Not much,' he acknowledged. 'Unless you want to go to the Gold Coast or something?'

'I'm too old for the Gold Coast,' she scoffed.

'Only if you're going with me,' her father teased. 'If a tall, handsome stranger like Eric asked you to go to the Gold Coast, you'd be there in a flash.'

'Maybe,' Kierney confessed with a smile, flinching at the reference to the security guard who had spent the last few days flirting with her. 'Except not Eric.'

'Peter then,' Jeff persisted.

'Oh, be quiet,' the teenager squirmed. 'I'll go if you want to go.'

'No. Let's go home. Gerry'll want to, and I know he feels obliged to stay with us. You don't have to come back on Monday either.'

'No way! I can't not hear the verdict after sitting through the painful parts,' his daughter bleated, eyes wide with indignance. 'Do you think Monday'll be it?'

'Who knows? Graham's message says the jury came back after five hours with no verdict, but that the judge sent them away again for another four hours. If they come back tonight with agreement, then it won't be long on Monday for sentencing, but if they still can't agree, she'll probably give them longer again.'

'What'll happen if they really don't agree?' the young woman asked, looking concerned.

'He walks,' her father raised a disillusioned eyebrow. 'They can't decide beyond reasonable doubt, so he walks.'

Kierney sighed. 'That's not right. Are they considering manslaughter instead?'

'I'm sure they'd be advised to, if only to reach a bloody decision,' Jeff guessed.

'But that's not right either, is it?' the prospective law student moaned. 'It gets back to your original point. Hurry up and decide. Never mind if it's the right one. Bye-bye, Juan Antonio.'

The dark-haired superstar chuckled. 'If you get any more like me, you'll...'

'I'll what?' the teenager replied, seeing her dad lost for words. 'So would that be it then, if the jury doesn't convict García? That's not good news.'

'If they find new compelling evidence sometime in the future, he can be retried,' her dad explained. 'Can't think how that might arise though. It'd be hard without knowing why the jury let him off this time.'

Kierney sighed. 'How depressing. All this effort and heartache we've been through, and potentially a total waste of time.'

'Yep. Be prepared for it, gorgeous. Winton's still confident, but I'm not so sure. I guess he has to be. Like a salesman has to believe in his product: fully paid-up members of the "Dead Horse Floggers Society". And the sick irony is the less sure I am, the more I want him to go down. How perverse is that?'

'"Dead Horse Floggers Society"?' the eighteen-year-old laughed aloud before returning to her father's last observation. 'But why?'

'I don't know,' the lost boy from Canley Vale replied. 'Probably because the more I found out about the man, the more it made me hate him for how futile it all was. He could've taken so many other steps to make his life better, but he chose the one that hurt us the most.'

'And what did he gain?'

'Potentially his freedom, or otherwise the opportunity to take advantage of Her Majesty's life improvement options,' the widower gritted his teeth, 'while your mamá's in a box in a drawer.'

Kierney leant over and hugged her father with all her strength. They were both nervous, knowing full well that it would only take was one or two jurors who were ambivalent, or worse, about the Diamonds to nullify the whole case. It was a real possibility. Jealousy was a powerful emotion, and didn't Jeff know it!

Sitting in their spartan room, the frustrated pair passed another two hours in quiet contemplation. Having scanned through the in-house movies, they had passed on watching "Seven", not only because they had both seen it before but mainly to avoid its bloodthirsty subject. They settled for "Apollo 13" and lost themselves in the amazing space mission, arguing about which scenes were true-to-life and which boasted cinematic largesse.

At four-forty, Jeff's mobile telephone rang on the bedside table. 'Winton,' he mouthed, seeing the name on the screen and answering the call. 'Hello, Graham. Yeah. We're fine, thanks. They're back? You're kidding? Yeah. We're in the hotel. We'll leave now. Thanks for letting us know. G'day.'

'The jury?' Kierney asked, sensing her father's excitement.

'The very same. Can you believe it?' he replied, dialling his manager's number. 'Let's get out of here... Mate! The jury's back with a verdict. I know. Winton texted me earlier to say Monday morning. Ha! Yeah. Probably. Great, mate. See you there.'

His daughter's eyes were full of questions. 'What did you laugh at?'

'Gerry said the jury's keen to get home for the weekend,' he told her, not finding the joke at all funny the second time.

As the taxi drove the kilometre-and-a-half back to the Supreme Court, Jeff could feel his chest tighten in apprehension. *This is it*, he thought. What would Lynn make of the verdict? He hoped she would be satisfied, whichever way the jury voted. He also wondered if a unanimous verdict had been reached, or if there remained one lone voice sticking to its outlying position. With his stomach doing its best tumble-dryer impression, he opened the rear door for Kierney to climb out, and famous pair ran past several loitering media teams who wasted no time in springing into action.

'Has there been a change, Jeff?' shouted a glamorous female journalist.

'Maybe,' the celebrity shouted back. 'Looks like it.'

With a growing cavalcade in their wake, the Diamonds rushed towards the lifts. Moments later, the sliding doors parted on the third floor with a Friday afternoon squeal, and the duo slinked into the public gallery as invisibly as possible.

The judge was in conference, but they couldn't hear anything above their own footsteps and the creaking of the plastic seats. Winton and Greenshaw were both on their feet in front of the bench, again looking like overgrown schoolboys who had been caught copying each other's homework.

Uniformed guards appeared at the rear of the court, shepherding García into the dock for perhaps the last time. The Spaniard's dejected demeanour spoke volumes, his face sallow and mirroring Jeff's own internal turmoil. Kierney gripped her father's hand, lifting it to her mouth and kissing it.

'Thanks, gorgeous,' the anxious man said, kissing her temple in return. 'I love you.'

The teenager's eyes scanned the elevated rows of seating, and her father followed her gaze. There were well over a hundred people present, some sitting alone and some in small clusters. The famous pair recognised almost all of them from the preceding few days.

Although there were fewer faces now, Jeff identified several loyal members of his fan club and others he remembered vaguely from particular events over the years. To his left, a couple in their forties caught his eye, and the woman gave him a thumbs-up sign with both hands. He nodded and smiled, turning back to his daughter.

'D'you see the woman over there, by the wall?' he pointed to a woman in a red jacket, with shoulder-length, fair hair. 'That's Wonderful Wendy.'

'Is it?' she stifled an exclamation, resisting the temptation to turn round again. 'Wow! Are you sure?'

'Yep. I remember her picture from the television news, the day her story broke.'

'I wonder what she's feeling now? Does she regret what she said, now she sees him down there?'

The peacemaker shrugged. 'Who knows? She's several hundred thousand dollars richer, with the prospect of more to come. That might go some way to offsetting her malaise. Wonder how that'd work in a divorce settlement? With any luck, our little spaniel'll be the richest man in D-wing.'

The eighteen-year-old smiled, seeing tears in her father's eyes again. Life was so full of ironies, precious few of which had landed in his favour lately.

Meanwhile, the judge had finished her mini-conference with the barristers. Duly dismissed, the two rather solemn men returned to their respective camps.

With a loud cough, Rosemary Milne turned to the jury, and the whole place fell silent in reverend anticipation. 'Thank you, ladies and gentlemen,' she began in a clear voice, 'for returning to the courtroom so quickly. I trust you found the extra opportunity to reach agreement worthwhile. *Foreman*, please could you pass the notification to the court officer?'

Three pieces of paper were handed over by a man in his early thirties, dressed in a dark suit. A consultant or middle-level manager, Jeff guessed. Self-assured, he turned to his eleven colleagues and gave a quick smile. There was little doubt he had nominated himself for the important role.

The judge unfolded the crumpled sheets and spread them out on the bench in front of her, one for each charge. The celebrity watched the woman's face, only able to make out a slight intake of breath, convinced he could hear every heartbeat in the room.

The authoritative woman took her glasses off, cleaned their lenses with a cloth and put them back on again. 'Ladies and gentlemen,' her voice rang out. 'You, as the jury in the case of The Queen versus Juan Antonio García Ruelas, were asked to return a verdict of "Guilty" or "Not guilty" on all three charges, and you have done this after considerable deliberation. Once a verdict has been given, it cannot be set aside by me, even if the jury reached the verdict under a misapprehension. Owing to the high-profile nature of this case, I've been at pains to ensure you were in possession of as much evidence as possible.

'It has been explained to you, ladies and gentlemen, that the aggravating factors in this case, such as the accused's motivation through jealousy and anger, must be proven beyond reasonable doubt.

'Mitigating factors are as follows: one, the accused has no prior criminal record; two, the accused did not commit these offences as part of organised crime activity; and three, he has complied fully with the investigation and court process.'

Judge Milne paused and waited once more for the jurors' acknowledgement. The accused stared at the floor, while up in the public gallery, his estranged wife continued to read her magazine. It wasn't clear whether García even knew she was there.

'Ladies and gentlemen, please will you confirm again that you're content with the verdicts I now hold in my hand?'

The *Foreman* glanced around his fellow jurors before standing up, proud as punch. 'We are, Your Honour.'

'Well done,' Kierney let out a discreet chuckle. 'He finally gets his moment of glory.'

Jeff laughed along with his daughter, but their attention was suddenly drawn to the back of the building, where the double doors swung open with an almighty crash. It was the indomitable Mr Blake, looking flustered and hot, as if he had been running. Judge, barristers and jury were all distracted as he located the Diamonds and sat down beside them.

'Did I miss anything?' he asked his old friend, holding out his right hand. 'Couldn't get off the bloody phone.'

'Nope. Just a knot of red tape so far.'

After a momentary pause to collect her thoughts, Judge Milne looked upwards again and made direct eye contact with the enigmatic superstar whose associate had made such a commotion at this critical juncture. Jeff dared to detect the tiniest of smiles on her face, but refused to be lured to any premature conclusions.

The weighty stare of the forthright, matronly woman turned back to the legal teams on its way to the accused, who sat in the dock with two police officers behind him. She signalled for him to rise to his feet.

'Juan Antonio García Ruelas,' she addressed the prisoner, 'you have been tried by this court in front of twelve of your fellow citizens. We've heard statements from the Prosecution and from the Defence, and the jury has taken great care to understand the ins and outs of this case thoroughly. They have taken their responsibility very seriously. I will now ask the Foreman to stand up and respond to my questions on their decisions. Do you understand, Mr García?'

'Yes, Your Honour,' the man replied in a tremulous voice.

Another freight-train of a shiver ran down Jeff's spine on hearing the distinctive Spanish accent. Despite being much weaker, it again reminded him of his maternal grandfather.

What must it be like to wait for such an eternity? How must it feel to be staring twenty-odd years of incarceration in the face? Or not?

'Thank you,' Judge Milne said. '*Foreman*, I shall now ask you to reply with the jury's verdict for each of the three charges individually. Are you ready to provide this information on behalf of your peers?'

The young man answered with less confidence this time. 'Yes, Your Honour.'

Gerry reached his right arm all the way across his friend's back and rested his hand on the eighteen-year-old's slender shoulder. She glanced across at both men, all three wan with the strain of apprehension. Her father leant against her, and she responded by resting onto his arm.

Twisting to see over to his far left, Jeff caught sight of Wendy García bending forward in her seat. Her hands were cupped around her face, perhaps to hide it. Fortunately, she was not looking their way.

'Thank you,' the judge said again, picking up the three sheets of paper and sorting them one behind the other. 'On the charge of the murder of Victoria Lynn Shannon Dyson Diamond, how do you find the Defendant?'

The widower closed his eyes and felt Kierney's hands grip his more tightly. His heart stopped for a second when he heard the full name of his beloved wife pronounced so purposefully, like on their wedding day.

The public gallery was on tenterhooks too, as were the barristers down below, the court officials and the accused wretch. Time stood still for everyone. Scarcely able to stand the suspense, Jeff forced his eyes open just as the *Foreman*'s shoulders lifted to take in a lungful of air.

'Guilty, Your Honour.'

Guilty. The three simple yet life-changing words clanged onto the courtroom's polished concrete floor, their impact reverberating around in the vacuous silence. Not a single sound came from the erstwhile opinionated dress circle, since all eyes were now trained on the Diamonds in their midst.

'Guilty,' the celebrity heard his daughter repeat under her breath in an almost involuntary response.

Blood draining out of his head, the musician shuddered and closed his eyes again. He couldn't see a thing anyway, largely as a result of a deluge of tears held in for so long that day. He put his arm around the teenager next to him, hearing her soft weeping. Spontaneous but polite applause broke out all around. Several people rushed forwards from the rows behind, eager to pat their hero on the back and show their support, soon turned away by the two tenacious men in uniform.

'Congratulations, mate,' Gerry whispered, twisting round in his seat so he could extend his hand to his old friend. 'Good result. The right result. And you, Kierney, darling. Congratulations too. This is for your *mamá*.'

The eighteen-year-old's dark eyes stared in their manager's general direction through long lashes, and she gave him the sweetest of tear-stained smiles. 'Thank you. He's guilty.'

Apart from a ringing in his ears, Jeff's senses had arrested. His brain and body had somehow suspended all function, replaced by an exaggerated stinging from the tattoo over his heart. It was not in the least bit painful; more a sweet, intense burn which lingered far longer than the sensations he had become used to. He squeezed his eyes shut and relished the pleasant feeling until it faded, at the same time as he received a kiss on the cheek from his loving daughter.

'*Papá*, he's guilty,' Kierney whispered, waiting for a reaction.

Still incapable of speech, the grieving husband opened his eyes and steered them downwards to the loneliest seat in the room, where they met those of his wife's convicted murderer. For the first time, he saw hatred in the man's eyes, most likely reflecting his own.

Don't blame me, mate, he transmitted to the Spaniard below. *What you did was entirely your choice.*

Taking the others by surprise, Jeff shook his head as an image of his own father filled his mind. Or rather, he realised as it became clearer, it was himself he was seeing in the dock, imagining the verdict handed down for his father's crimes.

'*Papá*, are you OK?' the young woman tried again. 'Did you hear?'

'Yes, baby,' her father whispered back without turning his head. 'I'm sorry. I don't know how I feel right now. Are you?'

The teenager kissed his cheek again. 'Sí. Very happy.'

A level of energy returning to the enduring inhabitants of the dress circle, they became more animated and impatient. The court officer banged the desk to bring order once again, summoning all present to hear the second verdict.

'Thank you,' Judge Milne responded to the jurors. 'Quiet please, ladies and gentlemen. *Foreman*, please... on the charge of intent to murder Jeffrey Moreno Diamond, how do you find the Defendant?'

The young man stood tall again, impatient to deliver his next piece of information. 'Guilty, Your Honour.'

A respectful but resounding cheer broke free from the crowd encircling the object of charge Number Two. The aforementioned Jeffrey Moreno Diamond exhaled and fixed the murderer's eyes in his own with renewed intensity. Vindication was surprisingly satisfying. This time, García was quick to look away, his body language now that of a defeated man.

A collective sigh of relief accompanied another subdued round of applause from those in the dress circle, some of whom had moved to sit much closer to the celebrities. The revered peacemaker made no attempt to acknowledge them at this moment.

The time would come to give thanks to the thousands, even millions who had stood by him and his family during this ordeal, but for now he was bound to resist any clamour for his attention. Despite all indications to the contrary, this was not his circus.

'Two guiltys',' Kierney stated, smiling. '*Mamá* would be happy too. I love you, *papá*.'

'Thanks, Kizzo,' her dad replied. 'She is, and we both love you.'

Gerry smacked his friend hard on the left thigh, causing the cramped muscles in Jeff's leg to jump. 'Two out of two,' he proclaimed. 'Was it worth it now then?'

Jeff shrugged, overwhelmed. He took in three or four deep breaths in an effort not to succumb to the tornado of dizziness which whirled round his head. His blood pressure was so high that his ears felt like stadium speakers pumping drums and bass out through the same channel.

'Don't know yet, mate. Ask me again later.'

Down on the courtroom floor, the jurors were all staring up to the public gallery, following the pointing finger of a woman in the front row, ecstatic with the outcome so far. The celebrity scanned their faces, wondering who among them had struggled with the guilty verdicts through the first few hours of deliberation. Which one or ones had voted "Not guilty"? And to which of the charges? He would never know, and regardless, it no longer mattered.

'Thank you again, ladies and gentlemen of the jury,' Judge Milne acknowledged the second verdict. 'And lastly, on the charge of possessing and carrying a firearm without a permit, how do you find the Defendant?'

'Guilty, Your Honour,' the *Foreman* answered with far less *gusto* due to the insignificance of this charge in the context of the prior pair.

A third, even louder set of cheers and applause went up however, and this time, the jury couldn't bear to be excluded from the celebrations. Seeing the judge had not moved to silence them, both Senior Counsels also turned around to direct their happiness into the dress circle, clapping their hands, while the thrice-guilty man sat alone, flanked by the stoic custody officers.

'Thank you, *Foreman*. Thank you very much,' Judge Milne said for the final time. 'Ladies and gentlemen of the jury, the court thanks you for the diligence you have shown during this trial and through the deliberation process thereafter. I'm pleased you were able to decide on a definite verdict for these charges.

'I shall move to sentencing momentarily, given that it's late in the day, but henceforth the jury is discharged. I thank you once again for your attention to duty and participation in this trial, and I wish you a safe journey home and a good weekend.'

An official opened the wooden gate at the back of the jury's section and signalled that the dozen citizens true were free to leave. Most continued to stare up into the public gallery for several moments, eager to share in the relief they imagined Jeff and Kierney to be experiencing.

The Diamonds watched as each juror passed the dock on his or her way out, the great man remarking that García showed no outward animosity towards them. Was the trial's adverse result Jeff's fault in this small man's mind? Why was it that some people seemed incapable of rationalising where responsibility ought to lie?

Still stuck in a bizarre no-man's land, the widower's thoughts turned again to his own father. He imagined him equally insistent that his punishment was undeserved and that his crimes were anyone else's fault but his own. It wasn't until much later in life that Paul Diamond took carriage of his fate.

'How are you going, mate?' Gerry asked. 'And you, Kizzy?'

The stunned father invited Kierney to reply first, more to buy time rather than out of chivalry.

'I'm very happy, thanks,' the subdued young woman responded. '*Papá?*'

Jeff exhaled, desperate to slow his heart down and regain the use of his senses. 'I need some time to think about it,' he confessed. 'All I can tell you is I don't feel anything, which leads me to believe that deep down I really don't give a shit.'

Gerry shook his head in dismay, and his daughter sighed.

'Or else I'm in shock, and it's going to hit me later,' the man added, seeing their disappointment. 'I'm sorry, guys. I'm not going to pretend I'm happy, 'cause I'm not.'

'Fair enough,' his manager acquiesced. 'Perhaps it's a bit of an anti-climax after sitting through everything.'

'Hey! I'll drink to that,' Jeff chuckled, doing his best not to bring the others down when it was clear they felt like celebrating.

Judge Milne and the two principal lawyers were back in conference, throwing the occasional glance towards García, who remained seated and silent in the dock. Several people had already left the court, but many were determined to see the trial out to the bitter end, rather than opting to learn the Accused's fate on the evening news.

Wendy García continued to leaf through a magazine as if waiting for a doctor's appointment. From time to time, she shot a look Jeff's way, which he would catch out of the corner of his eye. A number of court officials had also departed, leaving a single associate and the recording clerk to close the week out.

After a few minutes, several of the dismissed jurors appeared through the rear doors of the public gallery, eager to meet the famous duo.

'What happens now?' Kierney asked the two men.

'Sentencing,' her dad answered. 'I'd say the judge already has a fair idea what she's going to hand down, and she's just checking with each team as to the justification.'

'Does she need to justify it?' Gerry asked with a smirk. 'At this point, he's pretty much hosed, is he not?'

His client sniffed, finding solace in dispensing pearls of conventional wisdom to his excited companions. 'She'd have to be careful nonetheless. The minute the press gets hold of it, they're going to be grabbing for all the reasons why. I'd rather they were explicit than read some made-up crap in tomorrow's papers.'

'*Papá*, what does the judge use to determine how long García's sentence is?' the eighteen-year-old asked.

Pleased to be posed an intelligent, fact-based question which would focus his mind, the proud father thought for a moment. He had done so much reading on this topic over the years that the justifications were relatively easy for him to recall.

'Well...' he began, smiling for his young muse. 'First and foremost, make the punishment fit the crime, as per "The Mikado".'

Kierney giggled. 'Oh, OK.'

'Judge Milne needs to decide between custodial sentence or some other form of periodic detention, or even something like electronic tagging,' Jeff continued. 'For something as serious as murder, it'd have to be a prison sentence. Or a secure psychiatric facility, I s'pose, which isn't appropriate for this bastard. The sentence also has to send a signal to the general public that the Supreme Court views this as a serious crime against the Crown, and that García's seen as a baddie as far as the Queen's concerned.'

'Good man. That's better,' Gerry smiled, sensing his old friend loosening up.

The widower shook his tired head. 'Then it has to be long enough to act as a deterrent to anyone else who wants to do something similar.'

'You hope,' the businessman sniggered.

'Do I?' Jeff snapped back. 'Don't be so sure, mate. I didn't mean to me.'

'*Papá*, shhh,' the kind teenager urged. 'Carry on, please.'

The superstar reached for his daughter's hand. Relaxing his mind had also relaxed his heart, and a scarcely controllable urge to break out and run far away from the courtroom seized him.

'Thanks, angel,' he replied, wiping his eyes. 'Just ignore me, guys. I'm fucked-up right now, but I'll get over it. Now where was I?'

'Did you want to get going?' Gerry asked, also spotting a few of the jury members pointing up at them.

'No, not yet, mate, if you don't mind. I want to stay for the sentencing. Kizzy, the next justifications are community protection and the prisoner's rehabilitation. For how long does he need to be incarcerated to make sure he's too old to re-offend, or he's so well rehabilitated that he won't want to re-offend? Also, he's supposed to have turned into a good person in all this time, so when he gets out he can be a fully functional and law-abiding citizen for the rest of his life.'

'That's awesome, *papá*. Thanks.'

'My pleasure, *pequeñita*,' the father replied, leaning over and planting a kiss on the youngster's flushed cheek. 'You are beautiful. D'you know that? And so good for me. But then there's one more justification I always blocked out in the old days; one I'm finding it twice as hard to articulate this time.'

'What's that?' Kierney asked. 'Something to do with *mamá*, obviously.'

Jeff nodded, gazing down at the activity in the courtroom below to distract himself from acute emotional overload. The teenager took a guess at what her dad appeared unable to put into words.

'The sentence needs to be long enough to acknowledge the impact of the crime, like how much people were hurt. Is that it?'

'Yep,' the world-changer's voice cracked. 'Exactly. It's recognising the suffering of the Victim and its impact on the wider community.'

'So am I Your Smart-arseness again?' Kierney was chuffed.

Gerry let out a loud laugh. 'Your Smart-arseness? Where the hell did that come from?'

The trio's laughter disconcerted the remaining people surrounding them, and the widower glanced around, ashamed to have been seen to take their focus off the seriousness of the evening's outcome.

'You know...' the accountant reverted too. 'That last point you made is really important in this case. The level of community impact of what this arsehole did must be unprecedented in Australia.'

The grieving husband frowned and nodded. 'You might be right. Kennedy's assassination in the US obviously, and John Lennon. But here? Yeah. I think so. Sadly.'

Gerry spotted Graham Winton gesturing towards the Diamonds again, trying to attract their attention. He gave the barrister a quick wave of thanks, only to be distracted by the judge, who appeared ready to close the trial by issuing her sentences.

'Ladies and gentlemen,' she began, as she had countless times over the last few days. 'We now come to the final part of the proceedings. The jury returned a unanimous guilty verdict on all three charges, and it is now incumbent on me to pass sentence on the Accused.'

Judge Milne paused as if she still expected the crowd to catch up. Then, after a fleeting glance up at the handsome celebrity, she focussed back on the dock. An officer guarding the prisoner signalled for him to stand for sentencing. The small man heaved himself to his feet, sapped of all energy.

'Juan Antonio García Ruelas, you have heard the Foreman report that the jury found you guilty on the charges of murder, intent to murder and possession of a firearm without a licence.'

García nodded but said nothing while the judge continued.

'I've given considerable thought to the circumstances of your crimes and have taken into account your long-running impaired mental state in my analysis. Of utmost importance in a case as serious as this is the court's duty to recognise the harm done to the Victim who died as a result of your actions, Ms Lynn Diamond, to her family and to the Australian community... indeed the whole world... who loved her and respected her.

'Because you have also been found guilty of intent to murder, the potential harm that would have been done to those same people and communities if Mr Jeff Diamond had been killed instead of, or as well as his wife. I hope you have some understanding of the magnitude of grief and loss Australia has suffered as a result of your wilful act, Mr García.'

Jeff clenched his jaws as came once more eye-to-eye with the man now confirmed as his wife's murderer and who might as well have murdered him. Feeling again like the twelve-year-old denied the opportunity to watch his father receive such a lecture, he longed to hurl abuse at this repulsive excuse for a human being.

Furthermore, if he had possessed a gun at this precise moment in time, the forty-three-year-old was certain the child inside would have used it, thereby making himself no better than the beige weasel in the dock.

'Shit,' the widower cursed, closing his eyes and leaning forwards, with his elbows on his knees and his head in his hands. 'I need to hear this so badly.'

Kierney rested a hand on her father's back, as did Gerry. She glanced over towards where García's estranged wife had been sitting, but she was no longer there. Scanning from right to left in the steep hall, the young woman's eyes passed over the teams of reporters and journalists, with their notebooks poised and their microphones and cameras trained on Judge Milne, until they found Wendy García in the very back row, close to the exit door. The two women knew each had been spotted by the other, and both looked away swiftly.

'Next,' Rosemary Milne continued, 'is the taking of a human life. By your actions, Mr García, Ms Lynn Diamond has had the rest of her very important life taken away from her and from the family who love her a great deal. Do you understand how significant this is?'

'Yes, Your Honour,' came a sullen reply.

Peering down again between the dress circle railings to where the Accused had shifted sideways and almost out of sight from his vocal detractors on high, the victim's husband was surprised to hear such a ready acknowledgement. With it came a glimmer of hope that a stretch at Her Majesty's pleasure might rehabilitate this man. Despite the verdict's damning attribution, he was not bad to the core, although this further emphasised the futility of Lynn's death.

The judge paused and took in the Accused's response. 'Good. Now, disregarding the illegal possession of a firearm, which is incidental in this trial, I have many options available to me for the punishment of offences against the Crown. These range from nothing, by which I mean unconditional discharge, a monetary fine and various types of custodial sentence. I could also order you to perform a programme of community service for those people who have suffered as a result of your brutal act.'

Jeff almost laughed, sitting back and putting his hand over his mouth to stifle the noise. 'Now that *would* be amusing,' he whispered to Kierney. 'He could take *mamá*'s place in all her concert engagements, so Cath wouldn't need to cancel her next tour.'

'*Papá*, that's not in the least bit funny,' his daughter scolded with a smile.

'Yes, it is,' her father insisted. 'It's hilarious.'

Shaking her head and flashing dark eyes at Gerry, the teenager turned back to hear what else Judge Milne might have to say.

'Mr García, I have no alternative but to impose a lengthy custodial sentence on you, as expected for a murder conviction. A murder charge carries a minimum of twenty years, and often a lot longer. On top of the murder conviction, you also have been found guilty of intending to murder another prominent individual, and you've told the court that you harboured such intent for many, many years. Is that correct?'

Again, García answered straightaway. 'Yes, Your Honour.'

'Thank you. Therefore, I would be derelict in my duty to protect Mr Diamond, his family and anyone else who might find themselves in a similar unfortunate position as Ms Diamond, and who run the risk of being shot at by someone with a long-held grudge that renders him or her unable to make sound judgements. I cannot allow you to walk freely until the Crown is satisfied that you won't return to society with the same feelings of hatred and jealousy which could drive you to pursue another murder.'

The judge took a few seconds to gather her thoughts. The public gallery was losing interest, restless limbs shuffling, like banks of interpreters waiting for the string of verbs in a complex German sentence.

'Why is she taking so long?' Gerry hissed. 'Just say life, Madam, and we can go and get drunk.'

'For fuck's sake, mate,' Jeff shook his head. 'She's duty-bound to go through all this stuff. It's due process. The media'll crucify her if she doesn't, and the Defence can appeal if she doesn't go through why she's dismissed all the other options. You'll get your drink soon enough.'

'Far sooner than García will,' Kierney grinned, leaning into her father's tired body.

The forty-three-year-old chuckled at the not-so-innocent remark, then burst into tears again. 'Jesus. I'm sorry, guys,' he croaked. 'I'm a complete wreck, but so unbelievably grateful to have you here. Thanks for being here, just in case I forget to tell you later.'

'Juan Antonio García Ruelas,' Judge Milne pronounced again, in a louder voice this time. 'We must not forget that celebrities are also members of the public, and your victim, intended victim and their family are citizens of the Commonwealth of Australia. Presiding over your trial, I am obliged to provide my reasoning for the sentence I'm about to impose on you. Celebrities, solely by virtue of who they are in the public eye, perhaps place themselves at greater risk than ordinary people. However, this does not mean the Crown has a lesser obligation to protect them.'

'You should protect them more!' a shout came from the back of the dress circle, followed by several other exclamations and utterances of general agreement.

'Ladies and gentlemen, please be patient until sentence has been passed,' Rosemary Milne sighed, sensing the end was in sight. 'Lynn and Jeff Diamond are two of our country's greatest national treasures, as I have been constantly reminded during this trial. Therefore, for the murder of Ms Victoria Lynn Shannon Dyson Diamond, I am sentencing you, Mr García, to life imprisonment, with parole to be considered no earlier than twenty years after today's date, that is the nineteenth of April, two-thousand-and-sixteen.'

An initial gasp gave way to cheers and determined applause as if the loyal fans who had kept the famous company for the last five days had been sitting on their hands for the entire duration. Judge Milne also broke into an overt smile for the first time, delighted by the verdict over which she had restrained her most professional influence.

Several people called out Jeff's name, but he refused to stand up or make any type of scene for now. He couldn't bring himself to show disrespect for the poor man who would hardly see the light of day for the rest of his life. There was plenty of time to celebrate, assuming the notion would appeal to him at some point in the future.

'You have not expressed remorse during this trial, Mr García,' Rosemary Milne continued, 'and nor have you outwardly taken responsibility for your actions. Therefore I'm unable to give you any discount on your custodial sentence.'

She looked towards Stephen Greenshaw, who was sitting with his legs crossed in front of his team's bench, almost disinterested. He had likely expected to wait until Monday for the trial's conclusion, pondering when he might next be allocated a case he had a chance of winning.

'She's looking to Mr Floaty to lodge an appeal,' the wise man told his daughter, 'but he's not going to.'

'Should he?'

'Sure he should,' the angry humanitarian nodded. 'He's supposed to do his utmost for his client, but he's just going to let him hang. That's not fair.'

Moving on to the second and third charge, Rosemary Milne wasted no time in announcing a further eight-year custodial sentence for attempting to murder Jeffrey Moreno Diamond, to be served concurrently, and a negligible extra three months for discharging an unlicensed firearm in a public place.

'Mr García,' the judge said for the last time, 'I commit you to the services of the Commonwealth of Australia's prison system, where I hope you will avail yourself of opportunities offered to you to work through your depression and anxiety, with a hope that you can rationalise your unhealthy feelings of anger towards two of our country's most... if not *the* most... respected, hardworking and morally good people.

'I have familiarised myself with the extent of Mr Diamond's financial commitment to people who suffer much like yourself, and I also know the time he and his family put in to improving the lives of disadvantaged people. His equally impressive and vibrant wife did not deserve to die at forty years old after their dedication to charitable causes. I trust you will reflect on these facts while you're serving your sentence.'

They were nice words, the superstar thought, gazing down at the closing scene of this long, drawn-out play they had been watching. The gracious woman was kind to have said them, yet the cynic in him wondered if she would have embellished her language quite as much if he and Kierney had not been present. Regardless, her speech was now on public record, and he acknowledged her apparent sincerity with a subtle wave.

Turning towards the guards stationed behind the dock, the Queen gave García his leave.

'Officers, please remove the prisoner from the court.'

Those who had lingered in the public gallery, largely made up of the Diamonds' most ardent supporters, immediately stood and stretched. While they gathered their belongings together, Gerry, Kierney and Jeff watched the diminutive Spaniard being escorted from the dock. The hunched figure disappeared through the solid wooden doors without so much as a glance back towards his wife. He must have had no idea she was there.

WHAT NEXT?

Down in the courtroom below, Judge Milne drew the proceedings to a rather unceremonious close, with only three officials and the legal teams remaining. As soon as the door had closed on another convicted criminal, signalling the show's final snap of the clapperboard, the performers' disposition switched from sombre to festive, with the weekend upon them and the high-profile trial concluded just in time.

Defence Counsel tugged his Mr Floaty outfit over his head and became an ordinary man again, much to Kierney's disappointment. He looked up to where he knew his old school pal had been sitting all week.

Gerry leant over the balcony wall. 'Stephen Greenshaw, I presume,' he shouted to the erstwhile Mr Floaty. 'How are you? It's been a while.'

'Indeed, Blakey, me old mate,' replied the barrister. 'I knew you were wrapped up in the Diamond world, but didn't realise you'd be here. Are you going to join us for a drink or two?'

The former Head Boy glanced over towards Jeff and his daughter, who were also on their feet, mobbed by overjoyed and curious fans. At this moment too, the doors at the rear of the public gallery flung open and another swarm of media personnel streamed down the stairs.

Greenshaw would have to wait, the celebrities' manager realised, turning on his heels and leaping up the steps two at a time. He held his hands up to stop the marauding crowd from coming any closer.

'Give them some privacy, please,' the courteous businessman instructed the journalists and photographers, allowing himself latitude to modify his tenor as experience suggested would be required. 'They need some time to come to terms with the verdict and what happens next.'

The reporters were desperate for a comment. Gerry refused to be drawn, causing a few to try shouting in the Diamonds' direction. Seeing his faithful offsider under siege, the rock star apologised to the concerned group of well-wishers and dragged his heavy legs up the stairs towards the press gang.

He would have to face them sooner or later, so he might as well get it over with. Kierney followed out of the same duty, secretly hoping not to be asked any intrusive questions.

'Mr Diamond, can you give us your views on the trial?' one man from The Australian broadsheet asked.

'It's over,' Jeff gave a perfunctory answer. 'That's all I care about right now.'

'Are you happy with the sentence of life in prison?' shouted a woman from the ABC.

'Happy's not the word I'd use, but I'm pleased the jury reached a conclusive verdict,' he told the array of wavering microphones.

'Miss Diamond!' another reporter called out.

The handsome billionaire invited his daughter to stand next to him, resting a protective hand on her shoulder. Cameras flashed all around them, which was nothing new. Gerry stood back and let his clients do what they did best, turning round after a while and returning to the edge of the balcony.

'Are you pleased with the guilty verdict?' the teenager was asked.

'Yes, thank you,' she replied. 'It's been a tiring week, and I don't know what else to say. I'm sorry.'

'That's fine, gorgeous,' her father encouraged. 'We're all tired. We'll organise a formal press conference in a few days' time. For now, we just want to get out of this place, if you don't mind.'

Vince Allen, one of the best known journalists in Australia's entertainment industry, thrust his voice recorder towards the famous star. The two had grown into regular sparring partners over the years, since the African famine relief campaigns in the mid-1980s.

'So Jeff, how do you feel about García, knowing your father also served a life sentence?'

The great man shook his head. 'Vince, I'm not prepared to talk about that now. Of course I appreciate the irony of life's circular coincidences. García probably doesn't deserve to go down for murder, but then Lynn didn't deserve to die either. Justice has been done, of sorts. It was never going to be fair, but I can live with that. I'm as content as I can be with the outcome.'

The honest confession temporarily stunned the throng, captured on tape for broadcast around the world. As the widower forged a path to the top of the gallery steps, his gaze alighted on Wendy García lurking near the exit, also surrounded by a bunch of opportunistic reporters. He broke away and strode across to where she stood, and to everyone's astonishment, they embraced. Cameras again whirred and clicked in furious fashion as a perfect front-page news story evolved right in front of their lenses.

Kierney was filled with a surge of furious disenchantment, opting not to follow her father's example. She held no compassion for her mother's killer or his estranged spouse. Perhaps if she had been the direct descendant of a double murderer she might have thought differently. She wasn't, fortunately for her disoriented young conscience.

'How're you going?' Jeff asked the woman in the red jacket.

'How are *you* goin', more like?' Wendy answered with an awkward, grating western suburbs accent. 'I'm sorry Lynn passed away.'

'Thanks. So am I,' the superstar acknowledged with a sigh. 'So am I.'

'And I'm sorry that my bloody excuse for an 'usband killed 'er. I never thought 'e'd do it. Didn't think 'e 'ad the balls.'

The widower shrugged, absorbing the painful irony. 'No? I guess people can always surprise each other. You probably rubbed a little salt into his wounds from time to time, didn't you?'

Wendy stood aghast, unable to think of a comeback. By now, Gerry had arrived at his friend's side, marvelling at yet another priceless media moment being architected on the fly by the genius communicator and his latest puppet.

'We all do things that piss off our partners,' Jeff smiled, a tear or two escaping down one side of his face. 'I know I did. Lynn's endless patience was rewarded with eternal peace. You wanted someone like me but you married someone like him, and you made him pay for it. I pushed my luck and married someone like Lynn, and we both paid for it.'

The grieving husband took a deep breath, determined to control his anger in front of Kierney and the press. To his delight, he received a perfectly timed token of appreciation for his trouble, feeling his tattoo sting in response to his candour. All that remained was for him to deliver a parting shot on behalf of his beautiful best friend.

'You've chosen to live the rest of your life as Juan Antonio García's ex-wife, so we're both left to find our own way through what happened. Let's just get on with it and not drag each other through the mud any longer, OK? Juan Antonio'll be alright, and you will too. I wish I could say the same. Good luck, Wendy.'

The plain woman stood dumbfounded as the celebrity shook her hand. He then stepped to one side, as statuesque and dignified as ever, inviting his daughter and Gerry to walk up the steps and out of the public space ahead of him. Wonderful Wendy had been left to the lions in the waiting media rabble, much to the astonishment of everyone present.

'*Papá*, that was amazing!' the astounded teenager exclaimed once they were back in the third-floor corridor. 'She had no clue what to say.'

Jeff gave the youngster a bear-hug. '*Gracias*. That was the plan. Let's get out of here, *pequeñita*. I'm just about hanging on here.'

'Hold your horses, mate. We've been summoned to the judge's chambers for a drink,' their manager interrupted. 'Via Mr Floaty.'

'Have we? Is that appropriate?' Kierney asked.

'Yeah. It's appropriate,' her father sighed, ''cause the case is all signed off now. There's nothing I'd rather do less, but I guess we shouldn't snub them after they worked their magic on *mamá*'s behalf.'

His friend slapped the stalwart on the back. 'Good man. Let's get a beer into you.'

Shell-shocked and weary, the trio shared the lift with four strangers who were none the wiser as to the trial's outcome. Jeff and Gerry provided polite answers to their questions, giving no salient information away.

Upon reaching the first floor, where the law firms' offices were located, they found Stephen Greenshaw waiting for them by the lifts. He extended a bony hand to his schoolmate and then towards the man with whom everyone wanted to be seen yet who had no desire to see anyone.

'This is our daughter, Kierney,' the celebrity ceded, nudging the young woman forward while raising his right arm to her shoulder instead of shaking the lawyer's hand.

He was sick and tired of watching the graceful teenager being left until last during introductions. Such disregard for common courtesy would never have been tolerated around Lynn, therefore it was high time it no longer happened to their gipsy girl either.

'Pleased to meet you, Kierney,' the barrister responded, taking her hand instead.

'Thank you,' the father spoke on the youngster's behalf, finally extending his own hand. 'Good on ya, Stephen. Nice to meet you.'

'Likewise, Jeff,' the lean gentleman replied. 'Please accept my condolences for the loss of your wife. And for your mother, Kierney.'

Formalities over, Greenshaw directed the visitors down a narrow corridor. The chambers were almost deserted, being after six o'clock on a Friday evening, when legal eagles had much better things to do with their weekends than to hang around their place of work.

The familiar voice of Graham Winton could be heard through an open door towards the end on the right-hand side. He sounded full of the joys of spring, no doubt regaling tales of the glorious victory.

'We'll stay for half an hour, max',' Jeff told the teenager in a hushed voice. 'I promise.'

She grinned in assent. 'Are we going home tonight or tomorrow?'

'Tonight, if possible. Is that OK?'

Kierney responded with a childish nod, anxious not to be a burden on her exhausted *papá*, who wagged his index finger, scolding her for making him cry yet again. Gerry went ahead of the Diamonds into the enormous and opulently furnished rooms. Inside were Judge Milne, the entire Prosecution team and four others whom he recognised as the balance of Defence Counsel personnel.

Now minus her black gown and wearing a floral blouse and a light grey skirt, the judge resembled a normal businesswoman; not at all like someone who had sentenced a man to life imprisonment less than an hour ago. She stepped forward to greet the new arrivals and introduced herself, again being presented with Kierney first.

'Thank you,' the eighteen-year-old said with a broad smile drawn out of habit from her deepest reserves. 'Should I call you Your Honour?'

The kind woman chuckled. 'No. You can call me Rose. It's lovely to meet you, Kierney. And Jeff... Do you mind if I call you Jeff?'

'Absolutely not,' the diplomat answered. 'Thanks for the invitation down here, Rose. It's kind of you to include us. This is my business manager and long-time friend, Gerry Blake. As a matter of fact, he went to school with Counsel for the Defence.'

'Oh, sugar! Is that right?' their host replied, loud enough for the entire cohort to hear. 'Are there any embarrassing stories to be told?'

The suave executive took the judge's hand, all smiles. 'Good evening, Rose. I'm afraid not. I was too young to be let in on any of Greenshaw's secrets, so I'm going to disappoint you. His sister, on the other hand...'

Jeff shook his head and sniffed. 'Doesn't take him long to debase the conversation.'

'Well...' Rose let out a sunny laugh. 'Welcome anyway, all of you. I'm glad you felt you could accept our invitation. It must've been a very difficult week for you. First though, let me pass on my personal condolences. Your wife was such a wonderful person.'

The celebrity nodded. 'It has, and she was. Both still are, I assure you. We're very glad it's over before the weekend, so thanks for wrapping things up so fast.'

The attentive Irishman presented his clients with heavy crystal glasses, one containing beer and the other filled with orange juice and a few bobbing ice-cubes. In front of the judge, the playful father reached for the juice, causing titters of amusement, and it was Kierney's frustrated head which was left shaking this time.

Winton sidled up and rested a hand on the famous shoulder. 'So, sir... Here we are. We got him!' he claimed in triumph.

'You did. Congratulations, Graham. And commiserations, I guess, Stephen.'

The erstwhile Defence Counsel raised his glass. 'Cheers!' he shouted from a few metres away, where he and Gerry had already embarked upon their bawdy reacquaintance. 'Commiserations for having drawn the short straw, you mean? Defending the man who shot Lynn Diamond. It's not a case I would've taken voluntarily, I have to admit.'

Jeff's jaw muscles tightened as anger brewed inside at the metaphorical distance the cocky barrister had put between him and his beautiful best friend. Rose Milne sensed their guest's negative reaction and changed the subject, addressing the quiet teenager once more.

'Is this the first court session you've attended, Kierney?'

'Yes, it is. It was extremely interesting. Thank you for providing the jury with so much information about the process. It helped me understand what was going on too.'

'Oh, you're welcome, my dear,' Rose replied. 'It's important for people to be clear on why we follow all the various rules. I'm sure half of it must seem completely pointless to the average person. When I found out I was presiding over this trial, I made a mental note to be extra careful in explaining the technicalities. I wanted to get the right verdict.'

'The right verdict?' the victim's husband challenged. 'Why this case more than any other?'

The perceptive law professional nodded. 'I'm sure you understand, Jeff, the reality of being seen to get a high-profile case right. We always try to arrive at the right verdict in every case, of course, but when the Crown's prosecuting on behalf of a public that's so angry and upset by what happened to your late wife, and your late mother, Kierney, it's doubly important to be as thorough as possible.'

'Excuse me, Rose, but do you mind not using the word "late", please?' the brave young woman asked. 'I'd rather still think of my mother as my mother.'

The group of lawyers fell silent for a few seconds, taking in this heartfelt request. The only minor in the room had given those with many years of professional experience a simple reality check. And to congratulate her, her father did absolutely nothing. His daughter was coming of age rapidly.

'I'm very sorry,' Rose responded, putting her hand out to touch Kierney's forearm. 'I understand. We have a bad habit of getting lost in the detail of a case and forgetting the impact on the people it affects.'

To restore some lightness to the atmosphere, the two Sydney Grammar old boys struck up a conversation about which schools various prominent New South Wales and national personalities had attended. While the attention was on the others, Jeff gave his daughter an approving wink for sticking up for herself and her family, and she followed his eyes to the younger solicitors who had broken away into a separate *clique* at the far end of the office.

The teenager took the cue and excused herself to join Peter and Moira, who were eager to include the youthful singer-songwriter. They introduced her to their colleagues, much to the doting dad's pleasure as he watched her mingling with the twenty-somethings.

'Tell me, Jeff,' Graham Winton asked in a voice rendered even lustier by alcohol. 'What was your reaction when the *Foreman* pronounced the "G" word?'

The widower sighed. 'Jeez... Every emotion at once, pretty much,' he answered, 'and then very soon afterwards, nothing at all.'

'Nothing?' Stephen repeated, eyes wide with disbelief. 'I'd have thought you'd be cheering. I was, and I was representing the godforsaken pleb'.'

A sardonic chuckle slipped from the splendid philanthropist's lips, while Rose and Gerry stood back to witness the two senior barristers take the celebrity's comments as criticism of their respective performances.

'Actually, no,' Jeff continued. 'As I said to you several times, Graham, I just wanted to see the trial fought fairly. Guilty or not guilty makes no difference to me. But guilty's the right outcome for Lynn, for our kids and for her family. So in that respect, it's good to have heard the "G" word.'

The star's manager piped up. 'Well, for me anyway, I'm exceedingly pleased to have heard all three "G" words, and I'm sure you will be too, mate, once the shock wears off. One thing you need to know about Jeff Diamond, ladies and gentlemen, is that even after twenty-five years as one of Australia's richest and most influential personalities, he still considers himself a man of the people.'

Rose smiled. 'We're all people of the people, Gerry. Or we ought to be, at any rate. It's an important quality, and I admire it. Why else would I have had so much trouble controlling the public gallery this week? I don't preside over many trials where the phrase "I love you" is yelled out on a regular basis.'

Everyone laughed, including the humble megastar. The former Mr Floaty remained indignant however, keen for further sport.

'But with these low-life crims, we educated members of society need to take the moral high ground,' he insisted. 'Even you'd have to agree with that, Jeff.'

'Look... I'm not sure I do, Counsels,' the forty-three-year-old answered, raising his cut crystal beer glass to the others. 'I grew up in García's low-life world, despite having played in yours for a good while now. I know what it's like to be treated like a second-class citizen; a pleb', as you called our insipid little Defendant just now. As I said to the journoes upstairs, Lynn didn't deserve to die and maybe García doesn't deserve to spend the rest of his life in prison. Fundamentally though, Stephen, I do agree with you.'

Greenshaw's expression switched from derision to approval, with a hint of arrogance thrown in for good measure. Jeff braced himself to clarify his position to the audience who had taken him hostage at the end of an arduous week. He loosened his tie and undid the top button of his shirt, preparing to turn the tables on these righteous self-appointed custodians of the law.

Even though the entertainment industry's biggest draw-card cut a much less strident shadow these days, he couldn't help noticing the judge's eyes scanning him up and down in admiration. He still exuded the necessary magnetism to win over a crowd, needing only to trot out one more hackneyed *Spiel* before securing leave to rescue his gorgeous daughter and whisk her back home to the seclusion of their city penthouse.

'I believe people have to be educated to use power to their advantage,' he smiled. 'So in that sense, I agree with your premise. And for this reason, I'm comfortable with the power resting with people like you guys. Only up to a point though... I don't doubt the silver spoon brigade works very hard, both as students to make the most of their golden opportunities and later while building careers. For Christ's sake, Lynn was one of you, and Kierney over there is one too. I can see good and bad in growing up on either side of the fence.'

'So you don't consider yourself educated?' Rose asked in surprise.

'Yeah. Of course I do,' the celebrity replied. 'But being willing to learn and being given the opportunity for a decent education don't always go hand-in-hand. I got myself educated in spite of the uninspiring circumstances of my birth. I've turned myself into one of you. Well, to an extent anyway... But I'm determined to keep a foot in both camps.'

The skilled negotiator focussed on one of his feet and then the other, spreading them further apart to illustrate his point. As he spoke, he scraped the sole of his right shoe along the floor towards his left, making a point of tapping the two together to draw attention to the gleaming black leather percussion instruments. He felt all eyes burning into his scalp as he bowed to the traditional worsted carpet.

Lifting his chin again, Jeff stared into their worldly but over-privileged faces and carried on. 'If I don't, the "haves" will drift off in their self-indulgent ships of plenty and leave the "have nots" behind to fend for themselves. Ignorance is the biggest problem, not a lack of intelligence. People in both camps are intelligent, but they don't necessarily know they are. That's ignorance, no matter what other excuses we might make.

'García, as you rightly pointed out, Rose, had no idea about the counselling services available from DCF charities that could've helped him. Instead, he shot my wife. That's ignorance too, but his biggest handicap was not his fault. The fact we hadn't got our message out to him makes Lynn's death partially my fault, which eats me up inside.

'It's all our faults for not keeping the two camps close enough together. Those of us who understand this ought to do something about it, rather than hanging our hats on "G" words, 'cause by the time we get to guilty, there's already a victim.'

The tall, good-looking enigma denied himself a much-needed breath to reinforce the gravitas of his closing sentence. Judge and sparring barristers inhaled for him, appearing at once inspired and crestfallen. In the bereaved philanthropist's eyes, true justice had not been served today, even though tomorrow's newspapers would dole out wholehearted praise to the system which saw Lynn Dyson Diamond's killer behind bars for at least two decades.

Jeff took a gulp from his beer glass, waiting for someone to contradict him. It was high time to leave the New South Wales legal fraternity shielded by its expensive, taxpayer-funded office furnishings and return to a place where he didn't have to constantly defend his own sensibilities. He no longer possessed appetite or motive to woo these east-side snobs with his magic words like some up-market freak show.

'But hey!' the wise peacemaker closed. 'I'm just an ungrateful bastard who should shut up and let you get on with your weekends. Who knows? On another day, the result may've been different. Those who needed a guilty verdict got lucky today.'

'Amen to that!' Gerry chanted, toasting his friend with an empty tumbler.

The widower sighed at the array of confounded *illuminati* left gawping at his plain-speaking. 'And perversely, García may be a whole lot happier in prison 'cause the pressure'll finally be off. He won't have to struggle every day; won't always be made to feel inadequate by his wife, his boss and the rest of us, who can't help but look down on people like him. Having lost his freedom in the physical world, he's somehow freer mentally, emotionally. Ironic, isn't it?'

'Yes. Indeed it is. A very interesting way of looking at things,' Rose Milne replied, pausing for one of her minions to refill her gin and tonic. 'There certainly are plenty of documented cases where offenders use the prison system as a way of escaping the responsibilities of life.'

'Absolutely,' the son of one such offender agreed. 'That's exactly what I mean. If anything, the "G" word gave him everything he was looking for: licence to hand his list of seemingly impossible challenges to someone else and say, "OK, I give up. You tell me how I should do this." And you did.'

Winton, Greenshaw and Blake, the three successful private school boys, gaped at each other in tacit acknowledgement of a superior mind. Graham held out his hand to the celebrity, who accepted the gesture's magnanimity with reluctance.

'You've taught me a lot, sir,' the barrister said, turning to his legal colleagues. 'We all had dinner the night before last, for the team to get some background for our closing arguments, and I have to admit my eyes were opened considerably. I used the term "everyman philosophy", I believe, Jeff, didn't I?'

'Yep. I remember that,' the rock star answered with a chuckle.

'It's very apt, though I say so myself,' the prosecutor went on, drawing in his learned colleagues. 'In this profession, we spend our days with our heads buried in the text books, talking about interpretation of the law and legal precedents, all very theoretical and frightfully intelligent. Then you go and say something like "OK, I give up. Tell me how I should do it," and everything makes perfect sense.'

Tired of regurgitating details about the trial, Jeff smiled through gritted teeth, glancing over to his daughter to see if she was ready to leave. He would have taken Winton's comments as a compliment if they hadn't come across as so patronising.

'Thanks, Graham. We'd better make a move. Gez, did you want to fly back tonight too?'

The stars' business manager read this gentle hint and set his replenished beer glass down onto the table. Old school-friends were a hoot to catch up with, but his loyalties lay with the Diamonds. Never more so than tonight.

'Yes, mate. Great idea.'

'I'll walk out with you,' Winton suggested, reaching for a stout, bulging briefcase and his suit jacket. 'Stephen, are you coming? Rosemary, thanks again for your sound advice this week and for a job very well done. Next week is another day.'

The two barristers each kissed their superior colleague on the cheek and waved to their associates. Rose Milne shook the handsome celebrity's hand once more, and he thanked her formally. With Kierney soon at her father's side, they all left the judge alone in her chambers.

'We should've offered to wash the glasses,' the teenager chided, feigning innocence and swinging her dad's arm like a toddler.

'Shhh!' Jeff scolded. 'Now that wasn't very nice, was it?'

Their relief at being out of the stuffy corridors behind the courtrooms was short-lived. Lunging at the doors and stepping out into the main foyer of the Supreme Court building, the Diamonds and their companions were confronted by forty or fifty journalists and camera operators who surged forwards *en masse* on the first glimpse of their target.

'Hello! Here we go again!' Gerry bellowed to the startled lawyers. 'Just stand back, and let Lord Sparkle deal with it. That's what I do, anyway.'

The seasoned crowd-pleaser scowled at his friend in jest. 'Cheers, mate. I thought you'd at least carry my gun.'

Kierney watched the two straight-laced gentlemen grappling with this last throwaway line. She cringed at her father's wicked sense of humour and wondered what these fine, upstanding society figures might make of it. The reporters fired question after question at the widower, all of which he answered directly while supplying as little information as he could get away with.

Greenshaw and Winton stood in awe as Jeff courted the cameras and monopolised the microphones that surrounded him, thankful it was neither of their turns to be interviewed. The frenetic scene looked like the witness stand on steroids to them, a welcome diversion at the end of a long week.

'He's never made it easy on himself,' the billionaire's long-time manager explained, only half joking. 'When Shakespeare came up with the phrase "pound of flesh", I swear he was thinking of this particular Polish Jew.'

Prosecuting Counsel laughed out loud. 'The greats are the greats for a good reason, I'm coming to believe. I said it before and I see it again now. It's not just hype, is it? Those who depend on the hype get found out sooner or later, but people like Jeff Diamond endure and go from strength to strength. True greats stand the test of time.'

'Marianna, it's Jeff.'

The sophisticated accent of his mother-in-law sounded similar enough to Lynn's to tip the exhausted widower over the edge yet again. Taking pity on him, his daughter prised the mobile out of his hand and spoke to her grandmother.

'Hi, Grandma,' she said as brightly as she could. 'It's Kierney now. We wanted to tell you the trial verdict came through.'

'Oh, darling, thank you,' Marianna responded, concern in her voice. 'Where are you now?'

'In a taxi, going back to the airport,' the eighteen-year-old replied. 'Is Grandpa there too?'

'Yes, he is. Let me go track him down. Is your dad alright, Kierney?'

The young woman looked up at her father's closed eyes and placed her fingers over the tiny microphone. 'Grandma wants to know if you're OK,' she said, nudging him back into the land of the living. 'She's getting Grandpa. Are you?'

Jeff sighed and opened his eyes, smiling at Kierney's childish tone. He motioned for her to hand the telephone back. She shook her head, putting the handset back up to her ear.

'Sorry, Grandma. *Papá*'s OK. He's right here.'

'Good,' Marianna replied. 'So is Grandpa.'

'May I tell them, please?' the excited teenager whispered, dropping the handset down and squeezing it against her thigh so her request wouldn't be heard by her grandparents.

Gerry sniggered from the front seat of the taxi, and his mate shrugged. He didn't have the energy to fight with his daughter and sensed she needed to do her share of the news-mongering after such an overwhelming few days.

'Thanks!' the youngster smiled, giving her dad a peck on the cheek. 'Sorry. I'm back. Are you there?'

'Yes, Kierney. We're here,' her grandfather's deep voice answered, audible to the vehicle's other occupants. 'Tell us, please.'

'He...' the young woman checked her manners. 'García, I mean, has been found guilty.'

'Guilty?' she heard both grandparents repeat in unison.

'Yes! On all three charges.'

'Oh, that's such good news, darling,' Marianna sounded relieved.

'Yes. Absolutely,' Bart echoed. 'All three charges. At last, some justice for your poor mother. I expect you're very happy with the result, both of you. Your dad must be...'

The older man's voice tailed off mid-sentence, either overcome with emotion or unable to find adequate words to describe his son-in-law's state of mind. Jeff coughed and requested Kierney pass the telephone over again. This time she obliged, and he lifted it up to speak, taking a long, labouring breath.

'Sir, I'm here,' the exhausted man stated. 'That's the extent of it, I'm afraid, for the moment. It's absolutely the right outcome for the Queen, and for you too, I'd imagine. For this I'm grateful. Lynn's killer's behind bars and will be until at least 2016 or thereabouts. Life sentence with possible parole after twenty. Case closed. *Buenas noches, Señor García.*'

The Dysons were speechless, causing Kierney to stare into her father's face in anticipation of further extravagant observations. She knew her grandparents wouldn't be surprised at his obtuse turn of phrase but was nevertheless annoyed by such flippancy.

'Thank you, Jeff,' Marianna responded after a few seconds. 'I can understand it leaving you feeling pretty hollow. It won't bring Lynn back. We realise that. We'd much rather that too.'

The spent man broke down, unable to deal with sympathy from his mother-in-law. 'No, it doesn't,' he sniffed, leaning his head against the car window and struggling for breath. 'Thanks, Marianna. I know you're grieving too. I'm just a selfish arsehole at the moment. You're better off talking to Kierney.'

Jeff handed the telephone back to his daughter, who was also crying. She gave her father the sweetest of smiles in return, sending him once more into floods of tears.

'We'd better go, Grandma, Grandpa,' the young woman said. 'We'll give you a ring tomorrow once we're back home and after a good night's sleep. We wanted to make sure you found out before you turned on the news tonight. *Papá* was amazing! He did *mamá* proud on the stand and in front of the journoes.'

'I bet he did,' Bart replied. 'We'll hear all about it over the next few days. The good thing is the obnoxious little runt is where he belongs. Speak to you both soon, Kierney.'

'Bye, Grandpa. Talk soon.'

They ended the call, and the taxi fell silent. Fortunately for everyone, it was already circling the departures terminal, searching for a suitable place to let its famous passengers out. Gerry paid the driver while the others grabbed their suitcases from the boot and ran inside to a team of security personnel who were ready and waiting to usher them through the Friday night crowds.

Once in the bowels of the terminal, the threesome was shown into a private room in the Qantas lounge to while away the hour before their flight. Jeff checked the amount of charge left in his telephone's battery before dialling his son's number, pleased to hear a cheerful greeting.

'Hey, mate,' the father responded. 'Good morning. We got a verdict. Yeah. We're at the airport, on our way home. My battery's low so I might cut off.'

The young woman watched her father struggling to maintain self-control as Jet must have uttered some supportive words from his Cambridge digs. She held her hand out towards him, signalling for him to give her the chance to speak to her brother.

'True enough,' Jeff nodded. 'Guilty as charged, mate. Yeah. Unanimous, as far as we know. It doesn't matter, anyway. Oh, I don't know. Yeah. I guess so. Look, mate, I can't talk about it now. We're in the airport. Here's your sister. Have fun.'

He passed the handset to Kierney, who took it with a supportive smile. 'Hi, Jetto. It's excellent! I'm happy, but it hasn't sunk in properly yet. You'll have to see if it's on the news over there. We just want to get home now. He's a bit bent out of shape. No. It's OK. We'll ring you tomorrow. The phone's bleeping at me. See you later. Thanks. Shall do, thanks. *Te amos.*'

When it came time to board the flight to Melbourne, airline staff accompanied the special delegation from the lounge and shepherded them all the way to their seats at the front of the aeroplane. Across the aisle from Jeff, his business manager fell asleep within minutes of take-off, fuelled by the two double brandies he consumed while waiting. Looking at his gorgeous gipsy girl, tucked away from prying eyes in her window seat, the father cast his thoughts back to their arrival in Sydney almost a week ago.

Should he have brought his daughter to the trial? When was someone old enough to know the truth; to make up one's own mind about what one believed to be the truth? Had he given Kierney sufficient space to work out her own truth, or had he unfairly biased her opinion with his own experiences? At least she now appreciated the subtleties of the law without having to fall victim to them herself.

'Are you OK?' the young woman asked, seeing her father's tired eyes staring through her with a faraway gaze.

'Yeah, Kizzy, I'm fine,' Jeff said, knowing he couldn't hope for her to believe him if he didn't even believe himself. 'Please don't worry about me. From now on we're looking forwards. Right?'

Kierney frowned and shook her head. 'Right. If you say so.'

That night, back in their Melbourne apartment, the widower lay on his bed in the dark and resumed his own life sentence. Running through his mind were all those years during which Lynn had been around to help him break out of the obsessive "now or never" anxieties which had gripped him in his teens, as a result of the betrayal and abandonment he had suffered. How long had it taken him to believe in the mantra of "There's always tomorrow" which his guardian angel had bestowed upon him all those years ago?

Yet there wasn't always tomorrow, was there? García had seen to that. Jeff had enjoyed a comfortable twenty-year sabbatical from his old fears, but now the boy with the death-wish was back. For the sake of his children, he knew he had to rise above the despair somehow, or at least make a damned good show of doing so. Jet and

Kierney deserved to think positive thoughts about the future, even if he had no interest in it.

Unable to sleep, the loving father crept into the office to switch on his computer and then into the kitchen to make coffee. One of the many e-mails the star had missed while away in Sydney summarised the steady stream of tribute records being released by other prominent artists, all keen to publicise the influence Lynn had on their careers. Similar to the memorial service, the list contained virtually every chart-topping musician, including some from Africa and even a couple from China. Once again, the grieving husband was humbled by the love the world had for him and his dream girl.

In addition to these instant hits, the Melbourne Academy students had written to him to announce their intention to make a film tribute to their favourite school governor. Qantas had sought permission to use DVD footage of Lynn and the family for a composite clip to be shown for a month on all in-flight entertainment before the regular news bulletin.

The widower scoffed at Cathy's approval request for these projects to go ahead, and he typed a restrained response indicating that he could hardly put a stop to people expressing their grief, even though it might be seen to prolong it for everyone else. *Meaning me*, he insinuated.

The scroll of senders' names in his e-mail inbox also resembled a catalogue of contemporary public life. The former deadbeat kid from Sydney's western suburbs still found himself affected deeply when counted in their number. All these Very Important Persons had taken the time to write to him about the death of his wife, to express support for the trial and to find out how he was faring. He couldn't decide whether this was a good thing or a bad thing. He was grateful for their concern but wished he could disappear for the next six months, until the plight of his family was relegated to the inner pages of the planet's newspapers and magazines.

One particular letter that Cathy had scanned and sent to her boss captured Jeff's attention. It was written by a former university colleague from the couple's time in London. Naomi Whiting had risen through the ranks of the British Foreign Service and was currently posted in Oman.

She and her boyfriend of the time had been regular contributors to the dinner parties he and Lynn hosted from their St John's Wood flat, during which they had tried to solve the world's most pressing intellectual problems over copious quantities of alcohol and other, far more illicit substances. The couple had caught up with Naomi periodically over the ensuing decades, along with the husband she met a few years later, and they had always enjoyed each other's company.

It would be mid-afternoon in the small Middle Eastern nation state, the celebrity calculated from the clock on the office wall. The billionaire lifted the receiver and dialled the number printed on the Consulate's letterhead. A switchboard operator with a strong accent answered and put him through with only the smallest of squeaks.

'Jeff, how are you?' the sophisticated woman of the world asked in the Queen's English. 'I didn't expect you to ring.'

'Hey, Naomi,' he said, overcome with emotion again as he linked her voice with happy memories. 'Ask me a different question. How are you and Tom?'

'We're very well,' the ambassador responded less vociferously. 'I assume you received my letter. I'm so, so sorry. I don't know what to say. Oh, Jeff. You've caught me on the hop.'

'I catch everyone on the hop,' he chuckled at her quaint expression. 'It's like I've developed a stutter or a nervous tick. People can't deny its existence, yet they try to ignore it when sometimes it's just not possible. I'd far rather have an honest conversation, but everyone else is too polite or embarrassed. Whatever... It's my new job; the Chief of Grief. It's become my life's purpose to engender awkwardness and force people to choose inappropriate language.'

The senior Embassy official was relieved to hear her old friend's response. 'My God, Jeff! I'm amazed you can still find it in you to make people laugh. Are you in Melbourne? It's late where you are.'

'It is. Just after midnight. Tell me something interesting.'

'Interesting?' Naomi hesitated. 'Let me see... Arafat's making inroads with George Mitchell, and there are adjustments to the Palestinian National Charter on the cards. The Israelis will object to what's going on in Hebron. We're still hopeful of progress though. Oh, but you don't want to know about this rubbish, do you? You've got other things on your mind.'

'Yes, I have,' the widower affirmed, 'but I'm trying to get rid of them. Purge the soul, and all that. I need some positive stimulation. What are the kids up to?'

'Colin's doing well,' the proud mother said of her younger son. 'He's learning the electric guitar. Nothing tuneful yet, but it's only since Christmas. He tries hard.'

'Cool. Are you being deafened or did you get him a set of headphones?'

The diplomat chuckled. 'Yes. Headphones are essential. I took your advice, for the sake of the neighbours.'

'And Philip?' Jeff asked, of the couple's firstborn who had been diagnosed with autism as a young boy and was struggling with life as a teenager.

'Oh, hard work. He's lost, poor thing. Doesn't have any friends, which is hard when Colin has an endless stream of invitations here, there and everywhere.'

'Get him a drum kit,' the celebrity offered, knowing his facetious suggestion would get a rise out of the patient woman.

'Thanks a bundle! I can always count on you to be helpful. That'd see to our expulsion from the Embassy, I imagine. Anyway, how are Jet and Kierney bearing up? What a terrible tragedy for them too.'

Jeff sighed. 'Ah, yeah... They're pretty good, thanks. Jet flew back to Cambridge over a month ago. He's going OK. The epitome of strength in body and mind, just like his mum. A Dyson, through and through. I'm heading over there for a few weeks in June or July. We're going to watch cricket and ride motorbikes around the countryside.'

'Terrorising the sleepy villages of the Home Counties?' the Englishwoman's deep voice was soothing. 'And Kierney?'

'She's less OK, to be honest. Mostly as a result of hanging around me all the time. She was due to start a course at Sydney Uni' but deferred a year. She's trying hard to be all things to one man, and I'm trying hard to push her away without offending her.'

'Really? That's so sweet. But, Jeff, can I ask you something?'

'Sure,' he heard a melancholy tone in the woman's voice. 'Ask away.'

'Was there anything unresolved between you and Lynn?'

The lonely man moved the receiver away from his face as he fought the temptation to yell in frustration, much like the fridge magnet cartoon which his daughter had stuck to his steering wheel on the afternoon of the funeral.

'No, there wasn't,' he answered instead. 'We were a hundred percent. No need to worry about that.'

'Oh, that's so good to hear. I always wondered whether that old adage had any truth to it.'

'I'm sure it has,' Jeff ventured. 'It depends how much you talk to each other. We should know that, Nao. At least I don't have the terrible regret of not saying what I should've said to her. I'm confident Lynn knew exactly how I felt about her every day. She didn't die wondering. And neither am I left wondering. I'm just left.'

Silence clogged the other end of the line, punctured by a muffled cough and what sounded like sniffing.

'Oh, Jeff, you always express yourself so well. That was beautifully put, even though it's a tragic image. I'm sure you're right. Lynn loved you enormously. In fact, I never met a couple so in love. I was always very jealous, to tell you the truth.'

'Yeah, well...' the negotiator mocked. 'Not so jealous now, I bet. Listen... Is it easy for you guys to get to Dubai or even London, if I send you my UK dates?'

'Oh, yes. I'm sure we could,' the diplomat jumped at the chance. 'It'd be lovely to see you.'

'You too, Nao. Thanks for your letter. It was very kind of you. Excuse my darkness of heart.'

'You're excused. You're always excused, Jeff Diamond. Hope things get easier soon. Keep in touch.'

'Sure. You too. Say hi to the family. *Adiós*.'

Replacing the receiver, the forty-three-year-old leant back in his black leather executive chair and stared at the ceiling. An eerie shadow of himself moving among the furniture, elongated by the angle of the illuminated desk lamp, conjured up memories of the many nights he had slept as a boy, behind the piles of contraband stacked up in his family's living room on the Stones Road, unable to face the short journey down the corridor and past his mother's bedroom door.

OK! That's enough.

What had happened to Juan Antonio García's mother? Why hadn't she arrived off the boat in Sydney with her husband and sons? Why did he even care? Jeff shook himself out of the obsessive train of thought. The shithead had killed his wife, and this evening he had received a life sentence to prove it. The widower knew he must learn to accept the guilty verdict as justice.

Somehow.

So with what did society expect justice to furnish a victim's life partner? The Queen had removed one more murderer from the streets. Big fucking deal! There were plenty of far more dangerous criminals still roaming free, and with a much greater likelihood of striking again. The Sydney Mafia remained alive and well for example, Jeff had no doubt.

What would justice mean to him if he had the luxury of choosing its form? This was a tough one. Definitely not financial compensation, a concept which never ceased to intrigue the intellectual whenever he read about other cases. Was a couple of million dollars really going to ease the suffering after losing a loved one? No amount of compensation could bring his children's mother back, and the Diamonds had more than enough money as it was. The financial whizz-kid, Gerry Blake, had seen to this.

'What do I want, angel?' he posed to Lynn's spirit. 'Are you there?'

The intellectual inhaled sharply. His second question had barely left his lips before a tingling sensation in his chest broke him out of his morbid rêverie.

'Hey! So you *are* there. Christ, it's good to feel you again. I've missed you. He's going down, did ya see? I guess you know that already.'

Again Jeff's left pectoral muscle twitched. He had reached the end of one of the longest weeks of his life, and without question the most difficult. Kierney mustn't hear him crying. Not again. She needed her sleep.

'Come with me onto the balcony, angel, please,' the bereft husband requested. 'I want to talk to you. Our little girl's sleeping. She's so beautiful, Lynn. So, so beautiful. Just like you.'

Grabbing his cigarettes and lighter off the coffee table, where he had left them with his keys, the songwriter slid the glass door open and took a seat at the table overlooking the lights of the northern suburbs. The traffic was still noisy down below, and there was no breeze to speak of. Smoking his first cigarette in a while, he concentrated back on the subject of justice.

Within a second or two however, inspiration was upon him. On his feet again, Jeff ran through the apartment and back into the office. He rummaged around in the desk drawers until he found a small voice recorder, checking its batteries and testing it with a few choice swearwords to relieve some tension. There were memoirs to be captured for posterity. How had Rose Milne described him and his beautiful best friend? National treasures?

'National treasures, my arse,' he mocked the judge's words as he reinstalled himself in the open air. 'Did you hear that too, baby?'

Jeff picked up the remains of his cigarette and rubbed his tattoo through the fabric of his shirt. How did one document a national treasure? How would he do justice to Lynn's story? To their story?

'D'you know what I want, angel?' he asked into the chilly air. 'I want a long, lingering kiss that makes my insides burst into flames. I want the soft skin of your naked body wrapped around me, intent on speeding things up while you're urging me to slow down.'

The stinging was gone from his chest now, replaced by a dull but pleasant ache. This peculiar physical reaction was likely only generated by his own mind, the lonely soul recognised, yet it was helping. The small red light on the Dictaphone flashed to remind him it was ready for more.

'I want our kids to have a mother, and I want a friend to share my crazy ideas with,' he continued, in tears once more. 'Is that too much to ask? I don't want a man to go to prison for the rest of his life. How does this help Jet or Kiz? What sort of justice is that?

'I want our daughter to continue on the journey you were taking her on, towards the lady she oh-so-nearly is. And I want our son to be able to swap tales of Olympic glory with someone who gives a damn.

'I want this endless torrent of words to pour into your detoxicating smile. I want a reason to check my watch ten times every hour when I'm away from home, to see how soon I can get away.

'Jesus Christ! I want to stop describing my self-pity and get on with doing all those constructive things we were right in the middle of, angel.

'I want my level-headed wife to help me resist the temptation to ring our dark-haired gipsy girl every night when she starts her law degree at Sydney Uni', to make sure she's safe and happy and still misses her *papá*.'

With his head in his hands, Jeff wept away the stresses of the last few days. He was convinced he was being heard on some level, although the beating of his heart overpowered any other sensation right at this moment.

Sniffing back the tears, he lit another cigarette. 'I want my patient and compassionate lover to remind me I'm being unreasonable and hypocritical when I criticise our son for not coming home for Christmas just because he wants to chase girls.

'And I long to perform again on stage with our family and see you smiling with the joy I know it gave you. The same joy it gave me.

'And Jesus, Lynn... I long to have more of those long, in-depth discussions over dinner with Jet and Kierney about life lessons in humility. That's fucking justice, don't you think? We had all those things, angel. That's what he took from us. That's what a guilty verdict should buy us.'

Such restitution the Diamonds would never glean from the Australian judicial system. This type of compensation wasn't listed in the bound volumes of laws and legal practices he had seen in Judge Milne's chambers.

With a soothing melody lolloping around his head, no doubt introduced by his dream girl as an instruction to put such antagonism to bed, he switched off the voice recorder and let it drop with a clatter onto the glass table-top.

'*Mañana*, angel,' he promised the night air. 'Tomorrow I'll start afresh. I'll write our life story, baby, and therein you'll find justice. *En nuestra vida singular.*'

DIARIES

The trio's return to Melbourne after the trial was greeted by what could only be described as respectful euphoria. News of García's conviction had brought some element of closure to the hundreds, if not thousands of fans who besieged the office of the Diamonds' management company, either by telephone, electronically, by post or in person. Cathy had warned her boss to stay away for a few days, and he had been only too pleased to heed her advice.

Realising he appeared to be the lone voice in considering justice still undone, the widower felt more and more isolated from a world that had once been the famous couple's oyster. He instructed his staff to decline all requests for public appearances and media interviews, providing one sole press conference to an invited cadre of journalists who could be trusted to report the facts, the whole facts and nothing but the facts. Kierney was forbidden to attend, and much to Gerry's surprise, he was asked to extend a *bona fide* invitation for Bart and Marianna Dyson to take their seats beside him.

'I can't have it all my way,' the celebrity had told his manager. 'Lynn was no less their daughter than my wife. Just because I don't share their politics and resignation to the bloody situation, I can't deny them access to her fans.'

This was a wise move from every angle, and the philosopher cursed the stubbornness he had shown over the years by keeping a safe distance from his in-laws. Wasn't it he who preached tolerance of other people's views and lifestyles? His acceptance of theirs was long overdue, and the warm reception they received during the media event only increased his contrition.

A few days after the trial, the doting dad managed to persuade the ambitious girl to travel to the New York springtime and spend some time with her favourite collaborator, Youssouf Elhadji. She had taken some convincing, but he had brokered a successful agreement via a promise not to move into their new house before she returned.

Now, sitting in the apartment all alone for the third consecutive night, Jeff regretted his decision. The place was so quiet, and the temptation not to get up, dressed or fed was overpowering. If it hadn't been for Gerry "happening to be in the vicinity" the previous evening, he might well have still been in the clothes he wore to drop his daughter off at the airport.

The time had come for the surviving national treasure to put fingers to keyboard on the combined autobiography he felt so compelled to write. He wanted to establish some momentum without Kierney's inquisitive eyes urging him to share each early chapter draft.

He knew it would take several false starts before he would be comfortable with the tenor and flow. It wasn't a song he was writing this time. It was a bare-bones, honest account of the most perfect relationship that ever existed; a life balanced both to craft itself meticulously and to evolve with the continual injection of new ideas.

The widower's thoughts reverted to the theme of constituency. How should he define the constituency of one potential readership? Write with your audience in mind, one former professor used to remind his students. An author must resist the urge to document everything he or she knows. That was an encyclopedia. A good book should do so much more than entertain. It must enlighten, inform, challenge and inspire by mounting a friendly assault on the readers' every belief and sensibility.

Elucidating the couple's developing sense of right and wrong was paramount, the songwriter decided. The front-end of the greatest pantomime lion in living memory reflected on the decisions which had shaped their life singular, long having held the opinion that every decision must be made in equal part by head and heart.

Now here was an ethos to sum up his beautiful best friend, if ever there was one! Good decisions were made by good heads and good hearts, and vice versa. If one was flawed, the decision was likely to be flawed too.

Jet's reference to one of Lynn's greatest anthems during a telephone call the previous night still swirled around his father's mind. She had written in 1994 about the legacy she wanted to leave. Listening to this song for the first time since her death, its lyric shimmered like a premonition for her husband, who had seen it as nothing more than a noble ideal at the time.

Thinking back on the many discussions he had shared with his faithful confidante on the subject of constituency, Jeff realised their immediate legacy was already in action. He could take their offspring anywhere or drop them into any situation, and they would survive and most likely excel. They had good manners, easy conversation, rounded general knowledge and formidable powers of intellectual common sense and emotional intelligence with which to figure out life's conundrums for themselves.

This author's job now was to broaden this legacy, continuing *la Grande Oeuvre* which the couple had started through The Good School program. The autobiography he intended to construct must serve as a handbook for those who wished to hone the skill of choosing right over wrong.

Simply telling the famous family's exciting and romantic life story was pure indulgence; the vicarious ramblings of a lonely, middle-aged man longing for the past and lamenting a lost future. This was the role of a tabloid novelist and not the mission of a *cognoscente* who considered himself somewhat wise.

The billionaire sat back, overcome with shame. Who was he kidding? He *was* a lonely, middle-aged man longing for the past and lamenting a lost future. Tears pricked behind his eyes as his tattoo again doled out a sharp rebuke.

'Thanks, angel,' he murmured, wiping his eyes. 'What was that? Have another drink and get on with it? You're right. Allow me some measure of self-pity, will you? But I promise you I'll do a bloody good job of our legacy.'

The grieving man owed it to his wife to do exactly this. While the days had dragged by since her funeral and memorial service, her soul had followed him around, prompting him to act or not to act, sometimes subtly and sometimes downright painfully. He was in no doubt that their fabled invisible elastic connection was cut, daring to believe it replaced by some form of ethereal understanding in which he might learn to find solace.

The buzzing of his mobile phone against the mahogany desk interrupted the widower's murky daydream. Leaning forward, he saw his son's name on the small screen.

'Mate, how're you going?' he asked, pleased to hear from the larrikin again so soon.

'It's not mate. It's me!' Kierney laughed. 'I'm fine, *papá*. You sound happy. I should've gone away weeks ago.'

'Absolutely not, gorgeous,' her father objected. 'I was planning our book. You caught me dreaming about happier times. What are you doing with Jet's phone?'

'Oh, good. Sorry to interrupt you. We just wanted to see how you are. I'm in Cambridge, on my way to New York. I changed my flights.'

'Did you? OK. Great. Is Jetto there too? Are you having a good time?'

'Yes and yes,' he heard his son's voice loud in the mouthpiece. 'Except I can't get into nightclubs with my kid sister in tow.'

Jeff chuckled. 'I know how that feels, mate. You shouldn't be frequenting nightclubs anyway. You're an impoverished student.'

'Sure,' Jet grabbed the telephone from his sibling. 'It was an ace idea for Kizzy to come over, Dad. She's perking up, so you needn't be worried. Except she cramps my style with the girls too. They think she's my girlfriend because we don't look alike.'

'Oh, my heart bleeds for you, son,' the retired playboy joked. 'It'll do you good to abstain for a few days. What are you guys up to, anyway?'

'*Papá*, it's me again,' the excited eighteen-year-old interjected. 'I've been on the back of the bike at over a hundred miles an hour!'

'Jeez, baby! Be careful. Don't let him be an idiot. It's bad enough having you so far away. Tell you what? Don't even tell me this stuff, OK?'

'Yeah. It's all good, *papá*,' Kierney agreed. 'Sorry. I'm being thumped at this end too. It's exhilarating though.'

'Hey, gorgeous... Are you in the flat?' Jeff asked.

'Yes. Why? Is there something wrong?'

'No. I'll ring you back on that number. I want to talk to you about something, if you've got time.'

'Definitely,' the youngster said, overjoyed to hear some enthusiasm in her father's voice. 'We're here. Just ring. *Adiós, papá*.'

'*Adiós*,' Jeff said to a dead line, amused by the impetuosity his daughter had absorbed from her brother.

'Trinity Mandarin Restaurant,' a dubious Chinese accent answered as soon as the celebrity's fingers had finished dialling the long combination of digits.

'*Pang yau chui,*' the linguist sneered. 'I'll have a sizzling beef noodles, please, mate. Do you deliver?'

'Certainly, sir,' Jet played along. 'As long as you don't care if it takes a week and arrives stone cold.'

'Nice one,' his dad laughed. 'Anyway... I just wanted to run something past you two, and you have to listen with an open mind.'

'OK,' he heard both obedient children answer and then giggle at their simultaneous responses.

The lonely intellectual explained his theory on souls to his children over the course of the next fifteen minutes, expecting a good deal of cynicism, especially from the budding scientist. He thought his romantic gipsy girl might be give him the benefit of the doubt, although deep down she was likely to be sceptical too.

'Actually, Dad,' Jet said, at an appropriate point to interrupt, 'I'm going to surprise you. I agree, I reckon. I've been thinking a lot about that line in "World Children". You know... The one we talked about before. I've been talking to some philosophy lecturers and I'm gradually coming to the belief that how can people achieve such greatness and wisdom after only having gone round once?'

'That's excellent, son,' Jeff tried hard to hide his astonishment. 'I'm very happy to hear this. Tell me more.'

The nineteen-year-old obliged. 'What if we have to go round several times to get really wise? I think you've been round a hundred times, don't you? That's why you and Mum could see everything so clearly. The trick is to learn from each time you go round, and therefore your idea makes complete sense to me.'

His father was silent for a few moments, unusually lost for words. Kierney took up where her brother had left off.

'I don't know what to believe, *papá*,' the young woman let on. 'Sometimes I have difficulty believing in anything apart from what my five senses confirm. Why would there be anything more? But then I wonder why everyone at some point in their life

257

asks hard questions, like "What's it all about?" and "Why do I wonder about what it's all about?"'

The showbusiness legend chuckled at her natural comedic timing. 'Have you been smoking before lunch?'

'No, *papá*!' the teenager sounded indignant. 'I really love the idea of you being able to communicate with *mamá* still. Like somehow you can keep in touch until you're ready to inhabit new bodies and meet again.'

This last comment, plus the sound of Kierney's voice cracking, pushed their father over the edge, wishing he was there with them.

'That's beautiful, *pequeñita*,' he cried into the telephone. 'I don't want to con you into believing it's real, but I so need to hang onto something. And I'm not imagining it, baby.'

'No. I know. I saw it myself. Here's Jet. He wants to tell you something we talked about last night.'

Jeff listened to some heavy breathing and then to the receiver being passed from one to the other, thrown back to happier times when he would call home from some far-off land to two excited primary school kids, eager to tell him what they had learnt in class that day or how many goals they had scored on the soccer pitch.

'Dad, I just wanted to tell you I'm going to make sure the woman I pick to spend the rest of my life with has to live with some sort of mental trauma, because I'm equipped to help her when another bloke wouldn't be. I know you probably think it's only words, but I really want that. Like a calling, for life.'

'Callings are normally for life,' the father replied with a smile he hoped the young man could hear. 'Mate, you don't have to do this. You're still getting over all the shit of the last few months. Just go with the flow for a while. You don't need to be making those kinds of commitments to me. I believe you're going to make someone a great partner. Both of you are.'

'But no, Dad. I mean it,' his son insisted. 'Kizzy's told me about what happened during the trial and the conversations you guys had, and maybe that's my old soul talking. Perhaps I was destined to get practice at dealing with someone with PTSD because my soul-mate'll need me to understand. When I meet her, that is...'

'Whoa, mate,' the older man exhaled through pursed lips, having difficulty believing his ears. 'You're quite the romantic all of a sudden. Are you OK?'

'Yeah. It's all good, Dad,' Jet maintained. 'And I don't mean all those things I said about Kizzo being here. It's awesome to spend some time together now everything's kind of settling down. We can talk about things sensibly without dissolving into tears every five minutes.'

'And because I'm not there to dissolve into tears every two-and-a-half minutes right in front of you,' Jeff added.

'Yeah. Probably,' the lad replied, with a trace of a laugh. 'Here's Kiz back.'

'*Papá?*'

'*Sí,*' their father answered, feigning suspicion. '*¿Qué tal, pequeñita?*'

'Are you alright on your own? And be honest...'

'I am, baby. I'm fine,' he confirmed. 'Gerry came round last night, and we went for dinner and a few too many drinks. And Suzie and Steve have invited me there over the weekend, which I'll probably do, and some of the band were over the other evening. Tonight's my only evening off, I'll have you know. And I wanted to ask you guys something else, if I may...'

'Oh, yes? What's that?' Kierney asked.

'In order to write our life story, I need to get some information about *mamá*'s childhood. I want to know if you're OK for me to open her diaries from before I knew her.'

'Shit! Of course,' Jet chimed in. 'Why would we object?'

'In case you thought they were private, even to me?' their father explained. 'All that stuff was committed to posterity way before I came along.'

'They might contain stuff you don't want to read,' his daughter warned. 'Are you prepared for that?'

'Yep. Guess so,' Jeff lied. 'I don't think there's much she hasn't told me about boyfriends, *et cetera.*'

'What if she wrote stuff about you after your first few dates that you don't like?' the nineteen-year-old asked. 'You know... Before she knew the real you?'

'That's the chance I'll have to take, mate,' the grief-stricken man found himself crying again. 'It'll freak me out to read about those days anyway, regardless if it's good or bad news. She stuck with me, so it can't be too terrible.'

'We don't mind, *papá*,' the young woman confirmed. 'As long as you let us read them afterwards.'

'It's a deal, ' their father agreed. '*Muchas gracias.* I love you guys. I'm glad you're having a good time. Go careful on that bike, mate.'

'I shall, Dad,' Jet promised. 'Do you remember Nicola Harmer, by the way?'

'From school? I knew she went to London on the promise of a record deal. Why?'

'He's going out with her,' the kid sister laughed, unable to hide the fact she was being beaten up for giving away too much information. 'She's short though.'

'Whatever,' Jeff smiled. 'It doesn't matter once you're lying down.'

'*Papá!*' Kierney shouted into the telephone. 'That's disgusting!'

'Yeah, *papá*. That *is* disgusting,' her brother echoed. 'Have you got laid recently? You need to, sounds like.'

'Enough, mate,' the widower was keen to dismiss this latest line of questioning. 'I'll leave you to your exploits if you'll leave me to mine.'

'Sure, Dad. I'm sorry,' the embarrassed young man answered. 'I shouldn't have said that. I'm sorry.'

'*Tenga calma*, mate,' Jeff reassured his son. 'Get off the phone. I have to start reading.'

'Hope they're a good read,' Kierney yelled into the receiver her brother still had hold of. '*Te amo, papá*. Happy writing!'

'*Gracias, gorgeousita. Adiós.*'

Permission sought and granted, Jeff poured himself another glass of wine and reached for the pile of diaries sitting on the other desk. He knew the couple's autobiography could never give a well-balanced account of their life singular without including elements of Lynn's childhood.

She and her elder brother had served as Bart Dyson's early guinea pigs as he revolutionised training techniques and reversed Australia's stagnant sporting fortunes. Doubtless, there were many milestones worth mentioning in the book to satisfy lovers of statistics and those who found competition compelling.

However, the man who stood Accused of distracting the teenaged champion from goals for which she had been given no choice but to strive was much keener to document the tug-of-war that had been fought behind the scenes over her private passions: for music and the entertainment; for social justice and making a difference; and for a certain swarthy renegade who changed everything.

Anticipating his children's blessing to delve into the yearbooks of Lynn's youth, he had retrieved the collection some days ago from boxes shipped from Escondido, but they had sat unopened for several days. These pristine journals contained his wife's innermost thoughts and were in many ways none of his business. Whatever she had wished to share with him, she most likely already had.

The lonely husband felt like a voyeur reading the girlish memories, wondering which ones would have come to light had his beautiful best friend survived to write her own autobiography. He had seen an outline she created several years ago, which had given little away, being more concerned with structure than content in its initial draft. Therefore, a superhuman editing effort was ahead of him in culling her early reminiscences into a concise synopsis to introduce the combined Diamond anthology.

The idea of raiding his partner's diaries had come about to lend blunt contrast to his own bleak ancient history. Was he betraying her confidence? And at which point should he start? 1972 and back some, or from the very beginning? All good questions that would doubtless be answered in due course...

Jeff settled down to work through the diaries one by one, finding easy therapy in plunging into the mind of a clever, starlet who had loved every aspect of her privileged life and appeared genuinely grateful for the opportunities it presented.

In much less idyllic circumstances, the adolescent Jeff Diamond had fantasised about her incessantly. Now, with the benefit of considerable carnal knowledge and an unparalleled respect for her achievements, the middle-aged fantasist contented himself with imagining his dream girl sitting at her childhood desk at the Benloch homestead and preserving her thoughts and dreams in perpetuity.

The bewitched man read on. In what had started out as a need for factual insight for their life story, he found that in reality they told him far more than he ever expected to discover. With the utmost care, he sorted the leather-bound volumes into date order, guided as much by the maturity of the handwriting as by their labels.

1963 was the first year on record, when Lynn had been only eight years old. Former US President John F Kennedy's assassination was the first entry she had made, in late November, a few days after the young celebrity's world had rocked for what must have been the first time.

'You again, Miss Irony,' the songwriter cursed, his tired heart gripped by a constriction he recognised from deep within. 'You don't have to remind me. I'm perfectly capable of coming to this conclusion on my own.'

Jeff read the simple language describing the Texas shooting and the innocent child's inability to understand why someone might wish to kill such a popular leader. A similar reaction had triggered her decision to write special, annual letters to him and their children after John Lennon's even more pointless shooting.

Distracted, the grieving lover dared to speculate on how many new diaries had been started during February of the current year. 'Maybe you always knew it'd happen, angel,' he opined into the air. 'Did you? Subconsciously? Did you know what your destiny held all along? You never told me. I might've been able to protect you if you'd told me. I'd have been more vigilant.'

There was a separate book for each year, and the longhand grew up from the large, open lettering of an eight-year-old, through teenaged "cool script" and on to the flowing, stylish calligraphy her husband recognised from more recent years. Since 1993, Lynn's almost daily summaries had been typed into the computer, printed out on A4 paper and stapled. Organised, as ever!

On his way to February 1972, when a determined, long-haired pretender had met the girl of his dreams, there were confessions and admissions therein which cemented answers to questions he had never before dared to presume. What had his maxim always been? *Hope for the best but expect the worst?* No, he acknowledged in humble rapture. He should have expected the best too, in hindsight, since it appeared Lynn Dyson's love had been his for the taking all along.

Jeff turned each page with hefty trepidation until he reached the night of their first date. Rivulets of tears flowed from his eyes as he read the teenager's naïve summary of a trip to the theatre, followed by an assortment of observations she had posed to herself after their first adult kiss.

"Very hard to concentrate! I wouldn't have cared if it was the longest, most boring play ever. It was like electricity fizzing between us all night, especially when we kissed. Wow!"

Then a few weeks' worth of entries later, when her codified "mystery man" proclaimed his love to her, she had written that night in anguish about being too young to fall in love, comparing the intensity of this stranger to her handful of casual boyfriends up to this point.

"I want a man who kisses me because he likes how I taste, who touches me because I feel nice, who likes what I say and do, and not just what my surname is, what I look like or even to get the biggest 'O'."

The sole occupant of the huge penthouse apartment laughed out loud, picturing the well-mannered young lady unable to bring herself to spell out the word "orgasm", as if it were as *taboo* to ink the word onto paper as it was to utter it with one's own lips while still a minor.

"That's a man who loves me, and that's how I'll know when I'm in love. TODAY IS THE DAY!!!!!"

Lynn Dyson's benevolent lion gave an almighty roar into the night, too exhilarated to cry anymore. What a mind-blowing few weeks those had been for the headstrong nobody recently arrived from New South Wales! He had lurched between hope and despondency, delirium and heartache, while trying to figure out how to snare this most inaccessible of quarries. And now, over two decades later, learning about the same period from the sexy blonde angel's most intimate confessions supplied a much needed fillip.

The captivated widower pictured the pretty, fresh-faced schoolgirl on that unforgettable night in the State Library, under the cover of homework, when she had scribbled a note which he still kept in his bedside table drawer. She had handed it to him so casually, he recalled with a smile. On it had been written the simple phrase, "I definitely love you."

'I did like how you tasted, angel,' her handsome stranger murmured, scratching his chest. 'You got what you asked for. I'm glad I could give you what you wanted in a man because you gave me precisely what I wanted. Much more than, baby.'

Jeff sighed and re-read the last few entries, overwhelmed by the realisation that the lines written in this secret artefact bore witness to their destiny being sealed. Why hadn't Lynn ever shared this with him? How many more gems like these was he likely to find as he flicked through the years? He glowed inside for the first time in several months. His tattoo was tingling, and a sublime amazement he didn't recognise as his own replaced his tears.

'Climb onto my lap, gorgeous,' he invited his wife's ghost, his penis swelling in response to the sensuous fantasy.

The songwriter's hot-blooded son was right to bail him up earlier concerning sensual gratification. Now his life was set to stabilise into this new normal, so had his physical incarnation resumed its normal function. He did so need to get laid. His body ached to be touched, longing for some relief from the endless pressure building inside, and he despised himself for it.

'I want to make love to you so badly,' Jeff growled. 'I want to taste you, feel you, look at you, breathe you in and listen to you moaning in ecstasy. How does that sound, angel? Is that the man you always wanted?'

Unzipping his trousers, he imagined the lithe athlete's smiling face, her enticing breasts and her strong legs pinning her down while they moved together. Golden hair fell onto his face and neck as she sat astride his lap on the office chair, as she had countless times over the years. He took hold of the turgid, throbbing shaft and visualised his knuckles, rubbing against her clitoris in a steady rhythm, turning her on and making her writhe against him.

Yet as fast as this urge had come on, the widower found himself once more plunging into despair as his erection shrank in his hand and the tears came streaming down again.

'Fuck you, Gravity, you bastard!' Jeff yelled into the night. 'I should've known not to trust you to stay away.'

A week later, Jeff boarded a flight for New York, aiming to coincide with Kierney's homeward journey. The pair would spend two days together in The Big Apple, during which he hoped to arrange a few meetings at the United Nations' headquarters, to help her with the new university project she had undertaken. After this, he had accepted an invitation to stay with Kiley Jones and Guy Kahn in their luxurious apartment on the Manhattan's Upper East Side, looking after their children and capturing memories from Lynn's stateside friends into his electronic manuscript.

While in the art-lovers' Mecca, the superstar passed several productive, relaxed hours in the company of Lynn's fellow Melbourne Academy musicians, reconstructing episodes from her early career. Richard and John claimed their guest as an honorary member of the downtown gay community after he came clean as having lost interest in women since his wife passed away. He was happy to accept the dubious accolade, despite the unwanted attention which went along with it.

Another reason for the trip to Manhattan island was to deliver on a long-awaited promise to the virtuoso violinist, who had issued her fellow composer with a challenge several years earlier that he would never convince her to appreciate Jewish fiddle music. After being introduced to a *Klezma* band playing the Melbourne circuit, Jeff had asked Cathy to liaise with their North American agent for them to tour the sizeable Jewish musical communities of the eastern states.

'If you catch me with my toes tapping at this unmelodic music, I'll dance the Hora with you,' Kiley had insisted, screwing her face up in determined dislike.

'You're on,' the challenger had sealed the deal.

And sure enough, in a packed hall in Gramercy, a gaunt and pale Jeff Diamond enchanted the unsuspecting audience by whisking the flame-haired violinist across the floor as fiddle and oboe combined to raise the roof. He declined the band's eager invitation to sing as their guest but couldn't deny a definite therapeutic value in having adrenalin chased through his body by the infectious rhythms.

La Grande Œuvre was taking shape nicely, periodically transferred onto discs and mailed home to their safe deposit box. Three weeks spent overstaying his welcome with his genial and sympathetic hosts saw the widower homesick for Melbourne and desperate to see his daughter again. Their rental house was ready for occupation, having been secured to a sufficient standard and filled with new furniture and state-of-the-art equipment.

At the beginning of June, Gerry and Fiona threw a dinner party for their old friend's forty-fourth birthday, having themselves moved into a brand new Toorak mansion the week after Jeff and Kierney had taken up residence in the doctors' house in Burnley. The songwriter had voiced his objections at first wind of their plan, saying he would be poor company and that he had no interest in celebrating. Undaunted, Gerry, being Gerry, ignored his mate's concerns and steamed ahead, dispatching invitations to thirteen of the best conversationalists in town.

The birthday boy arrived first by taxi, after again threatening a non-appearance. Pitching in with the preparations alongside the couple, they swapped news about their respective moving experiences. He was in reasonable spirits, although these days looking lean and haggard. The other guests, all of whom the influential star admired and respected, dribbled in over the next hour, and the party was a huge success.

Instructed as he left the apartment by his fifty-four-year-old daughter to be on his best behaviour and not to tell any morbid jokes, Jeff was grateful the conversation stayed far away from his plight and allowed him to flex his under-used cerebral muscles. He had to admit to the restorative value of pursuing intellectual truths and suppositions with someone other than his elusive soul-mate for a change.

One of the invited couples reported a recent decision to invest in a 1960-model Ford Mustang, passing around photographs as if it were a new baby in the family. Everyone cooed and gasped appropriately, including the guest of honour. It was a stylish classic, with left-hand drive a rarity in Australia. The topic was one the celebrity could indulge without the interference of too many memories.

'We should go to Bathurst this year,' he suggested as an open invitation to Gerry and the other men seated around the table. 'We get asked every year, don't we, mate? And there's never been a good reason to go. We should do it this October.'

Fiona shot the lonely man an encouraging nod, overjoyed at one of the few positive suggestions their old friend's shadow had initiated in the last few months. He smiled a characteristic half-smile and refrained from shaking his head. She meant well, he kept reminding himself, wondering how soon he might be able to escape.

'That's an excellent idea,' Gerry agreed. 'It can be my pre-buck's-party buck's party.'

'Excuse me!' an indignant fiancée exclaimed. 'I hope you're not going to be partying for two months.'

'Ah, come on, Fi! This man's life's been one long buck's party,' Jeff scoffed, refilling his whisky tumbler. 'Why not? We can call it the "Mid-life Crisis Tour".'

'Are you insinuating an obsession with sports cars is a mid-life crisis?' yelped Roger, the Mustang owner.

The birthday boy shrugged. 'I reckon, Rodge. Don't you? We all have 'em, mate. Nothing to be ashamed of.'

'No, that's just a myth,' Roger's wife came to her husband's Defence.

'It's not actually,' the superstar contradicted. 'It's a transition phase, just like the "terrible twos" and teenage rebellion. Our brain's way of adjusting to physiological changes and the expectations we have of ourselves.'

'Like not being able to bowl Jet out anymore?' Gerry teased his VIP client.

'Yes and no,' the outstanding cricketer's father grinned. 'That's a combination of changes in him and me, but absolutely. Another one's the transition between promiscuous dating and serious monogamy, Gezza.'

His manager snorted in mock disgust at his buddy having trumped him again.

'What about having kids?' Fiona added.

Before the birthday boy could adjudicate, another guest offered an example. 'Another's moving between doing any old job to earn some money and building a proactive, deliberate career.'

'Maybe, Mark,' Jeff responded. 'Although I'm less convinced about that one. It feels like a symptom of something else, but it might also be where we're evolving to. Not many of us are that sophisticated, as a percentage of the world's population. I'm talking more about basic human and even animal instincts.'

The table rocked to a surfeit of supercilious nods from the well-educated, self-made millionaires, frantic to be seen as worldly as well as wealthy. The sight made Jeff cringe inside. Australia's élite class still had a long way to go before its proponents could hold their heads up high in a meritocratic world.

'Then, where we're all at now is the hare-to-tortoise transition,' the wise man continued, deducing he was in fact the youngest guest at the party.

'Hare to tortoise?' an awestruck woman exclaimed.

Jeff cocked his head and raised an eyebrow, daring her to disbelieve him. 'Yes, Cyn. That's when we come to the realisation that life's slipping through our hands. We've spent the first half of our lives running hell-for-leather for the finish line, and suddenly we think, "Jesus! My back's killing me," and "I'm so stressed at work," or "I never have time to play golf," and so on... So we start wanting to slow down and make the most of life in a completely different way.'

'With a Ford Mustang,' Gerry interjected, gesturing towards Roger. 'Well done, mate. You've become a fucking tortoise! That's really something to be proud of!'

Jeff shook his head while the rest whooped with drunken *gusto*. 'Mock all you like, Blake-san. You're no different. In fact, you're a transition behind the rest of us.'

'What you mean?' the inebriated businessman snapped in a strange half-Indian, half-Jamaican accent. 'I'm just getting to monogamy, and you're already at mid-life crisis?'

'I mean you've been forced to complete two transitions at once, old bean,' the celebrity laughed. 'Mid-life crisis looms, and you're still wearing short trousers in the relationship stakes. You've been resisting just that little bit too long, but now you've had to catch up fast 'cause you know instinctively that being a tortoise on your own ain't too damned palatable.'

Jeff's voice cracked, but he persisted with the topic, enjoying holding court after so long. This was where he used to belong, commanding the attention and dispensing the wisdom of ages to those who ought to know better. Sensing Gravity tightening the strings around his heart, he realised the temporary comfort zone he had settled into was about to dissolve and leave him bereft once again.

'I never really held much store in the effect mid-life crisis had on people before. But now I'm in it, I understand it much better. I always reach the transitions early. I've crammed so much into my life, y'see. And it's got to be pretty lonely slowing down to smell the roses on your own. Something I've become acutely aware of lately.'

Fiona's single friend, Toni, destined to be the best man's counterpart in December's bridal party and who had been drafted in to make up the numbers for dinner, sighed at the change in tone from the man whose company dazzled her.

'You'll meet someone else,' she offered.

The widower sniffed, watching everyone round the table nod in agreement yet again.

'If I want to,' he replied, unable to prevent himself from sliding down. 'Lynn and I were in tune through all our transitions. We were set up well for Tortoiseville. I don't think I dictated the pace of her life. I hope not.'

Before Gerry or Fiona could jump in to reassure him, the tattoo on the grieving husband's chest jumped to life under his shirt. *Nice timing*, he thought. He hadn't come on his own tonight after all, not prepared to reveal his secret social life in such unenlightened company.

Capitalising on a lull in the conversation, Fiona stood up to take the pile of empty plates into the kitchen. The dutiful guest of honour followed her with the vegetable dishes, setting them down on the counter top while his host refilled everyone's drinks. It was a skill the gregarious businessman had inherited from his father, and he fulfilled his obligations admirably.

'So how's it going, Jeff? Honestly?' the city lawyer asked. 'You seem more cheerful these last couple of weeks.'

The visitor liked Gerry's new fiancée well enough, but sometimes she was a little too over-familiar for his liking. She had arrived in their circle at the worst time. Unfortunate, because he was sure his resistance to her concern would be lessened if Lynn were still in their midst.

Fiona had many good qualities, and it pleased him to see his mate so happy with this novel domestic bliss. Two distinct characteristics were hard for him to support, however: her natural nosiness; and the fact she always presumed to know what was best for him and his children.

'Ah, yeah. It's getting easier slowly, I have to admit,' he replied, leaning on the wall next to the refrigerator while the evening's cook prepared dessert. 'Yet on the other hand, it's getting harder 'cause I can feel Lynn slipping away.'

'You're healing,' she suggested, accompanying the words with a patronising pat of his arm. 'You're beginning to let her go.'

'Is that right?' he heard himself answer, a little too rudely.

As luck would have it, his manager's partner failed to pick up the septic tone in the his voice. She made her way into the dining room with a platter of something sweet and sticky, and Jeff took advantage of her absence, slipping down the hallway and out through the front door for a cigarette and some time on his own.

Resting his hands on the railings of Gerry's brand new veranda, which had been complemented recently by tasteful outdoor lighting and café blinds to calm the wind.

He swore under his breath, looking up at the stars. 'There's a woman in there whom I've known for five minutes telling me I should let you go. What d'you think about that, angel?'

Nausea washed through the forty-four-year-old as he stubbed out his cigarette. Sitting down at the table, his sensible side knew Fiona was right, but how could he even entertain this concept? Back in the mid-seventies, he had endured two years of agony for Lynn to return from her sojourn overseas. He was barely at the four-month mark now, already beginning to recover.

'Christ, Lynn! You made me into this all-powerful, resilient superhuman, and now I'm able to let you go,' he cried to his absent wife. 'I never thought I'd be this strong, and I hate who I've become. I want to need you, angel. I want to still have you in my life every day. I can't believe I'm moving on, and I need to know if you've moved on too.'

Leaning his elbows on the glass-topped table, Jeff rested his head in his hands and wept from the heart. At first, his mind filled with a jumble of different thoughts; from how the children would react to an admission that he was leaving their mother behind to the stack of letters he received every week from women proclaiming they could make him happier than ever.

After a few seconds, the superstar's addled brain stumbled across the dark screenplay entitled "When You're Gone", which he and his creative inspiration had written and filed away several years ago. They had constructed two different endings, unable to agree which was better. The itch in his tattoo increased gradually as he recalled the two paths the surviving partner's character might have chosen for the film's conclusion.

'So which way does it end, angel?' he whispered. 'Does Marie hook up, or does she follow Lex?'

The sweet sensation under his chest hair stopped, leaving the abandoned playwright divested and confused. Why had his co-writer gone silent? He tried asking the question another way.

'OK, how about this... Do I hook up with someone else, or do I follow you?'

The muscle over Jeff's heart cramped so hard that he dared to think he was having a heart attack. Unwittingly, Gerry chose this very moment to burst through the front door.

'Hey! What happened to you, mate?' the bombastic voice shouted from not two metres' distance. 'We've finished dessert already. Did you want some?'

'No, mate,' the guest smiled, exhaling sharply. 'Thanks, but I'm not hungry. I'm going home, if that's OK.'

'You can't go now! We're just warming up!' the Irishman exclaimed, lighting a cigarette for himself and offering another to his buddy. 'Are you alright?'

'Yes and no.'

'Cryptic as ever. Shall I call you a taxi then? Are you sure you won't stay? This is supposed to be your night after all...'

'Yeah, I know. Thanks, mate. A taxi'd be great. Sorry to duck out on you. I'm just not into partying 'til dawn anymore.'

The two men sat and discussed the day's football results while they finished their cigarettes. All the while, Jeff resisted the temptation to massage his left pectoral muscle, which was serenading him with an almost constant, dull throbbing.

They adjourned inside for the birthday boy to bid *adieu* to his merry dinner guests. It was only ten-thirty, and his cab arrived within five minutes, the busy period still several hours off. He thanked his hosts for forcing him to celebrate his birthday and for inviting such interesting people to provide a diversion.

After trying so hard to persuade his daughter to go out more often, keen to stop himself clinging to her like a limpet, tonight the inspired father rushed home to tell her about his new plan. He was duly disappointed to find the place empty.

'¿Kizzy, estás aquí?' he yelled up the stairwell, greeted only by a loud silence.

Saturday night. Why would an eighteen-year-old be at home? No matter. His mind rushing at a million miles an hour, Jeff searched the computer's file system for the screenplay he and Lynn had written at the beginning of the nineties. It would be inspiring to work with his dark-haired, deep-souled gipsy on this project, providing she could bring herself to deal with its morbid themes. The veteran director had taught Jet at an early age about filmmaking and how to get a message across, and this old script now gave him the chance to pass these skills on to his daughter too.

Kierney and David returned home a little after one o'clock in the morning. From the breathless laughter outside the front door, they sounded every bit like lovers. The father's heart, although green with envy, warmed to hear the teenager enjoying herself.

He got to his feet and stood in the office doorway, intending to announce his presence early to ward off any potential embarrassment. 'Hey, guys.'

David Ekwensi froze to the spot, terrified at having been sprung by his famous girlfriend's even more famous father. The expression on the young Nigerian's face was priceless, and it was all Jeff could do not to laugh. Kierney was unabashed though, knowing full well her dad would expect nothing less.

'Papá!' the young woman cheered, running towards him and planting an affectionate kiss on his cheek. 'I thought you'd be sleeping at Gerry's tonight. Do you mind if David stays over?'

'No. Of course not,' Jeff answered, eager to sound as inviting and non-judgemental as he could. 'But please don't make noises that'll make me jealous. I came home from Gerry's early 'cause I've had an idea and want to run it past you. In the morning though. Whenever.'

'OK, papá,' Kierney shrugged, grabbing her boyfriend's arm and spiriting him away upstairs. 'Thanks. How was your birthday dinner?'

'Ah, pretty good, pequeñita. Thanks. All the talk about mid-life crises has spawned something inside me. So much so that I'm going to have to divide my time between the book and a new project I'd love to do with you. But not now, eh? Get out of here!'

The young woman appeared a little torn, keen to share in her father's overdue positivity. 'Oh, wow! That sounds exciting. I can't wait to hear about it. Come on, Dave. Let's go. Goodnight, papá.'

With an appreciative wave of his hand, Jeff turned back to the office, full of smiles. The tattoo on his chest was calling him back to the computer. There was work for him and his beautiful best ghost to do. It would also distract his mind from the image of a grown man playing with his daughter's precious youthful body, just like he had played with her mother's a generation ago.

'Luke!' he announced, hearing the telephone being answered in the English summer. 'It's Jeff Diamond. How are you?'

'Jeff?' the award-winning actor checked if he had heard correctly. 'How are you? I didn't expect you to ring me on a Saturday afternoon. Are you in London?'

'Nope. I'm at home in Melbourne. I have a proposition for you. Wanted to sound you out before my people approach your people.'

'My people?' the Englishman laughed. 'I am my people, Jeff. Tell me how you are though. How are you travelling? How long is it now?'

'Nearly four months, mate. And it's still shit, as you might expect.'

'Yes. That's what I thought. Are you filling the time at least? Working and stuff?'

'Well, funny you should ask...' the caller smiled at the perfect *segue*. 'I'm writing our autobiography, which is excruciatingly rewarding. Then just tonight, I've decided to resurrect an old script we wrote some years ago. That's why I'm ringing, mate.'

'Really? Tell me more.'

'Yeah. I'd appreciate you reading it, to tell me if you're interested in making it into a movie, in the lead character.'

The line was silent for a few seconds, before the rounded, thespian *timbre* returned. 'Wow... I'd be honoured.'

'Cool, thanks. You haven't read it yet!' the writer warned with a chuckle. 'And I'd like you to recommend someone to play the leading lady. Someone with whom you'd have significant chemistry.'

'Sure. So what's it about?' Luke asked. 'Is there sex involved?'

Jeff scoffed. 'Well, that's up to you, mate. It's all in the interpretation. Can I send you the script?'

'Most certainly. What's the timeframe on doing it? Have you got a producer in mind?'

'I'd like to do it with Kierney,' the celebrity answered, picking up on the actor's enthusiasm. 'In London, as part of this shithouse grieving process. When would depend on your availability.'

'Fabulous!' the actor gushed. 'Shoot it over, and I'll give it my undivided attention. Thanks very much for thinking of me.'

The two men signed off, and Jeff turned back to the closing scenes. So how should the story end? Did the survivor move on and release the dead man from endless purgatory, severing their connection once and for all? Or was knowing that the dead man wanted to hold on to this static past preventing the surviving woman from starting a new relationship with a warm-blooded mortal?

'What d'you want, Regala?' the bereaved husband asked. 'What happens? D'you want me to look for happiness without you? I'm not sure I could. The thought of touching someone else still repulses me, but maybe it's only a matter of time. What about where you are? Are there ghostly singles' bars up there? Have you got a string of cold admirers waiting to snap you up?'

Nothing. His bizarre string of questions circled around the study while the pained artist stared into the gardens, fondling the floppy ears of his new rent-a-dog. Indie, a rescue surrendered to Suzanne's boarding kennels, had developed an instant bond with his temporary owner, who had reciprocated without hesitation.

'What d'ya reckon, mate?' Jeff addressed his enquiries to his canine companion. 'What would you do? You'd hump anything, wouldn't you? It's simple for you. You didn't know her. You have no idea what I'm talking about.'

The Labrador retriever licked his master's wrist and thumped his tail against the floorboards at these words he took as expressions of love. Dogs were so easy to please, the widower smiled. Maybe there was something to be said for wanting to come back as a domestic pet.

If you were one of the lucky ones, that was. If you were allocated to a human who talked to you, fed you and exercised you. The superstar hadn't asked Suzanne how Indie had come to be a rescue dog, preferring not to hear about cruelty or neglect inflicted on such an open, adoring animal. Such abhorrence was only too familiar...

'Let's go, boy,' the night owl shouted, slapping his thigh and jumping to his feet. 'Let's take a walk while I figure out how it ends. But you have to promise not to get too attached to me. Suzie-Anna wants you back, you realise. And I warn you, it'll be bloody hard for me to give you back. So lighten up on the love, OK?'

In the extensive grounds behind and to the side of the Diamonds' new home, the forty-four-year-old yomped barefoot across the thick lawn, kicking a ball for Indie and slipping over several times. They were both soaked with dew by the time the game lost its attraction. Sitting on the decking, he rolled his damp trouser legs back down and fixed the panting dog with a stare.

'Lynn's getting colder the longer I take, boy. I need to go and warm her up.'

Jeff began to cry again, much to Indie's curiosity. Burying his gentle muzzle into cupped hands, he pushed as close into his master's lap as he could.

'Thanks, mate,' the lonely writer sniffed, ruffling the rolls of soft fur around the retriever's neck. 'You're very kind to humour me. It's all nuts, I know, but there has to be a cello. Lynn always loved the cello. Didn't you, angel?'

The "JL" tattoo caused his muscle to flinch straightaway. 'Whoa!' he cried out, lifting his head and looking around him. 'That was a clear signal. What else? I've got "The Sun Won't Shine" and "You're Gone" for the soundtrack so far. What else were we going to put on it? I've decided how it ends, angel.'

Breathing in the damp air, the widower stood tall, calling for the Labrador to follow him inside. 'I'm going to get Marie to hook up with the new guy, but I'm coming to get you. If you'll have me.'

Again Jeff's sincerity and patience were rewarded. His mind cleared, and his left pectoral muscle spasmed long and sweet. He grabbed Indie behind his ears and stroked his head, generating playful whimpers in return. The pair of new friends crossed the large patio and ran back into the house, with only two feet out of six taking care to dry themselves on the mat.

'Hey! Come back here!' Jeff scolded, holding up a towel kept by the door for this very purpose. 'What's the hurry? You can't type. You need me.'

The following morning, Kierney came downstairs and saw the office light on. It was seven-thirty, the sun already beginning to penetrate the shadowy house. The dog bounded out to greet her, and she yelped when his claws dug into her chilly toes as they danced around each other.

'Indie, stop!' the young woman cried, giggling. 'You're piercing my feet. *Papá*, are you still up from last night?'

'Yep,' came a scratchy voice which hadn't been used for some hours.

The golden retriever tore back on hearing his master's voice, worried he had deserted his post.

'Could you let him out, please? Is Dave still here?'

'Yes,' Kierney replied, pushing the door open and seeing her father hunched over the computer, typing like a fevered newspaper hack on a tight deadline. 'I'm making tea. Why didn't you go to bed? Are you still working on the book, or the new idea?'

Jeff leant back in his chair and held his right hand out towards the teenager. The lightness of spirit that had descended on him during the night had remained through the early hours of the morning. With his heavenly collaborator peering over his shoulder, words had tumbled out non-stop through his fingers.

'I'm finishing off "When You're Gone",' he said. 'Remember that screenplay your *mamá* and I wrote and then shelved? I've decided on an ending, made a few tweaks here and there, but it's almost ready to send off to Luke Darby.'

'Oh, OK,' Kierney nodded, picturing the talented actor from one of her parents' earlier films. 'Are you going to ask him to be in it?'

'Yeah. Already did. Why don't you go and get your lover out of bed, and I'll make the tea. I want to talk to you about it, and it's up to you if you want him to be part of the discussion.'

The teenager frowned. 'No. I don't think so.'

'Whatever you want, gorgeous. No rush. It can wait 'til you're finished with him.'

'*Papá*, you make me sound like a hussy,' she complained. 'David's going to work anyway, and so am I. We'll get up and join you for brekkie.'

The author saved the version he was working on, then stood up to give the youngster a hug. She looked alive with fulfilment, her long hair tangled from the night's action. Her man was treating her well, it seemed.

'Sounds perfect, baby. I want to send this off today, so I'll give you the edited highlights, and you'll have to trust me with the rest. I'd love it if you'd produce it with me.'

Still shy around his girlfriend's father, David opted not to stay for breakfast. Jeff was secretly pleased, and Kierney didn't seem to feel spurned. He set about explaining the screenplay's plot, his plans for casting and directing, and some details about the all-important finalé.

Tearful, the calm woman nodded. 'It's OK. I knew you'd make this choice. So did Jet. I haven't seen any other likely ending crossing your mind, even though I wish you could find some way of going to *mamá* while still being here with us.'

'Jeez. Thanks, gorgeous,' Jeff sighed. 'I don't expect you to understand too well, but I do ask you to try and be happy for me. For us. Leaving you guys behind'll be the absolute hardest thing I've ever done, believe me. But by telling you now, I'm hoping we can all say and do all the things we need to, so when the time comes, it'll seem like the right thing to do.'

Indie gazed up at the two dark-haired empaths under his protection, sniffing and snorting his commendation for their convoluted plan. Kierney ran her hands along his back and tickled the base of his tail.

'You're turning him on,' the comic winked. 'I'd be careful. He's not choosy. He'll break your heart.'

'*Papá*, what's got into you?' the teenager frowned. 'Just because I've got a boyfriend doesn't mean my whole life revolves around sex.'

'Why not?' her father teased.

'Argh! I'm going to uni'. I think the movie'll be amazing, and I'm really keen to do it. If Luke wants to, did he tell you when he'd be available?'

'No. We didn't get that far. I asked him to pick someone to play Marie.'

'Oh, cool. Good call. Do Marie and Lex have to be like you two?'

'What do you want?' Jeff turned the question back to the would-be producer.

'I don't think they should be too much like you,' she mused. 'It's not really your story, is it?'

The author shook his head. 'No, it's not. I can't wait to get back to that either. After last night, everything's somehow fallen into place. After weeks of confusion and consternation, it's like *mamá* and I've come to some sort of agreement. We took our time and made our hard choices. For the first time since she disappeared, I feel kind o' peaceful.'

Kierney smiled and took her father's outstretched hand. 'That's fantastic. I'm glad, *papá*. Really. I hate the thought of the next few months, but I totally support your choice. How's the book going though? You'll still finish it, won't you?'

'I thought you had to go to uni'! I don't want to hold you up. However, since you asked, it's going pretty well, thanks.'

The eighteen-year-old shook her head, embarrassed at her bluff having being called. 'Oh, *papá*. I'm itching to know,' she whined, 'but I'm not, at the same time.'

'Why not?'

'Two reasons,' Kierney confessed. 'One, because it's private, and I want you to know I respect that...'

'Cheers,' the widower acknowledged. 'It is. Intensely private at the moment. With all the hidden nuggets from those early diaries, it's almost too private for me. But I want to share it with you guys. It's the story of where you came from, *pequeñita*. What's *Número Dos*?'

'Two is wanting to wait until it's the finished article. I'm glad to hear the confusion's been replaced by peace, but I'm sure there are still chunks missing and you're not satisfied with it yet.'

'Will I ever be?' her dad replied. 'This isn't like a song, gorgeous, which captures a moment in time or a particular emotion. There's no room for convenient rhyme or poetic licence in what I'm writing now. These are facts and interpretations, and very complex emotions have to be put into words.'

Plunging back into his recent past was perfect therapy for the grief-stricken wordsmith, and Kierney saw light in her *papá*'s eyes for the first time in months. It stoked the fire in her heart, even though the end-game didn't inspire her at all. Quite the reverse, in fact.

'Is there a theme emerging?' she asked as they both walked into the kitchen to have breakfast. 'Or is it purely an account of your life together?'

Jeff scratched his chest without thinking, bringing tears to his daughter's eyes. 'Sorry, baby,' he whispered. 'I don't know I'm doing it anymore. I just feel so close to your *mamá* the last few days. Please don't be upset with me. I'm fine. Totally nuts, I grant you, but fine too.'

The teenager wiped her eyes and smiled. 'Yes. You are nuts, and I love you. So is there a theme?'

'A few,' her father nodded. 'Obviously the overarching theme is "one life".'

'Singular?'

'Singular,' the author repeated. 'It's becoming clearer to me every day that I was ready to devote myself to this one person from about ten years old, and probably even from birth. I just didn't have the maturity or capacity to make sense of it any younger. I did know whom I was ready to be devoted to though. How? Who knows?'

'The sceptic in me would argue you wouldn't have known who your soul-mate was if *mamá* hadn't been famous,' Kierney hazarded, knowing her dad wouldn't mind the challenge.

'Yeah,' he agreed. 'Part of me thinks the same way, but I'd counter it in my madness by telling you that *mamá* wanted me to find her. She made it very easy for me to find her.'

'So that means she must've known she was destined to be devoted to you too.' his daughter smiled.

'Hope so. *Exactamente*. I don't know if her instincts were as strong or as clear as mine. I don't think she knew what was going on in those terms until I mentioned it. She's a younger soul than me. That's what we used to say, anyway...

'This was our time though, baby. I have no idea if we'll endure into the next life, but I really need to find out. And I know how hard it is for you to comprehend how I'm willing to bet my future with you guys on such a ridiculous chance.'

The kettle boiled, and the inquisitive teenager jumped up to fill two mugs, accepting a milk carton from her father. He could see her mind was turning at a million miles an hour, as was his. The upcoming film project would set them on the right path for the months ahead, of this the handsome sage was in no doubt.

'*Papá*, do our current incarnations get to choose where our souls go next? Or is it totally random?'

'Jesus! I think about that all the time!' Jeff replied, lowering his tall frame down onto a kitchen chair.

'If *mamá* can pick who she inhabits next, it shouldn't be too hard to figure it out,' the youngster posited. 'Do you think?'

The grieving husband sighed. 'I ask her for clues regularly. So far, she's keeping me guessing.'

Kierney span round and put her hands on her hips. It was a familiar pose, used whenever the mini-humanitarian felt compelled to defend an innocent party against an over-opinionated parent, and it brought fond memories flooding back.

'*¿Qué?*'

'What makes you so sure she doesn't want you to know? Perhaps it's not up to her. Perhaps she hasn't got control of her life back either.'

'Perhaps, perhaps, perhaps! I have no more answers than you do. I thought you were in a rush to get to uni'?'

'Oh, but this is so much more interesting,' the teenager moaned, 'and it affects me personally. I don't want to miss anything.'

Jeff stood up and hugged the gorgeous young woman, who fell into his arms. 'I think something out there makes the choice for us,' he muttered, kissing the top of her head as he swayed from side to side in time to music playing on the radio. 'But I don't know if we can influence that choice at all, or how.'

'Like a god?'

'I have no idea, *pequeñita*. No effin' idea whatsoever!'

'Right! Oh, well... So how'll you find her?'

Her father shook his head. 'I have no idea about that either. Just a whole lot of faith in I'm not sure what. I've got no preconceived ideas about what I'll be looking for, and even what "looking" might mean in an afterlife.'

Kierney smiled at her dad applying quotation marks around this very Earthly function. 'And is it an afterlife or some sort of weird parallel existence where bodyless souls hang out until they find someone new to live in?'

'Indeed,' the dreamer said, sipping on hot, sugary tea. 'My inclination is maybe our souls never quite leave that other world. It's where we go to be home, and home for me will have *mamá* in it.'

'*Papá*, shut up,' his daughter requested, her eyes filling with tears again. 'Tell me about the book instead. You have my support. Just don't make it worse by reminding me all the time, please?'

'Yeah, sure,' Jeff sighed, taking stock of how long it had taken his gorgeous girl to reach the end of her tolerance. 'You're right. We should get going. Come on, Indie.'

Father, daughter and rented dog walked out of the kitchen and through the patio doors, into the garden. To both occupants this house felt so grand and imposing, although no more sumptuous than their own seaside paradise had been. It was older and much darker, lending extra solemnity, and its foreboding seemed to be heightened this morning by their shared contemplation of ancient souls.

The Diamonds had never considered Escondido to be grand. They had always had fun there; it had been a family home, full of running feet, music and laughter. Apart from the odd days and nights they spent in the city apartment, Jet and Kierney had never lived anywhere else, right from when their *hacienda* was first built. They had all grown up together. This house, nestled under a wide canopy of trees and behind thick hedges, had forgotten what it was like to accommodate young people, which gave it a tranquil but gloomy atmosphere.

'D'you like living here?' Jeff asked his gipsy girl over breakfast.

'Yes, I do. It's peaceful and very comfortable. Do you?'

'Yeah. Living in someone else's house is strangely soothing,' her father mused. 'It's as if we're being looked after by an invisible benefactor.'

'Ooh,' the teenager frowned. 'That sounds a bit spooky too. Where's he hiding?'

Her dad laughed. 'Have you been in every room?'

'Yes,' Kierney smiled. 'Except the attic. Maybe he's up there?'

'It's like our luxurious transit lounge, *pequeñita*. Neither of us'll stay here, but it's fine until we're ready to move on. D'you think Jet'll like it?'

'I'm sure he will. He likes old things. I wonder who my soul-mate is, *papá*?'

The comment took the introvert by surprise, and he fixed her eyes in his for a few seconds. 'You'll know in time.'

'How many people miss their soul-mate altogether?'

'Most, I reckon,' the widower shrugged. 'Are you scared you'll miss yours?'

Kierney's eyes widened. 'Yes, I am. I don't want to have an ordinary relationship. I want one like yours and *Mamá*'s.'

'Yeah. I really hope you do too. It's the best. Do you channel him?'

'My soul-mate?'

'The very same. D'you know who you want him to be?'

The young woman let out a shy giggle. 'I have an image of sorts in my mind.'

'Then work on it. He'll reveal himself at some point.'

'Do you talk to Jet about this too? About romantic things?'

Jeff's head nodded from side to side in a strange circular pattern, much to his daughter's amusement. 'Yes and no. I connect with him on a whole different level,' he reassured her. 'But yeah. We talk about his future. As a person, I mean. Jetto's interested in who he'll end up with, just like you are. He described her on the phone while you were over there, didn't he? But he won't admit to the whole soul-mate idea easily. Typical man, gorgeous. We don't like appearing vulnerable. Like David... He didn't want to let me see how much he likes you.'

'But why not?' Kierney asked. 'What are you all so afraid of?'

'Looking weak,' the teacher told his precocious girlchild. 'We've been conditioned to always be in charge, in control. To admit we're dependent on a woman to any extent seems like an admission of failure. It's not constructive, but somehow blokes do it instinctively. It took me a long time to rid myself of this particular trait.'

'So what are you afraid of, I say again?' Kierney mocked, picking up their empty cereal bowls. 'That women'll gain the upper hand and subject you all to slavery?'

Jeff laughed in return. 'Oh, we already have that, baby. And some do. Absolutely. Some women would leap at the chance of gaining control.'

'That's a shame. Why do some women have to spoil things for the rest of us? Jet said he wanted to be with someone with mental illness, didn't he?'

'He did,' the intellectual affirmed, amused by the sudden change of direction.

'Perhaps that was him channelling his soul-mate,' the dreamy student continued. 'He had a premonition, but he's like me; hasn't worked out who it is yet.'

'Maybe,' her father nodded, 'or maybe he's just watched me suffer too long. I wouldn't blame either of you if you switched off for a while, to be honest, in terms of looking for a partner.'

'He told me he wants to marry someone who speaks Spanish too.'

'*¿Verdad?* He never told me.'

'Yeah. He said it ages ago. Before *mamá*...'

The compassionate teenager finished clearing the table, filling the sink with warm, sudsy water, commanding her domesticated male slave to put everything else back in its rightful place. She still found it difficult to speak about the day her mother ceased to be, and her father played along with her diversion in silent compliance to make her feel better.

'Did you channel *mamá* back when you were ten?' the teenager asked a few minutes later.

'Yep. You bet,' Jeff answered, 'although I wouldn't have called it that at the time. I was desperate to talk to someone who might understand me. I had no clue whether she would or not, but Lynn Dyson was so unbelievably beautiful. I was drawn to her way more than to any other girl. Auntie Lena caught me talking to my posters many a time! It was all about sex for her though, so she let me off lightly.'

Kierney laughed. 'That's funny. I can just imagine Auntie Lena walking in on you. Was it embarrassing?'

'Not as embarrassing as when it *was* all about sex,' the father confessed, flicking the tea towel at his daughter. 'And now you're embarrassing me. You women are all the same. Just out to expose us for what we are.'

'And what's wrong with that?' she taunted. 'Isn't that honesty?'

'Fuck! Of course it is, woman,' he moaned. 'That's precisely what I mean. Women think they have a monopoly over weakness. Move over, lady. Give us some room.'

'Welcome in, *papá*,' the long-haired temptress smiled, standing back and waving an inviting arm towards the sink. '*Mamá* did understand you, and so do I. And so do a whole heap of other people these days, since you taught us all how.'

'I guess so. Whatever success I had, it was all your *mamá*'s doing. Man, this time around must have been the best for my ancient soul.'

'I'm glad.'

Nostalgia encouraged the romantic to carry on, hugging his daughter close and kissing the top of her head. 'We made you and your brother, for a start. Twenty years of high-octane happiness, *pequeñita*. That's a lot to be thankful for and a lot to live up to next time round.'

'Aim high,' Kierney said, twisted in her father's arms to kiss him on the lips and echoing one of their missing family member's favourite phrases. 'Aim high.'

The great man broke away, walking backwards, overtaken by a fear that he had opened up too far.

'Jesus! I don't know, baby,' he sighed, sitting down at the kitchen table again. 'What if it's all some stupid nonsense of my own design, to make these next few months bearable? I'm not even drunk or stoned. I'm hardly even smoking these days. Just retreating into my mind like a deranged lunatic.'

'It's all good. You don't have to explain yourself to me. It's awesome to hear you're finding a way to deal with things. I want you to be as happy as you can, and I don't care how that works.'

'Thanks, *pequeñita*. I'm sorry. You shouldn't have to listen to all this stuff.'

'I absolutely want to listen to all this stuff,' Kierney insisted. 'I want to feel close to you. I love hearing about all these ideas. I can make up my own mind about them. Please don't stop.'

Jeff stood up, and the pair embraced again. '*Gracias*,' he said, kissing her forehead. 'My body's healing. My mind's healing. Even my bloody heart's healing, despite trying to do everything I can to sabotage it. I'm getting ready to go round again, Kizzo. It must be what happened before. It must happen for all of us, except we don't often get to think about it for so long.'

'*Mamá* didn't get much time to think about it,' the teenager lamented, leaning into her father's chest.

'No,' her father agreed, cupping his right hand over her head and squeezing it a little tighter. 'But she's a quick thinker, gorgeous. She'll have worked it out. I'm impatient too, which is a good sign.'

HEALING

June made way for July in 1996, and the rambling house veiled in thick foliage turned out to be difficult to keep warm as the Melbourne winter took hold. The time had come for father and son to embark on their road trip, at the beginning of the English summer. The re-architected screenplay had been cast and would commence filming in London in a matter of weeks, and the diverse chapters of the Diamonds' autobiography were filling themselves in with comparative ease.

The man of the house was sick of waking up cold. Never before had he been cold in bed, or at least not that he could remember. He had no recollection of any heating appliances in the pokey Canley Vale flat where he grew up. Even if there had been, the family had no money to spend on such bare essentials.

When he ended up with the place to himself, Jeff had spent precious little time in his own bed as a self-sufficient and hot-blooded teenager! And then once the rock star became an overnight sensation and earned enough money to buy his penthouse apartment and later build their glorious *hacienda*, worrying about heating or cooling had become a thing of the past.

The widower also felt old. Old and cold. He had no meat on his bones these days, and no second body shared his bed to keep the room temperature from dropping too far in the dark hours. Leaving Kierney and David with Indie in the southern hemisphere chill, Jeff jumped a jet-plane for warmer climes. Or so he hoped...

However, Miss Irony made sure torrential rain lashed against the windows of the Boeing 747 as it landed at Heathrow on the morning of Jet's twentieth birthday. The impatient Business Class passenger waited for the aeroplane to come to a standstill, chatting with an elderly lady in the seat next to him, who had imparted every minute detail about her daughter and son-in-law in Somerset without once asking him a question about his own situation. Her self-absorption had been a welcome waste of time, in fact.

'Welcome to summer,' the star joked to the flight attendant, while they helped the frail passenger reach her bags from the overhead locker. 'What's the temperature? Did you decide not to tell us so as not to depress us?'

'Twelve degrees, sir,' the pretty young thing answered, grinning through bold red lipstick. 'Not deliberately, no.'

Jeff smiled. Once upon a time, this would have been the cue for him to ask her out; a quick romp before she needed to be back on duty to fly the next bunch of wealthy businesspeople and holiday-makers back to Singapore. The fact that his brain had joined forces with inspiration from lower down proved to him yet again that the healing process was advancing, despite the ultimatum he had set himself. As far as the outside world was concerned, he was a single man again. Wasn't this what single men did?

The handsome superstar glanced down at his left hand and the two wedding rings side-by-side, scolding himself for even contemplating such a disloyal act. With the onset of cooler weather, Lynn's ring had ceased to limit the circulation in his little finger. Even his own had worked loose with his substantial weight-loss, to the point where he had toyed with the idea of taking both off. However, now he was in the UK and about to enjoy a man's holiday with his son, he was content to be leaving this painted lady with a chaste kiss and an autograph.

Jet stood head and shoulders above most other relatives waiting at International Arrivals. He had cut his mop of blond curls shorter than usual. It was also growing darker with minimal exposure to the sun, but the smile he had inherited from his mother filled Jeff's heart with sunshine nonetheless. In front of his chest, the idiot was holding a homemade sign saying "DAD" which was generating a fair few takers as the disembarking passengers filed by.

'Welcome, Mr Diamond,' the young man said with great ceremony, his right hand extended towards his father. 'It's nice to have you back on British soil. Can I help you with your...'

The passenger had no bags, and he flicked the top of the lad's head with a swift left hand, surprised the teenager hadn't ducked out of the way in time. They embraced, slapping each other on the back.

'You're slipping,' Jeff teased. 'Happy birthday, son.'

They travelled in an anonymous Hackney cab to a West End hotel, where the visitor had suggested they stay for a couple of nights to catch up with the London scene. Jet had bought tickets to a show for his birthday entertainment, and the pair whiled away the hours between checking in and walking out into the chilly evening air by swapping news and shooting the breeze. Neither said so, but both were determined to keep the conversation light and positive, knowing they had five weeks of talking ahead of them.

The play, "Mojo" by Jez Butterworth, was perfect for their first evening's entertainment, wrapping the unsavoury but fascinating topic of gangland violence in gritty humour. They followed it up with dinner and a cigar at Ronnie Scott's jazz club, where they lingered well into the early hours. They agreed not to exchange gifts for their respective birthdays, instead opting to pay for each other's meal, a longstanding tradition which seemed inappropriate to break simply because the composition of their family had altered.

On Sunday, the duo slept in late and enjoyed a lazy breakfast in Little Venice, only a stone's throw from the modest apartment Lynn and Jeff had shared before they married. The forty-four-year-old told his son about the renaissance he had undertaken that year too, and how London had left such a deep impression on him for this reason. He had departed the UK in December 1975 to return to Melbourne and marry the girl of his dreams, in sound mental and physical health for the first time in his life.

The sentimental father, dosed up on coffee and greasy food to soothe his hangover, described how the sprawling, grey city had lost top spot on his list of favourite places in 1982, when the Diamond foursome had spent ten glorious days in Paris with Jet's Uncle Junior and family. Jeff described the pavement cafés and university bookshops near *la Sorbonne* more fondly than ever, and the young man was content to hear these stories again, these days spiced up by with a few more adult twists and turns.

The two men had decided to use one of the coming weeks to hop over the English Channel to France on the recently opened subterranean rail service. As long as they left on a Monday and were back for the following Friday, the champion's cricket commitments would only suffer the loss of one training session. They also bought a road atlas and planned the route they would take with their motorcycles around the hills of mid- and north-Wales, ending up on the tiny island of Anglesey as guests of an early graduate of The Good School.

Thus, their holiday itinerary was well-formed by the time they stepped off the train in Cambridge on Sunday evening. Jeff was pleased his son had inherited his mother's organisational skills, along with her smile, leaving the student better equipped than he had been at the same age.

Living independently in the UK had given the lad an added self-assurance that would serve him well in adulthood. He had a courteous but easy manner with all around him, ingrained in him and his sister by their globe-trotting parents, giving the visitor ample pride in the young man's winning personality.

Jet's brief affair with Nicola Harmer had ended almost as quickly as it had begun, and the ladies' man was eager to introduce his father to the current woman in his life. Lisa was a biology student at Newnham College, long-legged, dark-haired and broody, much like Kierney. The father kept his opinions to himself, a little worried by the uncanny resemblance so soon after his kid sister's recent visit. There was still some healing going on inside the cricketer's mind too, without doubt.

Ensconced in the pokey spare bedroom in his son's university digs, Jeff suggested the couple take him on a tour of their favourite haunts, to partake in a few local brews. Digby, a flatmate who looked as if he hadn't had a haircut in several years, accompanied them, full of inane babble for the icon in their midst, as if he thought it were his only chance to air his views.

Initially, the great man bit his tongue and shared furtive smiles with his son whenever a naïve or impractical solution to one of the world's problems was offered up. Yet as the enthusiastic, left-wing, would-be radical gained in confidence, his ideas grew wilder and wilder, and his mate's famous dad felt compelled to fight back.

The conversation became more robust with each pint of beer consumed, and the former party boy soon discovered the youngsters' drinking capacity was considerably greater than his own. With regret and under the cover of jet-lag, he made his excuses to draw the outing to a close.

Still not even sure whether Digby was a first name or a surname by the end of the evening, he shared a humorous observation with Jet that Digby might well be Gerry's political mirror image at the same age.

That night, the billionaire slept on a knobbly mattress, with the wardrobe bearing down on one side and a corner of the desk looming dangerously close to his head on the other. Nevertheless, it was a privilege to be living in his son's life for these next few weeks.

Before switching the lamp off, he rang the morning in Melbourne to find out how Kierney and Indie were coping without him. They were fine, of course. She was replete with stories of David, her friends' romantic and career escapades, and the human rights project she was running at the university over there.

'Time's getting closer, Lynn,' he whispered after ending the call. 'Did you manage to make it over here? Jet's doing well, angel. He's the perfect combination of you and me, I think, plus a smattering of your dad. I have to admit to that reluctantly, don't I?'

The muscle above his left nipple sang quietly to the melancholy man drifting off to sleep, dog-tired and anesthetised by too many whiskies. Tears rolled down his cheeks, and he kissed both wedding rings once more for luck.

The first night of their ten-day motorbike ride found the riders in Llanfyllin, a tiny town over the Welsh border from the picturesque English county of Shropshire. They had driven across country from Cambridge in a west-north-westerly direction, stopping in Shrewsbury for fuel and lunch. Jeff's 1100cc BMW was borrowed from the owner of the store whence the student had bought his pride and joy, the beloved Triumph Daytona Super III. It was his Aston Martin equivalent, the former tearaway joked without objection from his son.

Between the friendly shopkeeper and Jet's motorcycling cronies, they had rustled up all the necessary safety gear for the Australian holidaymaker, the twenty-year-old taking advantage of a rare opportunity to teach his father a thing or two about how to ride. The weather was mostly kind for their first few days, only raining on them for short bursts and never for long enough to make the road surface too greasy.

Their spirits were high, slipping undetected through towns and villages and only outed occasionally while paying for snacks or petrol. Jet had advised his father not to remove his helmet while in the gentlemens' toilets, to minimise delays caused by curious fans. The tactic worked, much to the amusement of the older man, as two urban spacemen stood next to each other at the urinals.

Jeff issued a challenge on their second night away, holed up in the almost as unpronounceable Llangollen in the Dee Valley, from where they would head westwards along the A5 to Mount Snowdon. Their task was to learn a minimum of five useful Welsh phrases every day for the rest of their holiday, and there was only one better way to accomplish this endeavour than in a pub full of locals, the father had offered. Jet smiled when he surveyed the clientele at the Bridge End Hotel, remarking that it was lucky they hadn't chosen the best way. There wasn't a single female in sight.

The quaint town, with its steam trains still running on viaducts and the odd horse-drawn longboat slipping along the canal, welcomed the famous pair like royalty; so much so that the Diamonds opted to stay an extra night. Keen to know how the autobiography was progressing, the young man plied his father with whisky after a hearty bar meal and encouraged him to open up about how he was coping.

'Mate, I'm fine,' the pale, thin man insisted. 'This trip's not about me. It's about you. It's me making sure you know everything you need to know. Your chance to challenge me for the position at the head of the clan.'

'What are you talking about?' Jet laughed. 'I'm not interested in being head of the clan. All this heathen history's gone to your head, My Lord.'

Alcohol rendering the songwriter uncoordinated, a clumsy left index finger stabbed at his forehead. 'Yeah, maybe,' he answered. 'But I'm serious. You're twenty, and I'm three hundred and five. There's a lot of shit in here, and I'm trying to tell you you're welcome to it.'

'Who says I want your shit?' the sportsman rolled his eyes. 'I've got enough of my own shit. You've taught me loads already.'

'Heaps,' Jeff translated this adopted English expression back into the young man's native tongue. 'Yes, I know, and I'm stoked you have. It's just that with the next few months seeing us on different sides of the world, I'm scared there'll be things we don't talk about.'

'Sure. When we get back to college,' his son offered, blowing air out through his nose as his emotions stirred, 'I'll introduce you to that philosophy lecturer I told you about. You'll like him. I'm surrounded by knowledgeable people, Dad. Probably more eggheads per square mile in Cambridge than anywhere else. That's why I want to talk about you. It's who I'm going to be. A glimpse into my own future.'

The billionaire nodded. The likeable blond cricketer had a fine mind and a polished way of showing humility to his old man. He reached out a long arm and squeezed the lad's broad shoulder.

'Alright, already. You've convinced me,' he capitulated. 'That's part of what I was going to say anyway. To remind you that you have Grandpa and Gerry to call on whenever you need something, and it sounds like there are several people around here whom you respect and like. It's important for me to know you've got plenty of avenues of enquiry. Don't take one person's word for things, mate. And especially not mine.'

'Why especially not yours? I thought you were the head of the clan. Now I'm supposed to ignore you?'

'Because I'm bitter and twisted. I have a strong bias towards the negative that you don't share. Kizzy does. I'm a bit nervous about that, but it's an irrefutable fact. She wallows in the pessimistic view, and it'll be a great asset for her chosen career. But you're an optimist, Jetto. You gaze upon the world and see joy first. I don't.'

'Have you ever seen joy first? Even while you and Mum were together?'

'Christ, mate... We were so unbelievably happy,' Jeff responded, tears filling his eyes. 'But no, I don't think I ever crossed the line into default happiness. It was always a conscious decision I had to make in the mornings, looking across at your mum's beautiful face. "Today is a good day," I'd tell myself.'

'Did she know?' Jet asked.

'Bloody oath, she knows,' the widower snapped. 'It used to bother her that she couldn't change me, but then she accepted that I was who I was. She always said she fell in love with someone who was much sadder than the man she married, so I'm glad I could kind o' meet her halfway.'

The younger man stared into space for a few seconds, absorbing his father's honest statements. 'I do have a question for you actually, wise, old man.'

'¡Excelente! Fire away.'

Jeff sat back in the lumpy, lopsided armchair and lit a cigarette, staring at the grown man whom he had helped bring into the world. This was truly a special holiday. His children were well-equipped to deal with life's transitions, and he hoped Lynn was listening in on this latest dose of drunken discourse.

'How will I know when I've met someone I really love?' his son said in an unusually boyish tone. 'The reason I ask is 'cause you already knew Mum was "the one" by the time you were my age, but I haven't got a bloody clue about what type of woman I want to spend the rest of my life with.'

'It's not an age thing,' the musician grinned. 'Look at Gerry. Fiona's the first woman who's captured his attention for more than a few hours. Don't put yourself under pressure.'

'I know, but I feel so much less grown-up than you were at the same age. And when you see stories in the paper about blokes becoming fathers in their teens, having to be good husbands when they're still in high school, it just makes me wonder if I'm ever going to grow up.'

'Jesus, Jetto!' the father leant forward. 'It's *your* life! Take it at your own pace. Look at your sister... She's already in her forties, but I can't see her settling down with one person any time soon either. It doesn't matter. You shouldn't use me as an example anyway, 'cause I was forced to be way more grown-up than your ordinary teen. I wasn't normal, mate. Trust me.'

The younger man also had tears in his eyes, and Jeff could sense his growing discomfort among the friendly locals. Swallowing the last mouthful of his whisky, he crunched down the remaining slithers of ice and beckoned for the cricketer to put his jacket on and head outside into the cool evening air.

'Half of me's jealous, Dad. I want to feel close to someone.'

'And the other half?'

The strapping athlete chuckled and shrugged. 'The other half wants to shag every woman who crosses my path.'

'Good on ya! That won't change, mate,' his dad smiled, punching him hard on the shoulder. 'It mellows, but it never goes away. We're programmed like that. Women aren't, and I've no idea why. Something very primitive obviously.'

'Shit! That hurt, you bastard. You're stronger than you look,' the lad bleated. 'But what about all those mature-aged women who hound you? They seem to be more hooked on sex than any man.'

'Christ Almighty! Don't remind me. There are extremes at both ends of the scale, I guess. Men and women. Y'know, I read somewhere that over the whole surveyable population of the developed world, one in twenty adults has no sex-drive whatsoever.'

'Wow! That's crap. What a waste!' Jet exclaimed. 'But that also must mean one in twenty has his or her tongue hanging out all the time.'

'*Exactement*,' the father raised his eyebrows. 'My point made very nicely. And all points in between. Cheers, mate.'

The two men sat on a park bench on the top of the hill, looking down on the small town's twinkling lights and the dark snake of the river winding through them. The wind blew icy cold, and both pulled their jackets across their fronts at the same time, making each other laugh.

'Kizzo told me about you knowing you wanted to be with Mum from ten years old. I want to know how. How could you possibly know Mum was the woman you wanted to spend the rest of your life with when you hadn't even hit puberty? How could you know you fancied her if you didn't even know about sex?'

'Because even men can distinguish love from sex if they can be bothered,' Jeff answered, shaking his head. 'You know that. Come on, mate! You can't tell me that after all the girlfriends you've known, you can't tell the difference between loving, liking, lusting and just fancying?'

Jet seemed perturbed. 'Damn you, Dad. Of course I can. But why do they call it "making love" then, if sex is separate to love?'

'Yeah, well... It's a valid question. I'd imagine it's a euphemism to make the thought of having sex more palatable to the prudish people of the nineteenth and twentieth centuries. After all, we're not supposed to have sex before marriage, so they kid themselves no-one'd have sex without being sufficiently in love to at least be on the path to getting married.'

The blond sportsman pouted, nodding. 'That makes sense. So it's not really making love at all?'

'Well, it depends...' the widower explained. 'And it's where we come back to your original question. If you're in love, the sex is a zillion times better. In a different league, honestly. That's what I prefer to think of when I use the expression "making love". The kind of feeling you get when body and soul are on the same wavelength. Doesn't happen very often.'

His son fixed him with a curious stare. 'So weren't you ever remotely in love with anyone else?'

'Nope. There were a couple who came close, but I soon understood them to be infatuation. Or a crush, I guess you'd say. Donna Jade was the closest. She looked like a poor man's version of your mum: successful, sexy and smart. I was a wreck at that point in my life, addicted to everything and really down on myself. I convinced myself I'd never meet Lynn Dyson, and much less be someone she'd be interested in, so I chose a substitute. I settled.'

'But you didn't stay with her for long, did you?' Jet asked, fascinated to hear such secrets from an era to which the youngster could now relate.

'No. Only a couple of months,' the celebrity confessed. 'Pretty soon we both figured out we weren't who we thought we were. I sabotaged it semi-deliberately because I knew it was going to be impossible to get her to admit to any failure.'

'Why is calling off a bad relationship a failure? Haven't you always said a cancelled project is a successful project?'

Jeff sniffed in amusement. 'I prefer not to think of my relationships as projects, if you don't mind. But yeah, exactly. You have to remember, mate, I was pretty sick back then. I felt completely trapped, and my brain was all over the place.

'Donna couldn't understand why I didn't sleep, and I wasn't about to come clean. I had no money and refused to let her pay for things she wanted us to do, and she became an out-and-out possessive monster when I tried to call it off. It was a crazy, fucked-up time. I ended up literally grabbing what little stuff I had and bolting.'

His son's eyes were alive with wonder. 'Bloody hell! And because you knew Mum was "the one",' he added, emphasising the word "knew", 'you were prepared to tell her about your nightmares, *et cetera*.'

'Not straight away,' the nostalgic man recounted. 'I felt trapped with her too for a while. I can't deny it, but because I wanted so much for us to work, I forced myself to go beyond my stupid male pride. Donna and I... That was one enormous, unholy mistake. As soon as I got past the successful, sexy and smart, I found out there was no connection. And one thing I knew I had to have was a deeper connection, just like you said you want. Or rather, half of you does.'

The younger man sniggered. 'Yeah. Quite! Do you think most people settle?'

'Absolutely,' his father answered without hesitation. 'All the time. As recent as fifty years ago... in the olden days, as you'd say... the vast majority of people got married because convention told them they should, and there was a bloody big stigma attached to being single beyond your twenties, especially for women. It's mostly the same today, I reckon, even when couples just live together, except the maximum advisable age to be single's risen by a decade or so.

'And also, it might well be that not many people are too interested in finding their soul-mate. Either they don't believe in them or they don't have anyone special in their sights. People get lazy, mate. It's easier to make a good enough life with someone who's there than an awesome life with someone whom you're yet to find.'

Jeff caught his breath as the tattoo on his pectoral muscle gave him a sharp serve. He stood up and turned away from his son, not wanting him to see this involuntary response. It was too late.

'Hey! Are you OK?' the teenager checked, moving around to see his father's reaction. 'What just happened?'

'Your mum reminded me she's not here.'

'The tatt'?' Jet asked, amazed. 'Does that really happen?'

'Yep. It really happens,' his dad replied, putting his arm around the sturdy hulk to turn him back down the hill and towards the hotel. '*Vamanos*. Let's get back. We need to get on the road early if we're going to get up the mountain tomorrow.'

'OK, sure. Can I ask one more question though?'

'I thought you didn't need to know anything?'

'Piss off, old man! As usual, you're right, and I'm wrong,' the student admitted. 'This has been so great, Dad. I love talking to you about this stuff. I'm interested in your thoughts on whether people in arranged marriages love each other.'

'Whoa! Arranged marriages? I don't know. Why? D'you want one? You'd have to ask someone who's in one. As far as I know, a well-meaning family... in India, for example... who want their children to be happy, will put heaps of effort into finding a match where there's a high likelihood they'll fall in love in time. They do all this horoscope alignment stuff and have endless profiles created by people who presume to know about compatibility. Although, in arranged marriages, it's more expected that you *learn* to love each other instead of *falling* in love.'

'Yeah. That's what I've heard too,' Jet agreed. 'But it seems pretty forced. So much pressure. Like it'd bring shame on the whole family if you admitted defeat. And no, I don't want one, thanks!'

'Absolutely, again,' the wise man grinned. 'Most Indian people I know grew up with the expectation that their parents'll find them someone to marry. They accept it as their fate quite happily. Some less well-meaning, unscrupulous parents are more intent on finding a match which brings the rest of the family enhanced prosperity or social kudos rather than producing a loving relationship.

'And that's when you hear terrible stories of women having to run away and hide somewhere for years, because the menfolk from her own family comes after her for deserting her husband and the overall union, or for not giving them an heir. They can suffer horrible persecution and violence, so I'm sure there are hundreds of arranged couples who simply learn how to stay together and make the best of it.'

'And the men have playthings on the side. Isn't that the way they escape?'

'Undoubtedly. But that's the same in any society. It's wholly more acceptable for a man to have women tucked away all over the place. In fact, in some cultures, it's positively heroic. But for a woman, it's a sin and totally reproachable. Yet another one of life's injustices that your sister's going to change in good time.'

The pair reached their accommodation, hands and faces numbed by the stiff breeze. Jet held the heavy, wooden door for his father as he stubbed out his last cigarette of the day. They climbed the stairs, both needing to stoop to avoid hitting their heads against the low beams as they turned down the corridor leading to their rooms.

'Do you think Kiz can make these sweeping changes?' the young man asked.

'I'm sure she can start the ball rolling,' the proud dad nodded. 'One, she's determined; and two, she's not in a hurry. These are two powerful ingredients for changing the world. Your mum knew that. I always got frustrated when I couldn't change things overnight. She was the one who taught me to have patience.'

Jet laughed. 'Yeah, I remember. I always thought that was a bit conundrumicious about you.'

'Conundrumicious?' Jeff echoed, unlocking his door and inviting his son inside. 'What the hell sort of a word is that? You attend one of the best universities in the universe, and all they can teach you is to make up stupid words?'

'You can talk!' the youngster snapped back, nudging his father's arm hard and watching him almost lose his footing. 'How can someone so keen to change the world be such a pessimist? Surely it takes optimism to make you believe the world's worth changing?'

His father righted himself, peeling off his coat and unzipping his boots. 'Hang about, squire!' he replied, mimicking the publican's strong Welsh accent. 'I don't subscribe to that at all. Being a pessimist is just a different way of looking at our surroundings. You and your mum see a glass half full of vodka and tonic, whereas Kiz and I see the same glass with half of it having already gone down someone's throat. It's the same fucking vodka and tonic, mate. The world still has the same issues, regardless of whether you see them in a positive or a negative light. You've done "SWOT" analyses, haven't you?'

The twenty-year-old stared at his opposite number as if he were crazy. 'Yes. What's that got to do with anything? Strengths, weaknesses, opportunities and threats, you mean?'

'Exactly,' Jeff affirmed, smiling at his son's reaction. 'Haven't you ever put something in the weakness or threat quadrant, only to have someone else say, "Well, that's actually an opportunity"?'

The student's eyes lit up. He grabbed his father round the neck and kissed his cheek.

'What was that for?' the older man yelled, pushing him away. 'I might be sex-starved but I'm not into queer incest yet, mate.'

This time, the sportsman shook his father's throat. 'Fuck off! That's amazing, *Maiastra*. I never thought of it this way. Thanks heaps! You *are* a wise old man after all.'

'Why, thank you, sir,' Jeff sneered, giving the sportsman a bear-hug. 'If I keep talking long enough, eventually you'll hear something worthwhile.'

Jet sighed. 'See? There you go again. We need a mixture of optimists and pessimists to make change. That's what you're saying, aren't you?'

'Yep. It takes all kinds of brains working together. That's what we've been preaching to you all your life. Use the fact that people aren't the same to apply creativity to solving the world's problems. You do it so second-nature that you're surprised to hear it articulated. Don't try and tell me you only just found this out.'

'No, OK. That's true. We need a mixture of strategists and tacticians, thinkers and doers, managers and workers. I get it. It just sounded so magical, how you described it just now.'

'That's what I do, mate,' the superstar smiled, again sensing his tattoo calling and rubbing the skin through his shirt. 'And you're going to make me cry again, between you and your *mamá*, so I'm going to kick you out. Go make love to an R-rated movie or something.'

'Shit, Dad! That makes me feel awful. By the way, it's X-rated over here. Did you want to go for another drink in the bar?'

The widower steered the youngster's shoulders towards the door. 'Cheers, mate, but no. Get out and get some sleep. I'll see you for a run in the morning. I need you to get me fit during these next few weeks.'

Jet got halfway through the door, only to turn straight round again with another question. 'So what am I going to change, as my contribution to the world?'

His dad leant against the doorframe and grinned, pointing a long finger at his son's forehead. 'Bingo! That's the question I've been waiting for. I'm very glad you asked.'

'Really? Is there a master plan?'

'Indeed there is,' the world-changer gave a knowing chuckle. 'That's a conversation I plan to have with you in Paris over *café-cognac*, while smoking some fine weed with a guy you already know who'll be joining us there.'

'OK...' the student nodded, satisfied but intrigued. 'Sounds interesting. Am I allowed to know who he is?'

Jeff eased the door closed on the huge wall of muscle, smiling and shaking his head. '*Adiós, chico. Te amo.*'

'*Te amo, papá.*'

Waiting while his son let himself into the room next-door, the sound of a bolt sliding and locking into place left the celebrity happy enough that his firstborn was safe. Shedding his clothes in a pile on the floor, he went into the freezing bathroom and squeezed some toothpaste onto his toothbrush. Staring at the mirror, he focussed on the symbol on his reflection's chest. He couldn't help but notice the man staring back at him was crying too.

'Did you hear him, angel?' he begged for a response. 'Our gorgeous boy? We're going to miss all these fantastic things our kids are going to do. Can you see what they're doing from where you are? Can you watch over them and still be following me around? I hope you can.'

No feedback was forthcoming. Perhaps Lynn was currently in Melbourne, keeping an eye on their gorgeous girl instead. One of Lynn's nicknames for her husband had been "Magic Man", and Kierney had written a song along the same lines. Now here was Jet saying, "It just sounded so magical." But what sort of lousy magician was he, if he couldn't *abracadabra* his dream girl back to them?

The lonely man turned on the television and flicked through until he alighted on a channel he hoped Jet would be watching. After two or three minutes staring at a bunch of naked, drugged-up actors with fake tans tangling limbs and other appendages while moaning with a distinct lack of conviction, he sought alternative entertainment in the late night news.

The grieving husband took a while to fall asleep, only then to find himself back in The Pensione Hotel on the morning he had last seen his wife alive. Juan Antonio García stood next to him in the lobby, his beige blouson jacket open to reveal a handgun he had recently fired.

In his nightmare, Jeff lunged forward and grabbed the weapon from its owner's belt and pointed the gun at the fearful man, shooting him in the head and in the chest. As the Spaniard collapsed to the ground, he turned the weapon on himself and pulled the trigger, the metallic chill of the silencer pressing against his left temple.

In an instant, the scene changed. The dreamer was transported to the familiar courtroom, where he sat beside García in the dock to face his accusers. Stephen Greenshaw, of floating gown fame, asked him question after question. Why was he parking the car? Why did he let his wife take the telephone call? Why did he plant the gun on this unfortunate delivery guy? Why did he conspire to kill his wife when the children they professed to love were barely adults?

The Defendant awoke, fighting for breath and in a pool of sweat. He threw the blankets off his blazing body, jumped out of bed and opened the tiny, lead-light window, frantic to suck in the cold air. The night was completely still over the dark and deserted street below, which was the only reason he didn't scream at the top of his lungs.

Closing the window, Jeff turned back to the bed and slumped down onto it. 'Take me now, why don't you?' he called out. 'I never asked to be here in the first place. You gave me happiness and then you took it away. You gave me this life, but as far as I'm concerned, you can fucking well have it back. Whoever you are, come on! I'm ready. I know I'm never going to see her again. You don't have to kid me along anymore with this stupid tattoo shit, for fuck's sake.'

Weeping inconsolably, the tormented soul's mind filled with a swirling mass of words, accompanied by a loud, tuneless noise that made no sense. He felt certain he was slowly but surely descending into madness.

The songwriter sat up, urging his pulse to slow down by taking control of his breathing and closing his eyes. An assortment of emotionally charged ideas drifted through his consciousness: open heart, freedom, prison... Yes, here it was. There was a song there, demanding to be caught and tied down. A good one too, albeit final.

The leather-clad boys returned to Cambridge unscathed, saddle-sore and much richer for their experiences. The piecemeal handover of the Diamond baton was well underway, with confidence growing each day on both sides that everything was falling into place.

Jeff split his time between lazy afternoons watching cricket with his laptop perched on his knees and long, intense periods in the old university libraries, researching all manner of topics and people-watching while he cogitated on various ideas. Living vicariously through the exploits of the eclectic bunch of students who passed by, some excited to come and say hello to their resident celebrity and some who would scurry past in a world of their own. The intellectual drew strength from the ambition and dedication he perceived in their continual pursuit of knowledge and cultivation of wisdom.

Every few days would see the busy writer and director jump into a rented sports car with heavily-tinted windows, driving back and forth, up and down the M11, to and from London, attending director's rushes with his daughter on the other end of the telephone, sharing video footage and making joint decisions on their upcoming movie release.

There were also frequent meetings with music company executives, charity representatives and government departments, making sure money kept flowing from one to the other in the right direction, preparing for the next few years of world-changing initiatives all over the world.

With his rambunctious personal trainer on his case, Jeff succumbed to the torture of recovery with minimal protest, knowing he was far from fit and healthy. Nonetheless, as the days passed, he began to build strength and appetite. His arms and legs sported distinct muscle definition again, and his abdominal muscles ached from the hideous number of press-ups, crunches, squats and leg-raises Jet made him do every morning. Their running pace increased steadily, and the older man learnt anew to look forward to the endorphin rush of aerobic exercise.

'Your soul-mate might be looking for you right now,' he told his son over a cooked breakfast in the cramped Cambridge student digs. 'The person who got your previous VIP's soul when she died.'

'Hmm,' Jet agreed with his mouth full, swallowing it down. 'I'd love to know who we used to be, if anyone. Were we a famous couple like you guys or just ordinary folk? Who would you like to come back as next time?'

'Haven't even thought about it. Indie, I reckon.'

'And Mum comes back as someone's leg?'

Jeff chuckled. 'That's disgusting. She'd be horrified to hear you say that.'

'I know. I'm sorry. It was a bit off. Anyway, Mum told me once that nearly every morning you'd thank her for being in your life. She said she always loved to hear you say it. Did you know?'

The widower smiled. 'Yeah, I did. And yeah, I know. I'm glad she told you too. I meant it, without question, but it was also my way of conning myself into the day. And then when you guys came along... used to run into the bedroom at daybreak and jump onto the bed... things got even easier. Even though my first reaction would be, "Oh, for Christ's sake, leave me alone," you always convinced me to get up and going. To put my grateful, happy face on. It's very powerful, son, the pull of family. The pull of being loved. I can highly recommend it.'

The student placed two steaming mugs of coffee down on the table. His flatmates weren't up yet, which was entirely normal, and it was handy to have the kitchen to themselves. Since returning from their motorcycling trip, the pair hadn't had much time to speak in private, prompting the twenty-year-old to turn to his mentor with a serious expression.

'I do want to have kids. Not for ages, but I will have them,' he made his subdued proclamation. 'And I'm determined not to have any by accident. You drove that home to me so well. To us, I should say. When my mates brag about not bothering to use condoms, I always keep quiet. I couldn't imagine having to talk to someone about getting an abortion. I know you did it with Auntie Lena. But for my own child? That must be truly awful.'

'Yep. I was bloody lucky, mate. I was always careful, for exactly the same reason, even when I was off my face with drink or drugs. There was always a chance something would go wrong though.'

'That's what I mean.'

'And when Gerry told me he'd got Heather pregnant, I was so thankful it hadn't been me. I really don't know what I would've done. I lectured him about getting married for Jenna's sake, and I told him I'd get married if I were in his position, but I think we both know that was a lie on my part.'

'Wow,' Jet whistled. 'Does Gerry know?'

'Nope,' his dad grinned. 'And you're not going to tell him either. I might be a hypocrite from time to time, but I'm also happy to go undetected.'

'So why did you tell me?' the student asked, wagging his finger.

'You remember we used to have the expression *"en famille"* for things you kids could only talk about between us?'

The young man nodded. 'Yes. We still use it.'

'*Oui.* From time to time. Well, I'd hope we can be in a position to protect each other's adult secrets as well as whenever one of you wet yourself.'

The boy cringed. 'Dad, why do you always remind me of those times?'

''Cause I'm your father. It's my prerogative, and you won't have to put up with it for much longer.'

'Bastard,' Jet moaned, punching the older man's shoulder. 'That was nasty. I hate it when you do that.'

The widower had tears in his eyes too. This preparatory work was hard going; these cruel-to-be-kind lessons...

'I'm sorry, *chico*,' he murmured. 'The press'll test you, mate. I need you to experience those "kick in the guts" moments. People are going to say some unkind things about me and what I'm going to do, and you're going to have to smile graciously and thank them for their valuable opinion.'

'Fuck that for a game of soldiers,' Jet grunted, clearing away their breakfast remains. 'I'd rather take my chances than hear it from you.'

'Fair enough, mate,' his teacher agreed. 'I shouldn't have gone in so hard. That's the end of the game. I promise.'

The pair of Diamonds spent that evening at home with Jet's flatmates and their girlfriends. They were a friendly bunch, having soon recovered from their initial shyness keeping company with the megastar living in their spare room.

Jeff had relayed story after story about recording and touring, also subjecting them to a fair smattering of tales from working in South Africa, the Middle East and Northern Ireland. They had partaken in philosophical discussions, political debates and uncouth bitching sessions about certain celebrities and wannabes.

After a shouted dinner of pizza and beer, the group settled down to watch a video that one of the guys had borrowed. The famous father stood in the doorway, surveying the happy scene of his son in the bosom of his friends. They were clearly fond of each other, and it reminded the older man of how close he had been to Gerry and Suzanne and to Gerry's sisters in those latter teenage years. This was like a second family for Jet, as the Blakes had been for him. Not so bad a substitute for the real thing. This was their time.

The Australian hero slipped unnoticed out of the flat for a walk around the magnificent university town. The following day, the Dynamic Duo would leave for Paris, and the great man needed to collect his thoughts for the next important lesson his heir was to learn.

After a few minutes, he heard running footsteps behind him. He turned around to see Jet catching him up.

'Hey! Why did you leave?' the sportsman asked, not even breathing hard. 'Stay and watch the movie with us.'

'No. It's all good. You need some time with your mates. You don't want me hanging around every minute of every day.'

'I do,' his son insisted. 'I really do. I don't want you to have to make yourself scarce. You're my guest.'

'I know. Thanks, mate. And I appreciate the sentiment,' the visitor said, patting the lad on the back. 'I wanted to leave you to it. Plus, I've got some planning to do for tomorrow.'

'For my special meeting with the man of mystery?'

'*Oui.*'

'*Bon. D'accord,*' the teenager was placated to some extent. 'Will I need to speak French all the time?'

Jeff laughed. 'No. 'Specially around him. I'm pretty sure he doesn't speak a word of French.'

'Oh, cool! But Dad, come back with me, please? We can do something else. I'm sorry. I know sex on screen isn't your thing at the moment.'

'No way!' the songwriter exclaimed, nudging his son's shoulder with one hand while lunging to grab his crotch with the other. 'It's fantastic to see you there with your mates. Exactly what I hoped I'd see you doing while I was here. It's breathing life into me, so please don't pay any attention to what I'm up to. Go back to Lisa, and I'll see you later.'

'Yeah? OK, if you're sure,' the youngster frowned, turning back in the direction of his digs.

'I'm sure, mate. Enjoy.'

Over an hour afterwards, Jeff stole back into the flat and resumed his position in the living room doorway. The tableau had hardly changed since he left, except perhaps that the couples had moved a little closer together. Some were stroking each other's limbs absentmindedly, and he watched others steal kisses every now and again. It made him proud of his larrikin offspring while also feeling insanely jealous.

The tape ended, and one by one the students stretched and yawned. The girlfriend of one flatmate had slept through nearly the whole movie, receiving a ribbing from the others when she awoke and asked what had happened.

Jet looked round, seeming to guess his father would have returned. 'Hey, Dad. How long've you been standing there?'

'Not long. I'm making coffee if anyone wants some.'

The rest of the flat's occupants declined, having the courtesy to leave their guest alone with his son and Lisa.

'You guys can go to bed too,' the older man said, winking. 'I'm sure you've got things to attend to.'

The young woman giggled. 'God! I could never have this conversation with my dad. There's no way he'd be able to joke about sex.'

Jeff shrugged, and the younger Diamond laughed.

'I don't remember when we haven't talked openly about sex,' he told his girlfriend. 'You can't imagine how good it felt when I could finally speak from experience.'

'Me too, mate,' his dad grinned. 'For months, I'd be waiting to see how your language changed. And then one day it came, if you pardon the pun. I can't even remember what gave the game away, but I remember thinking, "He couldn't have got that from a magazine."'

'Ew!' Lisa squirmed, pulling a face. 'What have you told your dad about us?'

'Nothing,' Jet insisted, blushing. 'He doesn't ask for specifics. I don't want to talk about it now either. Move on, old man.'

'It's fine, mate. Really. I've been there and done it all. Many, many times in fact. Now it's your turn, and that's exactly how life's supposed to go.'

'Not at forty-four though,' the student refuted, filled with sympathy for the man who had given him everything.

'Nope. You're damned right about that, mate, but we can't change it.'

Jeff gave each youngster a mug of coffee and pointed them back into the living room, bidding them to sit down. He told them he had started the chapter on his and Lynn's wedding, and how much easier it had been to craft than he had expected.

'I'm fine with watching and writing about sex. Just not doing it,' he confessed with a wicked grin. 'No "Nike principle" for me... It's better than nothing, I guess.'

With a restrained chuckle, Lisa excused herself with a kiss for her boyfriend and a tentative peck on the cheek for his father. The handsome celebrity accepted her friendly gesture, winking at his son as the attractive young woman left the room.

'Mate, if you meet someone like your mum, grab her with both hands. I guarantee you, you won't regret it. You won't miss out on anything. But if you don't meet her straight off, enjoy yourself with anyone you want for as long as it lasts. No-one gets hurt if you're upfront and honest. Not for long anyway... You'll know who's right and who's not.'

'Cheers,' Jet nodded. 'I'm more relaxed about things since we talked. Lisa's fun; I like her a lot, but it's not special.'

His father smiled. 'Go to bed, son. And believe me, I've done a whole heap more meaningless things than you give me credit for. Make her scream. Enjoy it for whatever you want it to be.'

'Goodnight,' the cricketer said, ruffling his dad's thick, greying hair in a sublime moment of role reversal. 'Hope you sleep well. Eurostar tomorrow.'

'Yep. Underwater train. Weird concept, but I'll go with the flow.'

The student groaned at yet another lame joke. 'Are you serious? Was that supposed to be funny? Jesus!'

'G'night, Jetto. Piss off to your woman, will you?'

'Does the guy I'm being set up with in Paris know about your plans?' Jet asked his father.

They were sitting opposite each other on a high-speed train with nothing but blackness and the odd bright light whizzing past them outside. And outside wasn't even outside. It was the inside of the outside. Their journey through the new "Chunnel", as it had become known, would only last twenty minutes at their current speed. Yet the fact they were barrelling along in a tube full of electricity inside another tube full of electricity under a large body of water unnerved both men somewhat.

'You're not being set up,' Jeff assured his son with a smile. 'I'll tell you who it is, if you're so curious. You're so persistent that it'll end up being an anti-climax if I leave you to find out for yourself. You're not six anymore. You can handle the anticipation.'

'Not sure I can,' the lad sniggered. 'Deal again.'

The older man shuffled the deck of playing cards on the shiny table between them and dealt two each. They picked up their hands, and Jet requested a third card, and then a fourth.

'Shit!' he said, throwing his hand down before his father had even checked his. 'I'm broke. Where did you get this pack from?'

'Sore loser!' Jeff taunted, extending a stockinged foot to kick the teenager's shin under the table. 'It's Julian Manolescu.'

'Julian Manolescu?' Jet repeated, a flicker of recognition appearing on his face. 'Oh, yeah. I remember him. He was at The Good School, wasn't he? Quite a while ago. From Melbourne?'

'Yep. He's at Heriot-Watt Uni' now, in Edinburgh, heading up a medical ethics community that's gaining an excellent reputation. He's also doing some interesting work on mental health and individuals' capacity for rational decision-making. And you're right, he was one of the early Good School graduates. And right again, he does know about my plans.'

'Oh,' the young man sighed, looking out of the window. 'So it's going to be another one of *those* conversations.'

The temerity in his son's enunciation of the fated demonstrative pronoun sent shivers down Jeff's spine. He didn't expect the discussion to be a bundle of laughs either, but hoped his son would glean inspiration from it. He dealt out ten cards each for a game of Gin Rummy, turning the top card on the remainder face-up to one side.

'Come on, mate,' he encouraged, tapping the table like Emperor Qianlong. 'There's no money on this one.'

The teenager leant forward and picked up his hand, sorting it as best he could. He reached towards the rest of the deck, laid a card down and took another from the pile. His opponent pounced on the discarded picture card.

'Cheers,' he joked. 'Good start. What's on your mind, son?'

'What are we going to be talking about?'

'Your future.'

'My future?'

'No. How to fry an egg,' the playful father snapped back. 'Parrot face! Stop repeating what I say. Saying my words back to me doesn't undo the fact I've said them.'

The younger man set his hand face-down on the table and slid himself out of his seat, standing to his full height in the aisle. '*Excuse-moi, Maiastra.* I have to piss,' he said, unable to stop himself smiling. 'Parrot face? *Embrasse mes fesses, mon père.*'

Jeff let him go, hoping the boyish humour wasn't hiding something more sinister. It was indeed destined to be one of *those* conversations. The Diamond Celebration Foundation had financed a research grant for Julian to work in the other Cambridge, in Massachusetts, on a topic dear to the philanthropist's heart. The promising academic had been over the moon to have been taken into the great man's confidences over the last few months.

The original plan for this trip to Paris was not meant to include either Diamond child. However, as the long night-time telephone calls between father and son had revealed a greater maturity and capacity for broad thinking than the billionaire had anticipated, it had been a most natural choice to invite him after all.

Within five minutes, the young man had returned to pick up his half-built hand again.

'Sorry, son. You OK?'

'Yes. Get on with the game. Ignore me. I'm nervous.'

'Sure. That's good. Me too, mate. We'll keep talking.'

The rest of their voyage passed quickly. The train emerged from the dark tunnel into bright European sunlight and rumbled past countryside where vehicles drove on the wrong side of the road. Ancient stone houses were maintained with a mixture of artisan materials, new technology and stoic Gallic pride. Even the livestock looked chuffed to be French.

Arriving at *la Gare du Nord*, the platform stretched a long way behind them by the time the front of the train reached the buffers. The Diamond men grabbed their bags and jumped off, both wearing baseball caps and sunglasses. They looked unmistakeably not French.

'*Bienvenu à Paris*,' Jeff shouted over the engines' loud roar. '*Prends un Pastis avec moi?*'

'Sure thing. Show me the way. I'm thirsty, big-time.'

The taxi queue was short, and within a minute or two, the pair were bumping over cobbles towards *la Boulevard Saint Germain*, bound for a bar which the romantic intellectual held dear. He had found himself at home in the Bohemian districts of northern European cities ever since 1973, when the rock star's début world tour brought them within his reach.

Being in his dad's favourite city gave the younger man a buzz he failed to comprehend, privileged to share in this vicarious escapism. It was as if the metaphysical years Jeff had gained since Lynn's death were stripped off him at Passport Control, and the teenager saw a glint in his old man's eye for the first time in many months.

'Why do you love it here so much?'

The songwriter shrugged. '*Vraiment, je n'sais pas.* Paris makes me feel free somehow. Being here is like suspended reality. It has ever been thus, mate.'

They checked into their usual Paris bolt-hole, opposite *Le Panthéon*, a few hundred metres from *la Boulevard Saint Michel* and *les Jardins du Luxembourg*. After battling with a stubborn door lock, they threw their bags onto Jeff's bed, along with the key to the second room. Within minutes, they were pelting back down two flights of spiral staircase and out into the late afternoon sun, in search of the cloudy aniseed spirit that was so undeniably French.

Students of all nationalities, colours, ages and religions thronged around the imposing university buildings in the narrow streets off *la Rue Saint-Jacques*. The faculties of Law and Philosophy attracted the scholars seduced by the mysteries of life itself. Animated discussions encircled the Australians, ideas elevating in curls of cigarette and cigar smoke while china clattered on table-tops and glasses hydroplaned on spilled beer.

'Now d'you see why I like it so much?' Jeff asked of his son, ordering their drinks and squeezing into the most inconspicuous table they could find. 'Can't you feel the minds melding?'

The cricketer could indeed. In fact, he could already feel his own mind melding, fired up by the scene's timelessness. "*Hic et ubique terrarium*", he recalled the university's motto from their undersea conversation; "Here and everywhere else", suggestive of a Jeff Diamond album title, had it not been copyrighted centuries ago!

Apart from fashions and hairstyles or the odd pop and splutter from a beaten-up Lambretta, it was easy to believe little had changed between the times of Louis Pasteur, Marie Curie and Henri Kagan.

There was an infectious vivacity about this erudite environment that Jet had been too young to discern when the family had last visited, barely two years ago. They had spent a few days in the same hotel during the superstars' recent monster tour, and he and his sister had rejoiced in being permitted to wander round the city on their own after dark.

'You know what Paris puts me in mind of?' the teenager ventured.

The older man blew a long plume of smoke into the air, shaking his head. '*De quoi?*'

'*L'indépendence.*'

'Excellent. *Parfait, mon ami.* What else?'

'Decadence,' the youngster offered. 'But not decadence in the context of wasteful. Hedonism, maybe?'

'No. It's not hedonism either,' Jeff mused, closing his eyes. 'I know what you're trying to describe, but I can't think of the right word either. Hedonism has overtones of immorality, whereas what we're both failing to articulate doesn't.'

'A place where you can experience everything at once,' the student added into the mix.

'*Indulgence, peut-être?*' the wordsmith suggested. 'Epicureanism. Pleasure, I suppose. Will that do?'

'*Oui.* All that,' Jet agreed, pointing to his father's empty glass. 'Another?'

'*Absolument. Merci.*'

The global citizen was proud to watch his confident twenty-year-old ordering another round of drinks, chatting to the waiter with ease. The exposure their children had received to various languages from an early age had enabled them to switch countries with minimal disruption.

Jet and Kierney had been schooled in the most valuable linguistic trick: if they were unable to summon a particular expression from one language, they knew to substitute the corresponding words in another. This way, there was always a fair chance the listener would be able to interpret whatever the children were trying to say, and the evasive phrase would be echoed straight back to them, rendering it all the easier to commit to memory in context.

'So what's the plan for the next few days?' the sportsman asked, returning to his seat. 'Is there one?'

'There's a strategy, but the plan's up to you,' Jeff replied, prolonging the mystery. 'Tonight you're going to get your connubials off with a beautiful stranger, and I'm going to sit here until they throw me out. Then tomorrow, we get up late, do some sightseeing and meet up with the others for dinner.'

'Others?' Jet pondered aloud, hissing the plural "s". 'Julian and who else? I still get the feeling I'm being set up.'

His dad chuckled. 'Gerry's flying in today. I wanted him to be across what we talk about too.'

'OK. Sounds ominous, but I'll bide my time.'

'And,' the celebrity continued, 'I was wondering if you wanted to give "Jet" away and start using your real name these days? Now you're your own man.'

Jet emptied his beer glass, tipping his head back to drain the last few drops. 'Actually, I have been thinking about doing that, yeah,' he affirmed. 'Occasionally I introduce myself as Ryan, but most people revert to Jet anyway.'

'Whatever you want, mate. Just tell me what you'd like me to call you or introduce you as, and I'll do it. Junior's still Junior after all this time, but it's up to you who you want to be.'

'Cheers,' the youngster replied, puffing out his broad chest and extending his right hand towards his fellow traveller. 'Ryan Diamond. How're you going?'

Jeff grasped his son's strong hand, looking him in the eyes. 'Honoured to make your acquaintance, Ryan, mate. And you don't have to call me Dad in adult company either, if you don't want to.'

'Hmm,' the student mused, waving to request another round of drinks. 'That'll be harder to grow into. You are my dad. You are, aren't you? Or is that what you've brought me to Paris to tell me?'

The dark-haired beatnik scoffed. 'Don't you start! You wouldn't believe how many people questioned that while you were growing up.'

'I know,' Jet replied, saddened by this offensive idea. 'Mum told me. Just for the record, I wouldn't want to be anyone else's son. And I'm not just saying it because of where we are and what's happened this year.'

Jeff coughed as his chest tightened. He heard the sincerity in the young man's voice, and it melted another layer of ice from around his frozen heart.

'Cheers,' he croaked, forcing a smile. 'It means a lot to hear you say that. I know it's tough at the moment, but it won't always be this way for you. Your patience'll be rewarded, my son.'

'Patience for tonight's beautiful stranger or for my time to be King?'

'Both, mate,' his father smiled. 'Both. Where d'you want to go for that? A night club on *la Rive Gauche* or somewhere a bit more classy?'

'Not Wild Horses?' the lad asked, referring to the cabaret joint his parents had owned for many years.

'By all means, mate! Are you looking for an education?'

'Maybe,' he smirked, awkward suddenly. 'Isn't that what this trip's for? To broaden my horizons?'

'Yeah. If you want your horizons broadened. Do I detect an element of boredom? Twenty years old and bored already?'

'Fuck, yes!' the lad shouted, making several people close by turn around.

'OK, OK,' Jeff whispered, batting his hand, palm downwards, encouraging the impetuous, alcohol-fuelled young man to keep his voice down. 'Steady. We should get something to eat.'

Jet apologised, leaning forward in his chair and softening his voice. 'Hey, I've been thinking heaps about our Welsh mountains conversations,' he confessed. 'You've made me question my motives.'

'Motives? Have I?' his dad chuckled. 'Sorry about that. You *are* entitled to ignore me.'

'But I can't. You've sown the seed, and now it's growing beyond my control.'

'Did I ever tell you my supermarket stories?' the former playboy asked, an impish grin spreading across his face.

'No, I don't think so. I'm guessing this is somehow connected, or have you gone off on some senile tangent?'

'Bloody cheek!' Jeff hissed, standing up and grabbing the back of his son's chair, doing his best to pull it out from underneath the heavyweight. '*Lève-toi.* Let's eat.'

After *Cous-cous Royale* and a bottle of fine *Beaujolais* in one of the better Tunisian restaurants in the Latin Quarter, father and son jumped into another taxi and headed to *l'Avenue George V*, to the nightclub the rock star had acquired early in his career. Its refurbishment had been a labour of love and a significant tax dodge rolled into one, and this was the first time he had visited with his adult son as a customer.

Thierry, the manager, was thrown into a spin upon seeing *le patron* turn up unannounced. He calmed down once Jeff assured him he didn't intend to stay but that he would appreciate if the twenty-year-old wasn't hassled while he took his pleasure. A fresh-faced student who hailed from Québec poured beer into two tall glasses, and a group of long-serving employees from behind the stage emerged to greet their famous employer.

Leaving the youngster to enjoy the show, along with any supplementary entertainment of which he might take advantage, the thoughtful widower wound his way through the narrow streets and wide avenues until he reached the river. He crossed the bridge to *la Place des Invalides*, in the seventh *arrondissement* where Napoléon Bonaparte was entombed. The impressive, early nineteenth-century buildings were adorned with spectacular illuminations, and the nocturnal tourist leant on the blackened wall which ran along the footpath above the banks of *la Seine* to smoke a cigarette and steep in the damp, aromatic annals of time.

'Are you here, angel?' he whispered. 'I wish you were. I want to love you in Paris again. Come back, Lynn, even if it's just for tonight.'

Jeff's aching body screamed for attention, triggering yet another counterproductive emotional outburst. Conflict raged within him as he fought his libido with threats of cracking up in front of an anonymous, unassuming female. He couldn't risk her wising up to the mileage she could gain by taking her story to the press. The likelihood of deriving any lasting satisfaction from the overdue mechanical act was so low that it wasn't worth taking a chance, although his physical longing had reached extreme heights tonight.

Back in the hotel, the celebrity lit a spliff and settled back against the pillow to ingest it, with a glass of malt whisky poised beside his left elbow. Paris transformed at nightfall into a hotbed of sexual delectation, yet here he was, Australia's sex-god, alone with a raging hard-on and no beautiful best friend to share the city's lustrous delights. At some point, he would have to break this impasse, and maybe tonight he should force the issue.

Jeff's thoughts turned to his son, talking trivia with a well-educated escort who would just happen by his table shortly after the show began. He pictured her leaning into him and soon found himself gazing at his wife's face. Her lips preparing to kiss his as their heads moved closer together, the neckline of her dress low enough to reveal the irresistibly soft, tanned skin of breasts which had spent a recent week topless in the south of France.

As the rock star's fantasy took flight, the tattoo on his chest flinched and rocketed him higher on the wings of desire. 'Oh, so you *are* here. Where've you been? D'you know what's going on inside me? It's hell, angel. I'm so horny for you, but I can't touch you and I can't see you.'

Chilled Scotch and warm smoke combined to relax the musician's senses, and he focussed his thoughts on the sublime tingling around the "JL" symbol etched onto his skin over twenty years ago. What would he have done without it these last few months? Lynn's distant presence had proved as invaluable after her death as it had before she had graced his humble half-life, in those dark, dark teenage years in western Sydney.

The boy from Canley Vale smiled at the doleful realisation of coming full circle. After more than twenty magnificent years, his existence had reverted to lying on a bed, talking to Lynn Dyson's absent soul and imagining she were about to touch him and coax him to the point of no return.

Umpiring his own private battle between body and mind, he removed his clothes and peeled back the sheets in front of the tall, wide-open windows. Outside, the traffic circling around *le Panthéon* droned on and on, hiding the *vignette* the lonely celebrity was about to enact from the rest of the world.

He and his dream girl had perfected the art of remote liaisons during the years of endless touring and international engagements, always with a friendly voice at the end of the telephone or the promise of a warm and willing body to come home to. The trick now was to bring the passion back to life somehow. He dared to dream his wife's spirit was as keen as he was to reignite memories of each and every night they had spent in this hotel.

'Work your magic, angel,' he invited, gripping his hardening shaft, desperate to ban all negative thoughts. 'Stay with me, *s'il te plaît, mon amie.* You look absolutely amazing. The sun must shine all the time where you are.'

For the first few minutes, the bereft lover struggled to maintain his erection, continually dragged back into the present by images of Lynn's murderer flashing through his mind. He pictured themselves back in their bed at Escondido, with the double doors open to the balcony and Port Phillip Bay's constellations shining down on the master bedroom.

Searching back through his vast back catalogue of momentous sexual encounters for the taste of his lover's kiss and the sound of her sighs, Jeff gradually felt the pressure building. Recall came fast and furious, but its effect was far less stimulating than he remembered. Despite every attempt by his heart to sabotage the pleasurable sensations, he was determined to see it through to climax in the couple's favourite hotel in his favourite city, if only to prove to himself that he was still a fully functioning human being.

Progress was painfully slow while his right hand closed in on his orgasm, the deliberate rhythm quickening in pace so as not to let his supplicating body off the hook. Then against all odds, just as he tipped over the edge, the rich bounty in Lynn's voice filled his head, and the last few torturous months through which he had persevered vanished in the flare of an ethereal high.

With a long, agonising moan, the solo act was over at last, in a Herculean flood of emotions. Sadness and elation, relief and anger, disappointment and satisfaction, love and hate crashed together as the acute physical paroxysm gripped his senses for several exquisite seconds.

'*Gracias, Regala,*' he whispered to the ceiling, holding his left hand over the stinging tattoo. 'I love you so much. I love you so, so much.'

Crying like a baby, Jeff rolled off the mattress and pulled open the door to the shower, feeling dirty and full of shame. Is this how life would be from now on? Managing to re-teach his body how to ejaculate, confirming that he was healing in spite himself, reinforced his overwhelming desire not to heal at all.

'Fuck you, García!' he shouted through the steady flow of cool water. 'Are you happy now? This is what you made me into, you fuck. A loser wanking in secret while his dead wife's singing in his insane, stoned head. You got your wish, you bastard. It *was* better this way. You were so fucking right.'

Finding an eventual calm, the spent man towelled himself dry and stood at the window to watch Parisians go about their late business. It was after eleven o'clock, and his son would leave Wild Horses soon, bound for who knew where? He re-lit the joint which had extinguished itself in the ashtray next to the bed, smoking the remaining few centimetres in frantic haste. The drug hit the spot within moments, and he began to mellow out at long last.

'Can we do that again, baby?' the bitter lover asked, laughing in the dark. 'Not sure why I want to, but I expect I shall. How was it for you?'

This time there was no response, but it didn't matter. His soul-mate had appeared when it counted, or he had conjured her up at least... Either way was good enough for the time remaining. There was no denying that his physical self felt better for the experience. His saviour had helped him subjugate the demons and become an ordinary man again, albeit temporarily.

THE BOY WHO WOULD BE KING

'Where did you end up last night?' Jeff asked his bleary-eyed companion.

The pair was busy helping themselves to fresh crusty bread rolls and buttery croissants at the small breakfast bar, savouring the aroma of coffee wafting from their table nearby. The rest of the hotel's guests must have already been through, leaving the Diamonds to feast on their own.

The cool, stone basement cellar was sparsely decorated and strewn with a random assortment of tables and chairs; a rough and rustic setting in the heart of France's noisy metropolis. In fact, the wandering minstrel couldn't detect a single change of décor in all the years he had been frequenting this trendy *auberge*.

'My new little friend, Emilie, showed me *une boîte* not far from Wild Horses,' Jet explained, ripping his croissant apart and applying a generous layer of apricot jam to the first piece. 'We danced for a while and had a few more drinks, and then we came back here. What about you?'

'Where is she now?' his father asked, smiling as he recognised himself in the man sitting across the table. 'Still upstairs sleeping?'

'No. She's already gone. She had to go to work.'

'You guys had a good night though?'

'Butt out, old man. I'm not giving you any salacious details to dine out on. She furthered my education. That's all I'll say.'

Jeff laughed out loud, clapping his hands. *'Magnifique!* I'll declare that "Mission accomplished" in that case. Onwards and upwards, Ryan, mate.'

'So what's the plan for tomorrow?' the hungry sportsman asked, chomping into his bread and jam.

Jeff tipped a cupful of coffee down his throat and refilled it with what remained in the pot. He had been dragged out of bed at daybreak by his draconian personal trainer, having slept better than expected, and was now wondering why he hadn't fought harder to stay in bed for an extra hour.

'No firm plans beyond tonight's dinner. Why?'

'I thought I might head out to EuroDisney,' Jet answered. 'Did you want to come?'

'Right,' Jeff smiled. 'Let me guess... Your throwaway invitation was made in the hope I'd decline, and there's a female reason for this sudden need for adventure.'

The lad sniggered. 'Am I that transparent?'

'Yep. Go for your life. It'll be good for you.'

'Thanks. What'll you do?'

'Depends what the others are doing. If I'm left to my own devices, I'll be perfectly well entertained hanging around *l'université*. It'll be just like the old days. Don't worry about me. I've got plenty on my mind, what with the book and everything.'

'OK then. If you're sure,' the lad agreed, finishing his breakfast and swilling down a large gulp of orange juice. 'I rang Kiz this morning.'

'Good on ya. Thanks for doing that. I left her a message last night too. Don't know where she was.'

'They went to some dinner party. Sounded quite official. She's going to ditch David.'

'Oh, yeah? Did she tell you that, or are you just assuming?'

Jet shook his head. 'Jeez! She told me. And she didn't say not to tell you, so you don't have to pretend you didn't know. Apparently, Dave objects to all the public engagements she attends, saying she's playing into the hands of the ruling classes.'

Jeff scoffed. 'Sounds familiar.'

'Did you do that to Mum?'

'I didn't flat-out object, but neither did I hold back on issuing the odd disparaging comment,' the veteran radical responded, 'until she convinced me those things were a necessary part of the job. David'll learn, but probably not fast enough for your sister. Is she cool with it though?'

'Yeah,' Jet replied. 'Completely fine. She's going to Sydney next month for the uni' project she's doing. She wants you to go with her.'

The celebrity frowned. 'Wonder why? Are you sure she's OK?'

'Dad,' the young man scolded. 'Do I have to tell you why?'

The father shook his head. Of course not. For Christ's sake, he was so wrapped up in his own world. His regular dips into selfishness in the face of his kids' wellbeing were reprehensible, and yet he constantly found himself caught out. He, of anyone, ought to know better.

'Fucking hell. I'm an arsehole, I know. Thanks for telling me, mate. And for keeping me in line. You're a good man, Ryan Diamond. Let's get out of here, shall we?'

The rest of the morning was spent in the fashionable shopping district around *les Galleries Lafayette*, where Jeff insisted the student buy a mountain of new clothes for the coming British autumn and winter. Their situation amused them: two shopaphobics let loose in the *chic* boutiques of Paris, badgered by a string of camp sales assistants who fell over the handsome stars in an attempt to purvey excellent customer service, but instead providing excessive customer annoyance.

Three suits, a dozen shirts and ties, copious designer underwear and a few stylish casual items later, the billionaire struck a deal with the overseas shipping department of one store, in which they agreed to parcel up the purchases from all their competitors' stores, in exchange for a handful of tickets to the Wild Horses Saloon. Jet watched and learned as his father's informal but persuasive style rendered officious managers putty in his hands.

After an afternoon spent apart, Diamond Senior in the business centre of the hotel, catching up on e-mail and telephone messages, and Diamond Junior holed up in his room with his head in a university assignment, the pair arranged to meet in the lobby at six o'clock for a pre-dinner drink. Jeff had advised his son to dress smartly, having booked a table at a swanky restaurant behind *les Champs Elysées*.

'Why all the cloak and dagger?' the sportsman asked, relishing a mouthful of the evening's first alcoholic beverage. 'It still feels like I'm on a movie set with a different version of the script to yours.'

Jeff chuckled. 'That's very good, mate. I like the analogy. Not long to wait.'

Another taxi spat the celebrities out in front of a renovated nineteenth-century *Beaux-Arts* terrace. They ran inside without delay to avoid a group of young professionals who had spotted them while enjoying their own *apéritifs* at the bar next-door. With the restaurant already filling up with wealthy tourists and small groups of businesspeople, the manager showed his new arrivals to an alcove off the main dining area.

The indomitable Uncle Gerry was already seated and poring over the enormous menu, with a small pile of folders and envelopes on the table next to his vodka and tonic. He stood up when the Diamonds arrived, giving them each a vigorous hug.

'Bonsoir, Ryan,' his booming voice rang out, '*et bonsoir, papa*.'

'Bonsoir, Monsieur Blake,' the young man echoed. 'You already know about the "Ryan" thing? No secrets around here! Is this where I'm supposed to say, "Fancy meeting you here?"'

'Indeed,' Jeff answered with a chuckle. 'You never know who you're going to meet next in this city. How're ya going, mate?'

The billionaire's business partner tapped the leather briefcase which sat on the chair beside him, directing a sneaky thumbs-up sign to the father while taking pleasure in jerking the son's chain. It was obvious the two old friends had colluded in the previous twenty-four hours, enjoying their opportunity to have fun at the twenty-year-old's expense.

'Oh, for God's sake,' Jet moaned. 'What the hell's going on? Is anyone going to let me in on your special, old men's secret?'

Jeff shook his head and proceeded to order some drinks. 'Keep calm, my son. Let's wait for Julian. Patience is a virtue, remember?'

'Right,' the student sneered. 'This'd better be worth it.'

The Australian party's remaining guest arrived within the next ten minutes. Julian Manolescu had come straight from a conference in London, rushing to make his flight from Heathrow after presenting to a packed house. He appeared a little dishevelled and was still not fully adjusted to the time difference after his long journey from Melbourne.

'Julian's been advising me for the last few months, mate,' Jeff explained. 'We have a shared goal, similar to the one I had with Sarah Friedman with the PTSD research.'

'Ah, yeah? How similar?' Jet teased, knowing full well that much of this research had been analysed in the same bed.

His dad grinned. 'Not that similar.'

'What happens on tour stays on tour,' Gerry warned with a wag of his finger.

'Whatever,' the celebrity smiled. 'Julian, please could you give Ryan an update on what we've been doing? Then I can fill in the blanks I'm sure he'll have.'

'You don't have to call me Ryan. It sounds weird.'

'Your call, son,' his empathetic father responded, 'but you'll get used to it. It suits you.'

The accomplished academic looked from one man to the other. 'Certainly, Jeff. As you know, the Diamond Celebration Foundation has partnered with my medical faculty at Heriot-Watt and MIT to undertake some research into the ethics of suicide.'

'Jesus!' the accountant exclaimed. 'No sugar-coating, to be sure. Should we be talking about this here? At least keep it quiet.'

'Only if we believe it's unethical,' his VIP client answered, refusing to lower his voice. 'If you're uncomfortable, you're free to stay out of the discussion, Gez.'

The truth was that the superstar and his long-time friend and manager held opposing views about the legitimacy of a person taking his or her own life. Even though Gerry was hardly a shining example of Roman Catholic virtue, he remained a staunch believer, having had the full gamut of sins drummed into him from an early age.

He and Jeff had argued on several occasions since Lynn's demise about the rights and wrongs of giving up the fight. "*La Lutte*," as the linguist often quoted, in deference to the Nobel prizewinning philosopher and novelist Albert Camus of this very city.

'I completely understand your position, Gerry,' Julian added. 'And we haven't heard Ryan's point of view yet either. There's plenty of time to talk, either tomorrow or once we get back home.'

Jet raised his head in surprise. 'Except I'm not coming home,' he reminded them, 'as in Melbourne, I mean. Or am I expected to?'

'No. Absolutely not, mate,' his father insisted. 'What Julian means is we don't need to finalise tonight's business at this table. There's no need to make any rash commitments or decisions tonight. I just want you to be aware of the work he's doing, 'cause it has a bearing on this evening's main objective, which we haven't got to yet.'

The other two sages nodded, leaving the youngster unable to stop himself laughing. Drama was unfolding around him, and he still had no clue what said objective might be. The others' excitement was infectious, but in a rather sinister way.

'This is a fucking conspiracy,' he cursed. 'Can we get it all out in the open as soon as possible, and then I'll tell you what I think.'

'Cheers, mate,' said the compassionate dad. 'There's no conspiracy. It is, however... believe it or not... all about you. As I said yesterday, this dinner's about your future. The next episode in your rite of passage, I s'pose.'

'Can I ask a question of you, Julian, please?' the lad requested, after a few slow breaths in and out.

'Definitely,' the academic agreed.

'What's your own personal view of suicide?'

It was their guest's turn to inhale deeply, but the imposition didn't faze him or his shrewd sponsor. Gerry, on the other hand, became further agitated, scanning the doorway in case they were being overheard. Or worse, recorded.

'Relax,' Jeff urged, putting a hand on his friend's wrist. 'Please?'

'My views are being shaped by this research,' Julian admitted. 'What started out as a study looking for answers regarding the ability of terminally ill people to make rational decisions extended into the whole argument of whether the ability to end one's own life should or shouldn't be a fundamental human right.'

'Self-determination, you mean?' Jet checked.

'Yes. But also to explore the reasons which lead people to believe that suicide is an immoral or illegal act,' the professor told the under-graduate, 'be they religion-based or ethics-based or whatever.'

The blond athlete fixed his father with a stern glare. 'So Dad, you think that by you participating in the research, it'll somehow give greater credibility and justification to your own decision?'

A thick, glutinous silence descended over the circular table, and the Blake & Partners executive buried his head in the menu once again. This time, the scientist was also confounded by such a direct question, and he slumped back into his chair, staring into his wine glass and wondering how the great man might respond.

'It has crossed my mind,' Jeff nodded. 'But no. If there's a positive side effect, then that'd be an added bonus. It's not part of my motivation, if that's what you mean. It's a worthwhile investment. Not for me, but for other people like me.'

'Good,' the cricketer replied, satisfied for the moment. 'Sorry to interrupt, Julian. Please continue.'

The decorated scholar smiled, also feeling vindicated.

'Thank you, Jeff. But to answer Ryan's question, my personal view is that I believe people can get to the point where they no longer want to live and that, as such, they ought to be free to make any decision which affects their life without judgment.

However, our shared area of doubt is the not insignificant fact that there's always more than one person who has a stake in someone's life.'

'Bloody constituency again!' Jet burst out laughing, pointing at his dad. 'I bet that's where you came in.'

'Exactly,' Julian affirmed with a knowing smile. 'As a modern society, we agree or disagree on whether someone can decide to terminate a foetus' life. This debate's been in the public domain for several decades now. This new research is all about finding out if society has the capacity or inclination to agree or disagree on whether a grown person can make the decision to terminate their own life.'

'OK,' the twenty-year-old nodded. 'And Gerry, you obviously don't agree.'

'No, I do not,' the Diamond family's most loyal and long-serving supporter answered with a sigh. 'I'm a middle-class, Irish Catholic, private school boy. What hope do I have at being progressive? And even more so when I look at what you and your sister have been through this year. Why would I approve of something that'll give you more pain?'

'Thanks! That did occur to me too,' the mature teenager grinned, while the widower exhaled and momentarily averted his eyes. 'So do you object to the issue itself or to the fact that it touches people you know? I know the two perspectives are linked, but they're two different arguments, aren't they?'

Jeff could see the research scientist lapping up these useful data points but called them to pause for a while so they could place their food order. 'Incongruous as it may seem, friends,' he declared, 'I can't help thinking about The Last Supper. Let's choose our fare before we get carried away and the kitchen closes.'

'That's effing gross, Dad!' his son pulled a face. 'But we will have a Last Supper at some point, and that's what's really scaring me, regardless of what you've dragged me through the Chunnel to talk about tonight.'

Jeff gazed into the deep blue eyes of Lynn's beautiful boy, a kindly smile on his face. 'This is the project plan for our Last Supper, mate.'

Silence overtook the quartet again, unsure of the world-changer's next move. He allowed everyone time for their thoughts to settle, neither regretting nor revoking his portentous statement. There was no point trying to dress their situation up. They were caught in a predicament of his making and for which none had much appetite.

'Denial's not an option,' he stated, hitting the table hard with his fingers. 'Your opinions are gratefully received, guys, but when it comes down to it, the choice is all mine. I've already promised not to make the choice without my kids' endorsement.

'Apologies if I'm forcing you to play a game you don't enjoy, but I'm anxious not to turn this into some blind hero-worship thing, where I arrogantly direct you guys towards my demise. I took the decision some months ago to be open about my intentions, and maybe it was a bad decision. If you'd rather I don't involve you any further, tell me now.'

'Dad, I support you totally,' his son replied without hesitation. 'Kizzy and I've talked about it *ad nauseam*, and we're on the same page about it. The only thing is we'd much rather know when than just find you one day and have all these unanswered questions.'

Their sensitive discussion was suspended briefly to allow a heavily starched head waiter to take their order. Choices were made with considerable difficulty, given the number of mouth-watering dishes available. Another two bottles of wine arrived soon afterwards, and the conversation was reignited by the Romanian-born academic.

'So, Ryan... If you and your sister decide at any stage that you don't want your dad to go through with it, do you expect or want him to change his mind?'

The young man blew out through pursed lips. 'Bloody hell... Well, I'd want him to change his mind, sure, but I'm not sure I'd expect him to,' he answered. 'And that's the whole point, isn't it? Whose choice is it?'

'But, mate, what if *you* change your mind?' Gerry asked, seeing his oldest friend nodding in approval. 'Is there any chance you could wake up one day and think, "Y'know, I don't feel so bad anymore"? Other people get over losing someone special. We're designed to. Time heals.'

'I know,' the celebrity nodded. 'And I am healing. No doubt about it. But no. The only thing that sways me in the slightest is these two.'

The widower sighed and gestured towards the strapping blond, brim-full of promise, sitting on the opposite side of the table. This short distance had turned into a veritable gulf in the time it had taken him to answer Gerry's question.

'Some days, like when we were in Wales riding our bikes through the rain, I'd test myself,' he confessed. 'I'd look at this perfect example of procreation and say, "Do I really want to miss out on spending time with you?" Many times I feel strongly that I don't. But I also feel like I'm three-hundred years old, guys. I've already seen more action than most people do in seventy or eighty years.'

The select audience watched their host wince as if a sharp pain had shot through his chest. The academic and businessman gaped at him and then at each other with concern in their eyes, but his son simply smiled and waited for him to continue.

'I know I sound like a spoiled brat for wanting to chuck away everything good in my life. And yep, I know exactly how good I have it. Believe me, I know. Every time my credit card buys a designer-labelled suit for my son and every time I smell a homeless guy in the street, I remind myself how lucky I am, but it's not enough to make me want to change my mind. I'm tired, I'm pissed off and unfulfilled, and I've had enough of being half of the whole I'm meant to be.'

'And that's the crux of my research,' Julian took over, watching the great man wipe tears from his eyes. 'It's not about what you have or don't have, or what your circumstances are. It seems some people don't value their lives as highly as others value theirs. Should we each be able to put a different price on our life, or do we presume to give every life the same value as we'd give our own?'

Jet grinned at his father again. 'Bloody utility now! You've infiltrated his brain. Be afraid, Julian. Be very afraid.'

Everyone laughed. Even the executive in the corner saw the humour in the young man's remarks. Unusually, he had retreated into his shell, being more at home with business cases and spreadsheets than philosophical arguments about life and death. Empirical information was the accountant's tool of trade, not the conceptual and cerebral tennis match in play around him.

'A good illustration is Rod Germany,' the intellectual explained to his riveted audience. 'Remember him, mate?'

'Yeah,' his son answered, thinking back to a fellow Melbourne Academy student who had committed suicide in his early teens after a brief but successful music career. 'And you would've known him too, wouldn't you, Julian?'

'Vaguely,' the lecturer responded.

'I spent ages talking things through with him,' Jeff continued. 'He was too good for this world, or so he thought. Just couldn't tolerate the fact that bad things happened around him that he couldn't do anything about.

'He didn't want to be part of what he saw as a broken system, and in the end I agreed with him. If this was a position his mind and heart both shared, and he couldn't see a point in trying to adjust his expectations, why hang around?'

'So did you help him do away with himself?' Gerry's voice sounded accusatory.

'No. But I didn't try and stop him either,' the songwriter responded, unabashed. 'I believed it was his choice, and he'd made it rationally.'

'Fair enough,' his manager said. 'I get the idea.'

'That discussion we had a few weeks ago with Fiona and her dad...' Jeff then asked the Irishman to recall. 'Y'know... The one about voluntary euthanasia for people with terminal illnesses? That's where Julian and I started. If a sane, rational person at their full intellectual capacity can travel to a secret location, drink a final glass of red cordial and go to sleep, then why can't those who're not terminally ill? That's discrimination.'

Their entrées soon arrived at the table, calling another temporary halt to conversation. For the ensuing ten minutes, the cuisine's superb quality distracted the foursome from the morbid topic.

Knives and forks set to work on the artistic creations, delivered on large white platters, putting the philosopher in mind of Honoré de Balzac's Human Comedy series. Another quote sprang into his mind, this time from "La Rabouilleuse". Being in France always inspired him...

He raised his wineglass, followed by the others. 'As Max Gilet said in "The Black Sheep", "He had eaten as much as a travelling actor and drunk like the sands of the desert." Let's enjoy and leave here replete, out of respect for this young bloke here.'

The tattoo on the proud father's chest pulsated with a discernible thrill, and his gaze fell on his son's flushed face just as he lifted a large piece of rare poached salmon to his mouth. The youngster blushed and nodded his thanks without speaking.

'This food's bloody tasty,' Gerry crooned. 'I hope it's this good where you're going, mate.'

Jeff parried his fork at his friend, swallowing a mouthful down. 'Nice try, you bastard,' he teased. 'I know I'm going to miss a whole bunch of amazing shit. It's true. There are still heaps of things I can enjoy about my life, like food and wine and a good book, *et cetera*.'

'But the sum of all those good things still doesn't add up to losing one extra-special person,' Jet came to his Defence, 'does it, Dad?'

'No, son. It doesn't.'

Without warning, the widower stood up and excused himself from the table. His boy's spoken gift had hit him hard. This was not a view he had expressed to his children before, so no-one could accuse him of planting it. Jet had come to this conclusion all on his own. Not only did the comment affect the great man profoundly because it was perfect for his situation, but also because he knew he was about to inflict a similar unbalanced equation on his precious offspring.

Gerry was right. Jet and Kierney... Ryan and Kierney rather, the father corrected himself... had already endured one round of pain and loss, and here he was, preparing to impose upon them again. Knowingly. What kind of humanitarian was he? Somehow, through his audacious, heart-on-your-sleeve grief, he had persuaded two smart and caring young people to condone his egocentric plan. How dare he?

Standing in the street outside, facing the wall while he smoked so as not to attract any attention from the busy bars on either side, Jeff dried his eyes as he saw Julian approaching. The celebrity offered his packet of cigarettes to the younger man, who declined. They walked back into the restaurant together after a while, having agreed to bring this conversation to a close and focus on the evening's primary purpose.

The celebrity squeezed his son's shoulder when he returned to his seat. Their main courses had been delivered, and Gerry's fingers were poised to leap on the next pieces in the ostentatious array of cutlery. The host held his hands up to request their attention for a few more minutes.

'Hold on a sec', please. Now, before any of you accuses me of having a Christ complex again, let's draw a line under this subject and enjoy what remains of our dinner,' he proposed. 'Instead of saying I'm terminally ill, you can say I'm terminally ungrateful. I'm fine with that.

'What's the difference, eh? I can't remember how old I was when I first started wishing a plane would crash on top of our flat or that I'd contract some deadly disease so people wouldn't label me as ungrateful for not wanting to be alive. And since your mum passed away, Ryan, those same old obsessive opinions are back, and although the rest of me is healing, they only get louder and louder. Who's to judge if being terminally ungrateful is wrong? That's all I'm saying.'

The student said nothing. Picking up his knife and fork too, he merely smiled at his father and began to eat. The others did the same, while the widower wallowed in the steady sting of his "JL" tattoo.

They polished off the wine along with their food, the recently arrived Melburnians updating the travellers on the last few weeks' football highlights, and revealing which of the usual suspects had been in trouble for off-field shenanigans.

Soon exhausting the sports news, they moved on to mount a robust exploration of a model for financing clinical research on a bigger scale, which was one of Gerry's ambitions for a refreshed Diamond Celebration Foundation strategic plan. Then on a much lighter note as the alcohol lessened their interest in crucial matters, there followed a period of merriment concerning the student's various forays into the intricate world of the female psyche.

His main course finished, the twenty-year-old visited the restroom, providing his father with the perfect opportunity to retrieve his props from the accountant's briefcase. When the young man returned, a small box sat on the tablecloth, in the spot his empty plate had occupied a few minutes earlier.

The lad peered at his gift and then at its donor, who sat with an impish grin on his face and a wrapped cigar twisting through his fingers. 'A new car?' he joked, picking up the package and shaking it. 'Thanks, but you shouldn't have. Matchbox cars are overrated these days.'

Gerry refilled their glasses with wine from a third bottle, twisting the neck extravagantly after each pour to prevent the loss of a single drop. Jeff cleared his throat and lifted his glass to eye level, which his son and his old friend both took as a signal that he was about to launch forth on another weighty address. Julian sat back, almost an innocent bystander for the next agenda item.

'Mate, this small gift is the reason we're all here in Paris this week, and why I insisted you go out and have a good time last night.'

Ryan gulped. 'Holy crap! You're going to make me become a priest.'

'No, mate,' his father laughed. 'Although it could be arranged, if that's what you want.'

The red-blooded student shook his head and picked up the small, plain-wrapped package again, bidding his dad to continue.

'Over the last few months,' Jeff gazed back and forth between Gerry and his son, before explaining further, 'a good many conversations have been had with a good many people all over the world regarding our business interests. The upshot of all that hot air is that we're going to move Paragon Holdings' headquarters to the US over the next five years. Not sure which city as yet though. And that's where you come in.'

The billionaire pointed again to the box in front of the young man, inviting him to open it. Jet obliged, carefully unsticking the tape on one end and peeling off the paper. An engraved business card holder was sitting on another small packet.

'Thanks. It's the same as yours. Very cool. This looks like grown-up stuff,' he hesitated. 'Do I open this too?'

The other packet contained a batch of two hundred business cards. The teenager thumbed a card off the top of the pack, turned it face up and started reading. A familiar logo was etched into the upper right-hand corner, below which was a cluster of words that blew his mind:

> Ryan J B Dyson Diamond
> Chief Executive Officer
> Paragon Holdings Inc.

Jeff watched his son's eyes blink as he mouthed "Chief Executive Officer" in stunned surprise. The athlete's ample lung capacity stocked up on air before breathing it all out again to steady his nerves. Such a measured reaction pleased his father; even more so when he felt his pectoral muscle spike with pain and then settle down to the same slow, sensual tingling.

'Gerry'll be your Chairman,' the patriarch carried on, 'and also remains as CFO for the next three to five years, during which time I hope he'll phase out and retire into married bliss. For as long as you want him there, Ryan. And believe me, you do want him there.'

'For God's sake, I'll need you there!' Jet yelped, seeing the successful executive nod in solemn confirmation. 'Are you sure? I can't believe it. CEO?'

'Very sure, mate,' his father affirmed. 'You don't have to take us up on our offer, but we ask you to give it serious consideration. You're the right man for the job, son. Your sister'll also be on the Board, and you're both ready to be appointed to the Ethics Committee, under Julian's tutelage.'

The initial wave of surprise beginning to wear off, the fun-loving sportsman's head filled with an emotional pride. The more he thought about it, the more he realised he had never thought about it. His parents had often spoken of how the vast fortunes of their venture capital company would be transferred into the next generation's control in due course. Yet after his mother passed away, the possibility of taking over the family business had not occurred to him even once.

'Isn't this nepotism, Dad?'

'Yep, sure is. Why not? My parting shot! I've never claimed to be a saint,' Jeff acknowledged the hypocrisy. 'You can resign on Day One if you don't feel comfortable, or you could put a team around you and learn the ropes just like I did. I'm about to go public with our esteemed colleague's appointment to Chair the Ethics Committee, and his main function is to prod your conscience. Plus, he has the casting vote, should you and Kierney disagree on project outcomes and policy matters affecting research.'

'Wow! Cool. So when *is* Day One? If I agree to accept your offer, that is...'

'Whenever you're ready, mate,' Gerry jumped in. 'Today, if you like, and you can delegate immediate authority to me until you graduate. Or we can appoint a caretaker until you're ready to take it on. We can work out a schedule over e-mail in the next few weeks. I'm totally flexible. We just need to be transparent for ASIC, and the SEC for when we move to the US.'

'ASIC? SEC?'

'Parrot face,' Jeff chided, needling his son's growing self-worth. 'The Australian Securities and Investment Commission.'

'Thanks, Dad. I *do* know that much,' smiled the boy who would be King. 'Though 'til now, ASIC's only been something I've read about in economics books or hear on the news when a company's in trouble. Now I'm going to be right in the middle of it. Holy shit!'

The outgoing CEO grinned. 'You shall indeed, son. Up to your neck in shit, just like I've been for the past twenty-odd years. You can leave all that stuff to the genius on your left. He takes care of all the governance bullshit... I mean, bureaucracy... You only have to sign on the dotted line. That's what I've done for all this time.'

'Including the memo about his pay rise?' Julian quipped.

'Shhh!' Gerry hissed. 'I told you to keep quiet about that.'

'Yeah. Not in front of the new CEO,' his mate uttered a theatrical aside, shielding his mouth with his hand. 'Anyway, Ryan... It's yours if and when you want it. Sleep on it, and we can talk more when you get back from EuroDisney.'

Astonished, the financial wizard's jaw dropped open. 'EuroDisney!' he exclaimed. 'We've just handed him the keys to a multi-billion-dollar conglomerate, and now you tell me he's off to EuroDisney tomorrow?'

Jeff shrugged, taking a mouthful of the smooth *Côtes du Rhône Grenache Mourvèdre* and savouring the pepper and raspberry in a liquid as dark as blood. He reached over and picked up the empty bottle to examine the label, distracted by another intense sensation which showed no sign of abating.

'You expect me to work with this man, Lord Sparkle?' his manager laboured the point. 'Jesus, Mary and Joseph! It'll be just like you all over again.'

'Well, you'd better hurry up and retire then.'

'No! Please don't,' Jet piped up. 'Not 'til I know what I'm doing.'

Back in Cambridge at the beginning of August 1996, the Diamond men spent the last few days of their bonding trip together at a three-day county cricket match in

Southampton, on the south coast of England. Warwickshire was second on the championship leader-board, with only four matches left in the season. Taking advantage of a warm, still afternoon, Jeff sat with his laptop computer on his knees for as long as its battery lasted, writing his autobiography with one eye on the men in white.

Since Paris, the billionaire had talked at length with the elated undergraduate about his new role as the figurehead of Paragon Holdings, nutting out a solid plan with their indomitable colleague over the telephone. A transition schedule in place, the proposal sat ready for the Board's endorsement later in the year.

Any residual guilt Jeff harboured for leaving his son in the lurch was dissipating, just in time to receive a new dose from his daughter. As far as he was concerned, his one saving grace was knowing the children were now speaking to each other regularly and about a settled future.

Another idea was germinating in the great man's busy head, desperate to fuel his flagging imagination with tasks he could dive into once he returned to Melbourne. Instead of flying directly home, he had plotted a course for Sydney to join Kierney, who had arranged for Suzanne to board Indie while the dark-haired pair attended a human rights symposium she had helped to arrange in her father's home town.

Late on this final Sunday afternoon, with the sun low enough in the sky to be dazzling his eyes, the illustrious father watched his son take a hat-trick of Hampshire tailenders. The drained laptop almost slid off his lap as he clapped and whistled along with a host of ardent fans. Before too long, the last man fell, and the match was over.

'Hey, Dad! How're you going?' Jet shouted, dropping his long, heavy cricket bag onto the ground and gulping his way through a two-litre bottle of water.

'Good, thanks, mate,' the vociferous fan answered. 'Why aren't you catching up with the lads? I'm fine to wait. You need to celebrate.'

'No. I'd like to get on the road, if that's alright. I promised Lisa I'd be home in time to take her to a party at uni'. You're welcome to come too.'

Jeff laughed. 'Cheers, but I'll pass. I'll only get stuck talking kindergarten politics again. I'm on a roll with the book, and my battery's flat, so I'll be fine at your place with mains power, a burger and *une carafe de vino viejo*.'

'OK, if you're sure,' Warwickshire's star player hugged his dad's shoulders, suddenly overcome with emotion. 'This has been a fantastic few weeks. I hope you realise how much I appreciate you being here.'

'I do, son. And me too. I think we've both learned a lot. I'm going to miss you heaps, but I've stayed long enough, haven't I?'

'Perhaps,' the lad hesitated. 'I'm glad you said it. It's not that I want you to go, because I absolutely don't, but it's getting to the stage when we're thinking each other's thoughts, which is kind of boring.'

'True enough. I'll piss off then, shall I?'

The twenty-year-old frowned. 'No. Or yes. How should I know? Are you going to be alright? Now I feel awful.'

The handsome musician grabbed the player's unwieldy bag, and the pair of Diamonds strolled towards their rental car. Several fans cried out to them, and a few scurried over to request autographs. Throwing the holdall into the boot and laying his laptop on the floor behind the driver's seat, Jeff slammed the door and started the engine.

'You played well, son,' he said. 'You never look rushed. That's a good skill, over and above all the technique and the killer instinct.'

'Cheers, but I'm serious. Are you going to be alright back home?'

'Yeah, mate,' the father answered. 'I'm off to the conference with Kizzy, then I'm going to be flat out organising Gerry's buck's party, for which I'd like your help at the end of next term if possible. And then there's his damned wedding. And on top of all this, I've got the book to finish.'

'Yeah. It's good to know there's a plan. How's the autobiography going? Can I see it?'

'Sure. It's in bits and pieces at the moment. I've yet to decide how it all fits together, but you're welcome to take a peek. Your sister's seen some of it.'

'Will I like it?'

'Hope so,' the author smiled. 'I hope your mum likes it, more to the point. I hope I do her justice.'

'Why the hell wouldn't you?'

His dad chuckled. 'Yeah, you're right. Why the hell wouldn't I?'

The next few months passed much faster than the widower expected. In the week before the start of his final year at Cambridge, his son made a flying visit home to participate in a concert to give the Australian athletes an appropriate send-off for the Atlanta Olympics.

The event was part of a long-standing pledge of Lynn's to make a fundraising album to help unsponsored sportsmen and women pay for their village accommodation. Her children had honoured this obligation with their father's blessing. The program of songs by various artists was to be called "A Thousand Voices", as a tribute to a similar project the renowned record producer had launched in the early eighties to coincide with her husband's thirtieth birthday.

Neither youngster put themselves up for selection for the Games themselves. Even Jet, the irrepressible champion whose training régime had suffered minimally from the turmoil earlier in the year, considered the extreme level of dedication required for competing against the best in the world was beyond him.

As they feared, Bart Dyson had exerted a certain amount of pressure on the duo, assuring them the extra routine of strict training would help them recover from their mother's death more rapidly. Jeff made it clear to the stalwart that his children would be making up their own minds about competing, despite being in no doubt that the elder statesman was correct in this instance.

He was secretly overjoyed when neither child grabbed an opportunity for sporting glory. He knew Jet and Kierney felt the lead weight of public sympathy weighing on their shoulders and wondered whether perhaps this was their way of ensuring there were no free rides in Georgia.

As the end of September clicked round, Jeff noticed a peculiar sense of euphoria creeping into his core, as if a momentous occasion were imminent. He and Kierney joined the Dyson family at Benloch on what would have been Lynn's forty-first birthday, for a quiet dinner and a chance to exchange happy memories.

After dessert, catching her son-in-law alone in the hallway on her way to make coffee, Marianna drew him to one side. She was nervous, her hands grabbing his forearm.

'May I ask you a question, darling?'

The tall man stared into the woman's eyes while trying to dislodge her determined fingers from his shirt sleeve without offending her. Physical contact from anyone other than his children was still hard for him to stomach, especially when accompanied by a voice which echoed his beautiful best friend.

'Sure. Are you alright?'

'Yes, Jeff.'

She stopped in her tracks at the sight of the willowy, raven-haired gipsy walking towards them, carrying a tray of mugs back to the dining room from the kitchen. As Kierney got closer, the others saw excitement on her face.

'Grandma, Brandon's on the phone,' she reported. 'I think Anna's had the baby!'

'Oh, my God!' Marianna yelped, abandoning her quest in an instant. 'Thank you, darling.'

Jeff watched his mother-in-law turn tail and almost sprint into the lounge room, whence they could hear cheerful voices. The Diamonds grinned at their host's reaction and followed at a steadier pace, the teenager still laden with china and silverware.

'What were you talking about?' she asked.

'Don't know. I think Grandma was about to say something serious but clammed up when she saw you. Obviously about your *mamá*.'

'Oh,' Kierney smiled. 'Probably. Or about me being left in the house on my own. She was fishing for gossip earlier, saying I must be scared. I told her you were mean and locked me in my room while you were away, so I wouldn't get up to mischief.'

The doting dad laughed. 'Gee, thanks! That's gotta go down well with the grandparents. Well done. Thanks for your support.'

'*De nada, papá*. It's a bit spooky that Anna's baby's born on *mamá*'s birthday, isn't it?'

They turned sharp right into the enormous living room, depositing the tray onto the sideboard. The others were gesticulating for them to come closer. The baby had indeed been born; a little girl. Already opening a bottle of champagne, Bart signalled for his son-in-law to fetch some glasses.

The widower's heart beat off the clock, overtaken by a bout of dizziness. What should he make of this event? It was still only the 19th of September in London, where his wife's younger sister and her husband lived. It wasn't yet Lynn's birthday there, but the baby's arrival unnerved him nevertheless.

Please don't let Lynn's soul be reborn already, he pleaded in silence, though he knew not to whom. *And not into the Dyson family again...*

Jesus Christ! The musician propped himself against the mahogany buffet, temporarily losing his balance. It was to his good fortune that everyone else was so engrossed in conversation, waiting for their turn to talk to the brand new father.

Jeff steadied his nerves and crouched down in front of the open sideboard door, buying himself some time by pretending to search for the right type of flutes. The tattoo on his chest gave him no clue, and tears pricked at the back of his eyes. His beautiful best friend would never play such a cruel joke if it were within her power...

Please, no. Please, no.

'What are you doing over there, Jeff?' Bart was growing impatient. 'Can I pop this bloody cork or not? The bottle's getting warm.'

'Sure. Yeah,' the forty-four-year-old answered, feeling fifteen again as usual. 'Sorry. Coming right up.'

He slotted four upturned glasses between the fingers of his right hand and returned to the others. Kierney's eyes flashed as she noticed the worry on his face, but he said nothing, twisting a flamboyant hand over and sliding the crystal onto the table with all the dexterity of a sommelier.

Before his daughter could press the issue, the telephone was handed to her. 'Hello? Hi, Brandon. Congratulations! How's Anna? Is she really tiny? Oh, that's so cute. Oh. Cool! Yes. It's lovely. I don't know. He's right here. Do you want to talk to him now? OK, thanks. Yes. Congratulations again. Say congrats to Anna too. Thanks. Bye.'

The eighteen-year-old held the receiver out towards her father, whose face had turned paler than ever. He smiled and accepted it, giving her a wink and caressing her flushed cheek with his left index finger.

'Brandon, mate. Great news! Congratulations from me too.'

The muscle above the songwriter's heart gave an almighty twinge, purging his lungs of every breath of air. What did this mean? Was Lynn still with him after all? He hoped so with all his might, sitting down on the arm of a convenient couch and beckoning for Kierney to join him. She leant into his body and kissed his temple, drawn in by a needy hand.

'Names? Why? That's your...' the widower sighed, unable to stem the tide of tears any longer while the others looked on aghast. 'Victoria? Sure. No. Of course I don't mind. Why should I mind? She's your daughter. Does Marianna mind, more to the point?'

Please don't let this little namesake be my next dream girl, his tormented brain stressed. *Please!*

Jeff looked up at his mother-in-law from under a furrowed brow. Her expression was one of confusion. Surely Brandon had spoken to the baby's grandmother about their decision to name her after the departed Dyson daughter. Instead, the quiet Canadian had sought permission from her lover.

'It's not my place to mind, mate. You'd better clear it with the proud grandparents. Here, I'll hand you over. Send my love to Anns.'

The emotional man heaved himself to his feet and waved the receiver in the air. Marianna reached for it and spoke with the caller while Kierney took a seat on her dad's trembling thigh and tried to feed him champagne to cheer him up.

'Are you OK? What's happened?'

Jeff played along, allowing her to tip the bubbling liquid into his mouth and laughing as it fizzed and spilled out on either side of the glass. He moved his head backwards and wiped his chin with the back of his hand, prompting her to pull her hand away and drink some herself.

'Do they want to name the baby after *mamá*? Is that what made you cry?'

'Yep. Partly. Tell you later. That's probably what Grandma was going to ask me before the news came through. Maybe she was supposed to sound me out before the baby arrived.'

The call from London eventually came to an end, though not before another round of raucous good wishes passed on by the baby's grandfather. Colour had returned to Jeff's face, and Marianna disappeared to finish making the after-dinner beverages which had been forgone in the commotion.

Bart told the others that the young couple had been planning to call their daughter "Vienna", after a song Lynn had written with Steve Christie a long time ago. The grieving husband backed up his father-in-law, saying he remembered this early choice had always been a favourite of Anna's.

His beautiful best ghost was still with him for the time being, judging by the persistent itching under his shirt, and it gave him hope that his wicked mind had jumped to an erroneous conclusion.

'What were you going to ask me earlier?' he asked the lady of the house, who was now pouring coffee for her family.

'Oh, nothing, dear,' Marianna stalled. 'I wanted to catch you in private. It can wait.'

Jeff smiled. 'Kizzy's much stronger than me, as you can see. Whatever you want to ask, she can handle it.'

The elegant woman let out a deep sigh, reluctant to raise the subject while the widower was still recovering from the previous assault on his precarious state of mind. She had been cornered though, and Bart's interest had now also been piqued.

She blurted out her question. 'Very well. I was daring to enquire as to the whereabouts of Lynn's ashes.'

Once again, the household plunged into an awkward silence, their eyes darting from one to the other. The Olympian shook his head, perhaps considering his wife's timing to be less than perfect.

Kierney fielded the question before her father could gather his thoughts. 'We haven't decided yet, Grandma,' her response gave nothing away. '*Mamá*'s at home with us. Isn't that right, *papá*?'

Her father nodded in gratitude, rubbing the front of his shirt. 'She is indeed. That's right. We'll let you know once we've figure out what we're going to do. Is that OK? It's a big decision, and we're not ready to make it yet.'

CLOSING IN

Gerry's wedding date was set for the second Saturday in December; the same week as his forty-seventh birthday. Fiona had asked Kierney to be a bridesmaid, and the polite young woman had declined, saying she wasn't up to participating in such a joyful occasion. On the whole however, despite this, the Diamonds were glad to assist with the grand affair.

The ebullient executive had been the linchpin behind Jeff's own bucks' party, all those years ago. Without question, it was a night still without rival. In return, his VIP client began to painstakingly piece together an event which he hoped would go some way towards paying his friend back for the loyalty, care and attention he had lavished on the family ever since.

In a lifestyle a far cry from the affluence and sophistication of the inner suburb of Toorak, the girlfriend with whom Gerry originally travelled down from Sydney still ran the boarding kennels she had inherited, hidden in the coincidentally named Diamond Creek. With the morning to himself, Jeff drove out with Indie at five o'clock to meet Suzanne for the early walk, as he had done after many a sleepless night in those first few months in Melbourne.

With the weeks ticking by, the ancient soul felt somehow compelled to tie his life's remaining loose ends together, as if it helped him leave everything in its rightful state.

'Suzie, if one more journalist writes about me being a shadow of my former self...' he complained, trudging through the paddock behind the back pens.

'What will you do?'

'Fucked if I know,' the tired man sighed. 'It's a very apt expression, I have to admit, but I've heard it and read it a thousand times. Can't they think of any original way to describe me?'

Suzanne was never one to refrain from offering a frank opinion, which was one of the main reasons for the morning's meeting. True to form, she rattled off all the remedies she thought would aid his recovery, unaware of his elaborate plan. The inquisition, peppered with these useful suggestions, came thick and fast. Was he sleeping? Was he eating? Was he happy in the house? Was he getting enough physical contact?

'Physical contact?' Jeff interrupted with a wry smile. 'You mean sex? Why don't you ask if I'm getting my rocks off?'

'Well, are you?' the conservative woman pressed, every bit the country girl these days.

'No,' the widower snapped. 'And neither do I want to, so leave my sex life alone.'

Suzanne frowned. 'Oh, shut up, Mr Precious! Steve and I care about you. We know full well how much you still miss Lynn. You need to satisfy your basic needs, or you won't recover for a long time. I've been reading all these self-help books, at first because of my own grief, but also on your behalf.'

Shaking his head, the celebrity put his arm around the carpenter's wife. It was flattering to hear she was going to such lengths to improve his lot, but her well-meaning intentions were absurd. Regardless, he thought better of being as forthright as to tell her so.

'You don't have to go to "Lost Lovers Anonymous" on my behalf,' he teased. 'Let me sort my own grief out, please.'

'But you do need to help yourself.'

'I know, I know. For Christ's sake! And please don't quote Maslow at me, Suze. I know what's on the foundation layer of Diamond's Hierarchy of Needs, and she ain't here anymore, OK? End of story.'

The kind woman pouted. 'Fair enough. I'm sorry. Are you talking to a counsellor at least?'

'I told you before, the kids are my counsellors,' Jeff replied, ruing his flippant comment but also interested to see how the amateur psychologist might respond.

Suzanne's eyes drilled into his. 'And I told you before, that's too much of a burden on them.'

The widower relented, knowing his friend only wanted the best for him and the children. She had been very fond of his absent wife too. The couple had invited him to dinner regularly in the early months after Lynn passed away, and he knew he ought to be grateful. The kids would benefit from such good-hearted friends in the near future, so he wasn't up for alienating anyone for the sake of his own bitter pride.

'Yep. I hear you, and you're not wrong. I do see counsellors, off and on. In fact, Kizzy and I are going out to Escondido for one last visit before it gets locked up, and we're taking one of the psychs from The Fellowship with us for exactly that reason. I don't want Kierney to have to cope with me if I crack up.'

'Oh, excellent. I'm happy to hear that. Really good, Jeff. When are you going? Would Kierney like some support too?'

'Thanks for the offer,' the father replied, not relishing additional company on what promised to be a harrowing day. 'I'll ask her. It's tomorrow actually. I'm not looking forward to it one bit. We've had everything taken out, so it won't be as bad as the last time I was there, surrounded by all Lynn's stuff and our photos, *et cetera*. It'll be like a "For Sale" house, I hope.'

'What about Jet? Doesn't he want to say goodbye to the house he grew up in?'

'He did already,' Jeff responded, impatient with the unending cross-examination. 'All good. I didn't leave him out. The kids went over together when he was here in early September. He hated it in fact. Felt nothing, or so he said. He told me he couldn't wait to leave.'

'What's happening with the cars?' Suzanne's questions kept coming. 'Have you got room for them at the new house?'

The visitor let out a melancholy groan. 'Yeah. We're fine, thanks. All taken care of. A few've been sold already. The old Aston's been boxed up in storage somewhere near the airport, and Kiz has laid claim to that. Jet's in two minds whether to hold onto Lynn's Maserati, and I'm still swapping between the Disco' and the new Aston.'

'Oh, yes! I forgot you got a new one. It's almost brand new, isn't it?'

'Why? D'you want it?' the billionaire snapped.

'No. I'm sorry. Of course I don't. What would I do with a car like that? Let's get back to the house and have some breakfast. I'm just saying you can keep any cars you haven't got room for here. You're welcome.'

'Cheers,' the celebrity acknowledged her offer, planting a fond kiss on her forehead. 'And I'm sorry too. I've got a pretty short fuse when it comes to too many questions. Brekkie sounds great.'

The billionaire and the kennel-maid strolled towards the ramshackle buildings and secured the fifteen bouncy charges into their pens. Washing their hands in icy water from the outdoor sink, Jeff made Suzanne squeal by flicking heavy droplets at her face.

Steve, the master tradesman, ran out of the house in response to the high-pitched screeching. 'You're looking much better these days,' he said, shaking their guest's hand. 'You've put on weight.'

'Yeah. Cheers, mate. I've gotta look my best in case Lynn decides to come back. Don't want to give her the idea I'm not up for it anymore.'

Steve frowned at his wife, not sure how to respond.

'Don't listen to him,' Suzanne instructed. 'He always gets sarcastic like this when he's hungry. Go read the paper, and we can have some coffee while the barby warms up.'

Dr Kenneth Cook arrived at the Diamonds' rented house early the following morning and drove with Jeff and Kierney out towards the coast and their former family home. A task force orchestrated by Cathy and overseen by Lynn's mother had kindly made an inventory of everything in the house, and many decisions were made independent of the grieving husband as to the fate of his wife's belongings.

Over recent weeks, the widower had noticed one or two familiar items appearing in Kierney's room, confident that much of her mother's clothing had been hung in her wardrobe too. She didn't tend to wear these pieces in his company. Apart from the contents of his bedroom, which had all been transported to the rental house anyway, Jet had shown scant interest in objects from the house.

He had asked no questions during this difficult process and now felt surprisingly at ease, driving along the Princes Highway towards sleepy Mount Eliza with his daughter to his left. In the back seat behind the rock star sat a long-time associate from The Fellowship, the charity that ran mental health drop-in centres all over Australia. Having used their services many times as an adolescent, their good cause had been adopted and transformed by the successful musician as soon as he achieved fame and fortune.

Several pieces of artwork and sculptures the family had collected were offered to the National Gallery of Victoria. The curators were delighted to add these to their display stock, excited at the prospect of attracting a whole new cadre of visitors. Cathy Lane had arranged for the recording studio equipment to go to the music therapy centre adjoining The Fellowship's headquarters in the inner suburb of Collingwood, while most of Escondido's furniture had been snapped up by Stonebridge Music employees as souvenirs of an era now passed.

'So we're pretty much going to an empty shell,' Jeff explained to the respected psychiatric consultant. 'The house'll be locked up until the summer's over, after which it'll be converted into a residence for people with acute depressive disorders.'

'Really? That's excellent news,' Ken responded. 'I hear the place is pretty well secured, so it'll be perfect. You're very generous.'

'My kids are very generous,' the humble celebrity corrected him, grinning at his daughter. 'They're allowing me to squander their inheritance.'

'It's not squandering it,' Kierney refuted with a smile. 'I really love the idea.'

The young woman also had mixed feelings about farewelling the house where she had grown up. Part of Cathy's task force, she had visited several times over the last few months, helping her grandmother and Michelle sort through her mum's personal effects.

She had needed no coaxing to participate, and the process had encouraged the significant females in Lynn's life to exchange fond memories and to express their feelings of loss with each other. The only one privy to the dark truth ahead, it had made her miss her mother more and increased her fears for the day when she would also lose her father.

Looking across at her dad while he drove at top speed down the highway, Kierney couldn't help but wonder whether he might regret his decision, or even change his mind altogether. His outlook seemed more positive in recent weeks, but she surmised this was only because time was closing in on his departure date.

Her brother had told her how adamant their father had become about giving up control of Paragon Holdings, which to the enthusiastic son and heir was a clear indication that the outgoing Chairman and CEO's mind was not for changing. The booming, publicly-listed enterprise was his pride and joy. He had built it from nothing into a corporate body with a heart and a soul; an entity the experts had assured him was impossible to sustain.

Indie barked in the rear of the car as Escondido's substantial automatic gates swang open. The Monroes' two diligent Jack Russells lolloped alongside the black four-wheel drive, escorting it past their own cottage and as far as the courtyard walls where a three-metre-high, wooden portico safeguarded the Diamonds' sanctuary.

'Shut up, boy,' Jeff growled, catching the doctor's startled expression in the rear-view mirror, the loud noise so close behind his left ear. 'Wait 'til we get out. Sorry about that, Ken.'

The housekeepers, Ross and June, heard the crackle and crunch of the Land Rover's fat tyres on the gravel and had set out across the driveway to greet their employer. Formalities over, the elderly couple made themselves scarce once again. They were moving out of the gatehouse too, into a spacious apartment that Jeff had bought for them in the centre of Melbourne. Having resigned themselves to a comfortable retirement, they were now enthused about immersing themselves in the many cultural and sporting events they had missed out on while living forty kilometres from the city.

June left the widower with a bunch of keys and remote controls. He rattled them to attract Indie's attention before handing them to his daughter, who could see several beads of sweat forming on his brow. His breathing was laboured too.

Taking the set of keys and making her selection, she took his hand when tears welled up in his eyes. 'It'll be fine, *papá*. It's empty.'

'*Gracias, pequeñita,*' her father whispered. '*Te amo.*'

Indie pawed at the closed door, excited to gain entry into this new playground. Using the dog as an excuse, Jeff backed off and allowed the teenager to unlock the door and enter first. He then motioned to Ken to follow her, bringing up the rear and hanging onto the collar of the bouncing bundle of potential energy.

The jaded father watched as his gorgeous gipsy girl walked through the hall and straight round towards the kitchen, slapped by a vivid memory from a day when he had collected the children from school and driven out of the city. Tears began to flow as he pictured Jet and Kierney running to find Lynn, bursting to tell her the day's stories, repeating lines identical to those he had heard in the car on the way home.

At the bottom of the stairs, Jeff stopped and sat down on the second step, hiding his head in his hands. The six feet of his two patient therapists stood in front of him, the hairy muzzle of one trying to force his master's hands apart so he could lick the salty tears he could smell.

'It's OK,' the two-legged one said. 'The shock'll pass. What's going through your head?'

'I'm seeing ghosts,' the helpless man laughed, looking up into Ken's eyes while fondling Indie's ears and neck. 'Little kids who can't wait to see their *mamá*. And a big kid who can't wait to see her either.'

The eighteen-year-old came running back into the hallway, wondering why no-one had followed her. It made Jeff cry all over again.

'What's wrong?' she asked, sitting down on the stair beside him. 'Come and walk round. It's like someone else's place. I can hardly remember where everything used to be.'

'Good advice,' the counsellor nodded. 'Take us on a tour, mate.'

With a deep sigh, the former master of the house heaved himself up onto his feet and slapped his thigh, sending Indie into a spin. They retraced Kierney's steps down the long corridor to the gymnasium and the changing rooms. The door out to the swimming pool was locked, and the water greenish and stale-looking after the winter's disuse.

'Fancy a dip?' the celebrity joked, giving his daughter a gentle nudge.

'Ew! No, thanks. Is the gym' equipment staying?'

'Yeah. For now. Most of this stuff's virtually new. Hardly run-in.'

The teenager groaned. 'Was that supposed to be funny?'

Ken Cook chuckled behind her, making her swing round in surprise. She had forgotten she wasn't on her own with her beloved *papá*. Jeff noticed her reaction and did an about-turn, opening the office door and stepping aside for the others to enter. Indie had wandered off in search of more exciting smells, since this room had been stripped of everything interesting, save two large mahogany desks and a few chairs.

Jeff leant against the doorframe. Marks of paint discolouration in certain spots gave away where enlarged photographs of various album covers and other significant posters charting the couple's careers had been removed. Following his eyes as they scanned the room with loving care, Kierney waited for him to rub his chest or provide some other signal that he and Lynn were in communication.

'Jesus, Kizzo,' he gasped, all colour drained from his face. 'All the momentous decisions made in this room... All gone. As if we were never here.'

'Where did the computers go?' the youngster asked. 'It does look very bare. And your beach picture? *Mamá* loved that picture so much. Where did it go?'

'Don't know, *pequeñita*. Cath's got it all somewhere. I've got the photos from our desks, piled up on the floor in the new office. Let's move on, shall we?'

The psychiatrist placed a hand on the struggling man's shoulder, and the threesome walked into the kitchen together. Again, except for the fitted cupboards and the modern, stainless steel appliances, everything was cleared out. Gone even were the table and chairs at which the young family used to eat breakfast while looking out over the patio to the pool and the gardens beyond. The absence of furniture made the space look vast.

Jeff unlocked the glass door and slid it open. Indie's acute hearing picked up a familiar sound, and he came bounding round the corner from the lounge room, his claws slipping on the polished floorboards. He raced outside, and his audience burst out laughing as he came face-to-face with a large expanse of blue-green water and was forced into an emergency stop.

Pushing the door closed again and leaving the dog to explore the gardens for a while, the forty-four-year-old continued the tour. They left the kitchen and turned towards the formal dining room, which was intact apart from some paintings which had also been taken down and packed away.

'I bet this room's witnessed some good conversations,' Ken chimed in, anxious to keep the patient from drifting too far into himself. 'And some very famous guests.'

The world-changer nodded. 'You're not wrong, mate. I can't think how many people we'd have invited here over the years. Musos, of course... Activists, politicians, sportspeople... And business associates, doctors, academics... The list goes on.'

'Did you keep a guestbook?'

Jeff let out a sarcastic chuckle. 'Nope! We didn't seek their feedback.'

'*Papá*, that's not what Dr Cook meant,' Kierney scolded. 'A guestbook would be very interesting to read all those names now. It'd be a fantastic historical record of your life and career.'

'Yeah, sure. That's very true. Sorry, guys. Just ignore me.'

His daughter skipped across the hallway tiles and took her father's hand, leading him through double doors into the large space they called the playroom. It had a low stage at one end, and the blackout curtains along one side were still pulled back from when the windows had been cleaned. Sunlight streamed in across the floorboards, over which a wide range of musical instruments, music stands, tables and chairs used to be strewn.

This room was where the family and their friends would gather to jam or to party. Hundreds, if not thousands, of hit songs had been written here. Countless spontaneous children's plays enacted during school holidays, and many a romantic encounter between husband and wife had begun at the grand piano that was now also elsewhere.

Jeff freed the young woman's hand and walked alone towards the stage to retrieve a scrap of paper which lay on the dusty wooden boards. He picked it up, yearning to find a special message from his beautiful best friend. It was blank. Screwing it up into a ball, he cast the crumpled missile aloft with all his strength, aiming for the back of the raised platform, and it rolled all the way to the far wall.

The award-winning performer span around and roared at the top of his lungs, desperate to purge the despair which gripped his chest and head. The acoustics of the high ceiling with its purpose-built baffle boards rebounded his voice, amplified still louder. The teenager put her hands over her ears and smiled in sympathy, while Ken stood by with the blank countenance of a consummate professional. They could hear Indie barking through the windows, probably wondering why his master was in such distress.

The widower's jangling emotions were now better under control, despite longing for a sign from his dream girl. The others had already returned to the hallway, so he followed them at pace, venting yet more aggression by slamming the grand doors closed.

Kierney jogged ahead to the kitchen to fetch the dog, who was pleased to find he had protected them all perfectly well from the outside. 'Are we going upstairs?' she asked. 'Do you want to?'

'Yes and no,' her father answered, making the girl giggle as usual.

'*Bueno.* I want to go on your balcony and look at the ocean. Can we, please?'

'Sure thing, *pequeñita.* Show me the way, *por favor.*'

Ken followed the loving pair up the dramatic, curved staircase and into what he assumed must be Lynn and Jeff Diamond's bedroom. Never in his life had he imagined himself in this location, and considering his position now, he would much rather it be in different circumstances.

Dr Cook had taken charge of the clinical division of The Fellowship five years ago. He had worked in London for the Maudsley Hospital, where he first encountered the work of Professor Sarah Friedman. He and his current client had become regular e-mail correspondents, and later firm friends after a particular case brought the lettered professional to Australia to speak at a conference at which the lyrical philosopher was also booked to deliver a keynote.

The doctor's specialisation lay in promoting the vital role of the sufferer's family in the treatment of mental illness, and he had been fascinated by Lynn's account of dealing with her husband in the early days, as compared to later in their marriage.

Now seeing the great man walking around his former home, disassociated and conflicted, Ken was grateful for the insights the stunning and compassionate beauty had provided during these times. The room they had entered was indeed the master bedroom, but it boasted no sumptuous furnishings and its walls were bare.

The widower stopped in the centre of the room and took a deep inward breath before expelling it again. 'This house is our marriage, our family,' he announced. 'It's everything I existed for, and yet this house is foreign to me now.'

'Even this room?' the doctor asked.

'Especially this room,' Jeff emphasised with little emotion. 'It doesn't feel like home. Or rather, it feels like it used to be someone else's home that I once visited. Maybe... Something like that.'

'Does it make you sad?'

'Actually, no,' the celebrity turned around and focussed on the psychiatrist.

Kierney wandered around in slow circles, lost in thought. She ran her fingers along the wall where their childhood had been mapped out by annual photographs. Even the notches in the paintwork which had marked their steady increase in height had been rectified.

'Whose house do you think it is, *papá*?' she asked.

'Don't know, baby. Whose does it feel like to you?'

'No-one's,' the young woman replied. 'It's vacant, like a museum almost. All the souls have left. I feel the same as you, pretty much.'

'Yep. Think you're right,' her father nodded, walking over and wrapping her slender frame in his arms.

He clung on to his dark-haired daughter as she cried. Strangely enough, even though he was only too cognisant of her pain, he didn't feel in the least bit like crying. He was at peace, if anything.

As they often had when his gorgeous gipsy girl was much smaller, the tall, handsome man walked her over towards the balcony, her feet balanced on top of his own. She giggled, resisting his movement like the playful toddler she once was. Kissing the back of her hand, he opened the left-hand door and invited her to step outside.

'Is *mamá* here?' the nervous teenager asked, hanging on to her dad's clammy palm with one hand and rubbing the breast pocket of his shirt with the other.

'No.'

Jeff wrapped her long fingers in his and lifted them to his mouth. With her fingertips pressed against his lips, they both stood together without speaking.

'I'll see you downstairs later,' Ken called out from the bedroom doorway. 'Call me if you need me.'

Turning around to thank the tactful doctor, the celebrity closed the French windows and let the strong wind from off the bay buffet around them. To his surprise, Kierney tugged on the handle again, propping the glass door ajar with an old stone which had sat there for as long as she could remember.

'This needs to be open,' she told her father, 'in case *mamá* comes back.'

Clenching his teeth, Jeff finally gave in to the intense but sweet, painful tears that had gathered behind his eyes. He blinked them away so as not to upset this caring, complex child.

'She's not coming back, gorgeous. Not here anyway.'

The doting father wished he had a camera to capture the expression on his baby girl's face. It was the most exquisite thing he had seen in a very long time. She was smiling as broadly as she could, and her eyes were wide and clear, yet tears streamed from the corners of her eyes, rolling down her cheeks and down both sides of her nose.

'You look so beautiful, Kierney Lynn Freedom Diamond,' he said, shouting her name above the wind. 'You used to be the most beautiful girl in the world and now you're the most beautiful woman in the world. Inside and out, just like your *mamá*. I love my two gorgeous angels so unbelievably much.'

'*Gracias, papá,*' the youngster answered, wiping her face with sleeves pulled down over her hands, as if she preferred to be remembered as a girl. 'I love you so much too. And I love *mamá* and Jet so much too. Thank you for giving me such a perfect childhood. I'll never forget this gift, for as long as I live. You gave me what you never had, and I'm so grateful.'

The bereft man laid a tender kiss on his daughter's smooth forehead, lingering for a while with his lips pursed against her skin. '*Y gracias a tigo, hija nuestra,*' he whispered, coaxing her chin around into the wind and holding her long, dark hair away from her face. 'Look out over the ocean.'

The matching pair stood side-by-side, leaning against the balcony wall. Jeff put his arm around her shoulder and at once was struck with an arresting image of himself with Lynn in the same pose. Although his first response was to pull clear of her body and leave without delay, for Kierney's sake he fought to rid his mind of the vision he needed so much to be real.

'We used to spend ages on this balcony,' his voice cracked. 'Talking, planning, y'know... Your education, your lives, our life.'

'And kissing,' his daughter added, unsure of what she was trying to say. 'It was worth it, *papá*, wasn't it?'

'*Sí, pequeñita.* It was worth it.'

The romantic eighteen-year-old leant as close as she could to her dad's strong torso, and he hugged her tightly.

'Before I die, I'm going to write the sequel to your book,' she proclaimed. 'I'm going to tell everyone that everything I achieved was because of you and *mamá*.'

The great man smiled, kissing her hair. 'Well, if you do, it'd be a book of lies, baby, 'cause you're going to achieve heaps of things *mamá* and I never even dreamed of. By the time you turn a hundred years old, you're going to have the longest list of achievements the world's ever known. There'll have to be a whole entire wing dedicated to you in the Hall of Fame.'

'Shhh, *papá*,' Kierney giggled. 'That's ridiculous.'

'*No es ridiculo,*' Jeff disagreed, tickling her in the ribs. 'Did you want to see your bedroom again?'

'No, thanks. I've seen it quite recently, and it's empty too. I've got everything at home.'

'At home? I'm glad to hear you say that.'

'Why?'

'Because it shows you don't need a place to be significant to call it home,' he explained. 'I hope you find home wherever you're comfortable with yourself, Kizzo. That's the important thing to remember.

'Pretty soon you'll have homes all over the place, like Jetto. He doesn't need to be in a particular place to be happy either. That's the main difference between being a child and being an adult, I reckon. And I do believe, Kierney Lynn Freedom Diamond, that from today, you are officially an adult.'

In the first of Gerry's many last hoorahs to his bachelor days, he and three friends took up Jeff's offer of a VIP weekend at Bathurst to watch the annual V8 Supercars race. All expenses paid, they were treated to unobstructed views of almost the entire Mount Panorama circuit from upstairs in the gallery above the pit lane. They were special guests of the Holden Racing Team, which was resting its hopes on veteran Peter Brock and newcomer Craig Lowndes to bring their VR Commodores in before Ford's EF Falcons.

The event's organising committee was thrilled to have the irresistible combination of Peter Brock and Jeff Diamond on board. The exponential pulling power of the professional and amateur drivers and self-confessed rev-heads would bring men and women flocking from all over Australia and beyond. The widower's unexpected decision to accept their invitation had assured the promoters of favourable and plentiful publicity this year.

The weekend was bound to be a tonic for the rock star too, as he confided to Kierney before leaving. There weren't any memories of Lynn to be found in this part of New South Wales, and the robust camaraderie of his manager's business associates would ensure no dawdling in the doldrums would be tolerated.

On the Saturday evening, the entire team, drivers, mechanics, managers and illustrious hangers-on, took over a local restaurant for a disorderly dinner before the main race. The celebrity shared fond recollections of coming to the famous weekend spectacular six years earlier with his son for his unusual *bar mitzvah*, much to the envy of one of their number, who had been subjected to the more traditional variety.

After their hearty meal and the obligatory speeches, the "girls" arrived, bussed in from Sydney. This was met with whoops of approval from Gerry and his friends, and Jeff found himself powerless to resist joining in. He owed it to his mate not to be a wet blanket, despite how awkward it was to have a nubile, twenty-something airhead sitting on his undersexed lap.

The rest of his party were high enough on alcohol, thankfully, not to pay attention to anyone else's exploits. This enabled the famous musician to switch Gemma, who had won a hard-fought race to the best looking man in the room, onto a vacant chair between him and the groom-to-be. To his continuing consternation, however, she and her scantily clad colleagues were so pumped to be at the same table as Jeff Diamond, that they refused to accept Gerry Blake was the centre of attention.

A parallel was drawn between the "gem" in Gemma and the superstar's surname. At first he went along with this harmless play on words, but it soon transformed into a millstone around his disinterested neck. And so did the clumsy limbs which found their way repeatedly to various parts of his body as the young women became more and more inebriated.

At one o'clock in the morning, the erstwhile party animal *extraordinair* stood up and broadcast his exodus for the hotel. Loud protestations were sounded from all quarters, but he held his ground. He felt physically sick and had no wish to spoil the evening for those whose nights were yet young.

'You go with them,' Jeff urged the devastated Gemma, who was still trying her hardest to kiss his lips. 'You'll have a much better time with these guys than you will with me.'

'Oh, but why?' she whined. 'I'm your biggest fan ever! We'll have heaps of fun. I think you're fantastic.'

The downcast celebrity responded with a humble smile. 'Thanks. You too, but it's not going to happen. G'night, guys. Enjoy.'

Dragging his fingers across Gerry's back as a momentary distraction from his own easy conquest, Jeff shook his hand. 'See you in the morning,' he mouthed above the music.

Over these high-decibel few days, the billionaire draw card fulfilled his obligations to the organisers by posing with the victorious Holden team and even completed a lap of the circuit with a television camera strapped on his shoulder and a microphone adhered to his cheek with masking tape. Despite the entertaining weekend, all things considered, he couldn't wait to return home to more serious pursuits.

Once more holed up in the rented home in Burnley South, Jeff sat at the computer and composed a long e-mail to his children. He searched around in the software's help files until he found out how to delay its dispatch until a certain date, and after several frustrating minutes wondering if he had set himself a technically impossible challenge, he sent it off into the ether.

Content with this achievement, the widower took Indie for a walk around the dark and deserted streets while waiting for Kierney to reappear after a night out with her girlfriends. Escondido was now a thing of the past; another task to cross off his project plan. He would spend the next few weeks transferring the rest of his interests to their new custodians, now almost excited at the prospect of putting his affairs in order.

His faithful business manager's bucks' party preparations were well and truly underway after the resounding success of their racing trip. At the end of October, the busy author saw his ambitious eighteen-year-old housemate head to New York to collaborate on an album with her hero, Youssouf Elhadji, and to make more contacts within the corridors of power on Manhattan's east side, where the flags of the United Nations flew side-by-side in a clear message for world peace.

After this recording commitment, father and daughter were to meet up in the UK with her brother for another quick break in London. Jet's examination schedule was tight leading up to Christmas. To give him plenty of time to complete the term's work and fly home in time for Gerry's wedding, they needed to fit in their few days prior to the period of virtual lockdown for all students.

Jeff's objective for this latest working holiday was to teach his children as much as he could about when to invest, when to spend, and when to cash out. He had been fortunate to have Gerry and the resources of Blake & Partners at his disposal when he was first managing his own finances, and he wanted Ryan and Kierney to understand their personal wealth too. In the meantime, he had also submitted the plans for dividing the family's city apartment back along its east-west divide, the architect henceforth instructed to deal with the next generation of Diamonds.

Somehow always faster than his time was petering out, the old soul despaired that psychologically more and more doors were slamming in his face, putting an ever greater distance between himself and Lynn. He realised, as each day went by, that her face no longer overlaid whatever appeared in his eyes, nor did he hear her voice in every dismal silence.

The grieving husband was healing behind his own back and in spite of his enduring grief, and this unpalatable admission only fuelled his determination to go through with his master plan. With his emotions so mixed up, being busy with their autobiography, best man duties, along with transferring businesses and charities into new hands, was all vital therapy. At least he wasn't sitting at home staring at photographs all day to convince himself he wasn't forgetting his beautiful best friend.

The screenplay "When You're Gone" had morphed into its film version under the budding directorial talents of Kierney Diamond. Luke Darby had not only leapt at the chance to play the role of Lex, but had enlisted the help of a young actress by the name of Natalie Edwards to bring Marie's character to life. Jeff had never worked with Natalie before, but she came with a formidable reputation and body of work.

The fruit of their collaboration delivered beyond any of their wildest expectations. It was slated for release in February, giving his daughter cause to brag that at long last she would be able to drink champagne at a première. Jet and Kierney were in good spirits overall, considering the year they had struggled through and the year which loomed large in front of them.

Cannabis and whisky were Jeff's drugs of choice these days, maintaining a semblance of sanity and forward momentum. One unfortunate side effect of the larger quantities he was consuming in recent weeks, however, was the onset of extreme hallucinations. Lyrics tumbled out of his mind in torrents, morose and confused; most of them too dark ever to become pop songs. Way too dark.

An infestation of rumours plagued the solo celebrity too, every time he was spotted with a female in public. Was Jeff Diamond dating again? Who was this mystery woman? Where did they stay last night? Like his undernourished physical being, it seemed the world was ready to leave Lynn behind too.

Finishing a late night session in the recording studio, during which he had laid down some tracks with his lead guitarist, a backing singer and her star-gazing friend, the songwriter invited the musicians back to the house for a drink.

The first warm evening of spring encouraged the host to switch on the lights over the covered patio and fire up a gas heater, more out of habit than design. As soon as the animated ladies made themselves at home at his table, the widower regretted his rash move.

Without thinking, he had created an impromptu party, and he cursed his own stupidity while preparing a tray of drinks to take outside. His gorgeous daughter would be home soon, only to be confronted by an all too familiar scene, but with a key participant missing. Still worse: substituted. This wasn't fair. How dare he send such conflicting messages to the sensitive and loving adolescent at this crucial time?

Just smile, the lonely man reminded himself.

A couple more rounds, and he would call it quits, using Kierney's impending return as an excuse. Jeanette, the singer's tag-along friend, had been flirting wildly with him for the last hour, much to the amusement of the other two. Her hands had wandered all over him, stroking the hair on his head, then his sinewy forearms before making a grab for his thigh.

'Well, at least Lynn's killer's going away for a very long time,' Sharon's loose tongue directed to their host. 'That fucking bastard... I hate him.'

Jeff winced, for once nothing to do with the tattoo on his chest. 'Cheers,' he murmured. 'I'm with you there. Though I fail to see what his incarceration compensates us for.'

'You're very forgiving,' Jeanette said, squeezing his knee and batting her eyelids.

Unable to bear the onslaught any longer, their handsome host threw an entire tumbler full of whisky down his throat in one large gulp and rose to bring the curtain down on their entertainment.

'No, I'm not,' he growled. 'It's got nothing to do with forgiveness. The trial couldn't bring us the outcome we needed; to see my beautiful best friend walk back into our life. Party's over, folks. Time to go.'

Stunned by the star's sudden change of mood, his loyal lead guitarist got the message through the alcohol and made sure the women were soon ready to leave. The celebrity apologised for the swift exit, and the merry but confused trio's taxi honked its horn at the end of the dark driveway.

'Jesus Christ, that was close, angel,' the songwriter sighed to his absent lover. 'I can be so obnoxious at times, can't I? I'm sorry. I've got to get out of here *pronto*. This is all getting way out of hand. Tell me where you are, Lynn, please. Tell me how I can get back to you.'

Having waited for Kierney to return and cheer him up with happy stories of a fun night out, Jeff went to bed sickeningly aroused from the attractive and over-attentive Jeanette's wandering hands and suggestive phrases. Over the last month, he had almost perfected the act of disassociated masturbation, even joking with his wife's ghost that he might make it the topic of a last-ditch volume of psychiatric research.

However, this night he couldn't bring himself to climax, no matter how hard he tried to focus on his lost lover's sexy smile and lithe curves. It was as if she were teaching him a lesson, knowing this was the closest he had come to choosing a new night-time companion.

The lonely soul eventually fell asleep on top of the bed, only to wake up cold and dejected a couple of hours later.

The hard-working celebrity arrived back at Melbourne Airport on an abnormally balmy night in mid-November, after a month away from home. Stepping off the courtesy bus, he almost forgot he had driven there in the old, black Aston Martin and had left it in the long-term car park before he flew out. He unlocked it with the key and dropped into the driving seat, dog-tired after his long flight.

The cowhide had sagged from supporting his considerable weight since the early nineteen-seventies. Jeff looked around at the dated design and the lack of modern features, remembering how superb this car had been in its day. He still found genuine enjoyment in taking it for a spin every now and again, even though he had upgraded a few times.

Although fastidiously maintained for all these years, there was no escaping the fact that the creaky, black monster was beginning to drive like an old car. The transmission missed the odd gear change, and the engine would often spit whenever the fuel lines blocked and then flushed clear.

Reading the odometer, the enthusiast smiled. Over two-hundred-and-fifty-thousand kilometres he and his trusty steed had clocked up. And what memories there were tied up in this aristocratic British sports car; the envy of all his mates when he had first taken possession!

It had been his second significant purchase on becoming a rock star, the first being a much more utilitarian washing machine. It had sped Lynn back to the city when she was so sick, after waiting a long two years for the entitlement, on the day her father gave their relationship his long-awaited blessing, and it had also brought both children home from hospital for the first time. Yes, he was glad he had hung onto the ageing beast for all this time.

Now, re-energised by blasting down the Tullamarine Freeway, bypassing the CBD and heading south to Escondido, Jeff was ready to make some more memories tonight. So unbelievably ready, he laughed out loud. His dream girl had sounded equally excited for his return, and his fantasies ran riot as he flashed through the dormant suburbs. The couple had spoken most nights while he had been away, and there had even been a naughty voicemail for him to pick up as soon as he switched on his mobile at the Arrivals gate.

With the music from Lynn's recent recording blaring out through the speaker system, the impatient lover sang along, desire building in his lap. Why did they build a house so far from the airport? He should have asked his lover to meet him in town tonight. That wasn't very good planning, was it, angel?

He shifted down a gear and pulled into the overtaking lane, relishing the surge of power which transferred from his bestial longing into the willingness of the old Aston. A speeding ticket was a small price to pay for the pleasures that lay in store for him at Escondido.

A lyric the prolific songwriter had written several years ago popped into his head; a perfect fit for his mood. He remembered most of its words, so vivid were the memories of flying back from South Africa after almost losing his life. For some strange reason, the two songs melded into one in the vehicle's darkened cabin. He was damned sure of one thing though: the sense of urgency he felt right now was no less keen than it had been back then.

The dashboard clock read after nine o'clock by the time Jeff steered the car into their quiet street in Mount Eliza. The electric gates swang open for the stealthy beast, and the billionaire hoon span the wheels on the gravel just for fun. One advantage of arriving home so late was that the kids would already be in bed. He couldn't wait to see them in the morning, eager to hear all their news after being awakened by the bouncing pair as only they knew how.

The imposing wooden door into Escondido's inner sanctum creaked as the weary traveller unlocked it and pushed it open. Lifting his luggage over the threshold, his eyes were met by the spectacular sight he had been hankering to see for way too long. She was framed in the glow from the dozens of tiny, star-like lights that ringed their courtyard.

'Hi,' the seductive voice greeted him. 'I thought I heard you. Welcome home, my beautiful black stallion.'

Lynn stood not ten metres inside the doors, wearing her knee-length, white leather coat with the high collar, which always reminded her husband of an Elvis Presley cape. A pair of sunglasses perched on top of her head held her golden hair clear of her face, except for one curled lock hanging down against her forehead.

Jeff dropped his bags on the ground and walked towards his prize, reaching out to take her in his arms and locking their lips in a hungry, passionate kiss. 'Whoa! It's so good to see you, angel,' he breathed beside her cheek, before succumbing to another deep kiss. 'You look amazing. I can hardly touch you, I want you so much.'

The traveller pressed against his lover's body, convinced there was nothing but lingerie under the soft leather. He walked her backwards towards the house, his erection throbbing with anticipation.

'Wait,' his wife whispered, holding a pen up to his face. 'The real estate people are here. They need us to sign the sale documents.'

'Now? That can wait 'til tomorrow, can't it? Where are we moving to?'

With only one thing on his mind, the red-blooded songwriter inserted his hand between two coat buttons and confirmed his expectations, slipping two fingers underneath the top edge of her panties and sensing her abdominal muscles twitch at the exhilaration of skin on skin.

He felt her lips smile against his. 'Nowhere. Only to Coldwater Creek. I want to be there with you forever.'

Lynn coaxed her husband's worn leather jacket off his shoulders, and the desperate man released his embrace to let it slide down his arms and fall to the ground. They kissed again, her tongue searching for his as their eyes gazed into each other's, drinking in their boundless love.

Jeff held her body tighter and tighter until his lover moaned sweetly and ran her fingernails along his spine towards his tense neck. Undoing the remaining coat buttons one by one, he allowed the exquisite woman to guide him ever forwards into the house.

'I love you so much, angel,' he whispered, kissing her collarbone. 'And I want you like you wouldn't believe. It's been so, so long since I held you.'

A monotonous buzzing tone reverberated in the air around his head, and the blonde beauty vanished from her lover's grasp. The incredulous man watched in despair as her radiant face faded into the distance, reaching to silence his alarm clock before launching it across the room into a pile of dirty laundry.

Returning to full consciousness, Jeff became aware of the hum of traffic from Punt Road, far away from where his dream had taken him. The intense letdown engulfing his mind and body caused his bedroom walls to close in around him, as the blissful dream faded to black.

The time was nigh, the old soul understood. Nine months had passed since his *regala* had been taken from him, and he now knew where she would be.

Despite how authentic the apparition had seemed, the lost lover conceded this was nothing more than another painful journey into fantasyland. This was exactly where he had intended to go on New Year's Day anyway and was far more likely to have planted the idea into his own subconscious.

Motionless and sobbing, he hoped Kierney was still asleep and wouldn't pass by his door on her way to the kitchen. He couldn't face her walking in on him after crashing and burning in such bittersweet fashion.

Lying in the pre-dawn darkness after this latest impassioned delusion, with limbs in need of caressing and fingertips that itched with the craving to stroke Lynn's skin, the widower's body pressed the point that sex was one of its basic needs. His muscles smarted with the disappointment of this unbearable limbo, unable to connect physically with the siren soul-mate who waited just beyond his reach.

All the while, Indie sat by the side of his bed in long-suffering empathy for his new master's pain. The stranded man wept loud and long, desperate and lonely, stuck in the doctors' house by the river. Another morning when his hand must force the issue, regardless of how agonising an emotional experience it would be. For his own peace of mind, he had to know that as a man he was not broken.

Jet returned home from Cambridge in the last week of November, his exams complete and set to prepare for the Australian cricket season. There he found a father frantic to talk. This anxiety worried the heir apparent at first, but after a few hours reunited, he realised his old man simply needed the company of another red-blooded male to share what was happening to him in these strangest of times.

'These days I wake up most mornings with a raging hard-on,' Jeff lamented, his expression one of agony. 'It's like my balls are saying, "Hey, mate. What's going on? You exercised us at least once a day for thirty years, and now nothing. Did you forget we're here?"'

The youngster chuckled, no longer embarrassed to have this type of conversation with his dad, and waited for the story to unfold.

'I can't have meaningless sex anymore, mate, can I? Even if I wanted to, which I don't really. All it'd take is one girl to blab to the papers, and I just don't want to have to deal with the fallout. Not for you two, or "G" and "G", for your mum's fans or even for me, but most of all not to debase her memory.'

His son nodded. It was clear he wasn't expected to speak.

'And ironically, she'd understand if I did, which makes the whole bloody thing ten times worse. I can't do it and I won't do it.'

'All good, Dad,' Jet smiled. 'It's fine. You don't have to justify anything to me. Not to anyone.'

'No, I know. I'm not. I'm justifying it to myself, I guess. When the flesh is weak, and I think, "Why the hell not?" Y'know what I mean? Your mum was worth too much, and it'd hurt all those people who loved the idea of us. Including me.

'There'd be so much media speculation and opinion from folks who just love to say they know me so well,' the celebrity complained. 'And I can't date anyone remotely nice because my heart'll never be in it. I don't want to let anyone down. So I'm fucked, basically.'

'Or not, more like,' the student replied, reaching forward and grabbing his dad's wrist for moral support.

The great man sniffed. 'Yep. You got it! So I use my trusty right hand whenever my mind doesn't get the better of my blood pressure and chase my libido away. I get it over with as quickly as I can, 'cause the emotions are overpowering: guilt, longing, shame, missing Lynn... You name it.'

'I'm sorry, Dad. I really don't know what to suggest.'

'Hey, don't be sorry,' he shook his head. 'I don't mean for you to solve my problems. I'm just fuckin' impatient and feeling sorry for myself. I still have so many unsullied memories of our fantastic sex life, and while I'm there with her, the world's bloody amazing again. Let's have another drink, shall we?'

That night, Jeff again took refuge in the book he was writing on Lynn's behalf. He gloated inwardly, albeit with a healthy dose of humility on the side, as he recalled the fervour with which he, as an egotistical twenty-one-year-old, had declared to a roomful of doubting friends that he would have the final word in his dream girl's life story.

How true this grandiose statement had become, although not at all in the way it was meant. Was it pure arrogance which had driven him to be so outspoken, or had he known all along that Lynn Dyson would see something in him that no-one else could see? Maybe a bit of both, he chuckled to himself.

The dedicated author had fashioned an authentic *atelier* in the doctors' dark study under the awning, looking out over the luscious established gardens. It was reminiscent of a professor's bolt-hole, like the one belonging to a close friend in South Africa, an academic with whom he had studied in London and later engineered an auspicious peace process for a country on the verge of transformation.

With a full bottle of whisky, an ice bucket, a packet of slimline cigars and a jug of cold water, the writer's latest date with his autobiography began. His wife's diaries and various other sources of reference material were scattered in untidy piles on the floor to his right, regularly dipped into to confirm details that escaped him.

On the table was a collection of the Diamond family's most symbolic photographs, distilled from the several hundred he had started with. They each represented a trigger for major milestones he must not forget, carefully sorted into chronological order by his two adorable assistants.

Jeff smiled as he ran his index finger across the interleaved pictures from left to right. The colourful assortment resembled a snake of dominoes which had tumbled together with a single push. Reaching the right-hand side, where he spied the couple's "official" twentieth anniversary portrait, he selected the first and last photographs in the long series. He wanted to examine the faces and measure how much he and his stunning partner had changed in the intervening years.

However, before the critic could consider this comparison, another picture from near the rightmost, more current end of the photographic spectrum caught his attention. He lay the other two down and picked up a shot of the entire Dyson clan, taken at Anna's wedding. The tattoo under his shirt spasmed in response, making him gulp.

Scanning the familiar faces, including his own, the melancholy man was hit with a profound sense of regret as he zeroed in on his forever lover's irresistible smile. Her untimely demise had denied her the chance to make a proper acquittal to whoever made the case for her to enter this lifetime.

Given the original, steely reception he had received from the blue-blooded family, coupled with the perennial status of "outsider" he was assigned from birth, the successful billionaire wondered if his wife's parents had any notion of the bitter irony which saw the privilege of documenting the lows, highs, and even higher, of their elder daughter's life fall to the no-good son of a murderer who stole her heart.

The philosopher swilled the mellow, amber liquid around his mouth, relishing its tantalising bite. In reality, he figured, precious few people ever reached the point of acquitting themselves. The vast majority finished their time on Earth with neither the desire nor the inclination to take stock of their achievements and failures, and others who might have prepared better were snatched rudely and too early, as in his beautiful best friend's situation. How was it that he, the same outsider, the no-good son of a murderer aforementioned, had ended up in this position? He was fortunate from this perspective, in a bizarre way.

Perhaps this was what set apart those souls who returned for another lifetime and those who did not. Here was a fascinating new theory the intellectual would love to prove if his whacky master plan were to succeed. Attaining full recognition for Lynn Dyson Diamond's significant influence on the world was the very least he could do, after her dedication to helping him rise above his suffocating ancestral scars.

His guardian angel had been instrumental in transforming her reprobate boyfriend into the somebody he strove to be: a giant among men, as was written so often by well-respected commentators. Of this there could be no doubt. She had selflessly cast aside her personal ambitions, for the most part dictated by her own accident of birth, to focus on Jeff Diamond's glorious quest. His odyssey, as she herself had once described it. For better or for worse.

The author glanced down at the completed manuscript underneath the picture gallery on his desk and smiled, fondling the soft fur behind Indie's ear. No matter whose body a soul was born into, life was full of opportunities. Many were seized upon with both hands, and some were left to fly by without even reaching up.

No-one dared disagree that Lynn and Jeff Diamond had snaffled their fair share of life's opportunities, and neither could one deny the vast array that they cast out for others to reel in. The forever couple's autobiography had been printed in its entirety for the first time that afternoon, bound up and ready for the editors. The most significant of these opportunities had found their way into this anthology for all to see and judge based on their individual merit.

Tired but satisfied, Jeff picked up the original pair of photographs again, leftmost and rightmost; the oldest and newest visual records of a remarkable partnership. Lifting them to eye level in the lamplight, he was struck by how little difference such a memorable quarter century had made on the surface.

The first photograph still tugged at his heartstrings, simply because it was the first photograph. When he received it, only a few weeks after meeting his dream girl, he had been quite sure this would be the one and only material souvenir of their relationship that he would ever possess.

How wrong could he be! As it turned out, the Diamond family became one of the most hounded and traded *paparazzi* prizes in history. The superstar couldn't count the number of times they had obliged their fans with spontaneous happy snaps in the street or at the beach, in shops and cafés.

Anywhere seemed fair game these days. In fact, he recalled with dismay, he and Jet were once even asked to pose together at the urinals of a putrid toilet block, which the young lad had found hilarious.

In his left hand were two fresh-faced teenagers with their whole lives ahead of them, dancing the night away at a twenty-first birthday party. The boy had long, dark hair and was smartly dressed in a suit and tie, eager to make a good impression on his new girlfriend's prominent parents and sophisticated friends.

And the girl? Whoa! Jeff exhaled deeply. She was so pretty... He had forgotten how gorgeous the sixteen-year-old had looked that night, wearing a knee-length red chiffon dress which swirled high up her long, tanned legs as he whisked her around the dance floor.

The mature couple in his right hand looked relaxed and happy, sitting close together on a park bench with Albert Park Lake glistening in the background, posed by a seasoned professional as if modelling clothes for a mail-order catalogue. The hair styles and fashions had changed, of course, but the love radiating from their smiling eyes was equally evident.

This image reminded the bereft man how tantalising it still felt to touch his only true love, no matter the intervening years. The stunning woman had recently turned forty; erudite, enlightened and oh, so very loving. So unbelievably sexy too!

And the bloke beside her? Well, he didn't turn out too bad, after all. Far better than his girlfriend's parents expected; that much had long been acknowledged.

About as well as his dream girl had known all along.

The final words had been written. This stage of the soul-mates' journey had been accounted for, along with a few pointers for the next. What lay in between was a vast gulf of uncertainty.

Would there even be a next stage? There was only one way to find out. After everything it had accomplished as Jeff Diamond, this was one golden opportunity the old soul was not prepared to let sail by without jumping on board.

Responding to Indie's adoring gaze by ruffling his hands through the long fur around his neck, the lonely man smiled. His vivid imagination recalled those early days of heightened anticipation and wondered how long it might be until he could experience the elation of falling in love all over again.

'Don't judge a picture by its frame, eh, boy?' Jeff cautioned his canine critic.

Without a doubt, the frame of their life singular had changed beyond recognition in the time that had passed between these two random snaps of the camera. Yet, as the book would soon testify, so had the man in the picture.

END OF VOLUME ONE

END OF VOLUME ONE

Lorraine Pestell
Visit www.lorrainepestell.com

Shawline Publishing Group Pty Ltd
www.shawlinepublishing.com.au

SHAWLINE
PUBLISHING
GROUP

CPSIA information can be obtained
at www.ICGtesting.com
Printed in the USA
LVHW031700041120
670706LV00008B/1344

9 781922 444110